Playing Dead

Return items to **any** Swindon Library by c
time on or before the date stamped. Only
and Audio Books can be renewed - phon
library or visit our website,
www.swindon.gov.uk/libraries

Deposits 02/13
Tel: 01793
465555

D3   B4   A5   C4
H1A   C1   B5   D2
            C2   B3
E7   D1   D6
F4   E2   G3   A2
G3   A   A8
A6   G4   B1
            G1

Swindon
BOROUGH COUNCIL

D1343789

Playing Dead

A Novel of Suspense

Julia Heaberlin

W F HOWES LTD

This large print edition published in 2013 by
W F Howes Ltd
Unit 4, Rearsby Business Park, Gaddesby Lane,
Rearsby, Leicester LE7 4YH

1 3 5 7 9 10 8 6 4 2

First published in the United Kingdom in 2012
by Faber and Faber Limited

A CIP catalogue record for this book is available
from the British Library

ISBN 978 1 47122 228 3

Typeset by Palimpsest Book Production Limited,
Falkirk, Stirlingshire
Printed and bound in Great Britain
by MPG Books Ltd, Bodmin, Cornwall

MIX
Paper from
responsible sources
FSC
www.fsc.org   FSC® C018575

For Steve, who reads to me

CHAPTER 1

Despite its name, Ponder, Texas, pop. 1,101, isn't a very good place to think. Four months out of the year, it's too damn hot to think.

It *is* a good place to get lost. That's what my mother did thirty-two years ago. The fact that she successfully hid this from almost everyone who loved her makes her a pretty good liar. I'm not sure what it says about me.

When I was a little girl, my grandmother would tell my fortune to keep me still. I vividly remember one August day when the red line on the back porch thermometer crept up to 108. Sweat dribbled down the backs of my knees, a thin cotton sundress pressed wet against my back. My legs swung back and forth under the kitchen table, too short to reach the floor. Granny snapped beans in a soothing rhythm. I stared at a tall glass pitcher of iced tea that floated with mint leaves and quarter moons of lemon, wishing I could jump in. Granny promised a storm coming from Oklahoma would cool things off by dinner. The fan kept blowing the cards off the table and I kept slapping them down, giggling.

1

The fortune is long forgotten, but I can still hear the anguished joy of my mother playing a Bach concerto in the background.

Two years later, on the worst day of my life, what I remember most is being cold. Granny and I stood in a darkened funeral parlor, the window air conditioner blowing up goose bumps on my arms. Cracks of September sunlight tried to push in around the shades. It was at least ninety degrees outside, but I wanted my winter coat. I wanted to lie down and never wake up. Granny gripped my hand tighter, as if she could hear my thoughts. Merle Haggard blared from a passing pickup truck and faded away. I could hear my mother crying from another room.

That's how I remember Mama – present but absent.

I'm not like that. People know when I'm around.

I've been told that I have a strange name for a girl, that I'm nosy, that I'm too delicate to carry a gun. The first two are true.

I've been told that it's weird to love both Johnny Cash and Vivaldi, that I'm way too white for a Texan and too skinny for a fast-food junkie, that my hair is long and straight enough to hang a cat, that I look more like a New York City ballet dancer than a former champion roper. (In Texas, *New York City* is never a complimentary adjective.)

I've been told that my sister, Sadie, and I shouldn't have beaten up Jimmy Walker in fifth grade because he is still whining about it to a therapist.

I've been told that growing up in Ponder must have been an idyllic childhood, picket fence and all. I tell those people I'm more familiar with barbed wire and have the scars on my belly to prove it.

I learned early that nothing is what it seems. The nice butcher at the Piggly Wiggly who saved bones for our dogs beat his wife. The homecoming queen's little sister was really the daughter she had in seventh grade. That's the way life was.

In a place like Ponder, everyone knew your secrets. At least, that's what I thought before. I never pictured my mother, the legendary pianist of the First Baptist Church of Ponder, as a woman with something to hide. I never dreamed that opening a stranger's letter would be pulling a loose thread that would unravel everything. That, one day, I'd scrutinize every memory for the truth.

The letter is five days old and I have read it forty-two times. It is pink and smells like the perfume of a woman I don't know. It arrived on a Wednesday, right to Daddy's office, sandwiched between a plea from Doctors Without Borders and a brochure on a new exhibit at the Amon Carter Museum.

Daddy's secretary, Melva, a former teacher and widow on the upside of her sixties, picked the envelope out of the stack as something I needed

3

to see. Personal, she said. Not spit out by a computer. A sympathy card, perhaps, because that was one of the few things people still felt obligated to write by hand.

When I opened it and read the careful feminine scrawl, I felt the earth shift. The tremor started low, in my toes, and worked its way up, although I can't say why the letter had such an instant effect on me.

The odds were that the woman who wrote this was a scam artist. Or simply had the wrong girl. The wrong Tommie McCloud, spelled with an *ie*.

Each of the forty-two times I read the letter, I wanted to hop in my pickup and go home to Mama, even though Mama isn't there and home is now an empty ranch house with faded flowered sheets covering the furniture like an indoor meadow.

But home is also endless rolling land, shimmering heat, sweet memories that thrum in the air with the cicadas. Home pulls at me like a magnet. Even when my body is hundreds of miles away, my soul stays behind, clinging to the live oak by the cement pond where I learned to dog paddle.

They say that Lyndon Johnson's shoulders rolled back and he relaxed as soon as he could see his ranchland stretching out below Air Force One. My Granny called LBJ an egotistical lunatic, but that profound connection he had with a patch of earth makes him OK in my book. I've tried to leave for good, to beat a new path, but I have been safest and happiest on Elizabeth Ranch, where my great-great-grandfather was born, where I grew up.

Less kind people would say I never grew up. They call me a runaway.

If anyone asked, I would describe myself as temporarily off-course ever since eight hundred pounds of steer stomped on my wrist fourteen years ago in a rodeo arena in Lubbock, Texas, knocking me from the pedestal of my saddle into mortality. It took two seconds for Black Diablo to crush twelve bones in my hand and wrist, and any wispy thoughts in my mother's head of tearing me away from the rodeo and turning me into a concert pianist. My fingers never worked the same again.

Goodbye to getting a master's at the prestigious Curtis Institute of Music. Goodbye to my collegiate rodeo competitions, because a year of physical therapy later, I couldn't swing a rope. I had the yips, like a catcher who suddenly can't throw a ball straight back to the mound after doing it thousands of times.

What else did I know besides Bach and rodeo? When the shattered bones healed, I left home, raw and angry, not sure whose dreams I'd been living. I spent a year in Europe as a backpacking, hostel-living cliché. Four years at the University of Texas getting a degree in child psychology, three more working toward my Ph.D. at Rice. Five years in Wyoming at Halo Ranch, a nonprofit that uses

5

horses to coax sick and emotionally distraught kids back to life, lured by an internship and an irresistible fellow Ph.D. candidate. Somewhere in there, I fell out of infatuation with him and back in love with horses.

Then, two weeks ago, Daddy died, and I came home to Ponder for good. I hadn't said it out loud, but I knew I wouldn't leave again.

My eyes close for a second and I can picture every word on the perfumed pink page in front of me, the spidery scrawl that is setting everything in motion.

Dear Tommie, it begins. *Have you ever wondered about who you are?*

Always, I tell myself. Always. But not in the way you think.

I'm looking for my daughter who was kidnapped July 15, 1981, when she was only one.

I do the simple math one more time. She was kidnapped thirty-one years ago and I am thirty-two years old.

Her name is Adriana Marchetti.

She's Italian, I think. I am pale. I freckle in the sun. My hair is untouched blond.

I've spent most of my life searching for you. I believe you are my daughter.

I want to shout at this invisible woman. My mother never lies. Never. It was the one thing that disappointed her the most, if her girls lied to her. And my father? Even less likely.

But I cannot lie to myself now. There was another

letter to consider. This one had shown up at the ranch in Wyoming. An official one, with my name, Tommie Anne McCloud, behind the envelope's waxy window.

The envelope contained a Social Security card with a brand-new number and a letter informing me that an extensive internal review of the past fifty years of Social Security numbers unearthed hundreds of clerking errors. The first three digits of my number did not reflect where my birth certificate said I was born.

Take this number instead.

No big deal. To *them*. But that number had been a part of me all my life. I was attached to it, like I was to my hair, my childhood cat Clyde, and the date of my birth. It was one of the few numbers I could spit out automatically, packed in my brain with all of the other passwords and security codes required for membership in the twenty-first century. It had been a nightmare to change it on my passport, insurance cards, credit cards.

But I'd never called to ask any questions. Why would I?

That letter was somewhere in a landfill by now. Daddy's Mac in front of me glowed, encouraging. I typed 'Social Security Administration' into Google, found an 800 number, punched it into my cell, and spent ten minutes bouncing around telephone menus that had no options for grieving, emotionally distraught daughters possibly kidnapped more than thirty years ago. I yelled 'Representative' into the phone until the fake voice gave up and transferred me to a live woman, who introduced herself as Crystal.

'I got a Social Security card with a new number in the mail a couple of years ago,' I told Crystal. 'My name is Tommie McCloud.'

'Uh-huh. Hundreds of people did. Is there a problem?'

'I just wondered . . . why? Where did the first three digits indicate I was born?' As I asked this, it occurred to me that I probably could have Googled this kind of information and saved a lot of time.

'You're just asking now? Never mind. Give me the first three digits of the old number and the new number.' I recited them obediently and she came back on the line a few seconds later. She had probably Googled it.

'Chicago, Illinois.'

'I was born at a hospital in Fort Worth.'

'Yes, ma'am.' Her tone was overly patient. 'That is why you got a new card.'

'This has been a huge hassle,' I said, irritated with her patronizing air, wanting to be distracted from the reason I called her in the first place.

'Ma'am, do you have any issues I can specifically help you with *now*? This is in response to our nation's heightened vulnerability to security threats and identity fraud. Do you not want a safe nation?'

Ah, the twenty-first-century tactic: Switch the

blame right back to the consumer. Yesterday, a representative for the phone company told me it would take a month to set up phone and internet service at the Ponder ranch. When I sputtered a protest, he asked whether I really thought I deserved to be put ahead of other consumers in line. And was I not aware of Texas flooding? I couldn't dignify that with an answer. The black earth in Daddy's fields was cracking from the heat. I pictured the phone rep shutting his eyes and stabbing his finger pin-the-tail-on-the-donkey style at a list titled *Natural disasters: Excuses they might fall for*.

'You're attacking my patriotism?' I asked Crystal, thinking that wasn't her real name or accent, that her own dry, un-American ass was probably sitting in India. 'Are you reading from a script? Because I'd recommend you get a new script.'

'I'm going to put you down as a customer hang-up,' she said.

'What?'

Silence on the other end. Crystal was gone.

It didn't matter. I couldn't avoid it any longer.

Rosalina Marchetti's letter was clear on this fact. Her daughter, Adriana, had been kidnapped in Chicago, Illinois. Rosalina wanted me to travel there sometime in the next few weeks, all on her dime.

Did she know that my father had just died? Wasn't that how these scammers worked, with a cold eye on the obituaries, one of the few places where unusual names are usually spelled correctly? Because that's the thing: Rarely did anyone spell my name right who wasn't a blood relation, and half of them didn't, either.

I read the letter for the forty-third time and it's like I'm twelve years old again sitting in the corner of a horse stall with a flashlight and a terrifying book, frantic to warn the heroine of terrible peril but secretly knowing I can protect her for a day, for months, for years, forever, by simply slamming the book shut. Ending her story in the middle.

I stare at Rosalina Marchetti's signature. It sweeps arrogantly across the right bottom half of the page, tall and loopy. Under her name, like an afterthought, she had scribbled:

And the angels cried.

CHAPTER 2

'Are you OK, Tommie?'

A familiar gravelly voice. A voice like my father's, worn raw by smoke and sawdust. I lifted my head from the pile of papers. If I squinted, I could pretend he was Daddy. Tall, angular lines, a fifteen-dollar haircut from Joe, jeans and boots that had met some cows, a face like the Texas earth, wrecked by sun and drought and cigarettes. The damn cigarettes. I pushed away the image of Daddy at the end, with his oxygen tank at his side like a loyal pet.

'Wade. Hi.' I finished pulling my uncooperative hair through an old rubber band I'd found in the drawer and flipped it down my back. 'I'm awake. Just unsure where to begin with Daddy's papers.' I wanted to say that the whole room made me physically ache.

Instead, I spread my arms to encompass the scarred oak desk in front of me, slotted and pegged together like a master puzzle by a cowboy more than two hundred years ago. Not a single metal nail. I took naps on top when I was three. Daddy bragged that it required five men to get the desk through the door.

The oversized leather couch in the corner still held the deep imprint of my father's lean body. A plastic hanging bag of dry cleaning, Wrangler jeans and lightly starched pressed western shirts, was hooked over one of the closet doors; a case of Corona Light and two cases of Dr Pepper sat by a small refrigerator on the plank floor, vices as hereditary as the cigarettes that killed him. I quit smoking at sixteen, the day Daddy slapped the first one out of my hand behind the barn, the only time he hit me. I stuck with the Dr Pepper.

My eyes lingered on the photo behind Wade's head, from another lifetime, a blown-up print of Daddy and Wade in federal marshals' gear. Arms around each other, cigars drooping out of their grinning mouths. A good day, Daddy always said. A bad guy went down.

This refurbished 1800s building in the historic Fort Worth Stockyards was once a place where bad guys went down every week, usually with a chunk of lead in the back. Sometimes in the saloon below, sometimes surprised in this very room while stuck in a woman spreading her legs for a few pieces of change.

Over the last thirty years, among these violent ghosts, my father turned his family's legacy of land into a multimillion-dollar oil and gas business, with the assistance of a secretary, seven lawyers, two investment advisers, and the man slouched in front of me the way only cowboys in jeans can get away with, a Tony Lama hat that had seen better days held with one giant hand over his crotch.

Wade Mitchell, ten years younger than Daddy, was the heir to the big job, so specified in my father's will, unless I wanted to step up. My sister, Sadie, had eliminated herself as a candidate years ago.

'I hate to ask, Tommie, but have you made a decision?' At first, I wasn't sure what Wade meant. Was he talking about his job? About Rosalina Marchetti? How would he know about that? I fingered the pink stationery nervously. Then I remembered, at Aunt Rebecca's house, at the wake, his urgent whisper.

'You mean about the wind farm?' I ask him.

'Yes. It's the one thing that we need to sign off on this week. BT Power wants to put up a hundred more turbines in Stephenville. If we don't, they're choosing another site. They've also got their eye on our Big Dipper property near Boerne.'

'I don't know,' I said slowly.

'Tommie, you need to leave some of these early decisions to me. We've got a good lease going with them.'

'Is there any controversy over the farm so far? The seventy-five turbines already in place?' I'd stood on our land just once since the turbines had been erected. I'd had mixed feelings. Nestled near an old farmhouse, they had a strange beauty about them, rising higher than the Statue of Liberty, gently whirring and spinning with the wind, turning the plains into an eerie, alien landscape when night fell, their red eyes blinking.

'What do you mean?'

'Exactly what I asked. A year ago Daddy put in seventy-five turbines on this land with an option for more. Do you think it has gone smoothly?'

Wade looked surprised that I had this much information. Or maybe surprised that I cared at all.

I'd never liked Wade much. He was brusque, always around, quick to shoo us away from Daddy when we were little. But Wade and Daddy once walked into bad situations with nothing but each other and a gun. Shared violence is like human superglue.

He decided to answer my question. 'The rancher to the north makes a lot of noise to the media about the way it looks,' he drawled. 'Says the turbines destroy his view. The town's happy about the taxes improving their school system. They got a turf field out of the deal.'

'I told Daddy a few months ago that the turbines are bothering the kids,' I said. 'And the horses.'

'What the hell are you talking about?'

'They put up a wind farm near the rehabilitative ranch where I work. We can't see the turbines, but they're close enough for the kids to hear. They call them the whispering monsters. The horses don't sleep as well. Some of the kids deal with constant nausea since they went full power. Wind turbine syndrome, they call it.'

Wade frowned. 'I can't deal with this damn hippie crap right now, Tommie. This is what your father wanted. You keep dawdling and we'll lose two million dollars like *this*.' He snapped his fingers, leaning over the desk, a little too near my face. 'You can't decide based on a few courses in psychology and a bunch of cancer kids and gimps and four-legged animals. That ain't how you make business decisions.'

He used *ain't* to underscore his irritation, since we both knew Wade was a literate cowboy with a master's in agribusiness from Texas A&M. But in his mind, the only kind of satisfactory therapy involved a bottle of Old Rip Van Winkle whiskey and an hour to kill with a gun and a bull's-eye.

'The Big Dipper is a beautiful piece of land,' I told him. I bit back that I was finally only a couple of months from my Ph.D. 'Untouched. There aren't that many properties with natural running water from streams and the river.'

'It's recreational property,' Wade countered. 'People aren't paying for it anymore, not a prime piece like this.'

We'd never sell that piece. I stared at him steadily. He was deliberately missing my point. I was deliberately missing his.

Grief for Daddy poured out of both of us, seeping into the cracks in the floorboards where blood used to run.

I knew that Wade fished with his twenty-five-year-old autistic son every Saturday, a promise he never broke. Wade's cowboy boots were custom-made at Leddy's down the street because of a limp that he'd never talk about. With that limp, he insisted on carrying my mother out of the house the day she left it for good, a rag doll in his arms.

He was mostly a good man, a smart man. I knew it. I just didn't like him.

'Get out,' I said, because I didn't want him to see me cry.

'Yes, ma'am. Call when you need me. It's going to be sooner than you think.' He gestured to the wooden file cabinets that lined the walls, to the mail stacking up on the desk, to the Apple computer that had yet to reveal its secrets, and my heart sank because I knew he was right: I would need him.

Wade turned with his hand on the doorknob.

'Tommie, you're going about this dead wrong. But I will say, it's nice to see a little fire in you. I thought that side of beef stomped it out of you for good.' His face softened. 'I hear you're still wicked on top of a horse. Maybe we should take a ride and works things out.'

He shut the door quietly.

My eyes roved over the walls, tears gradually softening the edges of the cattle drivers and whores and gamblers, historic photographs of Hell's Half Acre that Daddy picked up one at a time out of dusty boxes in antique shops.

I stopped at the picture of Etta Place, the beautiful, unfathomable girlfriend of the Sundance

Kid. Nailed in a place of honor over the doorframe, one of Daddy's favorite pictures, a Christmas gift from Mama pulled out of a shiny silver box.

Long, dark hair piled up, gray eyes, a slim, lithe body. Etta didn't look wild or cruel but they swore she was.

Why did no one know her real name? Was she really a prostitute when she met the Sundance Kid? And where did she vanish to? How do you live a life without a beginning and an end?

As a child, I would sit cross-legged on the hard floor directly in front of her, craning my neck up, willing Etta to speak, to spill her secrets just to me, until Daddy finally glanced over from his desk and said:

'She's a mystery, honey. A goddamn mystery.'

CHAPTER 3

Five minutes after Wade left, I decided to turn the page and allow the plucky, foolish heroine to plunge ahead.

I wondered what it meant that I was now thinking idiotically of myself in the third person and using words like *plucky*. My colleagues would offer up the fancy term *disassociating*. Sadie would say *not wanting to deal*.

Rosalina Marchetti could be a con woman, I told myself. Or a stalker. Emotionally unbalanced. Dangerous.

I had to know.

My fingers leapt over the keys of Daddy's computer, suddenly alive after a week of crippled hesitation. It took just thirteen minutes before I found the right Rosalina Marchetti in the *Chicago Tribune* archive. And, when I say right, I mean wrong, so wrong.

Rosalina Marchetti née Rosie Lopez, more poetically known in her stripper days as Rose Red, married Chicago mobster Anthony Marchetti on January 27, 1980. A month after that, Marchetti stood before a judge and received a life sentence, convicted on six counts of first-degree murder and unrelated charges of embezzlement and bribery. The sentence seemed light. Anthony Marchetti belonged in hell. He'd viciously murdered an FBI agent, his wife, three children, and an agent guarding them at a safe house. But the court left a chance for parole.

Marchetti stared coolly out of his wedding announcement, a dark and charismatic stereotype. He looked as if he would be equally comfortable attending the opera or chopping off body parts in a back room. The glowing woman is usually the star of these kinds of photos, but his new bride, Rose, hung back shyly, her face in shadow. It was ridiculous to think that either of these people had anything to do with me.

Their melodrama didn't end there. A little more searching confirmed that Rosalina's story held up. She'd given birth to an unlucky little girl six months later. I say unlucky because the child was kidnapped three days after her first birthday. My stomach hurt as I kept reading, one of the 'hot reads' on a true crime site with 136,000 hits. Days after the abduction, the kidnapper had sent Rosalina her daughter's finger. I looked down to confirm that my fingers were still attached. Why didn't Rosalina ask about the finger in her letter?

Details were scarce after that. I fought off another little chill after finding the girl's name – Adriana Rose Marchetti – still active on the FBI's missing persons list. She'd never been found.

Rose Red now lived in a lavish, gated Italian-style villa on Chicago's North Shore. Anthony Marchetti still sat in prison. She'd never divorced him. According to various society columns, she was a generous contributor to AIDS causes, missing persons organizations, and library charities.

But I could find only her name. After the wedding photo, there were no more pictures.

My eyes glazed a little. I hadn't slept more than four hours a night in two weeks, not since Sadie's pre-dawn phone call saying Daddy was gone.

I should go. This would be the first night I'd spend at the ranch instead of at Sadie's, and there weren't sheets on a single bed or anything in the fridge but Miller Lites and Cokes for Daddy's friends who dropped by the ranch to hunt. Daddy asked our longtime housekeeper to shut down the house six months ago, and Daddy had worked here, showered here, and slept here, unless he took a suite at the downtown Worthington.

It was at least a forty-five-minute drive home. Maybe the Worthington was a good idea for tonight.

I could see nothing but inky black out of the windows that lined the west wall, not even the brick of the building next door, so close I could touch it if I leaned out. The other offices in Daddy's building – an insurance agency, an orthodontist, and a law practice – had emptied by 6 p.m., so I was alone with the ghosts. The air-conditioning clunked on and my heart did a little frog jump.

Still, one more nagging thought.

It took only a few more strokes to find out where Anthony Marchetti wound up.

Twenty days ago, he had been moved from the Level 1 maximum security prison in Crest Hill, Illinois, to a jail cell in Fort Worth, Texas. Marchetti was up for parole. And he was about a five-minute drive away.

Someone was messing with me, either up there or down here.

My tired eyes processed movement, a blur of green.

Someone was in the room, at the door.

My right hand automatically took hold of the Beretta M9 my father kept in a special holster attached under the desk and I whipped it up, evening it directly at the head of a man I'd never seen before. This took approximately three seconds. Good muscle memory.

A long time ago, Sadie and I taught our little hands this move with a squirt gun. The object then: to get the other player wet and to wipe up the floor before Daddy returned from his conference room.

'Whoa.' The stranger stopped short, about a foot in.

This guy had to be a lost tourist. Not bad-looking, but not my type. An aging frat boy. He wore a lime-green polo shirt like a flag from another country, with a tiny pink pony on his left bicep. His ripped $150 jeans were made to look as if he'd worked a lot of cattle, but had instead been beaten and distressed by slave labor in Vietnam.

He was a pretender.

As a Levi's devotee, who'd worked cattle since age six, I counted this as the first strike against him. There were other strikes, like short hair moussed into an unnatural state.

'Are you lost?' I asked carefully. 'This is a private business.'

Eyes on the Beretta, he plopped himself in the leather chair facing me. He set a small digital recorder on the desk and a briefcase on the floor.

'I'd feel better if you put that thing away,' he told me. 'I'm from *Texas Monthly* magazine. We have a mutual acquaintance. Lydia Pratt? I didn't mean to scare you but I thought I'd try to catch you here and set up a time for us to meet. Here's my card. You weren't answering your cell.' He tossed the card across the desk.

His story rang a few true notes, but the man himself set my nerves screeching like teenage cheerleaders. I lowered the gun, returned it to its safe place under the desk, and picked up his card.

Jack Smith. Senior reporter. *Texas Monthly* magazine. Two phone numbers and a fax number with an Austin prefix, and an email address.

'Call me Jack,' he said, grinning, sticking out a hand I didn't take.

Get out. The words screamed in my head. I glanced down at my cell phone and considered a less lethal move. Two missed calls from a cell phone with an Austin prefix. So he probably wasn't lying about that, either.

'And?' I asked.

'And I'm working a story about the success of horse therapy with kids who have aggressive or antisocial behavior. Lydia said you two were doing research together. I badgered her to give me your cell number.'

True. Lydia Pratt was a former mentor and professor of mine at UT and a long-distance research partner.

'How did you get in the front door downstairs?' I asked. 'The computer security system locks it automatically after five.'

He shrugged. 'It was open.'

'How did you know I'd be here?'

'I'm a reporter,' he said, like that explained everything. 'I interviewed Lydia in Austin on Friday. She mentioned you were in Fort Worth. I flew in to work on another story and you and I happened to be in the same place at the same time. The guy I interviewed today said your father had an office down here.'

'Who is that? The guy you interviewed?'

'I gotta protect my sources.'

This guy was annoyingly glib, like he was speaking lines in a movie. 'This isn't a good time,' I said abruptly. 'And my part of the research is focused more on treating kids who've experienced a devastating trauma. The suicide of a parent, the death of a sibling. Horse therapy is only part of my research. You need to leave.'

'Think about it,' Smith insisted, not moving. 'I'm sure you could add something interesting. A story could help you get more funding for your research. I won't take much time. I'm at Etta's Place until Monday night.'

Etta's Place. This had to be some kind of huge cosmic joke. I forced myself not to glance up at her picture. Etta's Place was the downtown inn that thrived on the slim possibility that after the Kid died, Etta masqueraded in Fort Worth as a boardinghouse matron named Eunice Gray. Or, if you were reading something other than the slick hotel website, Eunice ran a brothel. I'm sure she didn't charge the website rate of $150 or more a room, no matter what salacious service was offered.

Sadie would call this serendipity. A sign, probably from Etta herself. An artist, my sister believed in magnet healing, braless summers, alien abductions, and that Granny's psychic bloodline ran through our veins.

As for funding, mine was plenty deep and directly from my trust fund.

Jack Smith uncrossed his long legs and stood up. I followed him, through Melva's office, down the narrow hall and stairs to the lock on the front door.

'I just want to check it,' I remarked sweetly. The lock appeared to be in perfect working order.

'How about that?' His grin widened. 'Must have been a little glitch with the computer.' I didn't reply. Daddy had told me the security company vowed the special feature was as reliable and about as technically complex as an alarm clock.

'What's the other story you're working on?' I asked. 'The one that brought you to Fort Worth?'

Smith's lips curled back up into that irritating grin.

'I know where Jimmy Hoffa is buried,' he said, and sauntered off, leaving that hanging in the hot air.

Our building's entrance opened onto a side street, away from the tourists and bars and the daily cattle drive. The city had been chintzy with the lighting here, so Smith turned into a walking shadow until he hit the end of the block. The streetlight illuminated his shirt like a neon glow stick before he disappeared around the corner. I waited until I was sure he wasn't coming back. Then I took the pistol out of my waistband, where I'd tucked it when he wasn't looking.

Jack Smith, reporter, would have been better off wearing American-made, boot-cut jeans for more than one reason.

For instance, they would have done a better job of hiding his ankle holster.

The jeans always told the story.

Jack Smith, reporter or not, was a pretender with a capital *P*.

A half-hour later, I put my father's Mac to sleep and turned out the lights, closing the door to

Daddy's office, checking to make sure it was locked. The 9 mm pistol was in my purse, right beside Rosalina Marchetti's letter.

I now stood in Melva's little piece of the world. The cozy space doubled as a waiting area even though Texans like my Daddy didn't make people wait.

Melva always left a floor lamp lit before shutting the door behind her every weeknight at precisely 5:31 p.m., but tonight, right now, it just lengthened the shadows. The twenty-seven-inch Mac on her desk glowed with a picture of her six-year-old grandson's Halloween impersonation of Frankenstein, casting an eerie high-tech rainbow on the Charles Russell print hanging behind it.

I was gathering up the courage to venture back into the dark hall.

In my mind, not moving an inch from Daddy's door, I walked the entire route to where I had parked the pickup truck. Down the hall and the staircase, out into the sweltering night, up two more empty blocks until I hit the parking garage. No tequila-soaked tourists in stiff new cowboy hats showed up to keep me company.

In my head, I rode up the creaky elevator alone to the third floor. I crossed a stretch of concrete and darkness to Daddy's beater Chevy truck, alone. I fumbled to open the door, panicked by now about getting inside fast enough and punching down the inside locks. No electric locks, no keyless remote for this old girl of a truck.

26

Standing there in Melva's safe world, staring into that dark hallway, I considered turning around and spending the night in Daddy's indent on the couch, the pistol on the floor right below my head. Instead, I punched a familiar number into my cell, hoping the creak above me wasn't Jack Smith or Etta Place. Or my dead Daddy, angry that some stranger was trying to lay claim to me.

CHAPTER 4

My breath came in short, quick gasps. I could see nothing but blackness and tiny fragments of light, glitter falling in a dark galaxy. My aching arms reached up and my palms pushed against the satin-lined lid of the coffin. I was getting weak. I'd been at this for hours.

A phone trilled, muffled but close. Someone was out there, six feet of packed dirt and red clay and crawling earthworms above my grave. They could help me. I began to scream so loudly I woke myself up.

This is how it always ended. The dream haunted me at least a dozen times a year, and the worst part was not knowing which night it would strike, when I'd wake up soaked in sweat, choking on my own spit, gasping for breath. There was only one night – the anniversary, September 3, when I always pulled an all-nighter with the horses, never letting my eyes shut – when I was free of it. On most every other night of the year, I fell asleep to the canned laughter of late-night reruns.

My dreams, since I was a kid, always had a

physical consequence. If I fell off a horse, I'd hit the ground with enough force to wake me up, and my butt would be sore for an hour afterward. Two nights ago, I woke up from a sex dream so close to orgasm that my fingers took me there in seconds. Of course, that could be because my sex life had been a little lacking lately.

It took a few beats for me to cross over the gray divide from dreamland to the deluxe king room at the Worthington. My body was slick with sweat, my hair damp at the base of my neck. My heart slowed at the sight of a gently starched white top sheet, the carved antique wardrobe, the cherry-red throw still folded neatly at the foot of the bed.

Victor from El Salvador had been only too happy to drive up to the door of Daddy's building last night in his Yellow Cab, pop me inside, regale me with tales of his own hopeless love life, then drop me into the waiting arms of a hotel doorman. Victor's card has been a fixture in every McCloud's wallet for the last decade, ever since the Christmas Day he slept near a DFW luggage carousel waiting on my long-delayed flight from Cheyenne that didn't arrive until 3 a.m. He drove the forty-five miles to the ranch as dawn broke and charged only a standard fare. All the McClouds had a stomach virus that year, buckets at every bedside, some pulled from the horse stalls. Still, Daddy crawled out of his sickbed in his pajamas and slippers to hand Victor a crisp $100 bill as a tip.

My niece, Maddie, is the artist behind the sign

29

pasted on the back of his cab's passenger seat. 'Best Cabbie on Earth!' it shouts, accompanied by a vibrant drawing of a taxi with a friendly brown man waving behind the steering wheel while driving atop a misshapen green and blue planet.

I hoped that in some small way Maddie's art negated some of the prejudice that flowed Victor's way since 9/11. I hated that he felt the need to paste three American flag stickers inside the cab for added passenger reassurance.

The phone shrilled two more times before I made a supreme effort to try to find it, lost somewhere in the puffy clouds of the comforter.

'Where the hell are you?' Sadie demanded as I pressed it to my ear.

'What time is it?' I asked groggily.

'It's eleven a.m. You're not at the ranch. I'm standing on the porch, so don't lie about it. You told me you were spending the night here.' Her tone, accusing, was justified.

'Oh, Sadie, I'm sorry! I was at the office late . . .' I wondered whether to tell her first about Wade or the obnoxious reporter or the woman claiming I was not Sadie's biological sister.

I chose none of the above.

'I decided to pull a Daddy and take a room at the Worthington. I thought I'd be up at seven and home before you got there.' Sadie and my niece, Maddie, lived two miles from the ranch in a doublewide trailer they dubbed the Can of

Dreams. It overlooked a sweet spot of the property that Sadie hadn't committed to building on yet.

'Uh-huh, right. Like you were going to pull yourself off of a million-count feather pillow-top mattress at the crack of dawn. Very optimistic. Well, at least you finally got some sleep.'

She changed the subject abruptly.

'Tommie, yesterday afternoon after you left, Mama had a little spell.'

I sat up, fully awake now, taking in the three tiny empty bottles of vodka on the dresser and the fact that I was completely naked except for a pair of purple striped bikini underwear.

'Why didn't you call?'

'I didn't want to bother you while you were trying to get a handle on Daddy's stuff because, Lord, we really need to do that. By the time I got there, she was calm. She said she just had another headache and asked why everybody was all bothered. Meanwhile, an orderly was picking up the lunch dishes she'd tossed across the room. She got a little V for that.'

V is for Valium. At some point, I think every single word in the English language will be abbreviated or eliminated if it cannot conform to one to four letters. Sadie, an iPhone addict, is on board with this; me, not so much. A hundred years from now, I believe linguists will study our language and write (brief) papers on how inefficient we were with our brains. Why use a complicated word when a shorter one will do? Why store fifteen words in

31

your head that mean essentially the same thing? The poetry, the nuance, the rhythm will no longer matter.

'Did she recognize you?' I asked my sister.

'No. Well, yes, eventually. After we got to Irene's.' She paused. 'We took a little field trip.'

I slid back down in the bed. No wonder Sadie was so eager to forgive me.

'And what did Irene have to say?'

'I can hear your tone, Tommie.'

There are words for people like my sister. *Kook* was harsh. I preferred *free spirit*. Sadie is both my polar opposite and my favorite person on earth.

There are words in my head for Irene not nearly as kind.

'She laid her out on her table. She thinks Mama stores too much energy in her head and that's causing some of her headaches and memory problems.' Sadie took a breath. 'I swear, Tommie, I think I saw something rise out of her like a fog. Mama kind of shuddered. And then we had a nice lunch at Catfish King. You know how she loves Catfish King. She called me Sadie Louisa. She hasn't called me that in ages.'

I stopped myself from saying that Sadie should be thanking a piece of fried fish for triggering Mama's memory instead of a lapsed-Catholic/psychic/yoga instructor with an occasional marijuana habit.

Two years ago, doctors diagnosed our mother with early dementia. Eleven months ago, Daddy gave in and moved her to a nursing facility that specialized in Alzheimer's and its many unnamed cousins.

No cure, just drugs that could help but often didn't. All of us took it hard, but Sadie still passionately sought the supernatural miracle that would bring Mama back to us.

'That's great,' I said carefully.

'Really?'

'Really. Good job.' I wasn't lying. It probably did Mama a world of good to get out of that place for a while. And who was I, the runaway, to criticize how Sadie took care of Mama when I was usually hundreds of miles north?

We hung up, agreeing that I'd be at the ranch by mid-afternoon, with CFS in hand as a peace offering. That would be text-speak for Chicken Fried Steak.

I spent twenty glorious minutes with my back to the shower's luxury hot water massager, the equivalent of a generous man giving me a back rub without expecting anything in return.

While I toweled off, my brain, still relentlessly processing, conjured up another picture. Mama pulling weeds in the garden, singing to herself, a mournful, bluesy song at odds with a bright day, knee deep in cilantro and lemon mint, the most cheerful of herbs. Still, it was a beautiful sound. Haunting. I was about thirteen, several yards away, cutting lilac for the sachets Granny liked in her underwear drawer.

When I asked, Mama told me the song was an Ethel Waters classic from the twenties. She said her mother used to sing it to her when she was a little girl. She seldom mentioned her mother, so those few words, that tiny glimpse, were a rare gift.

An odd lullaby, I thought. More of a lament.

Ain't these tears in these eyes tellin' you.

Right after Mama was diagnosed with Alzheimer's, I became obsessed with listening to every version of 'Am I Blue' in digital existence. Ella Fitzgerald, Linda Ronstadt, Ray Charles, Bette Midler, Willie Nelson. At the time I just thought I was missing the Mama who used to know the words, hoping to trap her inside a little machine and plug her voice back into my head.

Now I wondered if my subconscious had been bubbling up, telling me that even at thirteen, I already knew something was not quite right. That the song was a clue.

A finger of dread found its way under the thick cotton of the complimentary hotel robe. I shivered. I stared in the mirror and told myself to buck up, raking my fingers through wet, stringy hair that reached halfway down my back.

I'd never believed in layers or bangs or Chi irons. I washed my hair. I combed my hair. I let the air dry it.

I'd only seriously chopped it off once, three years ago, donating it to a little girl named Darcy. In her case, *A* was for alopecia. She'd arrived at the

34

ranch with a bad synthetic wig and the kind of emotional scars that only other little twelve-year-old boys and girls can scratch out on your heart. Darcy loved the horses first and my hair second. When she left, a hairdresser in town cut off fifteen inches. I put it in a plastic bag as a goodbye present, which sounds creepy but wasn't in the least.

Myra, a good friend and the psychologist who ran the therapy side of the ranch, pulled me in afterward.

'That wasn't exactly protocol,' she said.

'Do you think it was the wrong thing to do?'

'I don't know. It's not Darcy I'm worried about, Tommie. Or any of the other kids. You have the highest degree of success of anybody here. I give you the most messed-up kids for a reason. The person I'm worried about is you. You get in too deep. I'm afraid the next body part you chop off will make you bleed.'

I wasn't sure whether she was speaking meta-phorically or not.

'I don't know any other way,' I protested. 'And I always let them go.'

'Maybe you watch them walk away, Tommie. But you never let these kids go.'

I scooped my jeans up off the floor by the bed where I'd dropped them last night, smelled under the arms of the peach-colored Lucky Brand T-shirt I'd borrowed from Sadie because the clean clothes in my suitcase had run out, found my bra and one boot under the bed and another near the door.

I tugged it all on and checked my purse for the pistol.

A weapon didn't seem like overkill even in the light of day. Then I called down and asked for a cab to take me back to Daddy's pickup in the Stockyards. Victor, I knew, had a lunch date with a single mom he'd met online.

CHAPTER 5

I decided to take the stairs because all the magazines say you should.

Those same magazines also advise you never to walk into a parking garage alone, even in the daytime.

Later, when I thought about what happened, I wondered if it was sweat or intuition that sent a prickly feeling down my neck when I placed my foot on the first step. I'm not one of those women who walk with their keys poking between their fingers, ready to combat a would-be rapist, but I'm more wary than average and my paranoia had hit Level Orange about eighteen hours ago.

My father descended from a long line of federal marshals, soldiers, and Wild West lawmen, one said to have put a bullet into Clyde Barrow. My late grandfather – federal marshal, combat veteran of two wars, and one-time sheriff of Wise County – religiously trained Sadie and me in target shooting and hand-to-hand combat on Sunday afternoons when Granny took her nap. The combat part mostly involved lots of giggling and kicking the straw out of a homemade dummy's private parts while we knocked it around the trampoline. The goal was to empower us and it worked. Boys' private parts never scared us much.

Halfway up the second stairwell of the parking garage, I heard noises above me. A symphony of muttering voices, percussive thwunks, and intermittent groaning. Someone was getting beat up.

Should I go up? Down? Was I the hero type? My heart began a slightly faster pound, like I was five minutes into a treadmill workout with the incline rising.

Was my imagination working overtime? Yes. It was probably a couple of construction workers. Or tourists. What kind of bad guys struck on Sunday morning in the middle of a tourist haven famous for expensive western wear, saddle bar stools, and the Cattlemen's restaurant where J. R. Ewing ate his big rare steaks?

Sweat dripped little raindrop streams down my chest, my neck, my back.

Do not, do not, do not, DO NOT have a panic attack.

I whispered this to myself like a mantra, as if it would actually help, while I slipped off my boots and padded cautiously up the stairs, dodging broken glass from Coors Light bottles. The stairwell door was propped open on the third-floor landing, making me an instant target, so I dropped to all fours, jamming my left knee into a jagged two-inch shard of glass. I pulled it out without thinking, wincing, feeling blood dampen my favorite jeans.

Tourists.

I was wet with perspiration. I guessed that it was about 110 degrees in the unventilated stairwell. The concrete barriers blocked most of the brutal sun, letting in only slivers of light. It took a second for my eyes to adjust. Daddy's pickup was twenty feet from me, right where I'd parked it yesterday.

Ten other cars were parked on this level, leaving plenty of scary open spaces.

This was important to note because the action was taking place in the far corner of the garage, about seven car lengths away. Three guys. Two standing up, faces shielded by large cowboy hats. And one on the ground, flopped over like a cotton dummy, on the wrong end of the punching. So far, they hadn't looked my way.

I blinked twice, not really believing what I was seeing.

Today's polo was the color of the Caribbean.

What the hell was Jack Smith doing near my pickup truck? Staking me out? A self-centered reaction on my part, since he was the unfortunate man on the ground. I stepped back into the stairwell, ran partway up the next flight, and dialed 911.

'Help,' I whispered. 'Guy getting beat up. Third floor. Stockyards Station garage.'

'Ma'am, did you say someone is getting beat up?' I could hear the click of her computer keys.

I hung up.

The logical thing would be to retreat down the stairs and outside into the sunshine. I wanted more than anything to leave Jack Smith to his own problems, especially because I half wondered if these two thugs were doing me a favor. But the thump of a hard boot hitting soft flesh reminded me of an old man in Ponder who used to kick his dog in public.

One of the men continued to go at Jack; the other leaned against a car, arms crossed. Jack's groans had stopped, his body's reaction reflexive now instead of defensive. Not good.

I grabbed my keys out of my purse, sucked in a breath, and, crouching, made an awkward, limping run for the passenger side of the pickup. I knelt down on the concrete to fit the key in the lock. I might as well have jabbed a pocketknife into my bleeding knee. It took every ounce of willpower not to cry out.

I pulled open the door and gingerly stretched myself flat over the ripped Naugahyde bench seat. My hand groped for the gun tucked underneath the seat. I slid backward out of the pickup, peered around the bumper, and took aim.

Daddy's pistol in my purse wasn't loaded.

But the .45 under the driver's seat of the pickup was. Unlike Daddy's pistol, it felt as natural in my grip as a hairbrush or a tennis racket. My grandfather gave it to me on my twenty-first birthday after Mama had retired for the night.

Lots happened while the women in our family slept.

It was a big gun for a girl, my grandfather warned me, with a hell of a kickback if you didn't know what you were doing.

'But,' he added, 'you're going to know what you're doing. It needs to be second nature or you have no business carrying.'

Grip, stance, sight.

Practice, practice, practice.

It was a year before Grandaddy decided I had passed his training class and gave me permission to take the gun out on my own.

The two men seemed to be arguing over whether to dump Jack into the back of a black Escalade.

'OK!' I yelled, like an idiot, running straight at them with the outstretched .45. I imagined several generations of dead, experienced law-enforcing McClouds flinching from their bird's-eye view in heaven. 'Put your hands in the air!'

'What the hell?' The biggest guy swung my way.

I slipped behind a red mini-van, readjusting my aim over the hood to point at the guy's left shirt pocket.

'Bubba, I think we have a little girl with a gun.'

Bubba? The last time I heard that name I was sixteen, and dating one. Now Bubba walked toward me, unmoved and unarmed, into a slash of light. Brute nose. Evil grin. A black beaver-felt Stetson that cost about five hundred bucks new. Ostrich boots.

Not a pretender. A professional redneck.

'This ain't just any little girl, Rusty,' Bubba said, seemingly unconcerned that I might blast out his heart. 'I think this is *our* girl.' He punched at the screen of his iPhone. 'Lookie here, cutie, I've got your picture. I'm not going to hurt you.' He strode forward, holding out the phone.

'I *will* shoot you,' I yelled. 'Stop right there!'

He grinned and kept on coming. Thirty feet away. Twenty.

Grip, stance, sight. White noise roared in my head.

'I've already called the police. And you don't think I can shoot?' I took aim at a Jack in the Box ball grinning from the antenna of a white Volvo station wagon to the right of his head, and it exploded satisfactorily into a puff of plastic. The human Jack had managed to drag himself into a seated position, but his arm hung at a sickening angle. Jack Smith wasn't going to be any help. I guessed at least three broken ribs.

I didn't really believe I would shoot this guy, and by the look in his eye, he knew it. He would be on top of me in seconds. Grandaddy's combat training raced through my brain while he advanced again, still smiling.

When he was a yardstick length in front of me, I burst from beside the van and thrust an impressive high kick in the direction of his crotch. The ballet classes I still attended every Wednesday night paid off.

'You little bitch!' he screeched. He grabbed his crotch with one hand and my hair with the other as I ran past. Yanking me violently to the ground, he pinned me beneath the weight of his boot. I saw long blond wisps in his fist.

I don't like to admit it, but I have a thing for my hair. As he leered above me, holding material from my scalp, I forgot to be scared.

With both hands, I twisted the boot as hard as I could into the most unnatural and painful position possible. The steel toe made a ninety-degree turn, knocking him off balance. His phone clattered to the ground. He let out another howl. I flipped away from him as 250 pounds of hard fat and muscle hit the floor.

My left cheek was now smack against the cold concrete, inches from the pointy toes of his boots and from his phone. The screen glowed with a picture of me from the staff bio section of the Halo Ranch website. There was no time to think about this. I scrambled up and ran toward Jack and his other attacker, fueled by frustration and anger and hellbent momentum, without a single thought of a plan.

What was happening to me? I didn't want to mess with these redneck freaks. I didn't want the pink letter in my purse. I didn't want my Daddy to be waiting for a headstone covered with a mound of fresh earth and a blanket of a hundred long-stem roses fried brown by the August heat.

'GET ON YOUR KNEES,' I screamed at the other goon.

I hadn't even heard them coming, not until the two police cars screeched short behind me, and four uniformed officers, a bona fide battalion for a Sunday morning in Fort Worth, exited with guns raised. I braced, my own gun pointed at the head of bad guy No. 2.

I was only inches from Jack, who peered up at me with a goofy expression.

'Your hair. It's so pretty,' he said dreamily. 'Like an angel.'

A cop gently pried the .45 from my hand.

'Is this registered?' he asked me.

I nodded, mute.

'I'll take your word for it. Let's put it back where you got it.' Texas cops could be nice that way. His mouth was still moving, telling me how I should look into pepper spray or a more appropriately sized weapon. Texas cops could be sexist like that, too. Grandaddy's advice was to never argue with them. Eighty percent of Texas law enforcement, he claimed, was the same kind of man, the kind on a lifetime power trip.

The other cops were busy cuffing the two thugs, who turned as docile as little sheep and no longer had a word to say. The guy in the black hat winked broadly in my direction, though. He held up a few strands of my hair and tucked them in his shirt pocket like a souvenir, before a cop pushed his head down and shoved him into the backseat of a patrol car.

Smiling at me through the window, he mouthed: *You're welcome, Tommie.*

The cops insisted I take a short ride to the hospital with them so I could get 'checked,' although I'm sure they were thinking there is not a pill for a 107-pound woman who tries to take down a 250-pound man with a ballet move.

They reminded me about Texas's concealed weapons law when they glimpsed the handle of Daddy's pistol in my purse, and then proceeded with a barrage of questions about the events of the last twenty minutes. I told them the truth: that Jack Smith had showed up in Daddy's office last night but that before that, I'd never seen him. I knew nothing about him except that he clearly irritated other people besides me.

I had no idea why Jack and I ended up in the garage at the same time. It sounded unlikely even to my ears but the McCloud name gave me some clout ('You mean, of *the* McClouds?' one cop asked). I left out the part about my picture on Bubba's cell phone. That was too complicated to process.

At the hospital, while my bloody knee dripped onto a pristine hospital sheet, I punched *Jack Smith Texas Monthly* into the search function of my phone.

Nada.

All manner of Jack Smiths popped up, dead, alive, and Twittering, but none that appeared to be employed by *Texas Monthly*.

It took about a half-hour for a resident to cut away the left leg of my jeans at the thigh, cleaning and stitching up the messy gap with the precision of Granny's old Singer sewing machine. Then, an antibiotics prescription in hand, I tracked down Jack, parked on a stretcher in an emergency room cubicle, tied to a morphine drip. His faded gown bared nicely toned, tan arms with defined biceps, reminding me of a Harvard rower I once knew.

'Who are you?' I demanded. 'What do you have to do with me?'

'Blue popsicle,' he said.

'What? Is your mouth dry? Do you want me to tell the nurse?' I tried to casually examine the plastic bag that held his personal items, hanging conveniently on one of the bed's metal rails, courtesy of an efficient nurse.

'Angel,' he said.

'I'm *not* your angel.' My surreptitious attempt to dig out his wallet only succeeded in wedging it deeper into the bag. I didn't see a gun or an ankle holster. Maybe I'd imagined it. More likely, the cops took it. Where *were* the cops, anyway?

'Chicago,' he mumbled.

I pulled my hand abruptly out of the bag.

'What did you say? Stop punching the morphine button. Jack!'

It was too late. Jack was already drifting off into self-induced slumber.

Chicago.

A word that wouldn't go away.

CHAPTER 6

I slipped onto the highway about four, curving the wheels in Sadie's direction, my knee throbbing in annoying rhythm with a persistent headache at the base of my skull. My eyes checked the rearview mirror every few minutes: No one was following me.

My scalp still tingled. In the hospital's bathroom mirror, I'd discovered a raw pink space on the left side of my head, an injury to my ego that bothered me a lot more than my knee.

A fresh-faced rookie cop, Jeffrey something, was nice enough to retrieve Daddy's pickup from the garage and drive it to the hospital. He'd brought it to the valet at the front entrance, tucked me inside, asked six times whether I was OK to drive, then handed me his card, doing everything but directly asking for my phone number. Any other day, I'd be interested. I could use a little chivalry in my life.

I usually loved this drive – the desolate Texas plains dotted with baled hay and cattle, the expansive blue sky that made me feel freer than four shots of tequila, the lazy comfort of going home. Today, all of it flew by in a blur of anxiety.

I had to tell Sadie about the letter. Why hadn't I done that already? My mind raced during the forty minutes of familiar highway to Ponder, the small town that abutted our family's ranch, finally zeroing in on the one thing that bothered me most: Anthony Marchetti, the butcher who sat in a Fort Worth jail cell. I didn't believe for a second that Marchetti had anything to do with me but I was beginning to think that somebody or several somebodies mistakenly thought so, and that couldn't be good for my family, not if that scene in the garage was connected to him.

Maybe Jack Smith was an innocent bystander, just a reporter hanging out by my pickup, and he simply got in the way. Maybe I was their true target. But why? The only weird thing going on in my life was Rosalina's letter, and she didn't issue any threats. The note was just a grieving mother's emotional plea.

No, Jack had to be involved somehow. What reporter wore a backup gun, for God's sake? A gun in an ankle holster is always a backup to something else strapped higher up. The ankle holster is too damn hard to reach for a primary weapon.

Jack had said 'Chicago.'

Rosalina is in Chicago.

Anthony Marchetti wiped an entire family off the earth.

In Chicago.

The whole thing was weird, unbelievable. I

turned off I-35, sped by the exit for Dale Earnhardt Way. Minutes later, I entered the Ponder business district, which is, of course, a joke.

My hometown has been living off two things as long as anybody around here can remember: the Ponder Steakhouse and the ghosts of Bonnie and Clyde. The Ponder Steakhouse had served up bull testicles – more politely referred to as calf fries on the appetizer portion of the menu – and very decent steaks since 1948. Bonnie and Clyde actually had the balls to rob the Ponder Bank.

Years later, when Warren Beatty and Faye Dunaway showed up to shoot the movie version, they left it pretty much the same – a dusty spot in the road with twin water towers, three churches, and train tracks right down the middle. I'd like to say the founders named Ponder for its poetic sunsets, highlighted on the city website as some of 'the best in the world.' But the town was named way, way back in another century for W. A. Ponder, a big landowner. Land equals power in Texas. I should know. My family owns a lot of it.

I swerved onto the main drag of Bailey Street, and made a quick U-turn into a parking space in the half-full lot of the steakhouse, my stomach growling for the to-go order I'd called in for three chicken fried steak dinners. An early supper for Sadie, Maddie, and me, as promised.

The Ponder Steakhouse could be the only place in the world where you're required to make a

50

reservation by phone for your baked potato. When you sink your teeth into one, fully loaded, cooked to perfection in a giant oven for two hours at exactly 500 degrees, well, you try to remember to call ahead the day before. Today, I'd have to settle for fries.

The screen door clanged behind me and I could see Betty Lou in the darkened corner taking an order from a couple of old women wearing straw shade hats with jaunty ribbons, in a tiff about the three-dollar charge on the menu for splitting a dinner. Betty Lou was throwing in the senior citizen discount, while righting the tilted frame of a faded autographed picture of Faye Dunaway that hung on the rough-hewn wall.

'Is your top sirloin tender?' one of the women asked Betty Lou primly, pointing to the least expensive cut of meat on the menu.

'No one's ever said they can't chew it,' Betty Lou drawled. This was the kind of answer you got from Betty Lou.

'Excuse me for just a moment, ma'am,' she said, waving me over to the register. With a blond dye job from Dot's Beauty Shop, tomato-red lipstick, and a pair of Wranglers, Betty Lou didn't look as old as her weathered customers but probably was.

She glanced at me briefly, taking in the tangled hair, the state of my jeans, and the knee decorated with an Ace bandage. None of it fazed her. She'd seen me in much worse condition in the last twenty years, sometimes with a cast from a bull-riding spill, sometimes smelling like something that came out of the rear end of a horse.

Betty Lou and I went through our usual routine: She handed me three hot environmentally incorrect Styrofoam containers loaded with thousands of heart-stopping calories and I handed over forty-five dollars, which included a generous tip. 'How's your Ma?' she asked. 'Tell her I miss her. I tucked in the last piece of chocolate pie for Maddie, so don't you put your fork in it.'

'Thanks, Betty Lou. Mama's about the same. I'll tell her you said hi.' Also part of the routine. I loved that it was still not pointless to Betty Lou.

Five minutes later, I was back on the road through town, driving past January Lane (although there was no December or February), the feed store, and the veterinary, hungrily snatching French fries out of the top container. After a few miles, I turned onto a road that quickly changed from smooth black asphalt to vicious, spitting gravel to clouds of boiling dust. I bumped along until I could see the big family ranch house up on the hill, in a protective clump of live oaks, but before that I turned off on an even more rugged dirt lane, winding through the playing fields of our childhood.

I pulled up to Sadie's doublewide trailer, which she'd affectionately decorated with multicolored swirls of spray paint. She'd set her temporary home on a breathtaking spot of land. It faced the sunsets and overlooked a cement pond now shimmering brilliant orange, like someone had filled it with Sunkist soda.

For the first time, I realized how vulnerable Sadie and Maddie were, alone at night, smack in the middle of open land. Targets.

I got out of the pickup, then stopped. A new piece of sculpture rose three feet above me, a twisting tower of colorful recycled metal – Coke and beer cans, scraps of rusted tin, bottle caps, all of it attached to an ancient fence post running up the middle. An old doll that I remembered from Sadie's childhood collection leered down from the top, wired in place. Molly, I think she'd named her. Molly's blond hair and yellow overalls had seen better days. Her blank blue eyes remained as creepy as ever.

Apart from the doll, the sculpture was oddly appealing, an idiosyncratic complement to the trailer itself, covered with Sadie's bold pop art drawings. Window boxes spilled over with marigolds, white petunias, and Mexican heather, thriving despite a spate of hundred-degree days.

'Do you like it?' Sadie asked, emerging from behind the sculpture with wire cutters in her hands. An impromptu weapon, I thought, if she ever needed one.

'I'm calling it "Last Night," inspired by that blind date Irene set me up on. What is she thinking, really? He was at least fifty. He had five threads of hair. He tried to slip his hand down the back of my jeans while we were still in the driveway. Lucky

53

there's not much between me and my jeans.' She pointed the wire cutters at my legs. 'Nice look, by the way. What happened?'

'Inside,' I evaded.

While she gathered up her tools from the ground, I took special note of our physical differences. Sadie wasn't especially tall, but she was all legs like Daddy. We used to lay out in bikinis on rickety lawn chairs, greased up with Crisco or baby oil, eagerly comparing the progress on our arms every half-hour. I always lost. Sadie roasted a beautiful gold; the best I could do was a bubble-gum pink. Her dark hair grew straight like Mama's and mine but was usually cut ruthlessly short by her own hand. My sister was blessed – or cursed – with sweet, open features that reckless men always took as an invitation.

Today she wore her favorite summer attire. Paint-spattered cutoffs. A hot pink tank top that showed off two inches of flat stomach. Cheap plastic thongs on her feet that had seen better days. Minimal makeup. Big smile. Sadie made her living firing up tiny blowtorches and bending platinum and gold into breathtakingly delicate jewelry that looked like it was made by the hands of fairies. Her pieces sold for insane prices in galleries in New York and San Francisco. She refused to build a house yet, although she could well afford it with her take from the gas wells. Too permanent, she said, although her muses lived out here in the gum trees and live oaks. Inside, other muses entertained

54

her through her Bose sound system, iPod, satellite dish, and plasma TV.

'Tooooooooooooooooooommie!'

My niece, Maddie, jolted out the door behind her, barefoot, brown pigtails flying, wearing a faded Save the Gulf tee that hit her at the knees.

'What are we going to do tonight?' she wanted to know. 'Did you rent something really good?'

'Yes.' I handed over *To Kill a Mockingbird*, rented out of a Redbox inside the hospital waiting room, and the chicken fried steak.

'You're the best aunt ever,' my nine-year-old niece declared, throwing her arms around my waist, then bouncing away as if her feet had springs, a prime-time commercial for joy. A knot rose in my throat. As soon as Maddie disappeared into the trailer with her loot, Sadie turned from stacking tools under the awning.

'What's wrong with your face, Tommie? You look like you're about to cry.' Her eyes involuntarily fluttered, and I knew what was coming. 'Why did you shoot a gun today?'

This was one of the problems with Sadie. She'd inherited The Gift from Granny. The fluttering eyes, a couple of blinks that most people wouldn't notice – signals of some kind of premonition or 'feeling.'

She sniffed. 'I can smell it.'

'Really?' I asked, not believing her. Sadie liked to acknowledge other people's psychic abilities, but not her own, even though hers were, well, real.

She opened the door of the trailer.

'Let's get settled first,' she said.

It was like stepping into a walk-in refrigerator – a breathtaking blast of cold air. I threw the deadbolt behind us, Sadie looking at me quizzically.

'It's still light outside,' she said.

I only nodded.

The trailer gleamed, spotless, as usual. Maddie was already plopped on the floor in front of the TV, lifting the lid of the Styrofoam container. Sadie and I nestled into opposite sides of the red-leather booth in the corner of the kitchen and dug in.

A granola friend, born somewhere north, once asked in disgust, 'Why would any sane person want a greasy breaded crust around a slab of red meat?' If you had to ask, I told her, you'd never know.

I bit into a perfectly fried piece of heaven and, keeping my voice low, gave Sadie an abbreviated five-minute version of Rosalina's letter, my internet research into her brutal, mob-connected husband, the surprise visit at Daddy's office from the man named Jack, the violent encounter in the garage. Once again, I left out the fact that Jack's attackers knew who I was. There was only so much worry I thought I should dump on her.

'Don't tell Mama you took out that gun,' Sadie warned when I'd finished, which was ridiculous because Mama didn't even know who I was.

'And clean it tomorrow.' For someone who lived out in the ether, Sadie was remarkably practical. Cleaning guns had always been a religion in our family, with Grandaddy as the head preacher. 'Do you have the letter?'

'Yes.' I gestured to my purse while peering into the depths of her Sub-Zero refrigerator. 'There's only one more Corona.'

'Go for it.' She reached across the booth to my purse on the seat, pulling out the pink envelope, bent and creased from all its encounters with my obsessed fingers.

I settled back into my seat with the beer, watching her eyes as they moved over words I'd memorized, reading along with her silently even though I couldn't see the page, my stomach churning around the grease.

Have you ever wondered about who you are?

My mind finished the letter a few seconds ahead of her. I watched as she flipped over the front of the envelope, examined the return address and the postmark, then held it up to the light, illuminating a small square. She pulled out a tiny picture stuck inside the lining of the envelope. How had I missed that?

A lovely, dark-haired woman stood on ground powdered with snow, an austere building looming behind her. In her arms, she cradled a small child. Sadie's next words brought back that prickly feeling on my neck and a dread I hadn't felt since I was little.

'I want to tell you something, Tommie,' she said, and I felt the world I knew falling away.

★   ★   ★

Sadie slid out of the booth, found the sponge at the sink, and began to scrub and rescrub the bar counter nervously. Her eyes landed everywhere but on me. I had never shared her fanatical need to clean. It seemed an odd characteristic for an artist.

'It was the night after you left for Wyoming. The first time, to do the internship. I surprised them.'

She stopped.

'Surprised who?' My voice was impatient. I thought we'd always told each other everything. Well, at least I'd thought she always told *me* everything.

'Mama and Daddy. Tommie, please don't be mad at me.'

'Sadie, just tell me.'

'They were fighting in the kitchen. At the table. They didn't know I'd come in the front door. It was late. Dark outside. I'd been with the horses in the barn. It was raining and I was filthy. I started up the stairs to the shower, but then I stopped. I'd never heard them so angry at each other before.'

I watched her pretty throat constrict as she swallowed, hard.

'Mama said it wasn't safe for you to go to Wyoming, that it was too far away. That Daddy better stop you. Daddy told her that she needed to trust him. Hadn't he protected us so far? He said it might be the safest place on earth for you to be, in a place backed up to wilderness. That they wouldn't find you.'

Mama always worried we were too far away. In

our mother's perfect world, I would have attended the TCU school of music, become a teacher, married, built my own place on the ranch, and borne three children by now. After the bull crushed any future as a pianist, Mama imagined the most ordinary life possible for me.

But who were 'they'?

Sadie glanced over at Maddie, who was glued to a black-and-white image of the irascible Scout, and her tone dropped lower.

'Daddy said . . . Oh, I don't know if I can tell you this.'

She seemed close to tears.

'Daddy said what?'

'He said, "As long as I'm living and breathing, she's safe. You're safe . . . "' She faltered.

'Just say it, dammit.' My voice was urgent and angry. Something else was coming, something I didn't want to hear.

'"I love her like she was my own." That's what Daddy said.'

There it was. My first certain step into an abyss of lies.

'Tommie, it doesn't mean anything.'

We both knew it meant everything. But she kept up the pretense. 'That's why I never told you. The next morning, everything was normal. Mama made scrambled eggs with cheese and green chiles, my favorite. She was smiling, relaxed, like nothing had happened. It all seemed like a dream. Really, maybe it was.'

All that detail, down to the chiles in the eggs. Not a dream. Her next words confirmed that.

'It was selfish, keeping it a secret.' She hesitated. 'I was just furious that you were going so far away. Not fair to you, I know. But nothing was fair. Maddie had been diagnosed by then and we'd moved back to the ranch. Daddy had taken over. I was a mess, a single mom with no plan. I wanted you to come home and fix it all.'

She didn't need to tell me. I remembered. The need to carve out my own life, to be on my own, had overwhelmed everything else.

She slid back into the booth, reaching her hands across the table.

'Please say something,' she pleaded.

I ignored the gesture. I didn't want her comfort. My mind was numb.

'What are y'all talking about?' Maddie's warm body was suddenly pressing against me.

Neither of us answered.

'You know, you can turn those into jorts,' she said.

'What?' I asked. Maddie was dragging me back from the edge, one little girl tug at a time.

'Those jeans. We can cut them off into shorts. Jorts.'

CHAPTER 7

I left Sadie's trailer after an animated round of chess with Maddie where so many salt and pepper shakers and lipstick tubes were standing in for pieces that it was a game just to remember what was what.

I was beginning to think she was losing pieces on purpose to make the challenge more interesting.

Maddie is the great love of my life.

Sweet, eager, daring, and very, very smart. When Sadie got pregnant at nineteen and the boyfriend skipped, none of us had any idea that it would be one of the best things that ever happened to our family and, early on, one of the most gut-wrenching.

Maddie has a tiny, uninvited peanut in her brain. One afternoon when she was three, she fell off a live animal, a rite of passage for McCloud girls. The scan in the emergency room revealed a disturbing shadow. Instantly, Daddy took over. Trips to the Mayo Clinic, MD Anderson, Boston Children's, and several rounds of radiation later, the tumor didn't budge, seemingly oblivious to all of the hubbub on the outside.

But it didn't grow, either. For six years, Maddie has continued to outperform all her classmates in everything: running, reading, writing. Once a year, she endures an MRI and doctors on a Fort Worth tumor board meet to reach the same conclusion. The neurologists say that with every month, it gets more possible Maddie will live a completely normal life. It makes me think that sometimes it's better not to know what's inside us.

Watching her little face, the furrowed, intense brow as she devised a game strategy to eradicate me from the planet, I promised myself, not for the first time, that I'd never let anything take her down. Not the invader in her brain. Not any malevolent forces in the wind.

Sadie observed our antics from the couch while updating her jewelry website on her MacBook. We didn't say much to each other until I picked up my stuff to go.

This would be my first night out of Sadie's cramped guest bedroom and in the family ranch house up the road, a departure planned before the events of this long day. Now I had another very good reason to set up elsewhere. I wanted to draw away the evil thing smoothing out its map and plotting a fresh path to me.

Sadie walked me to the pickup. She handed me an old Nordstrom shopping bag filled with her clothes and a blue drawstring Gap bag with shoes. A peace offering.

'To tide you over,' she said.

We wore almost the same size, everything just a little tighter on me. I'd been in such a hurry to catch my plane after hearing about Daddy that I'd packed minimal clothing and only the pair of scarred beige cowboy boots on my feet.

Now I was down a pair of jeans. But up a pair of jorts.

'You should let me wash your clothes, Tommie. I don't mind. Who knows the last time someone has run that old Kenmore of Mama's?'

'I'm fine. Don't worry about it.'

She lingered outside the truck after I shut the door, her arms crossed in the same defensive posture I'd seen since she was four and furious that Daddy wouldn't let her drive the golf cart around the property. I rolled down the window.

'When are you leaving?' she asked. 'Going back to Wyoming, I mean? Get back to those kids and your research? You could just forget all this stuff. Leave the ranch and everything else for Wade to watch over.'

Run away again, she meant.

'That's the thing, Sadie. I'm not leaving. Not this time.'

In the dark, I couldn't read the expression on her face.

'Please be careful,' I told her. 'Lock everything up. Turn on that fancy alarm that Wade installed.'

'I'm well trained,' she replied. If the terseness in my voice worried her, she didn't show it. 'All of that is standard procedure around here.'

I shifted into first gear and sucked in a shaky breath. Everything I loved most in the world fit in this tin box on the prairie. I wasn't going to allow anyone to take it away. Or, for that matter, let Rosalina Marchetti make it anything less than it was.

'We're forever,' I said, the words we used to write together on the sidewalk at school, in the sand at the beach, in the glass fog on the car window.

Sadie watched me drive away, growing smaller and smaller in my rearview mirror, until the blackness swallowed her.

The pickup crawled up the curved drive. The timed security lights from the sprawling ranch house glimmered through the trees. A cleaning crew showed up once a month to throw open the windows and dust, but the house had remained empty since Mama left it. I can't say I was all that thrilled about walking into it alone after the events of the last twenty-four hours, not knowing what hid in the dark beyond the reach of the security lights and a moon that flitted in and out of smoky night clouds.

Stepping out of the pickup, I slung my backpack over my shoulder, gripped the .45 in my right hand and the suitcase in the other, and moved toward the veranda. I groped under the cracked pot near the porch swing for the key. The family ghost, propelled by a gentle breeze, rode the swing back and forth. The air smelled wet and fresh, like

64

a storm was coming. The door gave a familiar whine as I opened it, and I punched in the security code.

Sadie and I had yet to go through Mama's things. Neither of us wanted to admit she would never return.

But I was thinking the time had come to admit a lot of things.

The house felt hollow, empty, a shell of what it used to be. I quickly flipped on lights to dispel the shadows, dropping my suitcase and backpack at the staircase, heading down the hall, not to Mama's room in the newest addition, but toward the kitchen and the centerpiece of my childhood – a long oak farm table where we ate and laughed and learned algebraic equations that left their permanent imprint in the wood. Where Mama and Daddy had their fight.

I opened the louvered doors of the cozy utility room off the kitchen. This was Mama's favorite space. Her small antique desk still faced the big window Daddy had cut out for her, once a view of lazy cows and inquisitive wildlife and little girls thinking up games that occasionally resulted in stitches.

Here, I had curled up in a slice of sun on the pine floor, listening to the steady vibration of the dryer, watching Mama pay bills or write letters.

It had always been my safe room. If there was anything to discover, I was certain it would be here.

65

I set the gun on the top ledge of the desk, moving aside a Hummel figurine of a girl playing piano, a bowl of seashells, and a small blue-velvet-covered book of Emily Dickinson poetry.

The gun looked ugly beside them, its character changed forever today, the first time I fired out of fear.

Mama's window loomed, a big black hole into the night. The security lights shone only on the front of the house and tonight's schizophrenic moon was in hiding.

I imagined a face emerging in the glass like a floater rising to the top of a lake.

A man, an attacker, could be standing on the other side and I wouldn't know until the shards shattered and rained all over me.

Stop it, I told myself. *Stop it!*

I yanked at the cord of the blinds, slamming them down.

The desktop rolled up easily. Inside, the desk was riddled with cubbyholes and rows of tiny drawers.

The middle drawer in the top row always held the most fascination for Sadie and me, with its miniature keyhole and a crudely carved monkey gargoyle, its hands over its eyes.

The irony was not lost on me today. I pulled on the drawer, but it didn't open. I closed and opened ten other drawers, but they revealed only the usual debris: paper clips, old car keys, a bundle of rubber bands, a handful of buttons that weren't related.

I saved the large right-hand drawer for last, giving it a solid yank. I knew what was inside: a plain white business envelope grimly labeled 'Read After My Death.' As one of her last lucid acts, Mama made a specific point of showing me exactly where it was. Funeral arrangements, she said. I flipped over the envelope, tempted to break the seal. Instead, I slid it deliberately back into the drawer. There were other things to discover first.

I heard a scratching sound. A rat running along the woodwork?

No. At the window. Something outside.

It's nothing, I told myself. Just like all those times as teenagers when Sadie and I lay in our beds upstairs, egging each other on, imagining all sorts of things congregating in the dark.

I cautiously pushed aside the blind because the nine-year-old version of Sadie wasn't there to pay a dollar to do it.

Not a face. The fingers of a tree danced on the glass.

The wind was beginning to blow, the storm coming. The moon, gone. I dropped the blinds and checked the locks on every door and window in the house. I yanked every curtain closed, flipped on every light. When I was done, I felt marginally more secure.

Rummaging around in the large cabinet over the washing machine, I found a feather pillow with the right degree of mushiness and a set of striped blue sheets, smelling like they'd just been pulled from the line outside the window.

Halfway up the staircase, exhaustion overtook any paranoia about what lurked out there in the night. My bandaged knee ached. I turned on the light when I reached my room, taking in the bare twin mattresses, the bright yellow furniture, the red curtains running with black ponies.

With what little energy I had left, I thought about Fate. I thought about it as I kicked off my boots, as I tugged on the fitted sheet, as I yanked my hair out of its sloppy pin-up job, as I tucked the gun under my pillow, a big McCloud no-no.

I thought about my brother, Tuck, who used to sit on the edge of this bed and tell me stories before he died in a car wreck on his eighteenth birthday and left a bottomless hole in my child-hood. I thought about Rosalina, still searching for her stolen daughter. I thought about Anthony Marchetti, a killer of children, and wondered again what in the hell he had to do with me.

The rain came as I shut my eyes.

I never knew Roxy Martin, but I saw gauze from her prom dress hanging like a turquoise ghost from a hundred-year-old oak tree a half-hour after the breath left her body. It plays like a movie in my mind. The mangled Mercedes convertible in the ravine. The flashing lights of the police cars that blocked the road, their headlights pointed toward silhouettes of three men down by the river searching among the wreckage for pieces of a pretty girl. The loud drumming of the helicopter ambulance landing on the black road ahead of us.

I read about Roxy in the paper the next day and the next: a sophomore, a star volleyball player, a daughter of a single mom, and the victim of a senior boy who drank straight vodka out of a plastic water bottle at the dance and survived the accident with a bruised spleen and two broken legs.

That was four years ago. I had been in Wyoming, driving back to Halo Ranch on my day off after picking up a prescription for a sick horse. Sitting there in my pickup, the police lights strobing my face, I was unable to tear my eyes away from the scene. I couldn't breathe. A psych major halfway to a Ph.D., I could identify my first panic attack.

I could also draw a line to its source.

Tuck.

I'd never had a full-blown attack since. But this morning, after a brief, fitful night of sleep in my old bed, I sat at Mama's kitchen table and my hand trembled while I pulled my gun apart to clean it.

I could be the daughter of a monster. For the first time, I gave that realization the freedom to roam my brain. Sadie's revelation about Daddy's words had opened a dark chasm.

I love her like she was my own.

My childhood could be a complete fraud. My DNA, an especially sick, twisted double helix formed by a stripper and a hit man.

69

Mama and Daddy could be champion liars. Kidnappers. Sadie might not be my real sister.

When a sharp pain jabbed me in the chest, I stood up and sucked in some slow, ragged breaths, opening the refrigerator for something to do, for some way to avoid a trip to Panic City.

A twelve-pack of Dr Pepper sat in the front. Whenever in Texas, I lived by Dr Pepper's 1920s slogan: 'Drink a bite to eat at 10, 2, and 4.' It was inspired by a long-dead Columbia University scientist who determined we had a natural drop in energy at those times of the day. I added a Pepper between the a.m. hours of six and eight whenever necessary. It was 7:08 a.m. according to the rooster clock above the old gas stove, which used to crow on the hour until Daddy figured out a way to shut him up.

I popped the top of a can and drank an icy, luscious, sweet sip, my legal alternative to crack cocaine. The thirty-nine grams of sugar ran straight to my bloodstream, respectable only if you compared it with the fifty grams in a can of Orange Crush. Maddie shared these numbers in a born-again manner during a brief stint when she drank only water at the behest of one of her TV pop-star princesses. A true McCloud girl, she returned to the Dr Pepper fold in two weeks.

As my blood pressure dropped to an acceptable level, I pulled my purse off the floor and dug out my phone. Three messages waited on my voicemail.

The first, from the Fort Worth police. Jack Smith's arm was not broken, just sprained. His attackers had made bail. The two men explained the encounter as a case of road rage, claimed that Jack had cut them off on I-35, then flipped them off. They'd followed him to the parking garage for 'a conversation' and Jack had made the first move.

I didn't believe it for a second but it was a pretty good story because we lived in Texas, where the rules weren't always clear to people. I made a mental note to call the police and get the real names of Jack Smith's attackers. In Texas, Bubba wasn't derogatory. It was affectionate. It could be a nickname for anything.

I didn't like that I'd pissed off two violent strangers who carried around a picture of me and were now free.

The second voicemail, from Sadie, was short: 'Call me after your Dr Pepper.' The rooster said it was still a little early for that.

The third was Jack Smith himself. He asked whether I'd mind dropping by his hotel sometime this morning. No explanation.

Sorry, Jack, I have other plans today.

As an afterthought, I checked my email, which I was stuck doing on my phone until wireless internet and cable were set up at the ranch. I didn't much like reading email on a tiny screen; I'd meant to go through it on Sadie's laptop last night but forgot because, as Granny would say, things took a turn.

I glanced at fifteen new messages with familiar addresses. Chicksaddlery, Equineglobe, Texaslonghorns, Potterybarn, Amazon, iTunes. Delete. Delete. Delete. Delete. Delete. Delete.

Eventually I'd weeded out all but five emails. Four were from staff at Halo asking how I was doing. Kind, concerned. I would miss these people.

The last email fell into neither category. Not obvious spam, not personal. The address was madddog12296@yahoo.com.

Subject line: Don't let this happen to your loved one.

If an exclamation point had been tagged at the end, I would have immediately dismissed it as an ad for drunk driving or Lap-Band surgery.

But there wasn't, and I opened it.

The message was a yawning square of empty white. No words. No picture of a smiling, size 12, Lap-Band surgery graduate holding up a pair of circus-tent jeans.

My finger hovered for a second before I clicked the attachment. My phone screen filled with a pixelated blur. I closed out the screen and tried again. I got the same garbled mosaic of tiny tiles.

Nothing, I told myself. Nausea began a dance in my gut. An email lost in space, meant for someone else.

Still.

How easy would it be to trace the email or to sharpen the focus? I could email the image to my laptop, but I didn't have the necessary software.

Or the skills, for that matter. I didn't want to involve a commercial photo lab.

Or the police. Not yet.

If it was nothing, I could look foolish. If it was something, I lost control.

Once you went official, the game changed forever. Not always a good thing, Grandaddy said.

How clearly I heard his voice in my head these last few days.

The panic was awake again, stretching and yawning and curling inside me like a predatory eel.

I'm a psychologist, I reassured myself. Not a frightened girl.

I once won a collegiate prize for a thesis on Alfred Hitchcock and the cinematic techniques of the modern-day stalker.

I could play this game and win.

I knew the rules.

Even in my head, it sounded hollow.

I glanced at my watch, flexing the fingers on my left hand, an involuntary habit ever since the cast was removed all those years ago.

I needed to pull myself together.

Mama was waiting.

CHAPTER 8

I turned in to a parking spot in front of the Good Samaritan Center, my mind entangled in the past, suddenly bothered about Mama's desk, about the day she caught me trying to unlock the middle drawer with a bobby pin.

I was nine and had just spent a weekend in bed with Encyclopedia Brown and the flu. Mama's usually gentle fingers left red marks on my arm and a dime-sized bruise that took a week to fade.

Later that day, she apologized with a package of Hostess cupcakes and a Coke with crushed ice. Her eyes were bloodshot, like she'd been crying. She apologized, but she also made it clear I was not to do this again. Ever.

In my rearview mirror, I watched a man in a cowboy hat emerge from a black pickup. He seemed oblivious to my presence, but I waited until he entered the nursing home before I got out of my truck.

Jesus, I couldn't start living like this, afraid of every tall man in Texas with a cowboy hat and a black truck. I'd be certifiably nuts in a few hours.

For the last year, Mama had lived in this building

among a sad cast of people. The outside looked like an adult Disneyland, with a grandiose arched entrance and golf-course coifing of flowers and trees. Fake lily pads danced on the surface of scattered ponds. Wrought-iron benches waited for company that rarely came.

All of it cleverly disguised the reality of the place once you hit the door: another L-shaped hospital ward where people came as a last resort. Expensive wallpaper, nice furniture, and pretty paintings on the walls didn't make a bit of difference when there was only one way out.

Once Mama really started to lose her mind, Daddy hired a live-in nurse at the ranch, but the property was too vast and Mama liked to roam. After one final midnight search for her on horses and four-wheelers, he gave in.

The rancid perfume of Lysol and urine rushed at me as the glass door slid open, an odor that couldn't be covered up no matter how much money you threw at it. Specifically, $82,000 a year – the cost of keeping Mama snug with skilled nurses and therapists who specialized in dementia.

Our family's money was like a nice warm blanket folded at the end of the bed, dependable, always there, but not something to be used unless you really needed it. Unless it was really, really cold. Daddy hammered that into us at a young age. Our ancestors broke their backs to work the land we inherited, he'd remind Sadie and me.

Every time I walked in here, I said a grateful

little prayer to those ancestors. Today, I was also praying that the man from the pickup was already ensconced in a room with a favorite aunt, reminding her patiently for the hundredth time who he was.

Instead, his towering form leaned against the reception desk, his back to me. He was genially chatting up a white-haired volunteer with a freshly coiled perm. His body language was languid, but I'd seen plenty of languid men throw a fast punch. I changed direction and strolled toward a familiar female figure sitting in a wheelchair in the center of the reception area.

'Hello, Mrs Hathaway,' I said brightly, kneeling in front of her. I had a new angle on the man, but he'd moved. I didn't think he was one of the goons from the garage, but I needed to get a good look. Could there be a whole posse of rednecks after me?

I turned back to Mrs Hathaway, who, after seeing me, had paused her self-imposed daily eight-hour shift chirping back at the reception room aviary, a floor-to-ceiling cage in the corner fluttering with tiny canaries.

She wore a bright yellow robe, looking like something of a canary herself. Mrs Hathaway's daughter told me that her mother had been a lounge singer; now she never made a sound except when she was with those birds. I hoped she imagined herself flying away or bowing to generous applause. She wrapped me in a hug that transferred a smear of Olay lotion to my cheek and then went back to the business of chirping. Mama and Mrs Hathaway hung out together sometimes when the odd little planets where they lived aligned.

'See you later, sweetie,' I told her.

As I turned down the hall that led off reception, the man's head was down and shaded by the brim of his hat. He laughed. Maybe he was just a flirt providing an old lady with the high point of her week and a story to make her Bridge Club widows jealous. Because aren't we all still sixteen inside?

At room 125, I knocked three times. Mama didn't answer, so I turned my spare key in the lock. I closed the door, wishing it had a deadbolt. I had never trusted flirts and was pretty sure I was born thirty when it came to men.

She rocked back and forth by the window, staring at the slice of garden view that cost four hundred dollars extra a month. The room was like dusk, shadowy and depressing, because Mama didn't like the lights on in the daytime anymore. You could turn them on all day and she'd go behind you turning them off.

She showed no signs of recognizing me. I stopped being disappointed a long time ago. During Wade's eulogy at Daddy's funeral, she'd placed her hand on my arm and leaned closer to ask, 'Who died?'

'Can I brush your hair?' She didn't respond but she let me guide her up and over to the chair in front of the dressing-table mirror. I stood behind her, gently taking out the bobby pins holding up her hair. It fell like a snowy waterfall, still silky and long.

I picked up the brush and slowly began to count every stroke just as she did for me when I was a child and had a bad day. My scalp used to tingle for an hour afterward. My counting was often the only sound that broke the silence between us during this ritual and one of the few things that seemed to relax her.

Today I was angry. Today I felt like time was running out for good, maybe for all of us.

'Mama, am I your daughter?' I asked. 'Was I stolen?' My voice crept higher. 'Did you adopt me?' If Rosalina wasn't lying, this was the next best option. Mama and Daddy had adopted me not knowing I'd been kidnapped.

'Baby,' she said.

'Don't "baby" me,' I said, so sharply that she flinched. 'Look at this.'

I held the picture of a young Rosalina Marchetti cradling a baby, possibly me, in front of her eyes. She turned her head away from it, and her hands began an agitated dance in her lap.

'Who is this woman? Do you know her? She wrote me this letter.' I laid the single piece of pink stationery in her lap. She brushed it to the floor. I bent to pick it up, pushing down anger, knowing it would not help. I took a shaky breath.

'She says you lied to me. That she is my real mother.' I spoke gently. 'Her name is Rosalina Marchetti, Mama. She is married to a killer.'

'She's a pretty girl.' Mama's voice was like brittle paper. 'You're a pretty girl, too.'

She reached up with a hand cruelly resculpted by arthritis. One more body part that didn't cooperate. Those once elegant fingers had dipped and sailed across the grand piano every afternoon of my childhood, teaching me the chemistry and magic of the great composers.

Sometimes, she'd still my practicing fingers and tell me little stories: that Bach had at least twenty children; that Mozart was christened Johannes Chrysostomus Wolfgangus Theophilus Mozart; that Vivaldi was nicknamed 'The Red Priest' for his red hair and had been buried, broke and destitute, in an unmarked grave; that Rachmaninoff had giant hands with fingers that could stretch across the keys like rubber bands; that Chopin loved Poland so much he filled a small silver box with earth when he left the country and had it buried with him. That most of these men would never understand their genius before dying.

On the very best days, she would scoot me aside on the piano bench and play a little Duke Ellington or Billie Holiday and sing in her clear high alto. Mournful, playful, intelligent. My mother was all those things. Was she also a liar?

In October or November, when the embers of summer died down, we'd throw open the windows and Daddy heard the strains of our music all the way to the barn. He claimed that the horses stopped to listen. Mama said that she liked to believe the wind snatched up our notes and that they floated on the prairie, traveling forever.

'Did you take me?' I pressed. 'Do I belong to someone else?'

Mama reached up. I thought she was going to hug me, but instead she pulled skillfully at the messy knot that held up my hair.

She drew me down, turning my face to the mirror, and laid her cheek on mine.

I studied our features – the delicate bone structures, the soft, straight hair, the sad expressions.

'Mama, I need your help.' Pleading. 'I'm afraid,' I whispered.

It was the first time in my life I'd said those words out loud.

Her face remained blank, unmoved.

In the shadows of the mirror, I was the girl she used to be. There seemed no doubt.

Before I left, I asked for the key she always wore on a silver chain.

Without protesting, she let me unfasten it from her neck.

By the time I made it back to my truck, there was an empty space where the man's black pickup had been parked.

I reminded myself that I needed to find out the names of the men who'd attacked Jack. Maybe I could get a restraining order. But that might just tick them off more, serve to remind them of my pesky existence.

I wish I knew what the hell I was dealing with. One of those men had sought out and found a picture of me on the Halo Ranch website, for God's sake. I should probably tell someone that. I felt under the seat for my faithful .45. Still there. Some people sought comfort in the warmth of a furry pet; I was growing fond of cold steel.

The depression I always felt after seeing Mama was now compounded by the growing sense that something was very wrong, like invisible monsters were laying low, biding their time, traveling with me in the bed of the pickup. All I could do was keep moving forward, I told myself, and be alert. Don't freak out Sadie and Maddie too much, certainly not yet.

I'd asked Sadie to meet me back at the house by two, and she was already waiting in the driveway. Maddie sat cross-legged on the ground, sorting pebbles into piles of different colors, looking up as she heard my tires crunch the gravel. Her huge smile only swelled my apprehension.

'I think this is the right thing to do,' Sadie assured me, as we walked toward the front door, but I sensed that she felt guilty, too. Mama had worn the tiny key around her neck as long as we could remember. She never took it off, even to shower or swim, and always brushed away our questions about its history. As little girls, we were enthralled by the flea-sized red jewel embedded in it, certain it held some magic powers. We were convinced that the key belonged to a hidden treasure chest, and one restless summer afternoon we even dug holes around the property looking for it.

Mama grounded us for a week and made us pack up the holes. Didn't we know the horses and cows could break their legs in one of them? Later that night, when tucking us in, Daddy told us the key belonged to her mother's jewelry box. Mama, he said, had found it in the ashes of the house fire that killed her parents. At that time, Sadie and I had only a fuzzy understanding of Mama's past. Still, neither of us really believed Daddy's explanation. Why would she wear a reminder of something that hurt so much?

I was struck by a pungent fragrance the second we stepped inside the house.

Familiar.

Unsettling.

'Do you smell that?' I asked.

Sadie turned. 'What? Good smell or something-is-dead-in the-walls smell?'

'Lavender. It smells like lavender. The bouquets that Mama used to place around the house. And I don't remember opening those blinds this morning.'

'Tommie, are you sure you're OK?' Sadie studied my face. 'We can do this later. Or tomorrow.'

'I don't smell anything, Aunt Tommie.' Maddie was giving every corner of the room a vigorous sniff.

'Here, give me the key,' Sadie said, deciding. 'Let's get this over with, Tommie.' Her hand rested on my arm. 'Are you coming?'

'Yes,' I said, forcing a smile. 'Let's do it.'

Maddie grasped my hand with her small sweaty one, still gritty from playing in the gravel. When we reached the desk, she broke away and ran her fingers over the see-no-evil monkey carved into the drawer, the one that had so fascinated Sadie and me as kids.

'Is that monkey peeking?' Sadie teased, hoping to lighten things up, as she turned the key. Maddie rolled her eyes, too old for the game.

But nothing happened.

'It's stuck,' Sadie reported. 'Maddie, get the WD-40 under the kitchen sink.'

That or a little spit had been my Daddy's answer to fixing most of the things that were injured on the ranch. But WD-40 didn't help. Neither did Maddie spitting into the lock. This wasn't the right key. I let out my breath. It couldn't be simple.

'A sign that Daddy wasn't lying about the key,' Sadie said, 'which is almost worse.'

In the end, it wasn't Encyclopedia Brown but Grandaddy who taught me to pick locks. I'd never had much occasion to use the skill, except for once or twice. Or maybe five times.

I pulled a pin from my hair and went to work. The lock sprung easily and I tugged on the small, shallow drawer, which fell neatly into my hand. I saw what it held and my heart dropped.

'It's just an old deck of cards,' Maddie said with disappointment. A deck of cards imprinted with two faded swans, snapped together with a

83

pink rubber band, the kind that used to wrap around rolled newspapers that landed on the stoop.

But Sadie and I knew these were not ordinary cards. Reluctantly, I picked them up. They seemed hot to my fingers, alive with their own heat. The cards weren't a good sign. It was Maddie who saw it first, who said excitedly: 'Look!'

Taped to the back of the deck, to the four of hearts, was another key, this one modern and efficient-looking, stamped with a number.

The key to a safe deposit box.

Sadie and I never really believed these cards still existed. Our second cousin Bobby had embellished their place in McCloud lore, along with a lot of other things.

As kids, Bobby persuaded Sadie and me that aliens left crop circles behind the barn (Bobby was van Gogh with a tractor), that an ancient monster lived in one of the creeks on the property (it turned out to be a pregnant beaver), and that Dr Pepper's secret formula contained prune juice (that may be true). A boy of many strange talents, he walked around in the summer with a plastic Baggie full of dying flies, which he caught with his bare hand in mid-air.

Mama told us that didn't mean he would grow up to be a serial killer and asked us to be patient because his Daddy was mean. She didn't put it that way, but we knew. We'd seen the marks on

Bobby's legs, a telltale sign of parents who still thought it was OK to pull switches off trees and use them on little boys against the will of nature.

When someone asked me a few years ago why I chose to work with kids on a rough emotional path, I'd surprised myself and said, 'Bobby.'

One Saturday afternoon when I was in middle school, Mama dragged us to watch Bobby pitch a Little League game in 110-degree heat, and for once, he couldn't get the ball to fly over the plate. His dad yelled from the stands: 'You piece of puke!' and stomped off, abandoning Bobby to gut it out on the mound with no ride home. Bobby struck out the next three batters. Later, his dad took the credit for firing him up.

But on the day Bobby talked about Tuck and those cards, the adults had exiled us to the orchards, ordering us to pick up at least seventy-five peaches apiece. If we threw even a single peach at each other, Granny warned we'd be forced into summer slavery making jam – hot, steamy work, and I never failed to burn myself on the sterilizing pan.

Bobby, however, provided all the entertainment Sadie and I needed by immediately falling face-first into a trail of fresh cow patties. He was about ten at the time, too cool to cry and desperate to save face.

'Hey, I heard a story about your brother the other day,' he said, as the three of us walked toward a cement pond where he could wash up.

'Don't talk about our brother.' Sadie gave him a small punch in the arm. 'It's disrespectful to the dead. It's not your business. God, you *stink*.'

'Don't say "God" like that,' I said automatically.

'I swear, I think you'll want to hear this. It's spooky. My mom told me. Come on. It's firsthand.'

Sadie and I shrugged. Everything Bobby recounted was 'firsthand.' But we yearned for any details about Tuck, whose face was dissolving like a photograph under water. He'd died when I was six and Sadie was two.

Mama was at fault for that. She never spoke of our brother. She had erased all signs of his existence, removing every picture from the house with Tuck in it.

We sat Bobby out to dry on a patch of dry ground a smell-proof distance from us.

'Go ahead,' I commanded.

'My mom says your Granny is a good Baptist, but she does a lot of battle with the spirits. They come to see her at night in her dreams. Even a psychic at the Texas State Fair told your Granny she was one of them, but even more powerful. Did you know your Granny could tell the future with cards? Mama said she can tell when a tornado is whippin' up.'

Bobby watched for shock on our faces, but Sadie and I already knew this part of the story. We were familiar with Granny's 'feelings,' because they sometimes prevented us from leaving the house. We both knew she could do a lot more than predict the weather.

Because of that, we often begged her to read our fortunes, but Granny had to be in just the right mood. If she wasn't, she'd usually shoo us away and say gently, 'Life is meant to be a surprise.'

Bobby caught a fly in his hand, generously set it free, and continued. 'Well, the night that your brother, um, died, it was his eighteenth birthday. And your Granny was going to give him a special birthday reading. So your Granny laid the cards, and all these dark cards began to turn up.'

Bobby was clearly enjoying himself, and he could tell he had us. His voice lowered an octave, and he crept closer. I still remember the stench of cow dung and rancid creek water that clung to both him and his words.

'So your Granny snaps up those cards in a rubber band and refuses to read them. Tuck just laughs, kisses everybody goodbye, and heads out to ride around and do some celebratin'. Around midnight, he dropped off a friend and headed home. He took a shortcut on some back roads. They say he was goin' fast. That big eighteen-wheeler was sittin' with the lights off smack in the middle of a farm road, the driver drunk off his butt and asleep. Tuck was under it before he even knew it.'

I could feel the warm rush of blood to my face and a pain in my gut as if Bobby had punched me with his pitching arm, hard. Sadie's mouth was open in a perfect circle.

We'd never been provided details of the crash. In the years since, I've thought dozens of times about looking up the story in the Fort Worth newspaper archive to see whether the facts matched Bobby's story. I never did.

'Shut up, Bobby,' I said furiously. 'Just shut the hell up.'

'I think I'm going to be sick.' Sadie's little body was dry heaving, bent over.

Bobby being Bobby, he couldn't shut up, and I was too busy holding Sadie's hair back to stop him.

'Your Granny never touched those cards again,' he persisted. 'They had ducks on 'em, I think. I heard she burned 'em in a witch's ceremony.'

I took a threatening step forward and Bobby did what he did best. He ran.

Granny turned the peaches Sadie and I gathered that day into twelve pretty jars of jam, but that batch always tasted bitter to me.

CHAPTER 9

I turned the key over in my hand, grateful for the four-letter imprint on one side: 'BOWW.' Otherwise, the search for a mysterious safe deposit box somewhere in the behemoth state of Texas – or maybe anywhere in the forty-eight contiguous states – could have swept us on a useless, consuming journey.

Instead, it was almost too easy. Our search took approximately thirty seconds of old-fashioned thumbing through the Yellow Pages. There it was, a discreet ad in the bottom right corner of page 41. Bank of the Wild West, 320 West Third Street.

Quaint. I'd never noticed it once in all my years of traipsing around downtown Fort Worth. It certainly wasn't an institution I ever heard Daddy or Wade mention. What reason would Mama have to use it?

'Mom, we've got to go,' Maddie said, tugging on her arm. 'It's almost three.'

'We're registering for school today,' Sadie told me apologetically. 'The *M* through *Z*'s start signing in at three-thirty. And we're wallpapering her locker with peace-sign paper and buying a Taylor

Swift lunchbox. It's been a long-standing date. Maybe we could go to the bank tomorrow. I don't think we'll be back by the time the bank closes.'

She hesitated at the door. 'So what are you going to do?'

'I'm going to the bank.'

I desperately didn't want to go by myself. To open a box of Mama's secrets in a strange bank without someone to catch me when the earth shifted. But, even more than that, I didn't want to wait. Or involve Sadie and Maddie unnecessarily. I needed this to be over as quickly and cleanly as possible.

'Tommie, are you sure? You don't look . . . like you feel good.'

I knew she was thinking about the lavender. Wondering if her tough, fear-no-bull big sister was going the way of her patients.

'I'm fine,' I lied. 'I'll pick up the stuff, dump it in a bag, and bring it back here. We'll open up everything together tonight.'

Forty-five minutes later, an assistant bank manager quickly put that thought to death. Ms Sue Billington strode over when I stepped into the Bank of the Wild West as if she were on a mission to sell me the latest Buick. She was dressed in a JC Penney uniform: navy blue two-piece suit, starched white shirt, suntan hose, and black Easy Spirit pumps. I saw a bulge on the left side near her size 12 waist. She was packing.

She also carried invisible red tape, which she

had been wrapping around and around my head for the last seven minutes. We glared at each other across her shiny, glass-topped desk, empty of everything but a computer, a phone, a pen, and a spanking-new empty yellow legal pad.

Her voice was breathy, sweet, patronizing. I stared at her mouth, a leathery pink purse, the lines around it creased from an overgenerous application of Maybelline foundation a couple of shades too dark, maybe in an effort to match the suntan hose.

The little mouth kept saying versions of 'No way.'

'I'm her daughter,' I tried again. I slid my driver's license back at her, leaving a smudgy trail on the glass. 'I'm her guardian. My sister and I share control of all her legal matters. I have the key to her safe deposit box in my hand.'

'Please lower your voice, ma'am. I heard you the first time and the second time.' She spoke slowly, reminding me of the Sunday School teacher who'd slapped me with a name tag that said 'Sinner' after I'd raised my hand and suggested hell might not exist. I think I tried to pronounce the word 'conceptual' to no avail. Granny was big on jump-starting our vocabularies at a very young age.

'Ms McCloud, your mother has no other business with this bank. According to our computer' – she paused and tapped the space bar three times – 'the box has not been opened for a number of years. We are not privy to any legal authority you may have over Mrs McCloud's affairs. You brought no documents with you. You are not listed here as the one person who has permission to open the box.'

'Who is?' I asked impatiently.

'Ms McCloud, you must know I can't divulge that. All I know is that your driver's license says you have the same last name. A common last name, I might add. In this era of identity theft, I would think you would be grateful that we undertake such diligent precautions.'

The truth was, she was right. I knew it. I kicked myself for not talking to Mama's lawyer before showing up.

'Our father just died,' I persisted.

'I'm real sorry about that,' Sue Billington replied tightly, unmoved. As I stood to go, she beamed a row of snowy veneers at me, probably a month of her salary. She chose that moment to parcel out the piece of information she knew I'd want most.

'You and your sister should really coordinate with your brother, don't you think? He was here recently asking about the same box. He was much more polite, if I do say so.'

Then she bent, retrieved a paper towel and Windex from under her desk, and, with a businesslike spritz, wiped my fingerprints off the glass and into oblivion.

I slipped on my Maui Jims as I exited the bank into the blinding sun, wondering why people thought sunglasses helped them hide.

I'd never felt more exposed, more vulnerable in my life.

The perfectly innocent new mother pushing a stroller by me right now had no idea I wasn't staring at her sleeping baby because he was adorable under his ducky blanket but because I wanted to warn him that life was not going to be what he expected. That it was random and unforgiving. Forget Daddy's death, Mama's dementia, their apparent lies. Tuck's death alone proved that.

A fresh wave of grief rolled over me. For Daddy? Or Tuck? I blinked back tears.

Who could be impersonating Tuck? Why?

The man in a suit wrestling with an over-stacked Subway sandwich on the bench across the street had no idea that I wondered, *Is it you? Are you pretending to be my dead brother? Are you watching me?*

Get out of your head, my psychologist brain advised. *Do something.*

The sandwich guy tossed what was left of his early dinner in the trash and wandered up the street to report back in either at his boring office job or to a goon in a cowboy hat and a black vehicle.

I took over his spot and dialed up W. A. Masters, our family lawyer. A brilliant legal mind and an old University of Texas buddy of my grandfather's, W.A. didn't use office technology invented after the electric pencil sharpener – certainly not a cell phone. His equally ancient secretary, Marcia, promised to hunt him down the old-fashioned way, walking over to Riscky's, a barbecue joint and his favorite place to drink a tall glass of iced tea with four Sweet'N Lows in the late afternoon while he sorted through the next day's round of court appointments.

I assumed that W.A. knew nothing about this key or the contents of the safe deposit box, that it was another of Mama's secrets, popping up like dormant locusts released from years of imposed napping. At the moment, I actually felt relieved that Ms Billington, armed with window cleaner and her rolls of crimson tape, was an implacable fortress in the way of anyone trying to get in before I did.

I hung up and felt a little better. I did wish I hadn't worn such a short skirt, something plucked out of Sadie's bag, because the bellman across the street was enjoying the view. My sweaty thighs were sticking to the wooden bench like a pre-schooler's. Sadie's white T-shirt with a small pink sequined heart was like a second skin on me, the neckline a little too cleavage-happy. As for her short red cowboy boots . . . well, it was that or flip-flops and I could hear Granny nixing that from above as inappropriate going-to-the-bank attire.

I tipped up my sunglasses and checked the time on my cell phone – 5:14 – then slipped them back down.

'So you decided to show.'

94

The voice was low, rough, behind me, and I nearly fell off the seat.

I whipped around.

Jack Smith grinned and slid onto the bench, throwing his good arm lightly over my shoulders. The other was in a sling.

Surely I could take a one-armed man. My purse was on the ground by my feet. There was possibly some very old pepper spray in one of the pockets. Daddy's unloaded pistol was at the ranch. My .45 was in its home under the pickup seat.

Where the hell was that bellman now? The side street had emptied. Quitting time.

'Relax,' Jack said. 'What's wrong with you?'

'What are you doing here?' I snapped, throwing off his arm.

'Seriously? I'm living here.' He pointed across the street nonchalantly. 'Aren't you taking me up on my invitation to talk?'

I stared in the direction of his finger.

'The message I left on your phone,' he said impatiently.

Oh, shit.

Etta's Place. The name was barely visible from here, gold-lettered on an old-timey hanging sign over the door. I'd been too deep in my head for the past fifteen minutes to even notice the hotel. It was like Etta was pulling the strings and not necessarily for me.

'Let's go up to my room,' he said, rising. 'So we can speak privately.'

'You've got to be kidding.'

'Wound pretty tight, aren't you, Tommie? I just want to help. Come clean.'

'Really?' I asked sarcastically, my eyes sliding down his jeans. No bulge at the waist. No ankle holster. Loafers. No socks. White ankles, with a low-sock tan line, like a runner or a sailor.

He leaned his face closer, providing a graphic view of bloody slits and bruises. 'I've been lying to you, I admit it,' he said. 'About the story I'm working on. I don't really give a crap about horses.'

I stood shakily.

'Here is where we say goodbye, Jack Smith.'

I'd taken three steps in the other direction when he spoke again. His tone was overly casual, sending a chill through me.

'That's too bad, Tommie. I could tell you a few things about your mother. Ingrid. Except that's not her real name.'

'*What* did you say?'

He ignored me or didn't hear, moving quickly, already at the opposite curb near the hotel entrance.

He wanted me to chase him.

OK, Jack Smith.

I'll chase.

I reached the hotel about ten seconds after he disappeared inside. The bellman instantly swung the door open for me, his eyes glued to my ass.

'I'm five hundred an hour,' I snapped at him.

The expression on his face was worth about that much.

Jack opened the door of the room sweetly nick-named Etta's Attic before my second knock. He must have leapt up the stairs two at a time to beat my ride on the elevator.

'Welcome to the honeymoon suite,' he said with a wide smile.

Etta's Attic was on the fourth floor near a fire exit. Small kitchen. Cozy, colorful king-sized quilt on the bed. Comfortable-looking couch. An open laptop on the bed.

A Beretta M9 and a shiny silver Smith and Wesson Magnum on the antique writing table.

Jack drifted over and picked up the Beretta. Now was the time to decide this meeting was a bad idea, not worth the price of what he had to tell me. The .500 Magnum was a bastard of a hunting gun. I'd only shot one once and that was enough. Jack flipped the safety on the Beretta and set it back down.

'It's this story I'm working on,' he said apolo-getically. 'I don't want you to get the wrong idea. I usually don't carry a gun. I just use my hands as weapons.' He thrust two short kicks in my direc-tion and punched the air twice with his uninjured fist. I could see the bulge of a muscle. He offered up another stupid grin.

Those moves didn't work out so well for you yesterday, pal.

I stayed rooted to my spot in the doorframe, a decision to make.

Walk into the room and shut the door. Or run like hell. I was pretty sure this guy was crazy. Jack didn't fit neatly into any psychological profile. My mind ran through a list of possibilities. Schizophrenia, narcissism, bipolar disorder.

Mythomania, the art of making crap up.

'Here's the truth,' he said. 'I'm working on a profile of Anthony Marchetti tied to him getting out on parole. You know who Anthony Marchetti is?'

I barely nodded, immune to surprise, remembering the reason I followed him here. Information.

'I thought you might. Come in and close the door, will you?'

I shut the door, knowing that this is how young women disappear. The braided rug on the floor didn't look large enough to roll me up in without my feet sticking out. A plus.

I watched as he walked from window to window, pulling down the shades.

'Keeps it cooler in here,' he said nonchalantly. 'Texas sun is a bitch.'

Jack sat on the edge of the bed still close enough to reach the Magnum.

'I'm here because Marchetti threw out a few bribes to get transferred from Illinois to a Texas prison right before his parole. Odd, don't you think? He clammed up when I tried to interview him a few months ago. But I'm a pretty diligent investigator. I stumbled across a few things he didn't want me to know about. Like your mother. I'm pretty sure he sent those guys in the garage to suggest I drop the story.'

'There's been a mistake.' My voice sounded more vulnerable than I would have liked, especially in front of this man, this *Jack*, who had busted his way into my life. What an idiotic, ubiquitous name. Jack Ryan. Jack Bauer. Jack Ruby. Jack the Ripper. Jackass.

'None of this has anything to do with me or my family.' I realized that a very small part of me still believed that.

He studied me. 'Just what do you know about Marchetti?'

'Practically nothing.'

'I don't think that's the truth.' His voice was suddenly taut. 'I have a source who tells me that Marchetti's wife has contacted you. Rosalina. You know *that* name, don't you?'

Jack was bearing down on me now. Soft. Cruel. He was the frat boy who used to take pledges out for beers and then force them to their knees with a paddle, I thought. The one with the big smile on his face and a piece inside missing.

'OK, don't answer,' he said. 'But I've checked you out and found a few strange details.' He angrily pushed himself off the bed with the arm not encumbered by a sling.

'Like what?' I stuttered.

'For starters, your Social Security number belongs to a dead girl.'

My mother's first name was Ingrid. I learned later that wasn't the truth. That it was the name she chose for herself.

When I was sick, my mother wiped my face with a damp washcloth and told me a family legend, a fairly morbid one, looking back on it.

Her great-grandmother was also an Ingrid – Ingrid Margaret Ankrim, who crossed the unforgiving Atlantic from Germany as a teenager in the late 1800s. By the time the ship docked in New York harbor, battered and carrying a lighter human load than it started with, her sixteen-year-old hair had turned completely gray. Stress, they told her. Ingrid wanted to die herself when the captain buried three of her brothers and a sister at sea, wrapped in sheets and tossed like dolls into the ocean.

My mother's voice always dropped to a whisper at this point in the story. She said Ingrid watched her own mother grow silent and still on the voyage, imagining her babies lying in pitch-black, freezing waters with God knows what brushing by them.

She told me that we both inherited Ingrid's eyes – a bottomless green. My mother also inherited the other Ingrid legacy – she turned gray early. Her gray hair first appeared at twenty, a single stylish streak. One afternoon, as she colored it away in a monthly ritual in our kitchen sink, she told Sadie and me that strangers used to stop and ask 'where she'd gotten it done.' It never occurred to us to ask why she made it disappear.

Maybe every little girl thinks her mother is beautiful. Mine really was. You could tell by the way men acted around her, even happily married ones, with a charming awkwardness that made you embarrassed for them. Her soft blond hair, when she let it loose, fell, as Granny said, 'right to her rear.' The needle pointed to exactly 110 pounds whenever she stepped on a scale. She fit snugly into 27 x 27 Wrangler jeans, one of those rare women who could walk into a western store, pull her size off the shelf, and leave.

She hated violence – even spiders that wandered into our house got a free ride out on a magazine.

She never got used to the terrible storms that kicked up every spring in Texas. When the black wall clouds appeared on the northwest horizon, she'd orchestrate us in a dance of panic. We'd run from one window to the next, opening and shutting them to achieve the perfect air flow that a scientist she'd heard on National Public Radio said would keep the house from blowing away.

She was a terrible cook and a formidable chess player.

She was sad.

Sadie and I would wake up in the middle of the night to the mournful notes of her piano floating up the stairs. Sometimes we peeked over the landing to watch her play dressed in a black silk nightgown, her body moving like a sensual snake, to an audience of one cowboy, our father. We didn't understand the depths of her talent until much later. We just knew she was the best church pianist Ponder, Texas, had ever seen because everybody said so.

But these are not the things I told Jack Smith while I wondered whether every sentence falling out of his mouth was a lie.

'You look like you might faint. Sit down.' He patted the side of the bed. 'I'll stand over here if it will make you feel better.'

Soft again. I wouldn't fall for it.

'What's my mother's name?' I fought the desire to put my head between my knees.

'Genoveve Roth.'

Genoveve.

'It doesn't make sense,' I said, struggling for control. 'You don't know her. She wasn't the kind of woman . . . she wouldn't have anything to do with the mob. Or a killer. It's ridiculous.'

'You tell me what you know about your mother, then I can fill in details.'

Jack's hand was poised with a pen over a hotel scratch pad, ready to take down my words.

I answered reluctantly. 'Before she was married, her name was Ingrid Kessler. She was born in a small town in New York. She lost her parents in a house fire when she was a senior in high school.

She had no other close relatives. She told us that every piece of her past, everything she loved, had burned. She didn't have enough money to go to college, so she headed to New York City to pursue a music career. She played piano in bars, waitressed, and got pregnant with my brother, Tuck, on a one-night stand.'

I could hear voices in the room below us, a suitcase plunking down, the door of the room shutting. A man and a woman. Laughing. Separated from my nightmare by a floor. By inches.

'I'm sure she was lonely when she met my father,' I continued, stronger. Maybe the man and woman could hear me, too.

'He wandered into the diner where she worked. He ordered four eggs over easy with salsa and almost an entire side of bacon. He was a huge guy. Six feet, five inches. He drank two pots of coffee before she agreed to go out with him. Four months later, they married.'

I'm not sure why all of this was spilling out. Maybe because, out loud, it sounded more true. Maybe because I'd never gotten tired of Mama telling the story.

'She told us that my father saved her. He carried her and my brother away to his Texas ranch and his big family. Daddy always joked how she transformed herself from a Yankee to a Texan. I was born quickly; Sadie, four years later.'

'And they lived happily ever after?' Palpable sarcasm.

'You know, you're an ass. I'm surprised you're not beaten up every day.'

Jack's phone beeped. A text message. He glanced down.

'We'll have to continue this later,' he said. 'I'll call you.'

I was back on the sidewalk in forty seconds, dazed, angry, wondering how a professional like me, trained to strip away the layers of the human soul, had extracted so little from Jack Smith. He'd played on my fear brilliantly.

I uneasily entered the parking garage where I'd left the truck a couple of hours earlier. It was a different parking garage from the one where I fired a gun, at the opposite side of town, conveniently located near the Bank of the Wild West. Nonetheless, it was a parking garage.

It helped that I rode up in the elevator with a beautiful, ethereal-looking young couple, professional orchestra musicians, lugging their instrument cases from Bass Hall and arguing whether Rostropovich or Casals was the greatest cellist of all time.

Mama would have an opinion, I thought.

I got off by myself on the second floor, my eyes sweeping every corner of the garage as I walked to Daddy's truck. Neurotically, I peered in the pickup bed, then at the cars parked on either side of me. An empty blue Mustang convertible on the right, and, on the left, a green late-model Jeep. The interior of the Jeep appeared piled to the top with trash, leaving about a six-inch view out the back window.

A hoarder, I thought. Hoarders usually start their habit as teenagers. Most don't seek treatment until reaching fifty. A lifetime of pointless shame.

As I moved closer, I could see that there was more organization to the mess inside than I'd thought. The car was crammed to the top with papers and files, not garbage. Still, it appeared obsessive. A delicate chain with a small gold medallion hung from the rearview mirror.

As I pulled out of the parking garage, I mentally kicked myself again.

I hadn't asked Jack for the name of the dead girl, the one he said shared my Social Security number. And maybe something much worse.

CHAPTER 10

I no longer know who I am.

I said it out loud, in the pickup, halfway home to Sadie.

I am a product of lies.

The knowledge was making me reckless.

I shouldn't be doing this alone.

I should never have followed Jack Smith into that hotel. My cell phone buzzed in the seat beside me and I jumped, skittering into another lane, nearly hitting a Volkswagen Beetle.

I straightened out the wheel, grabbing the phone, staring at the readout, my heart tripping erratically.

Marcia. W.A.'s secretary.

I stabbed at the touch screen.

'Hello? Marcia? Hello?'

She started in immediately.

'Hi, honey. Just wanted to let you know that W.A. is in a five-foot hover. As you know, he does not like loose details. He had no idea, no idea *ta'tall*' – she emphasized these last two syllables with Texan flair – 'that your mother was carrying on secretly with that bank. He's over there right now. Made 'em open up past quittin' time just for him to get things settled. Thank goodness, I calmed him down a bit before he called the bank president.' She drew in an audible breath. 'Wild West. Even for Texas, that's a silly name for a bank. I'd sooner shoot off my right pinkie toe than put my money there or shop at Walmart on a Sunday afternoon. But the president was quite cooperative. Turns out his dad was Billy Bob Jordan, who used to go up against W.A. back in the day. You remember him?'

Marcia was always asking whether I remembered people I never knew. If I didn't hop in quickly, she was sure to give extensive details of Billy Bob's lineage going back to the Confederacy.

'Well, at least he's not in an eight-foot hover. Or a ten-foot hover.'

Marcia had been assessing W.A.'s hovers for many years. Anything past five feet required a bottle of whiskey and a policeman.

'Do you know when I'll be able to get into the box?'

'Well, honey, it's late. I told W.A. it would be best not to put out the bank any more than we have to. A Miss Billington over there seems to have quite a bird up her skirt. But they open right up at 8:30 a.m. I suggest you hustle over there first thing. Want me to have W.A. meet you there?'

Her curiosity was clearly piqued, but I didn't take the bait even though I trusted her to be discreet. Marcia once told me that a man with a hot cattle brand couldn't get a scrap of information out of her, and I believed it. What she knew and kept to herself about W.A.'s rich and powerful clients could fill every safe deposit box in Tarrant County.

'Thanks, but I'm good,' I said, watching the yellow Bug disappear ahead of me over a hill.

Daddy always said life was a game of inches.

A few more inches when I had swerved the wheel, and all of this could be over.

I could be over.

Just like Tuck.

Sadie's trailer door was unlocked.

Until two days ago, I wouldn't have thought twice about it. I also wouldn't have moved my .45 from under the seat to the glove compartment or put Daddy's pistol, which I'd stopped at the house to load, back in my purse. Or stood outside for five minutes after pulling up by the trailer to make sure that headlights weren't following me up the dirt road.

'Sadie, why the hell isn't the door locked?'

I had made my entrance into the trailer, fully meaning to say hello first, but spewing a furious admonition instead.

An iPod blaring in her ears, Maddie waved cheerfully while stirring yellow, toxic-looking cheese powder into overboiled noodles. Crumbled browned hamburger was in a skillet waiting to be tossed in. Two empty blue boxes stood on the counter. A double recipe. I was invited for dinner.

Sadie, immersed in her task at the red booth, looked up when I shot the deadbolt with more vigor than necessary.

'Maddie just fed the cats and probably forgot. No need to overreact.'

You don't get it. Something evil is parachuting into our universe. And you're playing cards.

'Maybe she left them in the same order,' Sadie said, acknowledging my presence, but as if we'd only been away from each other for five seconds instead of five hours.

Now I realized what she was doing. Laying each of Granny's cards in consecutive rows on the black Formica top. They stood out starkly, each one a knife in my chest. It seemed like a sacrilege to Tuck's memory to take ourselves back to that awful day. Sadie was too young to remember this, I reminded myself. All that pain. The sobbing and the screams. It was just a story to her.

'She probably did a quick spread,' she said.

Granny favored two techniques when telling fortunes. The more elaborate was called the Four Fans. Her subject randomly picked thirty-two cards out of a deck and she arranged them into four fan-shaped spreads of eight cards, each fan representing an aspect of the person's life – past, future, relationships, work. She'd do this mostly at Bible study teas for the ladies in her Sunday school class, who considered it blasphemous while believing every bit.

Before Tuck's death, Granny had always used the same cards – this dog-eared deck with two entwined pink swans. After his death, if you could talk her into a reading, Granny employed decks that Daddy and the ranch hands dealt at their Friday night poker games. I'd seen her use this deck only once after Tuck died.

For us kids, she favored a method she called 'the quick spread,' often accompanied by the words, 'We don't have time for this nonsense.'

She took fifty-two cards, plus one joker, and laid them flat on the table, facedown. We'd be instructed to move our hands over the top, spreading them into a chaotic mess until Granny told us to stop and pick exactly twenty-one cards.

We watched, hearts in our throats, as she flipped them over one by one.

Sadie continued her own reading. 'The jack of diamonds represents Tuck, followed by the three of hearts, which stands for celebrations. And his birthday was on the third of September. I bet Granny didn't think that was a coincidence.'

She flipped over the next card. The ace of spades. Why did it hold such power? 'The closer that ace is to the card that represents Tuck, the sooner the tragedy,' Sadie said.

She flipped over four more cards. The king of spades. The queen of diamonds. The queen of hearts. The joker.

'Look at all these face cards. At the king of spades. He represents someone evil, a man. Or it could be an authority figure.

'The two queens in a row suggest some kind of betrayal. Queen of diamonds could represent Mama – it's a blond woman – or she could be the queen of hearts – that's a mother figure. I'm not sure what the joker means.'

Clearly, Sadie had paid more attention to Granny's readings than I had. As if reading my mind (and maybe she was), she nodded to her laptop and said: 'I just gave myself a quick lesson online.'

My favorite reading from Granny included the ace of hearts – love, of course – and a jack of clubs, a promise that I'd meet a mysterious dark stranger. I kept my eye on one of the handsome young migrant workers on our farm all that summer. I blew off her warning about the card that followed – the two of spades. Deceit.

Snap out of this.

'Sadie, stop. Don't put another card down. It's crazy to think these are in the same . . .' I lowered my voice. 'That these are in the same order after all these years.'

Maddie was reaching into the refrigerator, pretending she wasn't listening.

'It's morbid,' I continued. 'And silly. Tuck had an accident because some stupid, selfish man got drunk. Unfortunately, it happens every day. How do you even remember Tuck's birthday?'

111

'Because it's the same date as his death. Because Granny told me to stay out of Mama's way on that day every single year. Didn't she tell you the same thing?'

She hesitated, picking up the cards.

'I know you believe,' she told me. 'You saw the cane.'

'The cane?' Of course I knew what she was talking about.

'The night of Granny's funeral. Mama let us sleep together in the guest room downstairs, in the big feather bed. In the middle of the night, I woke up. You were sitting there, just staring at the floor. On the carpet, we could see the shadow of Granny's cane.'

The cane, with a brass snake's head handle, that our grandfather massaged smooth out of an oak branch. The cane that trudged up and down Bailey Street on Granny's Saturday walk. The cane that snapped in two when she slipped and broke her hip on the back porch steps two weeks before her death from pneumonia.

'She came to say goodbye, Tommie. It was her way.'

Enough. I changed the subject.

'I saw Jack Smith today. Now he claims to be working on a profile of Anthony Marchetti. He says Mama is messed up in this somehow.'

Sadie looked up from the cards and stared at me. 'Do you believe him?'

'Yes . . . no . . . he's not very specific. And he's

a liar. But what about the letter from the woman who claims I'm her daughter? My mysterious Social Security number? Jack Smith says it belongs to some dead girl.'

Maddie handed each of us a bowl of macaroni and cheese and hamburger coagulated with powdery clumps. The wedge of iceberg lettuce was almost hidden by the glop of Hidden Valley Ranch.

'Will you please eat?' she pleaded. 'It's starting to look gross. And y'all are freaking me out.'

Sadie smiled at her. 'Just a minute, honey.'

To me, she said, 'You need to call Hudson Byrd.'

I woke the next day in my little-girl bedroom after enjoying a dreamless seven hours of sleep thanks to a pink pill I found in Daddy's medicine cabinet.

No hangover, no guilt, no worries about ill effects, at least not until the inevitable study years down the road finds otherwise. It seemed careless of me to knock myself out in an empty house with everything going on, knowing I wouldn't hear an intruder. But if I didn't sleep, I decided, there was no hope of surviving this anyway.

It worked. I met the morning with some semblance of the old me. The first thing I did was survey the living room, hands on my hips, dressed in a yellow cotton high-school-era nightgown I'd dug out of a drawer. I yanked the sheets off all the furniture, including the grand piano, and piled them in the laundry room. No more ghosts.

I took a deep breath before removing the old

quilt from Daddy's place, a worn brown easy chair that faced a large picture window.

The second move was to pop a Dr Pepper. The third was to call Wade and tell him to make the deal on the wind farm in Stephenville.

'But don't give them the Big Dipper property,' I said. 'I have plans for it. Also, you're in charge, officially. Just run the big decisions by me, like you would Daddy.'

'You're making a good call, Tommie,' Wade said. 'I'll take care of things. I'll honor your Daddy. And Tommie . . . I'd still like to take that ride sometime.'

As I hung up, I wondered again how much Wade knew about my family's secrets. His loyalty was impenetrable, like the black waters around Alcatraz.

Still in my nightgown, I headed back upstairs and dug a package of Post-its out of a backpack that held a tangle of printouts and notes related to my Ph.D., the one I was finishing up online, courtesy of Lydia Pratt, my thesis adviser and former college professor at the University of Texas.

I stopped briefly at a Xeroxed picture of Alex Wharton with his Harry Potter scar. Alex was a thirteen-year-old from Texas who visited the ranch a year ago. Daddy had read about him in the *Fort Worth Star-Telegram*. He'd worked with social services to send Alex to me at Halo Ranch, paying his full scholarship.

Two summers earlier, Alex had watched his father knife his mother to death on the sidewalk in front of their rent house because he didn't like his dinner. Pork chops with Campbell's cream of mushroom soup topping, mashed potatoes, and a frozen Green Giant medley. When that son of a bitch found Alex cowering in the laundry room, he stood up and shot him three times with the gun his mother kept buried in a box of Tide.

He'd paralyzed his father for life. Some people won't die.

'Put Alex back together,' Daddy told me.

I wondered if that was possible, if a soul could hold that much plaster, as I rolled up the gold cotton rug and set up trails of Post-its in the middle of the oak floor between the twin beds. This was my typical approach to research or to any problem with a kid at Halo Ranch that I couldn't reach.

The word *Mama* stood out on a pink Post-it in the center of my little project, with every question I could think of trailing chaotically from her in blue paper spokes. I'd written the names of all the other players on yellow squares and lined them up vertically. Anthony Marchetti. Rosalina Marchetti. Jack Smith. The mysterious 'brother.' Even Sue Billington, who I was certain knew more than she said.

I jumped as the thirty-year-old air conditioner thumped on, the rush of cool air from the vent making me shiver and the Post-its tremble, ready to fly.

None of it made sense.

It was the web of a demented spider.

CHAPTER 11

The high from the pink pill didn't last. By eleven, my gut was back to churning. All I wanted to do was swallow another one, maybe two, and crawl back into bed.

Dream it all away.

But Sadie and I had agreed to meet at the bank and face down Ms Billington together. She had an early rendezvous with her jewelry rep at the Dallas Market Center first, and by a miracle of God, the guys finally showed up about the same time to hook up my internet at the ranch.

I checked the parking lot for suspicious black trucks before dropping Maddie at a cheerleading day camp held four times a year by Ponder's high school squad. The logical part of my brain assured me that Maddie would be perfectly safe here. She loved this camp, a fact Sadie and I were mildly distressed about. In Texas, girls take lessons in cheering on boys practically from toddlerhood. I dreaded the day Maddie headed to middle school with girls who carried tiny two-hundred-dollar Gucci bags and considered chewing gum and a laxative a good substitute for lunch.

I reminded myself that I'd survived.

Sadie was waiting for me in front of the bank, chatting up a homeless man sitting with his meager possessions against the brick wall near the austere glass door, which discreetly advertised Bank of the Wild West in small gold letters. I immediately felt guilty about the four-dollar Starbucks in my hand. He laughed at something Sadie said, and she slipped him some cash. He tipped his dirty Dallas Cowboys cap in thanks.

'Hey, there,' Sadie said, spotting me. 'Let's do this.'

Our feet had barely touched the marble floor when Ms Billington, wearing an identical JC Penney suit, this time in brown, walked briskly over to us.

'You must be the sister,' she told Sadie, giving her a suspicious look. I couldn't wait to see who won this battle. I'd put my money on Sadie.

'What a beautiful set of pearls!' Sadie exclaimed, putting out her hand.

'Why, thank you,' Ms Billington said begrudgingly. And then, 'They've been in my family for seventy-five years.'

Ten minutes later, Ms Billington was 'Sue' and Sadie was the niece she wished she had, instead of the one in New Jersey who never called. Personal information flowed forth like a Las Vegas fountain – her cat, Shiloh, was diabetic; her Princess Diana roses were eaten up with black spot this year; she had almost saved enough for an over-forty singles cruise to Cabo.

Just who was the psychologist here? I asked myself.

Comfortably pulled up to Sue's pristine desk, we signed our names on the dotted lines, scribbled our initials in the right places, and showed our driver's licenses.

My hand shook a little; my signature was scraggly, uneven. I hoped Sadie didn't notice.

As a final show of kinship with Sue Billington, Sadie pulled a Kleenex out of her pocket and wiped off a drip of coffee that spilled from the lid of my Starbucks cup.

Sue beamed.

Sadie whispered, 'She's not so bad.'

I wondered, *What would life be like if I was as nice to adult people as I was to kids and horses?*

We trooped behind Sue in an obedient line, past wrought-iron teller windows and a life-sized Remington sculpture of a cowboy flying on a bucking horse. Surely it was a copy. I hadn't noticed any of this yesterday.

When we reached the far back wall, Sue discreetly pulled out a keycard and slid it into a near-invisible slot in the oak panel. A small door slid open. I was beginning to think Mama knew what she was doing when she left her secrets in the hands of the Bank of the Wild West.

The door shut behind us and we stood inside a wood-paneled room, large enough to hold about ten humans with very little breathing room. It was otherwise bare of anything except for cameras on spidery black arms hanging from the corners and a flat screen glowing like a blue aquarium window. It was positioned near a steel door. Sue punched six numbers into a keypad and placed her hand flat on the screen. It scanned her whorls and lines in seconds. James Bond technology still amazed me, although even Disney World scanned thumbprints at the front gate these days to assure that customers weren't sharing passes and avoiding Mickey's ninety-dollar-a-day fee.

The lock on the door clicked, Sue braced her hips and pulled it open, and we walked right into the muzzle of a gun.

Instinctively, I jerked Sadie's arm and yanked her behind me.

'Didn't mean to scare ya,' the man drawled, as he replaced his gun into a holster. 'It's just procedure. Hi, Sue.'

The ID hanging off a cord around his neck read 'Rex Ferebee, Security Systems Manager.' We now stood inside a glass box, the working digs of the overzealous Rex.

Through the glass, on three sides, we could see into a much larger room lined floor to ceiling with hundreds of metal boxes, each embossed with a large number and the same insignia of the Wild West Bank that had been stamped on the Yellow Pages ad: two derringers crossed over each other to make an X. Pendant lights hung from the ceiling, giving the room a cozy, modern glow. A gleaming maple conference table swallowed most of the floor space, along with a dozen overstuffed leather chairs.

'How much is it to own a security box here?' I asked, thinking this room was like something out of a John Grisham novel. His characters often started in hell and wound up on a sunny beach, I reminded myself.

Sue's smile was smug. 'They cost a lot. But our customers can well afford it.'

Rex waved his badge over a sensor. The glass wall on the right slid open enough for us to walk through. Sue marched over to Box 1082 and stuck in her key. I recognized this routine from the movies. I pulled out my keychain, inserting Mama's key into the other keyhole. We heard a loud click. Sue pulled the box easily from the slot, placing it on the table.

'Toodle-loo,' Sue said, and she and Rex exited the room. I imagined their leaving was just for show. They were probably pulling up chairs to TV monitors with enough angles to see up my nose.

'Hey, I'm Pee-wee Herman,' Sadie said, twirling her chair in circles.

'Wave to the cameras,' I replied, trying to match her light tone, as I slid open the top of the box.

And then I hesitated, the dread ramping up again, and Sadie stopped her game with the chair. Her head reached about halfway up the back of the plush burgundy leather; her feet dangled a good six inches off the floor. I would have laughed on any ordinary day.

'Maybe this is where professional basketball players keep their stuff,' she said. 'Or billionaire giants. Are those newspaper clippings?'

I reluctantly turned back to the box. Not a million dollars in hot cash. Not a cousin of the Hope Diamond. Instead, an odd collection of old newspaper clippings cooked with age to a golden brown. None of them appeared to be from the same newspaper, or from the same town, for that matter.

They seemed perfectly benign, which is exactly why they scared me.

I glanced quickly through several of the headlines: GARDEN CLUB MEETS THURSDAY, JOE FREDERICKSON WINS DISTRICT ATTORNEY'S RACE, WOMAN FOUND DEAD IN LITTLE RIVER.

The box held no clue to Mama's fascination with these particular articles or why she felt compelled to safeguard them. I set aside the rest of the clippings to look at later, and pulled out the last item in the box, a sealed plain white business envelope, thick with whatever was inside.

'Rip it open,' Sadie instructed. 'And then let's get out of here.'

I slid my nail under the flap and pulled out a wad of checks. Seven of them were made out to Ingrid Mitchell and the rest to Ingrid McCloud. My head was spinning. How many identities did my mother have? The checks were issued from the Shur Foundation, whatever the hell that was. They ran consecutively for five years starting in March of 1980, written on the first of each month for exactly the same amount of $1,500. I quickly multiplied: $90,000. Was it blackmail money? But she'd apparently never cashed them. Mama hid these checks for thirty-two years. Coincidentally, the same number of years I'd lived on this planet.

Sadie opened a large manila envelope helpfully provided by Sue Billington, gathered everything up, and placed it inside her backpack.

Then she pressed the red buzzer underneath the center of the table as we'd been instructed, so Sue and Rex could release us from this prison of sleeping secrets.

Blood pounded in my brain, drowning out every thought but one.

Mama was a liar.

After a quick lunch with Sadie at a new sushi joint, we parted ways so she could pick up Maddie. Nothing like eating questionable raw fish on a hot Texas day chased by an icy Dr Pepper.

Ten minutes later, I stood nervously at the front desk of the *Fort Worth Star-Telegram*, a venerable 106-year-old institution in mortal combat with iPhones and iPads like every other metropolitan newspaper in America.

One foot in front of the other, I told myself. *Don't trip.*

It was hard to say I trusted any newspaper completely, but I was counting on trusting one man inside this one with my life. He stepped off the elevator in a bright orange University of Illinois

T-shirt stretched tight across his belly, barely topping sagging Dockers that displayed signs of the something Italian he'd had for lunch.

Lyle Matyasovsky, managing editor for print and new bullshit media (the 'new media' was added in the publisher's fit of modernization; Lyle added the 'bullshit' in a fit of disgust), was old school all the way. I suspected that Lyle, nicknamed by reporters for his poofy Lovett-style hair and his poetic way with the language, bought his T-shirt wardrobe at the Dallas flea market.

He enjoyed letting Texans butcher his name before telling them that the first *y* and the *v* were 'kind of' silent. His résumé included stints at *The New York Times* and the *National Enquirer,* where he made big bucks to write headlines like DAUGHTER FINDS MOMSICLE DEAD IN BASEMENT FREEZER AFTER 20 YEARS. No one knows why this Yankee chose to land here. It's all part of the mystery of Lyle.

But the main thing: Lyle was an FOD. Friend of Daddy. Favors had been passed back and forth between the two for years. Daddy had insisted I carry Lyle's card in my wallet since high school, along with W.A.'s and, of course, Victor's. Like the spark that made the universe, no one knew how or why the relationship between Lyle and my Daddy began, just that it thrived.

'When you're a McCloud in trouble, you need a friend in the press, a friend in the court, and a friend on a horse,' Daddy used to say.

Lyle, W.A., Wade.

As soon as I saw Lyle, my face crumpled. Lucky for me, Lyle was an old hand at face crumples, because 60 percent of newsroom journalists are currently on a cocktail of antidepressants.

He ushered me into the elevator to the third floor, past the prying eyes of reporters shocked and hopeful that the newspaper might be hiring again (but surely not someone who wore red boots), and into his office, located in a tiny space in the corner. Lyle required nothing fancy.

Although I'd met Lyle fifteen or so times in my life, I'd never been in here. The 1950s-era metal desk – at least the parts you could see under the reporter notebooks, memos, and press releases – looked like chickens had two-stepped across it every night for years. The fluorescent lights were off, and a small antique desk lamp on a corner table was on. A brown and pea-green easy chair of indeterminate age sat crunched into one corner, possibly containing the contagion that would take out the *Star-Telegram* before technology did.

Framed newspapers lined the walls, not with Lyle's impressive honors and projects, but with headlines from other papers that struck him as worthy:

IRAQI HEAD SEEKS ARMS.

TYPHOON RIPS THROUGH CEMETERY; HUNDREDS DEAD.

DISCIPLES OF CHRIST NAME INTERIM LEADER.

IS THERE A RING OF DEBRIS AROUND URANUS?

124

I blubbered uncontrollably in the bio-disaster chair while taking in the satirical Onion headline MIT RESEARCHERS DISCOVER EACH OTHER.

Lyle shut the door, fiddled with the string of the dusty vertical blinds, then rolled his desk chair around to sit next to me, a clear sign the world was turning on its axis, because his reputation wasn't that of a touchy-feely guy. I hoped he wouldn't pat me on the head and trigger another round. A hug or any form of sympathetic body contact is the worst thing you can offer a Southern woman in tears if you're looking for her to stop.

Lyle kept several inches of distance and handed me a dusty box of unopened Kleenex resting on the top of his desk. Maybe journalists were all cried out.

'I'm sorry about your father. I didn't get a chance to talk to you at the funeral. I'll miss him. He had a way . . . with words.'

Lyle avoided my face, polite of him, because I could feel salty snot running down my nose into my mouth. Mascara bled into my eyes, stinging. I blurted out, 'That's not why I'm here.'

He watched impassively as I pulled my life's portable accessories out of my purse: a greasy bottle of Water Babies 30 SPF sunscreen, a half-eaten Hershey's bar, two mini-bottles of Germ-X (one empty), an envelope of outdated coupons, two sets of keys, a prescription bottle filled with Xanax (another of my discoveries in Daddy's medicine cabinet), a new horse hoof pick with the requisite curved metal hook that I'd purchased on sale the day before leaving Wyoming, and, finally, before I hit bottom, the letter from Rosalina Marchetti.

In Lyle's pudgy hands, the piece of stationery looked fragile. My life, in his hands. The cliché of all clichés. He read it quickly, read it again, then swiveled his chair back to his computer and spent a few minutes at the keyboard.

'She's the wife of Anthony Marchetti,' he said thoughtfully. Not, *What a nut* or *I wouldn't worry about this*.

But then, that's why I was here. Daddy said that Lyle would always tell it like it is, that he had a way of shutting out anything but the truth.

'You know him?' My voice sounded weak. 'Marchetti?'

'I know his history. Chicago Mafia, fraud, embezzlement, murder, up for parole. I know he's sitting down the street in one of our jail cells. Part of a new prisoner exchange program with Illinois and four other states. They're about to move him out to Odessa. Or at least that's the crap my reporter is getting. This makes me wonder. I assume you've looked him up yourself?'

I nodded, thinking that Texas had few reasons to say yes to Anthony Marchetti. The Odessa facility was in hot demand, a cushy place to hold such a violent offender, especially one Texas didn't have to take credit for.

Only two years old, the prison was touted as the

most high-tech in the world, with room enough to hold five thousand male and female prisoners. The operation was funded by a complicated equation of state and federal funds, making it a hodge-podge of inmates and a political nightmare, especially since Texas governors didn't play nice with Washington all the time. Or ever. One governor liked to remind everyone that the state could secede from the union at any time because that was the agreement in 1845 when Texas joined up, which, by the way, isn't technically correct. (Yep, the same governor whose name rhymes with 'scary' and who entered the presidential arena sounding like he jumped out of *Bonanza*.)

And then there's Trudy Lavonne Carter, the billionaire widow of a Houston oilman, who offered to donate the $600 million and fifty acres on which to build the Texas spectacle, but with a tangle of controversial strings attached.

The Texas legislature almost rejected her financial gift 'on moral grounds.' This was ironic like only things in Texas can be ironic. Trudy was a devout foe of the Texas death penalty and inhumane prison conditions. She informed her congressmen and state senators she'd only write the check if she could choose the architect and approve the plans. She insisted on skylights, air-conditioning, and enlarged cells. She'd once visited a distant cousin stuck in a suffocating Texas prison with no air-conditioning in the middle of July. It left quite an impression.

Trudy, bless her or not, won out.

'A guy named Jack Smith keeps . . . running into me,' I told Lyle. 'He claims he is a reporter working on a story about Anthony Marchetti for *Texas Monthly*. He says Marchetti bribed his way here.' For now, I left out the encounter in the garage.

'Never heard of him,' Lyle grunted, dismissing Jack as he rolled through his mental address book of Texas journalists.

'He claims that my mother is involved somehow.' Lyle's face was unreadable, as usual. 'I also got this anonymous email. It's probably nothing. But the subject line bothered me.' I pulled my phone out of an outside purse pocket and pressed on the screen. 'The third email down.'

He took it from my hand and read the subject line from madddog12296 aloud: 'Don't let this happen to your loved one.'

'Click the attachment,' I said. 'It's a blur.'

'Yes,' he agreed, 'it is.' He reached across to set the phone on the desk in front of me. I rummaged in my backpack, found the envelope from the bank, and tossed it across the desk.

'All of this is from a safe deposit box of Mama's that she never told us about.'

'Tell me this is off the record,' Lyle said.

'Why? I don't think you'd ever betray me.'

'Just say it.'

'This is off the record.'

'It's like handing a dollar to a lawyer. Just a little safeguard for you that I can repeat to anyone above

128

me. There's Rupert Murdoch and then there are the rest of us, who will forever adhere to a code.' He slid over to his computer. 'Forward that email with the attachment to llmat@fwstar.com.' I fiddled with my phone and we watched the email pop up on his screen in seconds.

'I'll have someone check this out. See whether we can follow the IP address and get this picture in focus.'

'So you think it's something,' I said.

He grunted in his characteristic Lyle way, which could mean yes, no, or maybe.

'Who will check it out?' I persisted. 'One of your reporters? A photographer?' He didn't answer. I knew from Daddy that Lyle maintained a few hacker contacts on the darker freelance side of journalism.

I inserted another question into the silence, this one personal.

'What do you think I should do next?' My voice wobbled a little.

'I think that you should sit here and tell me every burp and fart of what has happened to you, leaving nothing out, not even the damn color of Mr Jack Smith's eyes. I'll start digging around. You could tell the police about all of this, but I'm not sure at this point that they're going to be that helpful.'

He paused, taking in the tattered state of my being, the red eyes, the kidnapped Xanax bottle, the hair piled up on my head like an exhausted maid. I realized he was still considering my question.

'You should think about hiring bodyguards for your family, Tommie. Then get on a plane and grant Rosalina Marchetti her wish.'

CHAPTER 12

It was a quarter after six by the time I finished with Lyle and sneaked my way into a basement room in the downtown courthouse, about a five-block walk from the newspaper.

The room was crowded with the most diverse group of females I've ever seen outside of a baseball game. Baseball and fear, the great equalizers. Blacks, whites, Hispanics, senior citizens, teenagers, suburban housewives – all these women had one significant thing in common: They were terrified of something.

Hudson Byrd, the man at the front of the class, a military contractor who witnessed horror shows in Iraq and Afghanistan, who once melted his hard body around mine, was teaching them to respect that feeling.

I spent forty-five minutes in a folding chair in the corner while they took turns imitating Hudson's simple defense moves on training dummies lined up at the front – slamming the chin with the heel of a palm, jamming the eyes with their thumbs, thrusting a knee to the groin.

Hudson roved around. 'Come on, folks, we need

a little less Jennifer Aniston and a lot more Angelina Jolie. Make damn sure he can't continue his gene pool when you're done with him.'

With every jab and poke and giggle, I had time to doubt the sense of showing up here and getting Hudson involved. I glanced at the door. Maybe he hadn't spotted me yet. As if he read my mind, he caught my eye and winked. He'd known all along, probably from the second I walked in.

Sadie said he showed up at Daddy's funeral and sat at the back of the church, that I just didn't see him. It would be rude to go.

Damn Sadie. Damn her for telling me Hudson was back from the war zone, for finding out that he was teaching this class tonight as a favor for a friend, for writing the time and location on a piece of paper she shoved in my purse, for reminding me without saying a word that I'd never come close to finding any man I loved better.

Eventually, most of the class was exercising serviceable moves. The granny in the back row with a cane and an ass-kicking left leg was the one I'd bet on in a dark alley.

'Knees, eyes, throat, groin,' Hudson said. 'Repeat it back.'

'Knees, eyes, throat, groin,' they chirped obediently.

'Those are your target spots. Don't forget it.'

For the last fifteen minutes of the class, the women sat cross-legged on the carpet and listened to Hudson's no-holds-barred lecture on weapons laws in Texas and the advantages and disadvantages of carrying guns and pepper spray.

They were rapt because Hudson had that effect on women. Sadie put him in the category of guys you could take home to Mama, but Mama would be shocked if she knew what he'd do to you later that night.

When his mouth was curved up, emphasizing crinkly lines around his eyes and deep dimples, he was irresistible, James Franco and Clint Black rolled into one, a magnet of sexual energy and charm and intellect. When it didn't, when his mouth formed a tight, inscrutable line, you took a step back.

I stepped back a long time ago and kept on stepping.

'You shoot a gun in self-defense and the bullet hits somebody, that's just the beginning of your problems,' Hudson was telling the women, holding up his hand amid a spree of protests.

'It doesn't matter if you're completely justified. You'll have to hire a lawyer for the investigation. When you're cleared, you'll have to keep him for the civil lawsuit the "victim" will slap you with.' He grinned. 'Hey, ladies, that's life in America, home of the free.'

When he was finished, a teenager, her iPhone on the floor inches from her leg in case of a Facebook emergency, stuck her hand in the air.

'Should I get a gun?'

'No,' Hudson said.

She made a face and glanced down at a flashing text message. 'Should I carry pepper spray on my key chain?'

'It depends,' he said. 'How pissed off do you get at your boyfriends?'

'My parents are making me take this class.'

'Yes,' he said, pointing to a thin woman with wire-frame glasses who had raised her pencil, briefly halting her compulsion to write down every word he said in a black notebook. She had a bruise around her right eye. 'You have a question?'

She cleared her throat. 'What specific kind of gun do you recommend that I carry?'

'I don't recommend that you carry any gun at all,' he said gently, 'unless you've practiced with it until it is like a glove in your hand. That said, a lot of women like .42 caliber revolvers or 9 mms. Some of them carry .380s. They're all effective, fairly easy to shoot. With a lot of practice.' He paused. 'Never, ever use a gun if you're afraid of it.'

She wrote this down.

Who would be safer tonight when we drove home, I wondered, *her or me?*

I wanted to beg her not to return to the man who delivered that punch.

A thirtyish woman, poured like cake batter into a pink tracksuit, waved her diamond rings vigorously.

'OK, what about this situation? A man is coming toward me with a gun and I don't have one. What should my first move be?' She chopped her hands in the air, karate-style.

'He's got a gun?' Hudson asked.

'Yes, a big one.' She couldn't help herself. She lowered her eyes to his crotch.

'And you don't?'

'Right. What should my move be?'

Hudson crossed his arms and propped himself against the blackboard that listed two reputable shooting ranges, one that I used to frequent every Sunday night.

'Your move,' he drawled, 'should be the same as mine. Haul ass.'

The class erupted in laughter, the teenagers helped up the old ladies, the suburban moms swarmed Hudson for a few extra questions, and I waited in the corner, wondering how to smother the heat coming off my body before he got too close.

Finally, when the last woman scooted out the door and Hudson moved deliberately toward me, all I could think about was how he'd looked on the top of a bull, a moving sculpture of grace and power, fighting for his eight seconds.

His archnemesis was a one-ton creature called Drill, Baby, Drill, a name that had nothing to do with oil and everything to do with West Texas testosterone.

Hudson and I met on the competitive rodeo circuit the year I turned eighteen. Eight months of daredevil riding, passionate arguments, and sex that disturbed the horses. It was the most alive I ever felt. Now he was inches from my face for the first time in six years, and I could barely breathe.

'So Tommie with an *ie*,' he said, drawing out the words slowly, 'what can I do for you?'

For the first time in two weeks, I wished I looked better, as his eyes roamed my face, makeup free, which is the way he always said he liked it.

No prelude, I just spit it out.

'I need one of your cop friends to let me into the downtown jail tomorrow to meet the murderer who might be my real father.'

'Done,' he said. 'If you buy me a couple of shots of Dulce Vida.'

An hour later, we sat in a heavily graffitied wooden booth at The Rope bar, breathing the cloud of smoke puffed our way from a guy who looked like Santa Claus with a black leather fetish.

Underneath a studded jacket, Santa wore a T-shirt that read, 'You never see a motorcycle parked outside a therapist's office.' I didn't take it personally.

The downtown dive catered to cops and Harley riders who shared an unlikely bond after years of drinking beer and twisting on bar stools together. I didn't want to know what kind of life-and-death issues were decided in this room as the two tribes handed tips back and forth. Regardless, sitting here felt pretty damn safe.

After an intent half-hour of listening to my spew

136

of emotion and wild facts and then reading the letter for himself, Hudson made a few calls. My wish was granted. Tomorrow morning, 6 a.m. Everyone, it seemed, at least those in Hudson's network, either owed him a favor or wanted Hudson Byrd to owe them one. Now I could be added to the list.

I fiddled with the laminated list of 150 beers from around the world, wondering if the waitress would really bring me a Fredericksburg brew called Not So Dumb Blonde. Today I felt like Pretty Dumb Blonde, and the 'pretty' didn't refer to my looks.

Being this close to Hudson Byrd again, depending on him, was dangerous. He'd almost killed a man because of me. While I lay in a hospital bed with broken bones, he found the rodeo official who had substituted Black Diablo in the lineup at the last minute, a bull unofficially banned on the circuit that year for wicked moves that had nearly killed two other female riders. I was simply unlucky enough to get him in the draw.

Hudson didn't blame the bull. The bull was a first-class athlete doing his job, almost a thousand pounds of muscle who could leap six feet in the air and spin at a freakish hundred miles an hour.

No, Hudson blamed the human being who put me on that bull. I couldn't face Hudson after finding out what he did when he found the man at a bar in the Stockyards.

Or so I told myself. The truth was, I couldn't

137

face my own future. The bull had shattered more than my arm. I was in pieces, devastated, no longer sure what was left of me. We had one more date, an awkward one, and then he stopped calling. Sometimes I think that if one of us had made the slightest move, uttered one more sentence, we might be married and divorced by now, burned out by our passion and tempers.

The relationship was all heat, nothing more, I told Sadie at the time, a lie. We fought too much, the truth. It took six months of healing for me to realize that I loved Hudson, and eight years for us to connect again, unexpectedly, at a New Year's Eve party in Dallas thrown by an ex-rider we used to hang with. Hudson was flying to Iraq the next day. I gave him a send-off kiss at midnight, which I'd do for any guy going to war, or so I convinced myself.

'How's the horsey psychology biz?' Hudson asked, tipping his beer, bringing me back to the present. I wanted him to hit the pause button on the charm.

'Technically, I'm a licensed equine therapist,' I answered. 'It's going fine.' I shook my head. 'Actually, I love it. Horses are amazing teachers. There's no bullshit with them. No human emotion to get in the way. The horses don't feel sorry for kids, don't care about their baggage. Treat the horse with respect and control or he won't cooperate. But, of course, you know this.'

He grinned. 'I was trained by a stallion named

Wicked when I was six. Some would say he could have done a better job.'

The waitress, walking past, slid a cardboard container of fried jalapeños stuffed with cream cheese onto the table, her fingers brushing Hudson's on purpose as she picked up an empty glass. It ticked me off, a ridiculous, involuntary response.

'I'm running a program with juvenile delinquents, mostly boys who've shown aggressive behavior,' I said, trying to keep the conversation neutral. 'They train our wild mustangs. It is a beautiful thing to watch. One rebellious spirit against another.' I bit into a pepper, catching the cheese dripping down my chin. 'But what about you? How's Afghanistan?'

'A disaster in every way,' he replied grimly.

His lips curved into a slow smile. 'You've still got the softest, sexiest drawl on the planet. You used to drive all those rodeo boys crazy. They said you had the guts of a tiger and the face of an angel.'

I couldn't help it. I laughed. He was piling it on and the liquor was doing its job. I felt like I was rafting on a warm river.

'What, you don't think cowboys can be poetic?' He leaned in, tucking a stray piece of hair behind my ear. *Stop it,* I pleaded silently. 'You were hard to resist then and near impossible to resist now.'

I could feel the blood surging in my face, a tingling where his finger had grazed my cheek. It had just been two of the worst days of my life. I wasn't ready for a full-on advance from Hudson, especially if it didn't mean anything to him.

'Are you scared?' he asked gently, his voice low.

'Of you? Or Anthony Marchetti? The answer is yes on both counts.'

'You don't have to meet with Marchetti. There are other ways.'

'I need to do this,' I insisted stiffly. 'I appreciate your help. I'll owe you a favor.'

'That might be one more reason this is a bad idea.' His finger trickled over the back of my hand. 'I usually collect.' He leaned back. 'You understand you only have ten minutes? *Outside* the bars of his cage? With Rafael standing right beside you? You understand that now I know about this, I'm in all the way. I will be a wart on your very nice ass. You accept these conditions?'

'Yes,' I said softly. 'I do.'

'I'm committed to a job out of town for a few days. So don't do anything stupid until I get back. Just the Meet and Greet.'

I heard him, but my mind was on something else.

'Are you going back?' I pulled it out of the air, but he knew that I was talking about the desert, where I'd been afraid he'd vanish into the sand.

'No,' he said. 'Never.'

The next morning, in the pre-dawn, air-conditioned cool of my bedroom, I pulled on old Wranglers, my hair still wet from the shower. I refused to dress up

140

for my meeting with Anthony Marchetti. I stared at my extra-pale complexion in the full-length mirror on the back of the bathroom door, sorry that I'd let Hudson talk me into joining him for a couple of shots of tequila.

Then I bent over the toilet and threw up.

Last night, I'd done a little drunk Googling, unearthing a portrait of Anthony Marchetti worthy of a bad Hollywood script.

I found it on a website run by Horace Finkel, a native Chicagoan and twenty-four-hour plumber, who declared himself the 'leading historical blogger of Chicago's top ten crime lords.'

Marchetti's primary racket before the slaughter of the Bennett family was flooding Chicago's South Side with heroin. The blog casually linked him to ten gangland slayings and thirteen individual hits in the seventies, but nothing the cops (or Horace) could prove.

Horace painted Anthony Marchetti as a romantic figure known for striding down Rush Street in a black designer trench coat with a red scarf whipped around his neck and a seven-foot bodyguard at his side. Marchetti considered the red scarf to be a lucky charm because he was wearing it during a failed assassination attempt. Later he used a symbolic red scarf to strangle people who betrayed him.

It really didn't matter if any of it was true. What mattered was that Anthony Marchetti was a man about whom it *could* be true.

I cleaned my face with a cold washcloth and scrubbed my teeth for five minutes to wash the taste of bile out of my mouth. I brushed mascara around green, slightly bloodshot eyes, applied a little base to smooth out the sunburn. It didn't help.

I pushed away a brief recollection of Hudson and me tightly wrapped, dancing slow on the boot-scuffed floor to bad Santa's off-key karaoke rendition of Garth Brooks's 'Friends in Low Places.' We'd left the bar around eleven-thirty and, when I refused to follow him to the Dallas hotel where he was holed up, Hudson ordered a large cup of thick black coffee to go and walked me back to Daddy's pickup parked in an open city lot near the courthouse. He watched me drink half of it before letting me drive off. No kiss. A good thing, I told myself.

My hair was already beginning to dry and I combed it and left it straight. I kicked aside last night's clothes, tossed carelessly on the creaky wood floor, and made my way to the five-foot-tall dresser in the bedroom. The two top drawers had always been Sadie's, the other three mine.

I opened the bottom one and moved aside a disintegrating homecoming mum, a crown with three rhinestones missing, and a half-full box of tampons. The cigar box hid out in the corner, under a pile of fading horse show ribbons, where I put it a week ago after finding it in a drawer in Daddy's office. I lifted the lid, overwhelmed by the smell of tobacco and the ache of loss. I raked through the mementoes – cuff links, a few old photographs, a faded red handkerchief, a watch, Daddy's silver U.S. Marshal badge.

My fingers rubbed over the words stamped underneath an eagle's wings. 'Justice. Integrity. Service.'

Sadie and I were too young to remember his career as a federal marshal. I always had the feeling it was a career path chosen for him by our grandfather.

Either way, Daddy never talked about those years. He didn't talk much, period, about anything personal. As long as we could remember, he was the caricature of a Texas rancher. He hung his cowboy hat on the same hook in the kitchen every day as soon as he walked in the door.

He was sexist in the way that men of his generation could be. He didn't touch dishes or fold clothes. He expected his dinner on the table at five sharp and all of us kids to be there, seated. We could get grounded for not making our beds with hospital corners. If he and Mama had a disagreement, we knew she'd always defer.

But he was always *there*. When Mama disappeared into her room or into her head, he remained present. A rock. If he favored one of us, it was me, not Sadie. We hunted, fished, rode – all with a comfortable silence I'd never achieved with anyone else. I dropped the badge back in the box and dug until I found the old snapshot I'd been looking for.

A little girl with long, messy blond hair sat on a Palomino horse grinning at the tall man in a cowboy hat holding the reins. He grinned back, his tanned face prematurely lined from years in the Texas sun. It had been a good day, but I couldn't remember why. Daddy apparently thought so, too, or I wouldn't be tucked in this box.

Why didn't you tell me I wasn't yours?

I slipped the picture into my back pocket for luck or comfort. Or maybe a little of both.

My phone beeped on the bedside table. An early-morning email from Lyle, with an attachment. Maybe he was able to clean up the image already.

Subject line: Sit down first.

I didn't sit down or read the text of the email.

Instead, I clicked the attachment. Then I stood frozen as the screen filled with a tiny, lifeless form in Sesame Street pajamas, crumpled in a pool of blood.

I barely made it to the bathroom before I threw up again.

Hudson's friend Rafael escorted me by my elbow through a seemingly endless gray corridor, my sock feet padding on the waxed linoleum. I'd been asked to remove my shoes and all my jewelry by the stocky female guard who'd frisked me, like a gentle massage. I almost wanted to tip her.

I couldn't even remember the details of my half-hour drive over from the ranch. The beginnings of a hangover headache, the nasty kind that lies on one side of my temple, pounded out the thump of my heartbeat. My stomach still rolled around like a choppy lake, in no condition to be up and about.

Still, I kept moving.

Move or Maddie could die like that little girl.

'Hudson told you the drill, right?' Rafael slid his passkey through the slot of a heavy gate lined with black steel bars. 'Stand two feet back from the cell at all times. You have ten minutes. Maybe less. We'll see how he does. He's been a good boy. Nice and quiet. We don't want you to mess that up.'

Five identical cells lined either side of this block, usually used as a holding facility for prisoners destined for more dangerous quarters in the unforgiving state of Texas, where we boast the all-time record for legally killing people. The cells measured about the size of my walk-in pantry. A shiny stainless-steel toilet and a narrow built-in cot with a one-inch mattress took up most of the space, leaving no room for a morning session of yoga.

Every cell I passed was empty, a set of stiff, bleached sheets folded neatly on each cot for its next guest. It was colorless, freezing, claustrophobic.

I shivered. Even in the brief time I'd been there, I wanted to let out a scream. This was my idea of hell.

We stopped abruptly in front of the last cell on the left. Anthony Marchetti was already front and center, gripping the bars with clean, well-manicured hands, the faint sound of classical music, something familiar, drifting from the headphones on the empty cot.

I couldn't place it.

'Hello, Tommie,' he said softly.

His icy blue eyes sent over a shot of electricity that I thought existed only in the pages of pulpy fiction. It shocked me, this demand for immediate intimacy, the sensation of falling down a dark, infinite space. I had the bizarre thought that I was the one trapped, not him.

He did not look like an old man beaten down by life in prison. The faded newspaper picture had not done him justice. He'd grown more distinguished with age, his black hair threaded with gray, his lean, muscular six-foot frame a testament to prison workout facilities.

I knew from my research that he was remarkably well-educated for a drug lord, with a master's from Northwestern's prestigious Kellogg School of Management. Strap him into an Armani suit and he could slip easily into place as a corporate predator. But right now, I felt like his prey.

'They told me you were coming. Are you afraid of me?' he asked, with a slight Italian inflection. I tried to switch my expression from one of panic, but the muscles in my face did not cooperate.

I wondered for a second if he could see into me, if he knew that less than an hour ago, I'd gagged over the picture of a child he murdered.

Lyle's email said it hadn't been hard for his 'technician' to sharpen the picture, just a little tweaking with Photoshop. The 'technician' had also traced where the sender had downloaded the photo, a circuslike site that promised true crime scene pictures for a monthly rate of $19.99.

Alyssa Bennett, the little girl now stored on my phone, had 527,453 hits. She was the daughter of FBI agent Fred Bennett, whose entire family was slaughtered more than thirty years ago.

Madddog12296 was going to be trickier to trace, Lyle wrote. No luck on that yet.

Lyle never sugarcoated a thing, Daddy said. On balance, I liked that, but not so much right now, because I couldn't get that girl out of my head while Marchetti leaned casually against the bars, arms crossed.

Rafael, standing at my side, shifted uncomfortably. 'Ask your questions,' he urged me.

The speech I'd practiced obsessively broke into fragments. 'I want to know whether . . . you know my mother,' I began nervously, and started to pick at the dry skin around my thumb, a habit since childhood whenever I worked myself into a jam. I could tell Marchetti noticed, intent on making me as uncomfortable as possible.

'I have not had much opportunity to meet women in the last thirty years.' He gestured at the tiny cell.

'Your wife . . . Rosalina Marchetti says I'm her daughter,' I blurted out. 'She wrote to me.' I reached in my pocket for her letter, the single thing the guard allowed me to carry through.

147

I held it out, now folded small and tight like a paper football. A symbol of my desire to bend and crease myself into something as tiny as possible.

'I need your help,' I told Marchetti. 'I have to know if this is true.'

As I spoke these words out loud, it struck me how odd it was that I stood there pleading with a murderer, a stranger. He looked at me with something like pity, if that's possible from a man who reputedly thought up a torture technique that involved water and electricity generated from his custom-made silver Porsche.

He glanced at Rafael, ignoring the piece of paper in my outstretched hand.

'Why did you let her in here? She's a crazy girl, eh? As for Rosalina, she's a liar. And a whore.'

He smiled tightly. 'I'm done here.' And then, nodding at me: 'Be careful.'

A threat? Or a warning? I couldn't tell.

He moved away from the bars and fell back on the cot, turning up the volume loud enough for me to hear the strains of a sonata. He flicked his hand toward me like I was a bug in his face. Dismissed. I wondered how many lives besides Alyssa's he had ended as casually.

'I'm sorry,' Rafael said, genuinely feeling bad for me, drawing me away.

The music hummed.

I could place it now.

Marchetti was listening to the third movement of Sonata in C Major, K. 309, which Mozart improvised in a performance more than two hundred years ago.

I knew this arcane detail because Mama played it on Sunday nights before Sadie and I went to bed.

Anthony Marchetti was toying with me, pulling me along his dark highway.

Sending a message.

We had reached the exit door at the end of the row, Rafael already sliding his keycard, when Marchetti's voice traveled down the cellblock.

'Tommie.'

So commanding that I stopped and turned back.

'No time left.' Rafael's hand was on my shoulder.

All I could see of Anthony Marchetti were his fingers wrapped around the bars of the cage.

But in the stillness of the empty concrete chamber, I could hear.

'Tell your mother hello,' he said softly.

CHAPTER 13

*T*ell *your mother hello.*
     You twisted bastard. Playing that sonata from my childhood.
  Tell me, Etta, was the picture of a dead little girl in a pool of blood not enough for the day?

Now I was talking to dead people. Why not? The live ones weren't helping much. So far, Etta Place wasn't talking back. A good thing. No bossy voice in my head but mine.

The green light on my cell phone blinked insistently as I walked to the truck, the sun rising over the top of the eight-story city jail, already promising another blistering ten hours. I looked at the list of missed calls. Seven of them. Four from Sadie and three from Mama's nursing home. I glanced at my watch: 6:22. I immediately hit the 'send' button on the last call. Sadie answered before I heard the first ring.

'Tommie, something's going on with Mama. They had to sedate her about an hour ago. She was tearing up her room, like she was looking for something. Her blood pressure is off the charts and her heart is . . . I think they called it

150

tachycardia. The night nurse said she started acting strangely after a man visited her last night, but didn't flip out until this morning. Wait a minute . . .'

Sadie came back on the phone a few seconds later. 'I've got to go. The ambulance is here; they're about to take her to Harris in Fort Worth, Tommie . . . she's so pale.'

'I'm about fifteen minutes . . . Sadie?'

She was gone. My whole body started to shake.

The skyscrapers, the red Toyota parked in front of me, the blue sky, the orange sunlight – all swirled together like a kaleidoscope, breaking the windshield into prisms of color. The keys clunked to the floor.

I wondered whether I was dying. This seemed way beyond a panic attack. Four years ago, after the first attack, too embarrassed to tell anyone, I found a list of tips on the internet in case it happened again.

A voice in my head sounding very much like Dr Phil, my profession's leading hypocrite, was now reading it off. 'No. 1: Relax and change your breathing pattern,' he boomed in his Oklahoman twang.

To what? Trying *not* to breathe?

'No. 2. Take a "mental vacation,"' he continued cheerfully, and I imagined his $16,500,000 mansion and Ferrari 360 Spider.

Desperate to quell Dr Phil, I squinted my eyes shut and imagined myself with Maddie, down by

151

the pond, tying the Woolly Fur-Bugger, a new fishing fly we'd discovered last week on Killroys' website. I painstakingly tied the fly in my mind, step by step. My breathing eased slightly, and I moved on to the Pull Back Nymph. By the time I'd finished tying an Embellished Lefty's, it was all over, my shirt soaked in sweat, my breathing shallow but regular.

The attack lasted thirteen minutes.

I peeled out of the lot and hit the highway to the hospital.

'God, Tommie, you look as bad as Mama.'

Sadie glanced up as I entered the packed waiting room, stepping over two kids playing Pick Up Sticks. 'They're getting her settled. She's barely conscious, speaking gibberish, but hopefully that's just the drug.'

I held back from reminding Sadie that Mama was rarely lucid, even without chemicals.

She pulled me by my elbow into a corner and spoke in an urgent whisper.

'That reporter showed up.'

'What?' I followed the direction of her eyes.

Jack Smith, crammed against the wall between an elderly woman nodding off and a manically texting teenager, tossed me a friendly wave.

I strode over, furious, thinking that anger was a good emotion for me to hang on to. It cleared my head of all the crazy crap.

'What are you doing here?' I demanded with

152

enough venom that the old woman's head popped up. The teenager's thumbs never stopped moving.

'Sorry, ma'am,' Jack said to the woman, standing.

'In the hall,' I raged. *'Now.'*

Most of the waiting room, a crowd bleary with exhaustion and worry, stared at our little trio as we stalked our way through. We were probably a welcome distraction – Jack in today's orange Polo; me, a sweaty, disheveled mess; Sadie, who seemed unaware she still wore the large paint-spattered goggles that she used for blowtorching.

I sagged against the wall, rubbing my forehead. Sadie, arms crossed over her rubber-band-taut body, glared at both Jack and me.

'I waited to talk to you two at the same time,' Jack said. 'I just happened to be at the nursing home when the ambulance arrived. Don't look at me like that, Tommie. You can't expect a reporter not to try to get information from a primary source.'

'Did you see the guy who scared our mother?' I was thinking, *Hell, you probably* are *the guy.*

'No. I wasn't there last night. I never spoke to your mother. Everything was chaos by the time I got there today.'

'I'd like to talk privately with my sister.'

'Sure.' Jack moved about ten feet away and pulled out his phone.

'Sadie,' I said quietly, 'I need you and Maddie to move into the Worthington for a while. I don't like the idea of you out there in the middle of nowhere. Not until we figure this out.'

'Why don't we just move into the house with you?'

'Because I think . . . I'm more of a target. There's Maddie to think about.'

And you, Sadie. I'd willingly go down in a blaze of glory for my sister. The problem was, she'd do the same for me. And she wasn't quite as good a shot.

'I'm worried about you.' Sadie gazed at me steadily. 'The lavender you smelled. I read up on . . . olfactory hallucinations.'

'Phantosmia,' I said. 'Probably a one-time thing, possibly connected to some migraines I've been having since Daddy died.' I forced a smile. 'Besides, Hudson says he'll help me.'

I didn't say when. Or how.

That sealed it. She broke into a huge, relieved smile.

'OK.' She nodded. 'As long as Hudson's with you. I'm going to head back to Mama's room and let you deal with *him*.' She jerked her thumb in Jack's direction.

'I'll be there in just a second.'

I turned to Jack, enunciating each word.

'I'm. Sick. Of. Your. Games.'

Two nurses walking by turned their heads and slowed.

'A little quieter, *please*,' he said. He smiled at the nurses. 'Everything's fine, ladies. She's just stressed out.'

'You're a patronizing jerk,' I said loudly as they

154

disappeared into a patient's room. 'Was that quiet enough for you?'

'You call me a lot of names. I'm going to eventually take offense.' He tested a door to his left and pulled me into a linen closet, an insulated cocoon, every shelf stuffed to the top with white-gray sheets, pillowcases, blankets, and towels. Plenty of stuff to suffocate me.

'More than thirty years ago, your mother entered witness protection, along with a young boy,' he said, as soon as the door clicked shut. 'Your brother. And a baby. Labeled "unspecified."'

His words made no sense. My mother was in witness protection? Tuck? Was I 'unspecified'?

'And you know this how?'

'Sources. I laid my hands on some FBI and witness protection files.'

A rapid knock startled us, and the door cracked open. A gray-haired nurse peered in.

'Mrs McCloud?'

'No, no, I'm not married,' I replied automatically, realizing how inane that sounded as soon as it came out.

'Your sister told us to update you. She needed to run out and pick up her daughter. Your mother is now sedated and her vitals are improving. She's stable. Why don't you go get some rest?'

'I haven't even seen her yet.'

'It's really best not to disturb her right now.' She hesitated. 'Regardless, you need to get out of the closet. We don't allow this kind of thing in here. It's not sanitary.'

'No,' I said, horrified. 'There is *nothing* going on. With him. He'd be the last person . . .'

'We all say that, honey,' she said serenely, piling a stack of sheets and pillowcases into her arms and holding the door wide open for us with her considerably sized right foot.

'Perfect,' Jack said cheerfully. 'We can finish the conversation that we started in the hotel.'

I glanced toward Mama's room and decided to take the nurse's advice. I moved toward the elevator. Jack followed. We rode down six floors in silence.

'How about this,' he said, as it jerked to a stop on the lobby level. 'I'll buy you lunch.'

'I want to see those files,' I demanded.

Jack held the door while an elderly man wheeled in a teenage girl sporting a signed Texas Rangers baseball cap and the white pallor of chemo treatments.

Another of life's cosmic mistakes.

I needed to stop my whining.

Find the way out of this maze.

Even if it meant sucking up to this bastard to do it.

'You're a cheap date. That's nice.' Jack bit into his third pork taquito, which he'd slathered with about a half cup of Conchita's extra-hot sauce.

A red river dripped unattractively down his

156

chin, leaving an unfortunate, bloody-looking spot on his sling. I knew his mouth must be in some category of hell, but he showed no signs of it. More braggadocio. He reminded me of a goat roper I once dated who ordered his steak 'so rare it's still alive.'

Conchita's Taqueria consisted of an outhouse-sized shack with an aluminum roof that barely contained the plus-plus-sized Conchita, much less the giant metal canister of sweet tea, a grill, a small refrigerator, a metal cash box, and three Igloo coolers stocked with ice and Coke, the real kind, bottled in Mexico with so much Imperial Sugar it made your teeth hurt. It was the only soft drink she served.

Conchita was famous for telling new customers: 'If you want a diet drink, you are sheet out of luck. Go to Taco Bell.'

Last year, Conchita had sprung for a purple polka-dotted umbrella for one of the three metal tables that sat outside the shack on a blistering patch of concrete. It was the best seat in the house. Today she'd cleared it off for us, yelling out her window at the two startled power suits finishing up their lunch, '*Vamos!* It eez time for you to go!'

Conchita didn't hand out this preferential treatment for me, even though I'd been a loyal customer for years. Conchita liked men, preferably tall ones who looked capable of throwing a punch. She'd been robbed in broad daylight more than a few times. Conchita never exactly smiled, but she served Jack with her most charming grimace and threw in an extra-spicy taquito for free.

'So,' Jack said, wiping his mouth. It was clear he hadn't wanted to talk until his stomach churned happily. I wondered how happy it was going to be around two in the morning.

'So . . . why did my mother enter witness protection?'

'Tommie, we're kind of exposed here.'

He gestured to a nearby table of four: a small boy punching at an iPhone, a toddler sucking his pacifier like it was a chocolate milkshake, a tired mother with a pink zebra-striped diaper bag that could hold enough to feed and entertain a small nation, and an irritated-looking Texas grandma.

'I can't get Wi-Fi here,' the boy whined, shaking the iPhone like an Etch A Sketch.

'Eat your taco, Evan,' his mother said, while the grandmother opened and then shut her mouth, thinking better of it. 'Put my phone down.'

'It has little white and green things in it,' he complained, pushing away the foil wrapper. 'I want to go to On the Border.'

'Evan . . .'

'Take them out!' the little Nazi ordered, stabbing his tiny forefinger imperiously at the offending items in his taco.

'Jack, I really don't think these people are paying attention to us,' I said, watching the mom get to work obediently with a toothpick. 'I'm going to make a guess that the little boss over there isn't

158

mob-connected. So what is my mother's link to Anthony Marchetti? And why are you so interested?'

Jack peeled the wrinkled Saran Wrap off a half-melted homemade praline the size of a hockey puck. 'I'm interested in anything to do with Anthony Marchetti. The trail leads where it leads.' He stuffed his mouth and chewed in an exaggerated fashion. 'Sticky,' he said, pointing to his mouth, 'but tasty.'

'What did you mean in the hotel when you said that part of the story my mother told me about her past was true?'

'Both her parents died in a fire.'

'Do you know if there was anything . . . suspicious about it?'

'No. Meaning, no, I don't think so.'

'For the record, I feel like calling you a name right now, but there are children nearby. How did you know that Rosalina Marchetti contacted me?'

He shrugged. 'I told you, I have a source. The FBI is wiretapping her. She's the wife of a mob boss who's running games from prison. The Feds have been trying to get at him and his wad of cash for years.'

'You have a source in the FBI?'

'Yep. I'm terrific with sources. Most people find me charming. Smart, even. Phi Beta Kappa. Princeton. Lots of connections.' He grinned. 'Don't look so shocked.'

'Do you really believe Rosalina Marchetti is my

mother? That Marchetti is my father? That I was kidnapped? Do you know who Tuck's father was? He *was* my brother, wasn't he? And who's the dead girl with my Social Security number?' The last question rolled out of my mouth in an unexpected screech.

The boy looked up from thumbing the phone, ticked off.

'Mommy,' he said, pointing at me, 'that lady made me lose my place in Doodle Jump. I died.'

'Shut up, kid,' Jack said to him.

The mother had the grace to look embarrassed. The grandmother smothered a smile.

To me, Jack said, 'I don't know who Tuck's father was. That's your brother, the one who died, right?' He paused, sounding . . . sympathetic. 'I had a brother who died. Something else we have in common.'

Before I could respond, the toddler spit out the pacifier with enough velocity that it ricocheted off Jack's cheek. It took only seconds for the pacifier addict to recognize his terrible mistake in judgment. His wail resounded like a tornado siren.

Jack seemed a little stunned, by both the plastic missile and the decibel level a two-year-old can reach. I got up and retrieved the pacifier from under our table while the mother dug furiously through the sixty-three Velcro pockets of her diaper bag.

'Pacifier wipes,' she muttered. 'Where are the

pacifier wipes? Oh, here they are.' She pulled out a small plastic tub with antibacterial promises stamped all over it.

Grandma was now on her feet. 'Christ almighty, you actually *paid* for those? *This* is how you clean a pacifier.'

She grabbed the pacifier out of my hand, stuck it into her Styrofoam cup of iced tea, gave it a few good swirls, and plopped it in the mouth of the wailing boy.

Then she grabbed the phone out of her other grandson's hand and said firmly, 'Eat your damn taco.'

The kids shut up.

'Grandma should have a reality TV show,' Jack said.

'Smith, focus on me, OK? I want to see those FBI files. And my mother's. And my brother's. Uncensored.'

'Impossible. What I got is already censored. Stuff blacked out.'

I reached into my purse and pulled out a key.

'I recently discovered the contents of a safe deposit box in my mother's name,' I said. 'She never told anyone. Not even her lawyer.'

Jack leaned in, practically salivating.

This dance was one I had practiced over and over again with patients. Give some, get some. However, I was reluctantly coming to terms with the fact that Jack Smith was different, like no one I'd ever encountered. A whole new can of beans,

Granny would say. My usual tactics weren't going to work.

'Tit for tat,' I said. 'That's the deal. And I'm not talking about my 34Cs.'

It was my first pitiful attempt at a joke in two weeks.

Inside, I wasn't laughing.

Something else *we have in common,* Jack had said about my dead brother.

What the hell did that mean?

CHAPTER 14

Christy King was a sixteen-year-old sent to Halo Ranch from the Las Vegas foster care system, a one-time runaway who hyperventilated every time she stuck her foot in the stirrup.

I was suddenly, irrationally consumed with guilt about her.

Had I been kind enough?

Before the state snatched her up, Christy had been beaten by a pimp almost daily for a year. She had arrived at Halo near comatose emotionally. A couple of times at the stables, when I pushed her too hard to get on the horse, she keeled over at my feet.

I think I had been kind. After ten lessons, she was able to saddle up. After eighteen lessons, she sat on the horse. After twenty-five lessons, she walked the horse around the pen with me holding the reins. After thirty lessons, she rode the horse, by herself, fifty yards and back. She never worked up to a trot, but we declared victory.

I must have been kind, because she made progress both in the stable and away from it. She hugged me goodbye on her last day, as a social worker and her new foster family waited awkwardly by a Volvo station wagon. She said that I'd changed her life. That she'd never forget me.

Yes, surely I was kind.

But I didn't really *understand.* I didn't have a clue how it felt to have her breath sucked away, her body and brain collaborating in a war against her soul.

The helplessness.

The desire to run.

Not until now.

After lunch, I returned to the house, opened the door to Daddy's home office, and fired up his copier. In three hours, Jack Smith would be breathing down my neck again.

He promised to meet me back at the ranch with his notes and files on the Marchetti case. I promised to reciprocate with the contents of the safe deposit box.

I didn't mention to Jack that Lyle would be joining us. Lyle wanted his own copies of the checks and newspaper articles and didn't mind the drive over to pick them up. Neither of us thought it was a good idea to copy them in the middle of a curious newsroom. And he was eager to get a good look at Jack himself.

As for me, I wanted to spend a little alone time with the newspaper articles before either of them arrived.

I left my MacBook charging on top of the dryer and spread the seven yellowed articles out on Mama's desk. The late-afternoon sun drifted in like the cone of a spotlight, doing its best to comfort me.

My mother was a fan of riddles. Every kid in elementary school wanted an invitation to our Halloween parties because of the elaborate treasure hunts she devised.

Blood red and dead in a bed. A clue stuck in the thorns of a withered rosebush. *The only place where death comes before life.* A slip of paper peeking out of the *D*'s of our ancient Webster's dictionary.

I pushed away the memories. My clever mother's mind was gone, poof, like it had been sucked out by a vacuum cleaner, leaving a few dust bunnies and me struggling to figure out the most difficult riddle of her life.

These newspaper articles meant something important to her, I was sure.

I started with the murdered girl in Oklahoma. It was hard to glean much from the faded picture of Jennifer Coogan, except that she was pretty and wore a crown. The headline was brutal and to the point: OU STUDENT SHOT, RAPED, AND DUMPED IN LITTLE RIVER, with an insensitive underline: *Police Say Former Miss National Teenager Runner-up Unrecognizable When Found.*

Twenty-five years ago, on the last night of her life, Jennifer Coogan was nineteen. She had just finished her freshman year at the University of Oklahoma and was waitressing back home in Idabel for the summer, living with her parents. Idabel surely was the safest place in the world for her to be that summer, except it wasn't. After closing up after a late-night shift at a local restaurant called the Cedar House, she walked to her '72 baby blue convertible and met the devil that her Baptist preacher ranted about on Sunday mornings.

If I'd learned anything from Grandaddy, it was that small towns were microcosms of big cities. Evil thrived quietly behind the screen doors.

The article was brief and didn't get into a lot of detail. Nineteen-year-old Jennifer was raped, tortured, shot twice in the back of the head, and tossed into a local river. No suspects yet. The first inexplicable murder in Idabel in forty years. End of story.

I shivered despite the sun's efforts. Was Anthony Marchetti involved in this? Was that the connection? The murder could be his work, but why would a Chicago mobster care about a young girl in the boonies of Oklahoma?

I moved on, poring over every word of every article with Mama in mind, trying to find anything that would connect her to the stories or at least something that tied them together. Most had been clipped from unremarkable newspapers from far-ranging cities in Oklahoma, South Dakota, New York. Four out of the seven contained either misspellings or grammatical errors, a sad commentary on the future of the English language and journalism in general.

My favorite wasn't a story but a captioned picture of an ambulance driver in Boone, North Carolina, with a little gap-toothed girl who held the large bean he'd pulled from her nostril. The EMT looked about eighteen, the kind of skinny, pale kid who sat unnoticed at the back of science class until you needed a pencil and then he'd always loan you one. His sheepish grin lit the photograph with an element of wonder that he'd achieved the kind of hero status where flashbulbs go off.

Wait a minute. Staring at that ambulance driver, I suddenly saw a connection, one that seemed unlikely to be coincidental.

The picture and the six other stories each appeared on an inside page, at the top right or left corner, so every one included a dateline and the name of the newspaper. With the bean hero's photograph, the clipper had taken extra precautions to include the date and city, making an awkward dogleg with the scissors.

Maybe the *stories* weren't important. Maybe the *places* and *dates* were. I ran to the kitchen and rummaged through the junk drawer that used to hold our school supplies.

Way at the back, I found what I wanted, an old but extra-large map of the United States, last used for a weekend-killing geography project assigned by Mrs Stateler, known less affectionately in the halls of Ponder Middle as Mrs Hate-her.

I grabbed the newspaper articles from the desk, along with a black marker, and spread the map on the kitchen table. I attached a number, 1 through 7, to each of the articles, organizing them chronologically by date. Then I wrote the corresponding number for each town and city on the map. With an unsteady hand, I drew a crooked line on the map, connecting them.

1. Norman, Okla. (Oct. 7, 1986)
2. Idabel, Okla. (June 22, 1987)
3. Austin, Tex. (August 1, 1987)
4. Boone, N.C. (Dec. 24, 1989)
5. Boulder, Colo. (March 25, 1990)
6. Sioux Falls, S.D. (Sept. 7, 1992)
7. Rochester, N.Y. (Jan. 17, 1996)

Could this be the path of a serial killer? If so, why wasn't every story about a murder? Was it another of Mama's clues, the answer encrypted in the words? Or in the numbers? I stared at the map, trying different approaches, before total frustration kicked in.

Then I piled the newspaper articles onto the map and carried the whole mess back to the utility room. With random tacks from Mama's drawer, I stuck the map to the wall above the desk and tacked the newspaper articles near their cities of origin.

I still couldn't see a pattern.

I turned to my laptop with the idea of researching

the newspaper stories further, but the internet refused to connect despite the twenty-year-old technician who assured me this morning that it was up and running like a jackrabbit.

What the hell.

Was someone messing with that, too?

Lyle's T-shirt read: 'My Kid's an Honor Roll Student at CHHS.'

Lyle didn't have any kids at CHHS. He didn't have any kids.

'Jack Smith seems to check out,' he said, without preamble, as soon as I opened the door. 'The switchboard operator at the magazine did direct me to a voicemail box for a Jack Smith. I'd feel better if I'd been able to talk to my friend who works at *Texas Monthly,* but he's out of town.'

I pointed to a gray Buick sedan speeding up the road. 'Let's wait here. It will take him one minute and twenty seconds to reach the driveway.'

Lyle raised an eyebrow.

'Daddy exacted a curfew. In high school, Sadie and I put a stopwatch to almost every route we traveled.' Seconds mattered. Another of Daddy's life lessons.

I was wrong. Jack made it in half my time, kicking up a long tsunami of dust. He slammed the car door, striding up to the house with one hand empty and the other still encased in a sling.

'Damn GPS,' he grumbled. Then, rudely, 'Who's this?'

'Lyle, an old friend of the family's,' I answered. 'A journalist, just like you. An editor at the Fort Worth newspaper. Where are the files you promised me?'

Of course he wouldn't live up to his word, I realized furiously. What was I thinking?

'Nice to meet you, Lyle.' Jack stuck out his hand, surprising me.

He stared at Lyle's manic hair, the T-shirt that advertised him as a proud papa. 'What's your kid's GPA?'

Lyle grunted something unintelligible.

We settled into three chairs near the fireplace in the living room. I didn't offer the standard glass of iced tea, a requisite for any guest in the McCloud household when it was under Granny's thumb, even those guests we harbored ill feelings toward. Love your enemy and all that. Offer extra lumps of sugar.

'No files,' Jack said. 'My source started to freak out.' Before I could protest, he added, 'However, I want to share what I can. Do you remember someone named Angel Martinez?'

I shook my head.

'He was one of the federal marshals on the case when you were a kid. Your grandfather trained him in one of his recruiting classes and then hand-picked him years ago to protect your family one summer.'

'I don't know an Angel Martinez,' I insisted. But apparently my grandfather did. How many other people had lied to me? His days as a federal marshal were well behind him by the time we played the horsey game on his knee.

'Angel spent three months here at your place when you were little. It was the last time your mother accepted official witness protection.'

'You mean *Martin*?' I asked, numbly. Martin, the beautiful Mexican migrant worker, the beneficiary of my first crush. The dark stranger who showed up, just like Granny promised after she read my cards, with the word *deceit* attached to him.

In my mind, I was right back there at the kitchen table, wearing my best demure nightgown after a cool shower, twisting my wet hair into a long braid while Mama and Martin played chess by a dim lamp. At night, Mama always liked the lights low and the shades drawn. The radio blared tinny Tijuana brass, Spanish radio's Saturday night special.

Martin stayed by Mama's side for three months. Somewhere in the back of my brain I always wondered why it didn't make Daddy jealous, even though she called Martin *mi hermano pequeño* – my little brother. After all, *I* was jealous. Martin drove Mama everywhere – to the grocery store, to the Dallas symphony, even to church choir practice.

'She told me she was teaching him English,' I said softly. 'And he taught her Spanish. That's why he didn't work as much in the fields.'

'Angel was born in America. He has a criminal justice degree from Berkeley. He wrote one of the old reports my source gave me. I'm trying to reach him. Where's the stuff from the bank?'

'You aren't exactly living up to your part of the bargain. Is this all you have for me?'

'What do you want to hear? I don't know why your mother needed the services of WITSEC. I'm sorry. It's completely blacked out in the documents.'

I stared at him, exasperated. Angry.

'Give him the contents of the box,' Lyle said calmly.

'I was beginning to think you were some kind of mute,' Jack said to Lyle, 'but it turns out you're a very smart guy.'

'Mute does not mean you are stupid,' I spat at him, seething. 'Children can go mute at a young age after a trauma. Sometimes for life. But they are still in there. You can reach them.'

Lyle whispered in my ear, 'Trust me. Give him the stuff.'

I stalked to Daddy's office and retrieved the manila envelope with Jack's name on it. I tossed it at him like a Frisbee despite his sling, hoping for at least a paper cut.

Jack caught it easily. I had to comfort myself that he still had a small purple spot under his left eye from the pacifier bandit.

'This is it?' he asked, feeling the envelope. 'All of it?'

'Yes.'

He pulled out the contents and laid them in his

lap, disappointed. 'Newspaper articles. Weird. And checks. From the Shur Foundation. That's an old sham company the government set up to provide monthly allowances to witnesses. This kind of financial aid usually ends after two to five years.'

'In that case, there would be no reason to keep the checks,' I said. 'Especially since she didn't cash them.'

'Maybe it was a very mundane reason. My uncle stored ten boxes of canceled checks in the attic in case we were ever audited. People don't trust the government.'

This wasn't going anywhere helpful.

'Would you guys like a drink?' I moved toward the kitchen, both of them trailing after me. I popped open the refrigerator, sticking my head inside.

I heard Jack mutter, 'What the hell is this?' and I banged my head on the top shelf in my hurry to get out.

Jack and Lyle had halted by the door to the laundry room, mesmerized by my map display. 'I'm plotting my next vacation,' I said sarcastically, thrusting two bottles of water at them.

My phone, abandoned during my research frenzy, suddenly vibrated impatiently on Mama's desk, rattling the smiling Hummel girl. I brushed past Jack and Lyle to grab it.

'I'm going to the bathroom,' I said, letting it buzz away in my hand. 'Please don't follow me.'

I strode out of the room and down the far hall,

through Mama and Daddy's room and into the master bath, which smelled like the cloying 'vanilla-roma' air freshener the maids had plugged into the wall. Unnatural. Mama would have hated it. I snapped the lid of the toilet shut and plopped on it. The call had already gone to voicemail. Actually, I had two voicemails. I punched in my code.

'How ya doin', honey?' The drawl was unmistakably Hudson. *'My job is taking me a little longer than I expected, but you can reach me at this number anytime, even in the middle of the night. I hear from my friend Rafael that Marchetti wasn't too forthcoming in your little session. But I'm not sure that's why you went. I'll check back in tomorrow. Remember, night or day. Program this number into your speed-dial. You hear me? Now.'*

The phone automatically rolled into the other voicemail, a female voice chirping away, and I hastily turned the phone around and stuck it up to my ear.

'. . . ummmm, you don't know me but I'm Charla Polaski?' She squeaked it out, a question. *'I'm in prison out here in Odessa. I'm innocent, though. I like people to know that right off. I'm accused of shooting my asshole of a husband, but if I would have done it, I'd have used that knife he used to gut his deer and I would have gone real, real slow, startin' with that ugly callus on his big toe that bugged the hell out of me during sex. You could have named that thing. Long story short . . .'*

174

Then nothing. Empty air. She'd been cut off.

The phone buzzed again. Another call coming through.

'Hello,' I said.

'Whoa, I didn't expect you to answer.'

Her voice was unmistakable. It had the squeaky, grating quality of a seven-year-old's first attempts to play the violin. Or a duck with a Texas twang.

'Charla?'

'That's creepy. How do you know who I am?'

'You just left a voicemail,' I said impatiently.

'Oh, you got that. Sorry I hung up, but Bitchy Becky was walking by and I couldn't risk her overhearing. She's in the cell two over from mine and she'd rat out anybody for a bag of Skittles.'

'I think you have the wrong number—'

'Nope, I don't think so. He wrote the number right here on my hand in impermable ink. You're Tommie, right?'

Impermeable, I thought, but she didn't wait for me to answer.

'I'm gonna take that as a yes. Is anybody with you?'

'Yes. I mean, no, not right with me, I'm in the bathroom.'

'Oh. I haven't had a private poo for two years. I'd die for one. I'll be quick. It's probably best if you just answer yes or no anyway, in case someone is listening. They were real picky about you and me not telling anybody.'

Her voice started to quiver. 'This badass guard

from the G Unit came into my cell last night. He told me I had to use my one phone call today to give you a message from a new prisoner here. He said it would be very bad if I didn't.'

'This is insane,' I muttered, my finger poised over the button that would end the call.

'Your father,' Charla said. 'Your father says to tell you to *trust no one*. And that he is protecting you. Who is your damn father? And why the hell did I get picked to call you?'

A pause, an 'Oops,' and a click.

'Charla? Charla??'

The line was dead.

CHAPTER 15

By the time I finished wiping a cold wash-cloth over my face for the third time, Lyle was rapping on the door to the bathroom.

'Tommie? Are you OK? I'm sorry. This is a little embarrassing. I'm worried. It's been twenty minutes.'

I opened the door and pasted on a fake smile.

What does 'trust no one' mean, exactly, Mr Marchetti? Does that include Lyle? Hudson?

'Sure,' I answered, flipping the wet cloth into the sink. 'I'm good. Where's Jack?'

'He took off. To do a little research.'

'That's just great,' I said dully. 'What do you think of him?'

'He doesn't operate like any reporter I've ever met.'

'But you trusted him with Mama's stuff.'

'Can't hurt. Why antagonize him? *Texas Monthly* has an impeccable reputation. At this point, we just want answers, right? The more help, the better.'

I had to admit that Jack had been on his best behavior.

We moved down the hall, past the stern eyes of

a black-and-white framed collection of ancestors. Daddy said they never smiled for pictures back then because it was considered too vain. Wonder what they'd think about 'reality TV star' as a legitimate job title on a résumé and tweets like, 'Hey gang! Let's synchrofart at 20:00!'

'I feel like I'm getting nowhere,' I said. 'That it's hopeless.'

Lyle hesitated. He pulled a folded wad of paper out of his back pocket.

'I found the dead girl with your Social Security number. These are a few printouts. I'm trying to get your family's FBI files . . . another way. And we're working on tracking the anonymous email.' He hesitated. 'At some point, we should consider talking to the FBI ourselves.'

I nodded, wondering who Lyle's 'we' included. Reporters suspected him of superior hacking abilities, although I suspected that Lyle was too smart for that. He just knew superior hackers.

'You don't need to go over this right now,' he told me. 'Or at all. Just know that my posse is on the case, too.'

'Do you know who Charla Polaski is?'

'Sure. A seventy-two-point headline. She found her husband naked and soaped up with their daughter's gym coach, who happened to be the wife of a city councilman. Shots were fired to their hearts and genitals. A very messy scene in the middle-school shower. The story was a publisher's wet dream.'

'Was she for sure guilty?'

'A slam dunk for the prosecutor. The jury deliberated twenty minutes. Polaski claimed she was set up to the bitter end. Why are you interested in this?'

'Just something I . . . heard.' I didn't want to get into Charla's bizarre phone call.

'I've got to get back to work and rip up the front page. The Dallas Cowboys' star receiver broke his ankle in a team workout. It's bumping Afghanistan off the front page. But I hate to leave you alone. I take it you haven't hired protection yet.'

'Working on that,' I said.

As we reached the door, I could tell he was struggling with the decision about whether to hug me goodbye. I threw my arms around him first.

'Somewhere up there, Daddy is very grateful,' I said quietly, even though I knew Lyle was a staunch agnostic.

As soon as he left, I gave Sadie a call. Mama wasn't speaking at all, she reported, still on IV fluids. The hospital wanted to keep her a few days for observation. Most important, she and Maddie were now tucked into a Worthington suite. I grabbed a Dr Pepper out of the fridge and headed to the porch swing with the four printouts from Lyle.

He'd found the girl with my numerical identity, Susan Bridget Adams, by simply paying a fee to a national genealogy website and browsing the Social Security Death Master File.

I had heard of the Social Security Administration index. Because of a cousin who was fanatically into that sort of thing, I knew it was widely used by genealogists. What I didn't know was that it provided the Social Security number and date of birth and death for about sixty million people, plus the zip code of their last known address.

It was disturbing that the girl who shared my Social Security number was so easy to unearth. It certainly didn't bolster my confidence in WITSEC, but then again, thirty-two years ago when I was born, who could have imagined this stuff would be right at your fingertips?

The last printout, a single page, was different. No website marking, no hint at all of where it came from. The page listed people named Adams as if it had been ripped out of a phone book, except that instead of addresses and phone numbers, it gave their Social Security number, date of death, and a file number with an asterisk. The asterisk was explained at the bottom of the page. Police case files. Suspicious deaths? I wondered. Had this info been hacked out of a government file?

Susan Bridget Adams, born in 1977, was high-lighted in yellow marker right beside her police case file number. She died a three-year-old toddler. It was shocking to see the nine-digit number I'd recited automatically for years at doctors' offices and banks beside the name of a little girl on an official death list, to know that her premature dying somehow brought me protection.

After swallowing the last drop of Dr Pepper, I headed back inside to my computer, praying the wireless internet gods were shining on me. And they were. I connected immediately and typed the zip code of Susan Adams's last known address into the search engine. The zip code matched someplace on the south side of Chicago. More links to the Windy City.

Then I searched 'Adams and genealogy.' With such a common name, I didn't expect much but was rewarded twenty minutes later at a website ranked fourteen on Google's list. A fuzzy black-and-white photograph of an angry-faced man named Uncle Eldon welcomed me to his surprisingly sophisticated page for the Adams Family.

I clicked 'family tree' and almost immediately found 'Susie' Bridget Adams and the single word description of her death: *fall.*

Her father still lived in the same Chicago zip code, possibly in the same home; her mother died in the late 1990s of cancer. It consoled me to see that she gave birth to five other children after Susie, all still living when the site was updated two months ago.

This page shared a link to 'Southlawn Cemetery Records.' Once there, I typed in Susie's name, all the while thanking Uncle Eldon for his overzealous details.

In seconds, the screen displayed a crude hand-drawn map, studded with coffin-shaped rectangles. I don't know why it bothered me so much. I'd seen a similar computer-generated map two days before we buried Daddy. In little Susie's case, someone scanned in the original pencil rendering in the old family plot where she rested.

Each rectangle bore a number. The numbers were assigned to ten names, all Adamses, all listed in old-fashioned, respectful calligraphy at the bottom of the page. It wasn't hard to find little Susie's coffin, a rectangle half the size of the others, crammed at an angle in the corner.

Grave number 426 – Susie's grave – wasn't expected. Grave diggers had made room.

She had been reduced to another number, a piece of geometry on a page. I hit the 'print' button and listened to Daddy's machine down the hall clear its throat.

Frustration gnawed at me, mostly because I knew that I was only working on the periphery of my own story. Susie was a single, sad note that led to a Chicago gravesite, more proof of my family's secrets, but little else.

An hour later, I lay on the couch wrapped in my old fluffy Peter Rabbit comforter. I was sailing on a highway with no speed limit after tossing five milligrams of Xanax from Daddy's bottle down my throat and chasing it with a whiskey. The

Rangers/Yankees game hummed pleasantly on the 42-inch TV nestled in the corner.

I closed my eyes and pictured my little place at Halo Ranch. The Tahitian beach scene that hung over the fireplace, the bright Mexican rug that covered the beat-up pine floor, a friend's photograph in the tiny kitchen of a heart-patterned quilt blowing on a clothesline in a West Texas landscape as bare as the moon. I'd have to arrange to move all of it back home. And harder, I had to break the news to colleagues and kids at Halo that I wouldn't be coming back.

I dozed and when I opened my eyes again, a large shape was slouched in Daddy's chair.

And he had something gripped in his hand.

'You had me worried there for a second,' Jack Smith told me. 'I knocked. Called your name a couple of times.'

His eyes lit on the prescription bottle on the coffee table and the empty glass. 'How much did you take?'

'Not enough to kill me.' I tried to claw my way out of the fog. How did he get in? The object in his hand appeared to be a small vat of blood.

Jack transferred the prescription bottle out of my reach, onto the mantel.

'I make an excellent doctored-up Prego.' He held up the jar. He had a new sling, I noticed. Bright blue. 'Are you in for dinner? I came by to do a little more research with you.'

Well, I was in no shape for that.

But, to my surprise, I was ravenous.

'Go for it,' I said, my eyes drifting closed.

He didn't seem to expect any assistance in the kitchen and I was incapacitated enough not to give him any. He efficiently turned out a Caesar salad, warm French bread, and a decent 'doctored' sauce piled with a mountain of snowy Parmesan cheese. He brought our plates out on two old metal Beatles TV trays he found in the pantry.

I didn't want to think too deeply about where Jack learned to provide such a simple, warm act because then I'd have to accept Jack as a human being with actual feelings. One-dimensional asshole Jack was enough for me.

He hinted that he could spend the night so we'd be ready to get to work in the morning. In my chemically induced haze, this seemed perfectly logical. Like a civilized divorced couple, we agreed he could take over the guest room downstairs for the night. I told him where the sheets were. Making his bed seemed a little too intimate and I wasn't sure how steady I'd be on my feet. He insisted on cleaning up the kitchen by himself and later, while I cuddled with Peter Rabbit and kept my eyes half-open to the game, he texted his boss.

As Jack settled in to watch the eighth inning of a Rangers blowout, I pushed myself up from the couch.

'Let me know how it ends,' I told him. 'I'm going to bed.'

'I'll go with you. Help you navigate the stairs.'

I shrugged and headed for the staircase, my comforter slung over my shoulder and trailing behind me, Linus-style. Jack caught me when I tripped on it a few steps from the top.

In my room, I kicked some clothes on the floor out of the way and fell on the bed, not bothering to untangle the sheets or say good night.

A wispy thought floated to the surface as I drifted again on that lovely sea.

Wasn't it most likely that Anthony Marchetti was warning me about Jack?

Wouldn't a reporter choose to do his research with a fellow reporter? Or by himself? Why the hell had I let my guard down?

Jack was busy at the window, checking the lock, pulling down the shade, before moving deliberately toward the bed.

He reached down, looming over me.

I wanted to protest but I couldn't.

He grasped my wrist firmly.

He was feeling my pulse.

The last thing I remember is Jack's silhouette, carved out by the hall light as he leaned against the doorframe.

I have no idea how long he stood there.

CHAPTER 16

My eyelids struggled to open, and when they did, I was confused. Lights out, shade pulled, a glimmer of gray coming through.

Music drifted up the stairs.

Dreamy. Sad.

Mama playing.

Am I still asleep? Thunder rumbled like distant drums, and the first drops of rain slapped the window.

I pinched my arm. It hurt for a full five seconds. Definitely wide awake. Still, the music drifted up.

Where in the hell is that coming from? Where, I suddenly remembered, *is Jack?*

I sat up abruptly. Last night's clothes, still on. Thank God.

I stumbled to the hallway.

Chopin.

'Hello?' I called, moving tentatively down the stairs, the grand piano emerging into view like a black, shiny beast. I half expected to see Mama sitting there in her hospital gown.

The piano bench was empty, coated with a fine layer of dust.

The living room, empty.

The music still playing.

Nocturne No. 19.

One of three nocturnes my mother loved to perform.

Now its notes were filtering under the closed kitchen door.

Physically, achingly pulling me against my will.

I held my breath and threw open the door.

My eyes set on it the second I stepped onto the cold tile. Mama's old radio by the kitchen sink, blaring. I thought it was broken.

I made four quick strides and flipped it off, whipping back to survey the room, getting my bearings in the sudden silence, trying to slow my heart. One of Granny's pale green antique McCoy mugs sat on the table holding the dregs of cold coffee. It was next to a cheap fold-out driving map of Oklahoma I'd never seen before. The newspaper story of Jennifer Coogan's murder was paper-clipped to it.

The louvered door to the laundry room began to slowly slide open.

Suddenly, the house wasn't silent anymore.

It was filled with a bloodcurdling scream. Mine.

Jack emerged.

'What the hell is wrong with you?' he snapped.

'You purposely scare me,' I said, breathing hard. 'Did you mess with the radio?'

He gave me an odd, pitying look.

'It's a nice station. Classical. Out of Dallas.'

'Mama's favorite,' I said dully.

'That's where the dial was set when I turned it on.'

He stepped toward me and I lunged a step back.

'Is there anything that would calm you down? That's not in the Xanax bottle?'

You getting the hell out of my house.

'Dr Pepper,' I said.

I dropped into a chair because my legs had turned to rubber. Jennifer Coogan's sweet face smiled up at me from the newspaper article, telling me I was overreacting.

'I borrowed your computer.' Jack handed me my drink. 'Checked into the newspaper articles. My FBI source emailed me some information on that girl who was murdered in Oklahoma. Are you calm enough to hear more?'

I nodded, itching to slap his patronizing face, considering the possibility that he had done more with my computer than use the internet. Most reporters – hell, most *people* – wouldn't be caught dead without their own laptops or smartphones. I dredged my brain trying to remember what would be on mine that I didn't want him to see.

'I thought it was possible that Jennifer Coogan was a hit.' He pointed to the headline on the table: WOMAN'S BODY FOUND IN LITTLE RIVER. 'The FBI was called in briefly on it because it was unusual. Two agents from Oklahoma City. Both retired now. Jennifer was raped and shot in the back of the head, then dumped here.' He took a pencil and circled a blue squiggle that represented the Little River.

'She was duct-taped to a jumbo can of hominy and a six-pound can of ready-made nacho cheese sauce from the restaurant where she worked. One was strapped to her feet, the other around her chest. But everything else about it looks kind of professional.'

'A can of nacho cheese sauce,' I echoed miserably.

'The cans are details not released to the press. The killer or killers weren't too bright if they intended to send her permanently to the bottom of the river. Kids out fishing found her body around dawn three days after she went missing. She'd washed up between a couple of rocks in a tiny inlet. The thing is, the girl was no one. A college student home waitressing for the summer. No criminal record. Conservative family. A career beauty contestant in high school. Runner-up in Miss National Teenager her senior year. Traveled very little outside the confines of her pageant schedule and her move to college. Not many girls her age lived a safer lifestyle.'

The idea that Jennifer Coogan was 'no one' said volumes about Jack.

'How did you really get this stuff?' I asked.

He dumped the cold coffee in the sink, as if he didn't hear me.

'There's never been any connection drawn between Coogan's case and your mother's,' he said. 'We probably shouldn't read too much into them. Your mother does have mental issues.'

She didn't when she put those articles in that box, I thought. *And when did Jack and I become a 'we'?*

'So, one of your FBI sources found this information in an old file? Jennifer Coogan's file? He just came up with it this morning?' My voice was sharp with skepticism.

'It's a pretty sure bet that murdered girl and Anthony Marchetti have nothing to do with each other.'

'Whoever said they did?' Interesting that Jack had been drawn to Jennifer Coogan, too.

'You know, Tommie, I think it's a good idea if I head out. I seem to be making you . . . agitated.'

And you've gotten whatever you could out of me, I thought.

As soon as the door clicked shut, I tossed the Dr Pepper can into a paper bag under the sink I'd rigged up for recycling and walked a direct path to the living room, where I threw the dead-bolt. The prescription bottle was there, perched on the mantel, beckoning. My hand closed around it, and I wondered, not for the first time, why it had been prescribed for a man who hadn't shown me a moment of visible panic in his life.

In seconds, I stood over the toilet in Mama's bathroom, tossing the pills into the water and flushing them away.

I headed back to the laundry room feeling a whole lot better about myself.

Personally, I wasn't done with Jennifer. My laptop was still on the dryer, fully charged. I unplugged it and powered it up on Mama's desk. It didn't take long to figure out that Jennifer's sensational murder had resonated throughout the state of Oklahoma and into bordering Texas towns.

Beautiful, popular girl, brave enough to tackle Whitney Houston songs for the talent portion of her competitions. She dreamed of world peace and a career teaching deaf students, until she was raped, shot, and tossed in a river like trash in the town where she trick-or-treated and got her first kiss and made brownies out of a box at slumber parties. She'd been turned into a terrible cliché a hundred times over on blogs and murder websites that thrived on digging up dead girls.

I hit the jackpot with *The Oklahoman*'s coverage. When I searched in their archives for Jennifer Coogan, eighty-two stories popped up. They could be mine for $3.95 apiece or I could pay $19.99 for a bundle of twenty-five. Otherwise, I'd have to be satisfied with the headlines, the bylines, and the first two lines of each story.

I could tell just scrolling through the list that two ambitious reporters churned out double-bylined 1A stories for three weeks, inside follow-ups for months, and a front-page one-year anniversary piece headlined WHAT HAPPENED TO JENNIFER? The most recent brief, only six months ago, said

191

that *48 Hours* had been sniffing around, considering a segment. The producers were following up on a tip about Jennifer's boyfriend at OU, who had disappeared around the same time as her murder.

I whipped out my credit card and spent the next hour and a half printing, reading, and highlighting.

Jack might not think Jennifer Coogan had anything to do with Anthony Marchetti, but I wasn't so sure.

Then, in the schizophrenic manner that had become my life, I ran upstairs, dug the pink letter out of my purse, and checked to be sure, even though I'd memorized the telephone number days ago.

I dialed before I could change my mind.

A brisk secretary answered: 'Pfieffer, Smith, and Zemeck. How may I direct your call?'

Jack Smith had searched the house while I slept.

If I hadn't been in my current obsessive-compulsive, paranoid state, I probably wouldn't have noticed. But there were signs. The blue and white plastic ice trays in the freezer were stacked in a different color order. Blue, blue, white, white, blue, blue. A drawer in my mother's room stuck out a quarter of an inch. The contents of my backpack were still messy, but slightly neater.

I stared at myself in one of Nordstrom's three-way mirrors, thinking I'd dropped at least a size in the last two weeks. A pretty export from Britain named Beatrice was eyeballing me at a 6 and asking whether I thought jade, mint, or celadon would work better with my coloring. I was wondering whether Jack Smith was a professional investigator for hire or a hit man.

Today, though, it was Rosalina Marchetti who was pulling at the strings, the zippers, the snaps, the buttons. Mr Zemeck, her Chicago lawyer, had been terse in our two back-to-back conversations about my trip tomorrow to see her. He wearily recited Rosalina's instructions for me.

'Show up at two. Dress for high tea. Wear green. Turn off your cell phone. No perfume.'

'Green? As in the color of the Grinch and dill pickles?'

'There's no need for sarcasm. She's eccentric.' And then, a little huffily: 'If you have to buy something to wear, send the receipt to my secretary.'

'Money's not an issue,' I said.

'I'm sure.' A small sigh escaped through the phone, and I pictured a rattled little man with a paunch, ready to retire from a life attached to a mobster's wife.

Less than an hour later, his secretary had reserved a room for me at a downtown Chicago hotel that she cheerfully described as 'the hippest thing' and emailed my ticket with an open-ended return. Sadie consulted me several times by cell, on both fashion and my impending trip. Mama was going to finish out the week at the hospital before returning to the nursing home, probably with no memory of ever having left.

Beatrice handed me a pile of greenery and in a few minutes I ventured out of the dressing room in a mint-colored sundress with so many inside hooks and strap crossovers that it needed a book of directions. But it worked. Oddly elegant. Cinched in all the right places.

Beatrice gave me a thumbs-up.

'I'm going to look for shoes,' she said, glancing at my scuffed cowboy boots. 'Back in a sec.'

It was late, almost closing time for the store. She'd left me alone with a three-way mirror and a row of closed dressing-room doors. Ten of them. Taunting me. I fell to my knees and almost stood on my head to check for any feet. My phone buzzed in my purse on the floor, near my ear, and I banged my head hard on the leg of a chair.

'Dammit!'

I wanted to throw the phone through the mirror but that would be bad luck.

I looked at the screen. Private caller. I never used to think of that as a bad thing.

'Tommie, are you alone?' Today Charla's voice sounded like it belonged to a member of the mouse family: squeaky and barely audible. 'You need to get this guard to lay off. I don't want to be involved in your family shit, OK?'

'You need to stop calling me,' I hissed. 'I got the gist the first time.'

'Be nice, will you? I'm under a lot of stress. Last

night, the girl across from me hung herself with a pair of silk thong panties her boyfriend snuck in on his own ass. How would you like to wake up to *that* picture?'

I wasn't sure whether she was talking about the hanging or the cross-dressing.

Charla carried on her rant, now at opera-level pitch. 'The food is starting to make my butt look like a beanbag. Even if I get out, nobody's gonna want me except some loser with a small weenie who bags at Walmart. And now I got myself an exciting new career working for the mob. So don't you be a-messin' with me. Do you want your message or not?'

'Not really,' I said.

'Honey, you better want it. This is scary shit. Word is, your Daddy has some super-impressive connections, inside and out. I've been here six months and I can't even get a guard to bring me an extra piece of pie unless I let him touch a boob. Today, a bad-ass guard showed me a morgue picture of someone they cut in Huntsville two weeks ago. Said it was just to give me a little incentive to do my job with you properly.'

Don't call him my Daddy.

'Girl, are you listening? Your Daddy wants you to know that quote unquote: "Chicago is a dead end." Do you think that's one of those double entendors or whatever they call them?'

CHAPTER 17

I threw a beat-up old Samsonite of Daddy's onto one of the double beds and applauded myself for arriving intact in Chicago, for not strangling a hapless man in the airport security line who looked surprised – surprised! – at the order to take off his shoes and remove his laptop from its case, for not succumbing to a panic attack when the plane suddenly swayed fifteen thousand feet above the earth.

The suitcase – hard maroon plastic with a lifetime of scratches – looked anachronistic against an austere modern room, not my taste but high above the noise of Michigan Avenue. The focal point was a sleek floor lamp with a blue neon light shooting up the side that could serve double duty as a nightlight.

Almost everything in the room was coolly neutral – either white, off-white, gray, or black. In $300-an-hour-decorator-speak, the colors were likely something more poetic, like Lovers' Moon, November Rain, and Midnight. Yep, the smart-ass part of my brain continued to click along. Maybe inspired by staring at the pink-purple OPI polish on my toenails named My Auntie Drinks Chianti. Pedicure by Maddie. You had to drink to make this stuff up.

Three hours to go.

My body had been buzzing like a dying fluorescent light since I woke up. Maybe a quarter of a pill of Xanax would have fixed that if I hadn't been so rash.

Plopping onto the other bed, I decided I'd rather be sitting on Black Diablo than alone in a hotel room in a strange city, wondering if I might be shot at in the next few hours or poisoned with a cup of high tea. I'd had plenty of time to interpret Charla's warning about a dead end.

I eased the green dress out of the hanging bag in the suitcase for something to do, wondering how many minutes I should allow to strap it on. It was the only dress I tried, but Beatrice insisted it was the one. Would the girl I had been a week ago have so docilely obeyed Rosalina's peculiar request?

I opened the mini-bar. No Dr Pepper. I grabbed a Milky Way, a Sprite, and a small can of cashews. When I finished downing that, I took a long shower, carefully applied makeup, pulled my hair off my face with two of Granny's antique silver hair combs, all while trying not to think about how Rosalina Marchetti could destroy my world with just a few words.

At one-thirty, when my nerves were about to explode, the doorman helped me climb into a cab. I barely noticed the buildings whizzing by, except when my Armenian driver screeched to a halt to deliver a stream of American curse words at pedestrian tourists. He specifically targeted anyone carrying a red American Girl bag. I counted thirty-two of them in one block and then stopped counting. I knew some mothers of Maddie's friends who thought nothing of dropping two thousand for a mom-and-daughter weekend trip to the flagship store on Michigan Avenue.

We cruised down Lake Shore Drive, the hot wind blowing through the windows, tearing apart my hair. In Texas cabs, air-conditioning was as certain as four tires. In the Windy City, apparently not. Half-moons of armpit sweat now stained the green silk. I stared into the beautiful blue of Lake Michigan on my right, punctuated with parasails and boats, its beaches packed with every skin and bikini color.

Snapshots flew by – a pretty girl in a bright pink sports bra bounced by an emaciated homeless man wearing three baseball caps and hoisting a bulging plastic bag. A cyclist knelt with a bloody knee to examine a flat tire on the concrete bike trail. A mother shouted into the wind as her toddler unexpectedly ran toward the waves. Lives that would never touch mine again.

Lake Shore Drive turned into Sheridan Road, connecting the city's busy ant farm with a life of stratospheric privilege. We passed lush, rolling lawns, every blade of grass the same color and height, as if a band of Oompa Loompas used a paintbrush and manicure scissors each morning to maintain perfection. And the houses – if they could be called that – stood against the clouds as stunning specimens of architecture: Spanish-style villas, colonials, and modern geometric shapes that took cues from Frank Lloyd Wright, a hometown boy.

The cabbie turned off Sheridan Road and wound his way around, toward the lake, eventually pulling up to a massive black iron gate. He pressed the speaker button.

'What's your name?' he asked over his shoulder.

'Tommie. Just say Tommie.'

'You don't look like a Tommy,' he said, turning around. 'You sure?'

'Just say it, please.'

He pressed the button again impatiently. 'I got Tommy here. You going to let me in?'

'We'd prefer that you drop off Miss McCloud at the gate. She can walk up.'

The voice was male and stern, like a former military man. Or a Texas football coach. The cabbie shrugged and asked me for eighty dollars. Not knowing whether I was being ripped off, I gave him five crisp twenties and told him to keep the change. Then I hesitated, holding out a bill. 'There's another hundred if you wait. And another hundred when you deliver me to the hotel. It will be at least an hour.'

He weighed the possibility, running a mental cash register.

'OK.' He shrugged. 'I'll circle. But I leave after an hour and fifteen minutes.'

He left me standing alone in front of the monstrous twelve-foot-tall concrete wall that curved like a snake around a large property, its look somewhat softened by branches with tiny pink flowers that dripped over the side.

A security camera on top of the wall adjusted robot arms to direct its lens on me. I considered my tangled hair, perspiring face, green dress clinging in places it shouldn't be clinging for tea of any kind with an elderly socialite. Nervously, I rubbed the key around my neck, which the hospital wouldn't let Mama wear when I tried to give it back. I glanced right and then left. No sign anywhere of thugs in cowboy hats.

A small metal door to the left of the main gate, practically hidden by foliage, swung open because someone, somewhere, punched a button. I walked cautiously through, into the land of Rosalina's paranoia, my body on high alert. I found myself in a narrow, arched tunnel of vines. The end was not in sight. I jumped as the gate snapped shut behind me.

I walked steadily for about three minutes as the path inclined toward what I assumed was Rosalina's house. Five times I considered turning around. Twice, the heel of my brand-new metallic copper sandals got caught in the dirt until I finally yanked them off and trod onward barefoot.

Occasionally, the vines parted a little above me to let in more light. I could see they covered a continuous metal arbor that acted as a cage; plant life covered it so densely I could not see out on either side, and I assumed no one but the cameras I occasionally spotted could see in. By the time I arrived at a stone staircase embedded into the earth, I was trembling.

I counted twenty steps before reaching the landing. It took me a second to get my bearings once I reached open sunlight. I stood on the second-level terrace of an impressive replica of an Italian villa. On one side I faced floor-to-ceiling windows that framed a ballroom hung with three massive crystal chandeliers. The room was designed so that on special nights guests would spill out onto this balcony.

When I turned around, Lake Michigan slapped me in the face with an unexpectedly cool breeze. In Texas, you only caught one of those in summer by standing near an air-conditioning vent. I couldn't see water, but I knew it was close.

I knocked the bottoms of the two-inch heels on the tiled ground to get off the dirt and strapped them back on before peering over the balcony into the most elaborate garden I'd ever seen, a maze of arbors and stone pathways and fountains. Someone could get lost in there. Which was probably the point.

'It's beautiful, isn't it?' asked a slightly accented voice behind me, and just like that, I was face-to-face with Rosalina Marchetti. The first thing I noticed was that she'd had her cheekbones 'done,' pulled higher and sharper, making her look more Italian than Mexican.

Few vestiges of the Rosie from that faded newspaper picture remained. Her silvery white hair was orchestrated into an elegant bun almost as twisted as her garden. Her pale green pantsuit flowed from her slender body like a loose skin, a subtle background to the diamonds glinting on her fingers, in her ears, at her neck.

Rosalina was more beautiful than ever. And I looked nothing like her.

'Oh, my God,' she said, a mist over her blue eyes, which I knew were really plain, ordinary brown. And then she swept me into what seemed to be a very genuine hug.

I felt absolutely nothing. *Shouldn't I feel something?*

'Shhh,' she warned, as I opened my mouth to speak. 'Not here.'

She tucked her arm through the crook of mine, and led me down two more flights of rocky stairs that spiraled their way into the garden. The paving stones looked ancient enough for Michelangelo himself to have picked over them.

In the center of the garden's opening courtyard, a life-sized copper statue of a small child with angel wings tilted her head to the sky, her arms open with glee as water spilled over her. 'That's Adriana,' she said. It took me several seconds to figure out who Rosalina was talking about. 'I put the fountain in on the three-year anniversary of her kidnapping.'

Please, God, don't let that girl be me.

Four other garden paths led off the courtyard into a dense, tamed jungle, and Rosalina tugged me along on one rampant with honeysuckle, oblivious to the effect of her words on me. From above, the garden gave the appearance of well-groomed symmetry, but once inside I gave up trying to keep track of all of the turns. I was hot, tired, and pretty certain Rosalina wasn't much of a physical threat. Besides, I had always cheated with a pencil and eraser at childhood maze games.

'I feel safest in here,' Rosalina said, pulling a branch aside for me to step through. 'This garden was designed for me many years ago by a University of Chicago math professor. He's dead now. I'm the only other one besides my security guards and a gardener who knows every way in and out, and it's locked without a key inside my head.' As she tapped her forehead, I prayed that the math professor died of natural causes.

She glanced at my dress, and my fingers awkwardly adjusted the neckline. 'Thank you for wearing green,' she said. 'It's better camouflage.'

This was beyond bizarre. Had Rosalina lived her entire life in fear, grieving for a stolen daughter, a recluse trying to disappear into her landscape?

'Don't feel pity for me,' she said, as if reading my mind. 'I made my deal with the devil. Your father, that is. I was still young, but I knew what lay ahead for me if I didn't marry him. Venereal disease, abusive men, an overdose. In some ways, your father saved me, although, of course, it was for his own selfish reasons.' Her voice trailed into bitterness. 'I'm assuming you know the story, at least that part of it.'

Your father. Did she mean Anthony Marchetti? She dropped the words so casually.

'Why would you assume that?' I stuttered. 'I don't know anything.'

'This is my favorite space,' Rosalina said abruptly, as we stepped into the colorful chaos of a small Mexican garden. Bright blue tile covered the ground, overflowing Mexican pots held lemon trees and wildly colorful flowers. A parakeet cackled and swooped by several inches from my face. Two green-striped padded lounge chairs were neatly divided by a small green table that held a green pot of tea and a basket of scones. I guessed we stood on the south side of the maze, but who knew?

'Sit down, dear,' she said abruptly. 'I'm not your mother, of course. Surely you never really thought that. You're the spitting image of Genoveve. I always found that pretentious of her. Her name was probably something perfectly ordinary. Jenny with a *J.*'

I clung to the important part.

Rosalina Marchetti was not my mother.

My mother was the one who tucked me in at night like a burrito. Who had closed her eyes and held her breath every time I threw my body on top of a bull.

My mother was lying in a hospital bed in Texas, her mind wandering through a demented dream of her own.

'You don't need to look at me like that,' Rosalina said haughtily. 'It was just a little white lie. I wanted to present my case in person. You wouldn't have flown all this way to see me otherwise; you would have simply tracked down Anthony. I figured you'd be curious. You're a psychologist. You help small children. And this is *all* about a small child. My daughter. I need to know what happened to her. And I know Anthony knows. I want you to get him to tell.' She swatted at a wasp with a wrinkled, French-manicured hand. 'Surely he can't pass up a plea from his long-lost daughter.'

I was thinking, yes, Anthony Marchetti definitely could. I was thinking I wasn't about to accept a word Rosalina was saying as the truth.

'You owe me.' Her face revealed a disconcerting glimpse of the stripper, the Mafia hooker, the survivor. 'You and your mother owe me. My daughter is gone because of you.'

'Tell me. Please.' I barely got it out, but it was all the encouragement she needed.

'I was Rose Red,' she said proudly. 'No other stripper pulled them in like I did. Anthony and his boys showed up almost every night. I dated one of his bulldogs. Arturo.'

She took a dainty sip of tea and crossed her legs primly.

'If alcohol and drugs in exchange for blow jobs counts for love,' she continued drily, 'then Arturo and I were in love. Anthony was the stud, of course, but he was out of my league. We spent a lot of time over at a Rush Street piano bar, where your mother played and sang after ten. Anthony would listen to her and drink martinis until the garbage trucks rolled.'

She gazed at me with a mixture of jealousy and fascination.

'It's eerie how much you look alike. That hair, the way you move. Anthony and your mother fascinated each other. She couldn't resist him. All that darkness and charm.' Her voice grew heavy with sarcasm. 'Thus began their great romance. The story goes to hell from there. I got pregnant. Your mother got pregnant. Difference was, one of Arturo's buddies raped me in the alley behind the bar. Every which way, if you know what I mean. Arturo wouldn't even look at me after that.'

'I'm sorry,' I said, meaning it. 'What happened to my mother?'

'Anthony went down for a hit on an FBI agent. It was ugly. He shot the man's whole family. Somehow, your mother was mixed up in it. Anthony pled out to get her protected. Kind of a grand gesture for someone with Anthony's résumé. To plead, I mean. I figured he'd just threaten a jury and get off.'

How, how, how could Mama be mixed up in this?

She paused, looking satisfied. 'But there Anthony sits, more than thirty years later.'

'I don't understand,' I stuttered. 'You said you and Anthony weren't . . . a thing.'

'He brought me an offer right after the murders. If I married him, my baby and I would be taken care of for life. But he made no bones about it: I'd be the new target for his enemies while your mother and his unborn baby got out of town. She already had an older boy. She never said who *his* father was. Not as pure as she put on.'

She was playing the role of martyr and enjoying every minute of it. I held back angry words because I didn't want her to stop.

'Anthony always called me Red after that. But as in red herring, not Rose Red. I can't say that he wasn't straight about the risk in marrying him. I just never expected anything to happen to Adriana. You know that whoever took her had to think she was you. Anthony's baby. I've been watching my back ever since.'

Something about this part of the story rang false, but I couldn't put my finger on it. I was schooled in the facial tics of a liar, but she displayed none of them, her eyes focused on me, never darting away.

She gestured to the house. 'That's my prison. My fortress. I can flip a switch in any room and see every corner of the house and grounds. I think my security boys like to watch me in the

207

shower sometimes, but' – she grinned – 'that's the price I pay. Every now and then I'll do a little striptease around the four-poster. That's just a bonus. They're well paid.'

I brushed aside this image. 'I still don't understand. Why now? How did you find me?'

'Do you believe in Fate, Tommie?'

I thought about Granny and her cards, about how I sat smack in the middle of a tangled garden that was a metaphor for my life.

'Well, I believe that Fate brought you to me,' Rosalina said.

'Someone told you where I was,' I said flatly.

She turned coy. 'I really can't say.'

It suddenly occurred to me that I'd brought a tape recorder and never once thought about turning it on. I reached into my bag, ostensibly for a tissue, and flipped a switch and the direction of the conversation.

'So you don't know what my mother knew about those murders?'

'Not a clue.'

'What makes you so sure Anthony Marchetti is my father?'

'I'm sure. Track him down. And while you're at it, ask him about my Adriana. Beg him to give me some peace.'

I looked at my watch. I'd been there an hour. Screw subtlety. I just wanted answers. 'Do you know why Anthony Marchetti has been moved to a Texas prison nearer my family?'

'I didn't know that.' Rosalina seemed authentically surprised.

'I feel like my family is being threatened, but I don't know where it's coming from.'

'Maybe you should ask the Feds who are trying to peer over my wall right now.' Rosalina let out a snort of laughter. 'Actually, honey, you can't believe a word the FBI says. Of course, you can't believe Anthony, either. He's the master of illusion. The FBI guys, though – they lie, lie, lie to get what they want. Try to make us nervous. They've been bugging my phones for a decade. Don't they think I know? They want to track all that money still drifting here and there.'

She brought the teacup and a flash of diamonds to her pale glossy lips, and I thought how her striptease was probably still worth watching.

I didn't care what else she had to tell me. I desperately needed to get out of there. As I pushed myself out of the chair, she tugged me back down.

'Not yet,' she said, glancing around. 'I want you to have something.' She reached into her pants pocket and placed a small red jewelry box in my hand, the elegant kind with the spring catch on the back.

The kind that promised something good.

It seemed odd that Rosalina would want to give me a gift – maybe something Anthony Marchetti had bought her once upon a time? Whatever it was, I didn't want it.

Rosalina quickly shattered that sentimental thought.

'My daughter's finger is in there.'

There weren't words in the English language to respond to that, or at least I couldn't find them.

'Be careful, don't drop it!' Rosalina grabbed the box to keep it from falling. My hand didn't seem to be working.

'Are you going to faint? *Ay, Dios mio,* don't faint!' Actually, I didn't think I was going to faint. I took a bottle of cold water from the ice bucket near my feet and placed it on my cheek.

'I'm sorry, Tommie,' she said. 'I shouldn't have surprised you like that.'

And then, 'It's mummified.' As if that made everything better.

Desperate not to lose me, she rattled on. 'The cops gave it back to me years ago, six months after the kidnappers sent it. They told me that this could be my piece of her to bury. That she was dead, and I needed to accept that.'

'Have they tested it for DNA?' I heard my voice, calm and logical. An invisible part of me wandered up there in the lush foliage of the Mexican sage trees, an impartial observer to this mad tea party. I wondered vaguely how a gardener coaxed them to grow so well in Chicago. I could almost feel the leaves brush my cheek.

'No,' Rosalina replied. 'They didn't do DNA testing much back then. They seemed so certain it was her. And, frankly, I've never wanted to know for sure. Until now. I'm getting old. I don't have that many years left.'

The box sat between us on the table, reminding me of the red coat in *Schindler's List*, the single piece of color in a world gone insane. The red of Anthony Marchetti's signature scarf. I picked up a cube of ice and rolled it around my neck. I tried not to let my imagination wonder what a thirty-one-year-old severed baby finger looked like.

'What do you possibly think I can do with this? I assume you've had investigators working on Adriana's case for years.'

'Whatever you think you should,' Rosalina told me. 'You are the daughter I never had.'

Her last scripted line.

The afternoon light had faded, and she sat in the shadow of a tree, Rose Red exposed. Somewhere along the way, she'd lost her Italian accent. She sounded like what she once was, a Mexican-American girl from the South Side, a scrapper who bent her morals until they strangled her. Despair leaked out of every pore. I could now make out the edges of her blue contacts. They couldn't hide the misery that lurked behind them. I'd seen those eyes before – on my mother's face, at Tuck's funeral.

I willed myself to pick up the box. I could do this. Perhaps I had lived every moment of my life to get here, to this spot inside Rosalina's vine- and pain-infested jungle. Maybe every research paper I'd ever written, every case I'd studied about childhood trauma, was preparation for this moment. Perhaps I was meant to find Adriana. Maybe she was still alive and held the answers.

I thought these things even while recognizing Rosalina Marchetti for what she was: a brilliant manipulator, a pathological liar.

I asked one more question, to test her.

'When you hugged me up on the terrace, you were looking for a wire, right?'

'Of course,' Rosalina said. 'You can't be too careful.'

CHAPTER 18

I let the water from the hotel's luxury shower massager run like hot spikes down my spine. Rosalina and I parted on pretty good terms, considering – not enemies, not friends.

She seemed satisfied that I would at least make an attempt with Anthony Marchetti. I made no promises about the finger but placed it carefully in my purse, unable to bear the thought of opening the box, not yet, and certainly not in front of her.

Rosalina allowed me to walk out of the mansion grounds on the winding driveway much less dramatically than I arrived. I was two minutes late, but my cabbie had waited.

Even with all the lies, details in Jack's and Rosalina's stories matched so closely they were impossible to ignore. I turned and stuck my face in a blast of hot water, my mind drifting to Sadie and our conversation yesterday at the hospital.

I'd gone to check on Mama, but the truth is, I needed a Sadie fix more, my little sister's assurance that it was all going to be OK before I took off for Chicago. We sat in a booth in the hospital cafeteria drinking cups of black coffee from the bottom of the pot and sharing a piece of dry lemon pound cake whose only saving grace was a drizzle of white glaze.

I had laid it all out: my jail visit with Anthony Marchetti; the details of Jennifer Coogan's unsolved murder; the little girl with my Social Security number buried in a Chicago cemetery; the emailed photo of Alyssa Bennett, slaughtered with her family in a Mafia frenzy more than thirty years ago; the almost comical warnings from a rodent-voiced husband killer on death row. My concerns that Jack Smith wasn't really who he pretended to be.

'Three little girls,' Sadie mused, smashing the last crumbs into her fork. 'If you include Rosalina's missing daughter.' I hadn't thought of parsing it that way. Sadie always had a way of tilting the world a little to change my view.

Her long legs were stretched out across her side of the booth. She wore a fitted white T-shirt, low-slung jeans held up by a tooled leather western belt, brown Reef flip-flops, and pink toenails with daisy decals, courtesy of Maddie. Silver hoops in her ears, not a whisper of makeup except a little black eyeliner, short wild hair she kept pulling her fingers through, big blue weary eyes, and still, the kid sweeping the floor two tables away couldn't take his eyes off of her.

She cast a spell. Maybe this was a curse for the McCloud women or at least for whoever ran into them.

Later, Mama lay motionless between us, heavily medicated, her hospital bed at a forty-degree angle, the IV pumping in nutrients, the lines of the heart monitor spiking in a choreographed pattern. She was too young for this kind of ending. Some people were destined to live the most significant part of their lives all at once, in a brief, intense span of time. Maybe Mama was one of them. Maybe, I thought, she'd lived that part of her life before she ever saw my face.

'I can't believe she told us all those lies,' I said to Sadie, finally, to break the depressing silence. 'And maybe Daddy, too.'

I expected sympathy. I didn't get it.

'Why not?' my sister shot back. 'You always thought Mama was perfect. That our childhood was perfect. You just wouldn't look at the signs. Mama put on a good show, but she never, *ever* got over Tucker.'

She realigned the sheet over Mama for the third time since we'd been back in the room.

'After you left for college, I'd find her alone, staring at his high school baseball picture. She kept it in a box under the bed. She and Daddy officially moved into separate bedrooms my senior year, although I think they'd been sleeping apart for years. He loved her, but he couldn't get inside her head. None of us could.'

'I didn't,' I said, at a loss as to how I missed all the gouges in my family's psyche, the ones I was trained to spot and buff out for everyone else.

While Sadie plumped up the pillow, I saw Mama and me at the piano. A hot afternoon. My little fingers, sweaty on the keys. I kept playing B flat instead of B sharp. I was doing this on purpose, angry that Mama wouldn't let me go riding with Tuck.

I heard the normal tumbling sound of Tuck plowing down the stairs. He jumped over the last three stairs to the landing, sunglasses propped on his head, big grin, ready to fly. Reckless, Mama often said. I always thought he was just a boy.

He yanked on my ponytail. 'B sharp, not B flat, Tommie girl.'

'Thanks,' I said sarcastically.

'Don't be long,' Mama said to Tuck. 'I'm having one of those days.'

Something silent and unhappy passed between them.

Words were Mama's rope, always thrown with perfect aim, pulling you in, wrapping you a little too tightly. You never knew when she'd pick up her rope. She missed wide with Tuck that time. He and his horse didn't come home until midnight. The tension in the house was so charged and heavy for the next three days that I didn't speak, terrified that a single word in the air would blow all of us up.

Was this normal? Kids don't know what is normal.

But I didn't express that to Sadie as she refilled Mama's water, opened a new box of Kleenex, and set it on the tray. Pulled the call button closer even though Mama was too out of it to know.

'I'm so sorry,' I said. 'I should have been there for you.'

'Don't be sorry. I'm not really angry with you, Tommie. I'm not even angry with her. I'm just confused. And scared. I'm worried about Maddie's safety. I want this to be over.'

Then I heard the tone, the pleading one she used all her life when she needed backup, when I was the big sister who secretly finished her report on the Roman Empire or helped her slip out our bedroom window on a school night for a quick make-out session in the dark.

The McCloud sisters were tight.

'You know you are my sister no matter what you find,' she had said. 'Figure it out, Tommie. Make it go away.'

I pictured it like a Frito. Or maybe more like a Bugle.

But still I did not open the box.

It was 7:22 a.m. and I'd been awake in the hotel room for two hours, mesmerized by the stripe of the lamp's blue neon light, thinking nightmarish thoughts about a decomposing baby finger while Rosalina's bitter voice swam around in my head. Odd that I'd never seen another person besides Rosalina at her mansion. Not a maid. Not a security guard. Just that disembodied male voice over the speaker.

I didn't wait on the hotel operator's wake-up call for permission to get out of bed. I took a quick shower and threw on some jeans, another of Sadie's slightly too tight T-shirts, this one etched with a cheerful blue Buddha, a little mascara, and clear lip gloss. I jabbed two yellow No. 2 pencils into a makeshift bun on my head, the hairstyle I wore for studying since high school. Because, today, I planned to study.

I stepped out of the hotel into the pedestrian traffic on Michigan Avenue, which was vibrating with aggression to a ranch girl like me. A bike messenger cursed and swerved when I stepped into his path; a grinning homeless person punched me, hard, on the arm; a swinging briefcase rapped one of my knuckles, all before I reached a café a couple of blocks from the hotel. The businessman with the briefcase kept on walking and barking into his headset. In Texas, I would have wound up with an apology and maybe even a date.

I appreciated a city with a pulse, but I needed to live where I could see the sky. At home, sky loomed everywhere, a blue marble cereal bowl a benign giant child turned over to keep us safe from his dog. Here, it was an afterthought, little slivers between the walls of the skyscrapers if you happened to look up.

On the plus side, safety in numbers.

Once I retrieved my coffee, I walked as far to the right of the sidewalk as I could, balancing the paper cup in one hand while watching the traveling red dot on my phone's GPS. I was the dot, of course, on a twenty-minute stroll to the Harold Washington Chicago Public Library, a granite and red-brick behemoth squatting on the corner of State Street and Congress Parkway. I stood still for a moment and endured the battering of passersby just to appreciate it.

Tall arched windows filtered in light from all sides, while creepy winged gargoyles leered from the top, waiting for someone with a wand to bring them to life. Inside, thousands of visitors a day chose from among six million books, further proof that books would survive catastrophic events alongside the roaches.

I closed the door behind me, instantly insulated from the madness of people rushing, rushing, rushing. I drank in the silence like precious water.

Here, the world slowed to school-zone speed, controlled by librarians intelligent and methodical enough to be either great presidents or serial killers.

Visiting libraries in foreign cities was a hobby of mine. College libraries, city libraries, itty-bitty libraries. It didn't matter. Today I had the bonus of a purpose, a suggestion from Lyle.

'Turn Off Your Cell Phone and Pagers, Please,' a sign asked politely. No exclamation point needed. With the help of an ancient docent at the front desk, it didn't take long to pinpoint my destination: up three flights of sweeping marble stairs.

I moved past a reading area laid out with dozens

of current newspapers from all over the world and entered a glass-fronted chamber crammed with rows and rows of scratched-up metal file cabinets.

The room held only one other occupant. A tiny punked-out girl in head-to-toe black with a single skull earring, grad student written all over her, who looked up from her thick book on Sartre and asked in an unexpectedly sweet voice, 'Can I help you?'

She led me to the cabinet with the microfiche reels, helped me collect the right dates and publications, walked over to a nearby machine, and provided an efficient lesson in the ancient art of reading and copying microfilm. I wasn't a novice, I assured her.

I'd done a sweltering summer of research into old microfiche records at mental institutions as an intern for two cantankerous UT professors who squabbled constantly about whose name would go first on a joint journal article that is still unpublished ten years later.

Punk Girl smiled, offering a glimpse of the innocent still in there, while the skull in her ear leered like the gargoyles. I wanted to ask whether she was buying Sartre's take on existentialism, if she believed our lives were blank pieces of paper on which we wrote the story with no help at all from God. I wondered if she'd gotten to the concept of *mauvaise foi,* bad faith, the part where we deceive ourselves in order not to take blame.

I figured she would think I was nosy and crazy, which I pretty much was at this point, so I kept my mouth shut. As she walked away I snapped the first roll in place, switched on the light, and whirred past ads and headlines until I found the date I wanted: January 3, 1980.

I could have found this in the *Chicago Tribune*'s online archives, but Lyle said there was nothing like experiencing the stories in real time, as they appeared in print. I could appreciate this. Researching online was a sterile experience. I liked original packaging.

The headline was direct and screaming, in 72-point type: FAMILY BUTCHERED.

The accompanying photograph showed cops throwing up in snow-covered bushes in front of an unremarkable saltbox brick house marked off with crime scene tape, the best action shot a newspaper photographer could get on a late-night deadline.

I pressed the button to copy the page, scanning the brief story:

CHICAGO – A family of five and an unidentified female were found shot to death execution-style last night in a home in a quiet Polish neighborhood on the North Side.

Police identified the victims as Frederick and Andrea Bennett. The names of the three children and the second woman were not released.

Police broke into the house about 9:30 p.m. after neighbors complained of a barking dog.

Stefan Pietruczyk, a next-door neighbor, said the family moved in only two weeks earlier and kept to themselves.

'Me and the wife thought it was strange that the kids didn't come out much,' said Pietruczyk, who has lived in the neighborhood for twenty-five years. 'And the parents weren't that chatty. But we were real happy someone had finally fixed up that house. Now we wish they'd taken their troubles somewhere else. Our property values are shot to hell.'

FBI agents swarmed the house shortly after Chicago patrol cops called in the murders. An FBI spokeswoman on the scene said further details would be revealed at a press conference today.

I scrolled ahead. The next day's front page featured a slightly more sedate 60-point headline: FBI FAMILY SLAIN BY MOB. Below were the headshots of the victims, including school pictures of the children: Alyssa, six, and two brothers, Robert, ten, and Joe, four.

They were *babies*. How could anyone look into those innocent faces and pull a trigger?

I peered closely at the main photograph – shuttered windows, empty driveway, anonymous landscaping – the earmarks of a safe house. According to the FBI, the Bennett family had been moved there from their home in an upscale neighborhood in Naperville. The unidentified woman with them was an FBI agent assigned to their protection.

The story unfolded on the front page for five weeks, eventually revealing that Fred Bennett was an undercover FBI agent investigating the mob. And, finally, swift justice: the plea deal of mob boss Anthony Marchetti, who told the judge in his allocution that he flew into 'an uncontrollable rage that I deeply regret' when he discovered Bennett deep inside his organization.

The prosecutor took the death penalty off the table since Marchetti spared the families and the state of Illinois the misery and cost of a trial. It left a horrific killer a shot at parole. There was no mention of evidence of any kind, of how the FBI fingered Marchetti almost instantly for the six deaths.

So far, none of this contradicted Rosalina.

I looked at my watch. Two hours gone. A middle-aged woman in a pink sweat suit and brighter pink Puma running shoes walked past, flashing a shy smile. I made the mistake of smiling back.

'How are you?' she asked, with the emphasis on the 'you.'

'Fine, thanks.' I cast my eyes down and silently begged her not to start a conversation. A genealogy chart peeked out of the canvas library bag hanging over her shoulder. There's no such thing as a short

223

genealogy conversation. Existentialism takes less time to explain.

She instantly picked up on my body cues, and I felt a little guilty. She wandered over to a reading chair in a far corner, where she found her place a third of the way into a weapon-sized paperback copy of *Anna Karenina,* which was farther than I'd ever gotten. She turned the page, the movement of her arm revealing a lump on the right side of her waist. Insulin pump? Heart monitor? Gun?

Somewhere in the back of my mind lurked the fact that Illinois had the toughest restrictions on weapons in the nation. Carrying a concealed weapon was prohibited for civilians.

Keeping a wary eye on the diabetic genealogist in the pink tracksuit, I refocused on the microfiche and snapped in another reel, this one for July of 1981.

WHO CHOPPED OFF LITTLE ADRIANA'S PINKIE?

I swallowed a gasp, startled by the headline even though I'd purposely picked a reel from a Chicago tabloid that gorged itself to the popping point on kidnappings and murder. In the next hour and a half, I discovered at least thirty stories from a dogged reporter named Barbara Thurman who had no ethical problem flaunting unnamed sources and sticking in her own opinion.

Thurman hinted that Rosalina was a drug addict and possibly involved in the disappearance of her daughter. Rosalina claimed that the girl had been torn from her arms in the front yard of her grandmother's home on the South Side, where she was visiting for the day. But no one else heard Rosalina's screams or saw two masked men tear off in a black Mercedes. Not the grandmother, not the gang members who skipped school to roam the block, not the old man across the street planting petunias in his postage-stamp yard.

One story delved into gruesome detail about the finger: how it arrived (regular mail, in a plain brown padded envelope, with a small brown bloodstain smudged in the corner); what the ransom note inside said (*Nine left. Chop, chop. You know what to do.*); how Rosalina reacted (she swallowed a bottle of aspirin and tried to stab herself with a steak knife before being transported to the hospital).

Thurman's final piece, a startlingly blunt opinion column, ran inside on page 3 with a headshot of an adorable brown-eyed baby and the headline: WHAT ARE THE POLICE HIDING?

On every front, the cops had shut down reporter Barbara Thurman. Only two short months of investigating and the case of the missing Adriana Marchetti was marked unsolved and stuck high on a shelf. For the next twenty minutes, I punched the appropriate buttons to copy each story about Adriana, racking up sixty bucks on my MasterCard and a frustrating headache.

I rubbed my temples. The books crowding the shelves felt like cold strangers, pressing in on me. The library was no longer my refuge.

Pink Lady had disappeared.

She represented good things, I had told my cynical brain the last time my eyes lit on her tapping Puma foot, about an hour ago.

Breast cancer awareness.

Excellent taste in literature.

She was probably the kind of mother who cut the crusts off her child's peanut butter and jelly sandwiches for a few formative years even though she thought it was silly, like mine did.

And now, as I felt so utterly alone and scared, she was gone.

CHAPTER 19

Punk Girl was fiddling with her skull earring and doodling a pretty good caricature of Rod Blagojevich in prison stripes when I approached her with my load of paper and film.

'I see you were successful,' she said. 'Just leave the film canisters here. I'll put them back. I need to earn my minimum wage.'

'Good job on his hair,' I replied, pointing to the puffy black mop on her piece of paper.

'I'm doing a paper on corrupt Chicago politicians and their early childhoods. Did you know this dude shined shoes as a kid to pay the family bills? You'd think he'd be a better person.'

You'd think. Or not. Some kids think they deserve more, and others think they deserve nothing. I haven't figured it out yet.

'Can you direct me to the bathroom?' I asked.

'The bathroom of the day is in Humanities on the seventh floor. There are plumbing problems in several of the closer ones, so it will be worth the walk.'

She pinched her nose to make the point and

when she released it I could see a tiny hole where another skull might live sometimes.

'Take the center staircase. Go up four flights. Turn left and head back through the stacks. The bathroom's in the corner.'

I walked up the four flights slowly. No one followed. I wandered through the stacks, breathing in a deep whiff of old leather and paper, feeling safer, as if the books were saying, *Calm down, we are still your friends.* In better circumstances, I'd love to bring a sleeping bag and live here for a month. I also said that about Daddy's barn. My hand ran down a copy of *Ulysses*, which caught my eye, like it always did. Maybe someday I'd read it and a thousand other works of great literature not included in the Ponder High School curriculum.

'Excuse me.' A man appeared suddenly, brushing across my body to reach for a book on the top shelf.

He smelled sexy, like expensive cologne and untamed hormones. He was twentyish, with a slender athletic build. He smiled at me under the brim of a Chicago Cubs hat. I liked the Cubs. Everybody liked the Cubs. Except the White Sox. And the Cardinals.

'How ya doin', Tommie? I'm Louie.'

Before I could ask how he knew my name, he provided a full frontal view, and I wondered, dizzily, if a villain had leapt out of the dusty pages of a noir novel.

'I'm not so pretty, eh?' A vivid red scar ran from his right eye halfway down his cheek. Whatever unlucky thing had happened, the lucky thing for Louie was that it didn't happen a millimeter to the left. He would be blind in one eye.

He leaned back, relaxed, against the shelf. 'The first thing I tell people in your situation is that this is an old high school football injury. Not everybody believes it. The second thing I tell 'em is that I made the most of it. Ask the bastard who chop-blocked me at the goal line in the game against Hubbard South. Knocked off my helmet. Five guys piled on. I couldn't see for the blood.' He drew a finger lazily down his scar. 'There was a cleat. Stuck in my face. Got it pictured?'

He pulled out a pack of cigarettes. I felt sure he knew he was breaking library rules, so I kept my mouth shut.

'I held on to the fuckin' ball, though,' he said, lighting up. 'And the jerk-off who hit me . . . I *own* that asshole. Still. His girlfriend. His money. His life. His face don't look too good, either.'

A disfigured lunatic hiding out in Modernist literature. Who knew my name. Possibly related to a Bubba I encountered not so long ago in a parking garage.

'I don't have a gun on me,' he said.

'Good,' I said. 'Great.' I glanced around uneasily, hoping to catch sight of a motherly woman in pink. Hoping the smoke detector would go off.

'I think you're gonna do what I want anyways.

People usually do.' He slid behind me and draped an arm around my neck like a lover.

I nodded mutely, filled with a powerful desire to pee.

'I know where that cute little niece of yours is. At the skating rink. Wearing purple shorts that say "Cheer" across her butt. Tell me, why do mothers let little girls out of the house in shorts that advertise their butts?' He took a drag on his cigarette and blew it into my face, which wasn't a problem because I had involuntarily stopped breathing five seconds ago.

'She's got on a Tweety Bird shirt,' he continued cheerfully. 'Her hair's in a ponytail. My friend thinks she's a cutie. His type. But I'm pretty sure every little girl's his type.'

He smashed his cigarette out into a green book binding, making a small dark O, like a tiny terrified mouth.

With his free hand, he pulled a cell phone out of his pocket. 'Let's check in with my buddy. See how it's goin' there in Texas.'

I had a flashback to Maddie's body in a hospital bed with tubes feeding in and out right after doctors first discovered the tumor in her brain. Now, thinking of a stranger touching her, I was overcome with the same sickening, helpless rush. Louie removed his arm from around my shoulders, pressing me against the shelves with his body.

'I'll give you anything you want,' I said. 'Money. Just leave Maddie alone.'

His arm gripped me tighter, enough to make it uncomfortable, but not enough that anyone walking by would think it was anything more than a boyfriend's casual embrace, a little prelude to sex in the stacks.

He pressed 'redial.' My bladder lurched again and I regretted the coffee and a trip to the Coke machine. Fear for Maddie squirmed like an alien life-form in my gut.

'Hey, there,' he said into the phone. 'What's our little kiddo doing? She's at the concession stand . . . ordering fried dill pickles, a Dr Pepper . . . and sour gummi worms. Oh, come on. Tommie here is not going to believe that one. Who would eat *that*?'

Maddie.

Maddie would.

She had a weird thing for pickles. She even put them in macaroni and cheese.

Tears stung my eyes. 'Please stop,' I begged. 'Please tell your friend to go home. I'll pay him. I'll pay you.'

He tilted my chin up and scraped a rough, nail-bitten finger along a trail of my tears. He stuck his finger in his mouth and tasted them. Then, with one slow, sensual movement, he pulled the pencils from my hair and let it fall, arranging it around my breasts. A simple act, but it was the most violated I'd ever felt.

I couldn't speak. I stood there. Frozen. His eyes and the lump in his crotch confirmed a sexual power trip. No wonder rape victims felt guilty. How could I be letting this happen? I was from Texas. I was a card-carrying member of the NRA. My senior class voted me 'Most Likely to Kick A — .'

Because, I reminded myself, he held the glittering key to my world above his head and was about to drop it in the ocean. He had Maddie.

My tormentor abruptly mutated, as if he knew he'd gotten off track.

'Anthony Marchetti went down for those hits, you little bitch. That's the way it needs to stay. You and your mother leave it the fuck alone.'

He wrenched the canvas bag off my shoulder and tossed all the work of the last four hours onto the floor. Marchetti's unsmiling face stared up from a mimeographed photo that fell near my foot, not looking as fierce as I remembered. Could he possibly be innocent? And why did this brute care?

But Louie was done sharing. 'You came in looking one way,' he said. 'You'll go out looking another.'

He pulled my hair straight up, until the rest of it fell in a shorter loop at my shoulders. He took off his cap and placed it on my head to hold it in place.

'Instant haircut.' He grinned, as if he'd invented something that hadn't been practiced by pre-teen girls for years.

He yanked his bright red T-shirt over his head, revealing a white Cubs T-shirt with a sweat stain

232

down the front. He watched my eyes travel to the outline of a gun tucked inside his jeans.

'I lied.' He shrugged. 'Bad habit. I used to get beat for it. Put this on, over your shirt.'

I hesitated.

'Do it NOW.'

Here's what I was desperate enough to think: Pink Lady might have needed a pee herself. She might notice me walking stiffly, awkwardly, down the center staircase with Scarface and postulate that he might not be the love of my life. She might spot his gun. Call a security guard.

'Don't say shit, got it? Hold my hand. Keep your head down.'

We merged awkwardly into the open reading area in the center of the floor, boyfriend and girlfriend. Loyal Cubs fans. Then he tugged me toward the stacks on the opposite side of the floor. Not to the staircase. He watched my expression morph.

'Oh, come on, you didn't think I had a plan?' A man at the table in front of us gave us a hard stare.

'Smile at him,' my kidnapper crooned into my ear. 'Do it for *Maddie*.' So I did. We both smiled at him, and the man smiled back.

'It's their year,' the man said, in library sotto voce, pointing to my hat, and returned to reading his paper.

My hope drained away as we moved out of the man's sight-line, traveling at Louie's quickened

233

pace through the stacks to the far wall. He pushed open a door labeled 'Authorized Personnel Only,' and we entered a chilly concrete stairwell.

'My father can get the floor plan of any building he wants with a single phone call,' he bragged. 'There's a bomb shelter under this place.'

He wasn't lying this time. He led me down to the basement, a huge, brightly lit room containing countless locked cages of books and artifacts. Shivering, I imagined a closed-door session with Louie in the bomb shelter, but my escort had other ideas. He made a direct line for the heavy black door on the far right wall marked 'Tunnel. Emergencies Only.'

I peered into the shadows of the dimly lit corridor and felt a wave of optimism. The playing field would be more even in the dark. Louie read my mind better than Sadie could. In a second, I was down, my cheek pressed against the gritty floor, my arm twisted excruciatingly high behind my back.

'Don't even think about it.'

He forced me up, stuck the gun in my back, and I stumbled ahead of him, the muffled sounds of honking and construction shaking the ceiling above us. Louie worked in focused silence, pushing me through the narrow tunnel. In minutes, we stepped into the basement of the building across the street, piled high with office supplies.

Louie quickly found the stairs, shoved me up two flights, through a door and out into the blinding sun, and we were instantly lost in a crowd of tourists on Michigan Avenue. I felt a momentary, unreasonable flash of anger at Hudson, who I'd never bothered to tell I was leaving the state. How could he let this happen?

Louie gripped my arm and urged me through the wall of bodies on the crowded sidewalk. What would happen to Maddie if I escaped? What would happen to her if I didn't?

'What do you expect to learn from me?' I asked desperately, stumbling beside him. 'At least tell me that.'

'Don't pretend you don't know. Mothers and daughters yap about everything.'

'Are you going to kill me?' I purposely stopped at a store window and faked interest in a thousand-dollar Louis Vuitton purse, spotlighted on a pedestal like a rare da Vinci sculpture.

'*Shut up!*' This time, it came out in a hiss, and a woman passing us shot Louie a dirty look. To me, the abused girlfriend, she offered a sympathetic one.

'You don't have to take it,' she said. 'There are places that will help you.'

'Mind your own business, lady.' He tightened his grip on my arm, dragging me away. 'Come on, we're crossing here.'

Actually, I had looked forward to coming 'here,' to Millennium Park, Chicago's most divine public place, replete with a stunning open-air band shell that looked like a spaceship had landed. I wished my first view of the Bean sculpture wasn't under such duress, but, still, it awed me: 110 tons of shiny stainless steel in the shape of a giant kidney bean. Blue sky, floating clouds, the city skyline, tiny figures of gawkers – all of it reflected back at me in the beautiful distortion.

But the most beautiful thing of all? Staring into the Bean, I swore I glimpsed a tiny pink tracksuit standing out in the crowd of about fifty people behind us. I didn't know whether pink tracksuits were as popular in Chicago as bright red American Girl bags, but, ludicrously, preposterously, hope surged.

'Stop fuckin' turnin' around,' Louie said, glancing behind him. 'Move it. Under here.' We stood with about twenty other people under the bottom curve of the Bean, gazing up at our reflections. I looked very far away. And skinny. Like a sad potato stick.

'Do you see how easy this was?' Louie asked me softly. 'In the daytime. Out in the open. Imagine me coming at you in the dark.' His arm held me close. 'I'm going to let you go this time. But give your mother a message. If she doesn't keep her mouth shut, if *you* don't stop your digging, your little Maddie won't be doing her cheerleader jumps anymore.'

He was going to *let me go*?

Inspired, I twisted his crotch as hard as I could, and my other hand reached for his gun. But his T-shirt, soaked with sweat, stuck to his ribs and I only succeeded in pushing the gun farther into his jeans.

I hadn't dug so awkwardly down a guy's pants since the senior prom, and I nearly knocked over an elderly woman as I wrestled Louie to the ground.

'Jesus! There are children here,' said a father, who clearly thought our fantasy perversion was a hand-job in the reflection of the Bean. He tugged his two small daughters away in disgust.

Louie yanked my hair back, knocked my face into the concrete, and for an instant I saw my frantic expression contorted back at me like a funhouse mirror.

And then pink. Oh blessed pink.

CHAPTER 20

I woke up in the back of a car with my head faceup in the lap of Hudson Byrd.

'Get Louie's cell phone,' I croaked, struggling. 'Arrest the last person he called. He's stalking Maddie at Skatepark.'

One of Hudson's best qualities was that he didn't ask a lot of unnecessary questions. He jumped out the door just as Pink Lady slid in the other side, gone so fast I wondered whether I had conjured him up.

'Good, you're conscious,' she said. I closed my eyes to avoid the psychedelic effect of her pink outfit and my bad decision to sit upright. My head was spinning like a helicopter on its way down.

'The ambulance is almost here.' She patted my shoulder. 'Bless your heart. Don't worry, we got him. He's in the car behind us, about to take a trip to headquarters.'

'Maddie . . .' My throat felt like I'd swallowed sand. 'My niece. One of his guys is following my niece—'

To her credit, Martha disappeared just as quickly as Hudson, whipping out a walkie-talkie and barking into it as she ran out of my view. Apparently, she wasn't just a nice mommy with a taste for Russian classics. I could see the shiny Bean in the distance like a huge bubble that had miraculously landed without popping, tourists cluttered around as if this were a perfectly ordinary day.

The seventh-floor Cubs fan popped his head in the window and grinned.

'How ya doin', kid? Any decent Cubs fan would have stopped to argue that we have no pitching. Agent Waring is going to ask you a few questions if you're up to it after this nice young lady here checks out your vitals.'

Agent Waring. The FBI.

I nodded, wishing everyone would go away. *Find Maddie.*

An EMT with a first-aid kit and a blood-pressure cuff appeared. A large black woman with gentle hands. She checked my pupils with a tiny flashlight and asked me a series of questions for a test that I evidently passed. As she worked, the world stopped dancing around. She responded to my half-hysterical request for antibacterial wipes so I could kill any cooties on my hands that had been living down Louie's pants. Only this and Maddie seemed important.

'Your blood pressure's not bad, considering,' she informed me. 'And your wounds are fairly superficial. The bump is on your cheek, not your forehead. Your eyes look good. I'm thinking you might have passed out from shock.' She pulled out a kit and went to work on my cheek. 'As long as you've got someone watching you for the next twenty-four hours, I'd just as soon let you go. The Chicago emergency room on a hot summer day – it's nothin' you want to experience if you don't have to.'

She smoothed on a Band-Aid with cool fingers and got out of the car, closing the door and poking her head back in the open window.

'Any dizzy spells or a sharp headache, you come on in. Somebody should check your eyes every now and then for twenty-four hours to make sure they aren't dilated. Don't get up. Wait here.'

'Thanks,' I said tonelessly.

I sat perfectly still, imploring God.

Save Maddie, save Maddie, save Maddie.

In ten minutes, God answered. A breathless Martha Waring plopped beside me.

'Your niece is OK. Your friend Hudson knows the owner of the Skatepark where she was hanging out. Buford somebody. Buford found a guy in the parking lot and, frankly, I'm not sure I want to know how things went down from there.'

I closed my eyes and pictured Buford Bell. Balding. A potbelly. A former champion skeet shooter and one-time Olympic alternate who still displayed his dusty trophies in the Skatepark lobby five miles outside of Ponder.

'Buford got the guy to admit he was hired anonymously through Facebook to give a scouting report on your niece over the phone. No plans to kidnap. Buford is holding him for the police, who should be there any second.'

Maddie was safe. Hudson was real.

She stared at me directly. 'Did you know your attacker?'

'I never saw him before. He said his name was Louie.'

'That's right. Louis Cantini. That name doesn't ring any bells?'

I shook my head.

'I think you were just in the wrong place at the wrong time,' she said soothingly, even though we both knew that wasn't true.

Should I disavow her of that wishful thinking?

'Why were you following me?' I wanted to know.

'I got assigned to tail you after you visited Rosalina Marchetti.' She hesitated, clearly deciding how much else to say. 'She's part of an ongoing investigation.

'When Louie Cantini showed up at the library, I figured, not a coincidence, so I called in some backup. The Cantinis and the Marchettis have an antagonistic history. Plus, Louie is probably lucky if he can read a soup can, much less a book. I apologize for not getting to you sooner. Louie jammed the lock behind him.'

'It's OK,' I said, trying to process the entry of yet another mob family into my nightmare.

I craned my neck to look out the rear window and was rewarded with a sharp pain.

'Where's Hudson?' I asked. *And how did he get here?*

'I told him I'd take care of you for a while. He tagged along to watch them question Louie.'

'He's not FBI.'

'No, but . . .' She paused. 'He has a lifetime of free passes, apparently. I heard it this way: Several years ago, a local Afghan interpreter opened fire on an army unit. Your friend Hudson and another security contractor ended up saving six soldiers. One of those soldiers happens to be the son of someone very high up in the Bureau.'

Ah, the legend of Hudson Byrd. Nothing could contain it. Not deserts, not oceans, not lonesome prairie.

My collection of injuries began to sing in chorus. My spine ached like I'd fallen off a wild bull; my concrete-grazed cheek and knees stung like the burn of multiple angry hornets; my throat felt like a night spent screaming at a TV in a sports bar. Nothing I hadn't experienced before.

I would live.

More important, Maddie would live. I would make sure of it.

When Agent Waring dropped me off in front of the hotel with two of the Chicago Bureau's 'best' rookie agents to guard my hotel room door for the night, I had to ask.

'Is genealogy actually a hobby?'

'When you have five hours,' she said, 'I'll tell you how I have about three-fourths of an ounce

242

of Tom Cruise's blood running in my veins.' She grinned. 'Enough to brag about at parties but not enough to drop Jesus for Scientology.'

She tossed off a two-fingered salute. 'I'll be in touch.'

As nice as she had been, I knew what that meant.

Pink Lady didn't think I was her problem anymore.

My temporary guard detail consisted of two nervous-looking guys in their early twenties assigned to stand outside my room. I knew that nervous and young wasn't necessarily a bad thing. It meant they'd stay alert, worried about not screwing up, and I guessed they wouldn't mind checking my eyes for dilation every now and then.

I slipped the keycard in the door, promised the boys hamburgers from room service in an hour or so, and stepped inside.

How could I ever think this room felt cold?

The lamp's blue light stood like a welcome home beacon. Tiny chocolate truffles rested on top of the oversized down pillows, perfect fluffs of cotton candy that I couldn't wait to mess up with my aching head. The pale gray comforter – what a soothing color! – was turned down with a military precision that my own bed could only fantasize about.

I walked only a few feet inside before dropping my bag and stripping every disgusting bit of clothing off my body, things that he had touched. I even wanted to burn the lacy black underwear that I'd paid fifteen bucks for at Nordstrom. I can't say that Hudson's ripped chest hadn't crossed my mind when I'd swiped my MasterCard in the lingerie department.

Where the hell was he anyway?

Instead of lighting a match to my underwear, I limped into the bathroom, knelt by the marble bathtub, and twisted the faucets all the way until the sound of the blasting water drowned out my sobs. I wrapped myself in a fetal position on the cold black tile floor, naked, head down, tears running down my legs, until I got it out of my system. By then, the tub was filled to drowning level, not that I planned to. I tipped in a generous amount of bubble bath, turned the spa jets to 'gentle,' and dipped a toe in. Perfect. Then I hustled out butt-naked to the mini-bar, retrieving a supremely overpriced bottle of screwtop Chardonnay to celebrate the fact that I wasn't being tortured or raped tonight.

If anybody ever asked me, the psychologist, what to do in a meltdown when therapy wasn't available, I'd tell them that I considered hot water to be the emotional equivalent and a lot cheaper.

I slid under, closed my eyes, and counted to sixty, a habit since Sadie and I competed for best underwater time one summer at the lake. Then I barely exposed my face, my ears still filling up with water, and let the minutes tick by with excruciating slowness. I'd always done some of my most rational thinking in the bathtub.

I sunk a little deeper in the water. Every cell in my body fought the idea that Anthony Marchetti was my biological father.

There could not be a human being more different from the salt-of-the earth rancher who raised me. No matter what facts were placed in front of me, I still could not believe that Daddy would lie to me, especially a whopper like this one. He got on to Sadie and me for the smallest infractions of the truth. 'White lies are lies just the same,' he'd say, even though most Texans found white lies pretty damn useful.

The tub had already cooled off. I used my big toe to turn on the hot water faucet. Mama used to say I liked to poach myself. Satisfied with the temperature, I closed my eyes again and returned to a half-formed plan that I'd thought up at the library. It had nothing to do with today's research or my family heritage. It involved a trip to Oklahoma to investigate a murder. More than anything else, those newspaper articles in Mama's box pulled at me like a magnet. They meant something. They dated back to the days when Mama was meticulous, when she made sense.

Two rough hands grabbed under my arms, yanking me out of my reverie and into the cold air. In that fraction of a second before my eyes flew open, I knew that Louie was back to finish the job.

'What are you doing?' Hudson's angry voice destroyed every bit of effort I'd made to decompress. He picked up the bottle of half-drunk

Chardonnay and dumped it into the tub. The other hand gripped my elbow a little too tightly.

'I'm trying to relax after a bad day,' I said with controlled fury, moving my hands fast to cover my breasts. But Hudson seemed not so much turned on as fascinated by the artwork of bruises that covered my body.

'Ouch,' he said, wincing, loosening his grip.

'The boys outside are getting hungry. I called your name at the bathroom door five times and you didn't answer. I got worried.'

I knotted a towel around me and changed the subject, struggling to regain some dignity. 'How did you get here?'

'The usual way,' he drawled, 'in one of those big things that fly.'

'*Why* are you here?'

'I made a promise to you over tequila. I always keep promises when tequila's involved.'

He saw the anger in my face and held up his hand. 'I talked to Sadie. She told me what you were up to. She already had the impression I was protecting you. How did that happen, I wonder?'

'Um.'

'Yeah . . . um.' Hudson sat on the edge of the tub, feeling right at home while I stood clutching a towel around my naked body.

I stalked around him to the hotel robe hanging on the door. 'I can't reach Maddie or Sadie. They aren't answering their cell phones. I tried calling from the car.'

'No worries. They're on their way to your cousin's house in Marfa for a little safekeeping. It's a long drive. Sadie said she'd call you tomorrow.'

Would Marfa be far enough?

'By the way,' Hudson said. 'Louie refused to talk until his lawyer gets back in town tomorrow. His father and Anthony Marchetti were big-time rivals in the drug trade in the seventies. Maybe still are. The FBI was a little tight with me on details.'

I reached for the robe and he turned his head. Nice, I thought grudgingly.

'Louie threatened me.' My voice trembled a little. 'He hinted that this has everything to do with the murders that Marchetti went to prison for . . . OK, I'm decent.'

'You were always *way* more than decent.'

I was suddenly too exhausted to carry on the banter, and he sensed my mood, following me silently into the bedroom, where my clothes were still strewn across the floor, not saying a word as I picked them up and stuffed them in the trashcan under the desk.

'How did you know to find me at the Bean?' I demanded.

'The bellman who directed you to a coffee shop this morning saw you Googling the library on your phone.'

Spies, spies, everywhere.

'From there,' he said, 'I just followed the action.'

Was he really this good at his job? Or was he one more person lying to me?

An hour and two beers later, I almost didn't care. I was dressed in a deliberately unsexy pair of cotton granny pajamas littered with tiny flowers, my hair dangling down my back like a wet rope. Hudson had rescheduled the flight I missed this afternoon for tomorrow night and booked himself in the seat next to me. He didn't think I should fly until we were pretty sure a blood clot wasn't forming in my head.

Now he lay beside me, propped up on the bed with the best view of the TV. No touching, I'd told him, before we settled in to watch the last half of the Cubs game.

Things were fine, until Hudson broke my rule in the bottom of the seventh. He turned on his side and ran his finger alongside a bruise.

'Tommie, I think you should disappear for a while until I figure this out. If I know the FBI, and I do, they aren't going to share much. I've got a place in Cabo. Take Sadie and Maddie. You could be a thousand miles out of danger and on your way to a nice tan by tomorrow night.'

'I burn,' I said, unable to focus much on anything but his finger traveling up and down my arm like the tip of a hot poker. It reminded me of something else.

'Hudson, there's a dead girl's finger in my purse.' My laugh sounded slightly hysterical.

'What?' Hudson raised up, his foot knocking over the half-finished beer on the side table behind him. He hadn't asked me a thing about my meeting with Rosalina Marchetti, whether I was or wasn't her daughter.

'Yesterday, at Rosalina's house. She said she's not my mother. But she gave me her daughter's finger. The kidnappers sent it to her in the mail thirty-one years ago. She wants me to find her. She's convinced Marchetti knows where she is. That she might be alive. She says my mother and I . . . owe it to her.' I realized I was babbling. 'I haven't worked up . . . the nerve . . . to open the box.'

'Jesus,' Hudson said, resigned. 'This is a very complicated soap opera you are living. You couldn't have picked a more effective mood killer. Go get the finger. Otherwise, I'm not going to be able to sleep.'

I retrieved the box, wondering why I hadn't chucked it and its contents into the Chicago River.

'Go ahead,' he urged, 'open it.'

I snapped up the lid and pushed down the urge to throw up.

The finger, the size of a doll's, rested on black velvet.

It was dusty gray, wrapped carefully in Saran Wrap like a tiny leftover.

I cleared my throat. 'I'm going to get it tested for DNA. I have a friend from college who works in a medical lab. I have multiple DNA projects in mind for him. Including my own.'

'Are you sure you want to do that?'

'No,' I said.

I snapped the box shut.

I was about to say more, to tell him that Rosalina claimed I was the child of a liaison between Anthony Marchetti and my mother. But Hudson pulled off his sweats, revealing pale blue boxers against beautiful desert-browned skin and the most amazing calves I've ever seen outside of a professional baseball catcher. He yanked off his T-shirt. Everything was as I remembered, only better. Perhaps I hadn't completely killed the mood, after all.

'The Cubs are up by six,' he said, sliding over to the other bed and popping the mint in his mouth before punching his pillow into a hard, tidy square. I watched those legs disappear under the sheets, thinking about being entwined between them, desperately wanting to taste that mint by putting my mouth on his.

'You need to work on your bedtime stories,' he said, turning over to face the wall. 'Sleep tight.'

In two minutes, he was snoring, leaving me to stare at the ceiling and think.

I knew Hudson too well. Maybe the finger was a surprise, but he knew more than he was saying about Rosalina and Anthony Marchetti. Or he would have asked more questions.

Oh, the irony. In less than forty-eight hours, I was breaking a promise to myself, about to close my eyes and leave myself vulnerable to another man of unnerving contradictions.

CHAPTER 21

It surprises me that Adriana Marchetti looks so much like Maddie did at that age. That fact surprises me more than her wings made out of bright green leaves and her ability to fly. I look but can't tell if she has all her fingers. She is waving, her hands a blur of motion. She dips into a puffy white cloud and disappears. When she appears again, her mouth is moving but no sound is coming out. She's trying to tell me something.

I can't hear. I can't hear!

She swoops nearer and nearer like a creature in a 3-D movie until all that fills the screen is her perfect pink mouth and rows of tiny white teeth. She's opening wide, her tonsils flapping. I'm about to be swallowed.

'Find me,' she taunts, as I slide down her throat and into the warm ocean. 'Find me.'

I sat up, soaked with sweat, my heart pounding out of my chest. I stripped off my pajamas and lay back, shivering gratefully as the air-conditioning hit my wet skin.

Ever since I could remember, dreaming had been like stepping into a dark universe as vivid as real

251

life. The coffin dream was the worst. Sometimes the two worlds collided and I woke up to ghostly faces at my bedside that vanished when I reached out to touch them. My eyes, wide open. My fingers stabbing the air to be sure I was alone. Granny called them night visitors. Scientists explain them away as a trick of the mind, a sleep disorder.

Just a dream, I assured myself. The child looked about three or four. Adriana wouldn't be three. That was just her age as a statue in a garden. She was only one when she was kidnapped. There is no proof she is dead. And there is absolutely no reason to think that I have latent tendencies to communicate with spirits, especially since that gift ran on Daddy's side of the family and I wasn't at all sure who my Daddy was.

I glanced over at Hudson, breathing quietly and deeply in his soft gray cocoon, and thought how many times I had been uselessly naked in his presence today.

The clock flipped to 3:07 a.m., casting a blue glow. My heart slowed to a normal rhythm. My nerves, however, remained lit up like a string of chasing Christmas lights.

It seemed as good a time as any to check my email. I noticed that Hudson had brought my canvas bag, probably retrieved by the FBI in the library. My research had been picked up off the floor and was now tossed inside like a pile of trash. My laptop lay safely where I left it, inside its case on top of the desk. I threw on the T-shirt that Hudson had thrown off and sat down and powered it up. I went straight to email.

The third subject line screamed.

DO YOU REALLY WANT TO DIE THIS WAY?

Madddog12296 was definitely getting more direct.

This time I didn't hesitate. I opened up the email. Blank space, except for an attachment labeled 'The Bennett Show.'

My virus software went to work.

No virus detected, it told me cheerfully. I clicked 'continue download.'

The first image filled my screen from edge to edge, familiar and confusing at the same time.

It wasn't a virus, but it was very, very sick.

I couldn't take my eyes from the slick horror show running on automatic in front of me. I had only several seconds to absorb an image before it faded out to bring another. And another.

Fred Bennett died violently in the kitchen while making popcorn. He'd put up an intense fight for his family. Every surface, every wall, every tile sprayed red like they'd battled with ketchup bottles.

The female FBI agent fell at the back door in the laundry room, her bloody head resting awkwardly in a laundry basket of unfolded towels.

Alyssa Bennett died with her beautiful blue eyes open. In the first picture from madddog12296, an image tormenting me since I'd opened it up on my phone at the ranch, her face had been turned away. It occurred to me now that was probably because he wanted me to imagine Maddie in her place.

In this one, Alyssa lay on the same ugly gray carpet and appeared to be reaching for her dead mother's hand six inches away. The blood-spattered leg of another child stuck out of a doorway behind them. The boys' bedroom?

I was familiar with crime scene photos. Before treating children, I insisted on seeing any tangible evidence of the horrible things they had witnessed. These pictures defacing my computer screen were definitely snapped with the aloof, detailed eye of a forensics expert.

The crime scene photographer never knew what might wind up being important, so his job was to shoot it all, the ordinary and the unimaginable: half-unpacked suitcases, the dirty contents of the dishwasher, a worn copy of *Goodnight Moon* on a nightstand, the Herbal Essence shampoo bottle in the shower. And, of course, every angle of every dead body, every single drop of blood.

About thirty pictures in all – probably not nearly everything that was shot that night, but the goriest highlights. These weren't downloaded from a website. These were hacked from a police file or from the FBI's photo archive.

I glanced over at Hudson. He hadn't moved. My fingers stumbled over the keyboard while I forwarded the slide show to Lyle so his practiced, less emotional eye could run over this carnage.

It was still too early to get up, but I couldn't imagine closing my eyes, knowing my brain would play the images endlessly. Better to focus on another task. Lyle had provided me with the password and access code for an extensive open-records site that the newspaper paid dearly for every year. Birth and death certificates, phone numbers, addresses, court documents – all only seconds away.

It didn't take long to find Barbara Thurman. She was now Barbara Monroe, in her fifties and no longer a reporter covering kidnappings for a Chicago tabloid. I wrote down her phone number and address on the hotel notepad and shut down my computer.

Adriana Marchetti's kidnapping, the murders of Fred Bennett's family, the newspaper clippings from my mother's safe deposit box. How were they connected?

An hour later, when Hudson's watch alarm beeped, I was showered, dressed, and ready for a little more business in Chicago before my flight out tonight.

Madddog12296 had done his job. He'd dragged me to a hellish, fertile playground in my head that I hadn't known existed.

Barbara Monroe lived in one of the renovated stone cottages in a gentrified neighborhood on

Chicago's South Side. A chaotic herb and flower garden meandered up the stone walkway, fighting off weeds, giving me a good vibe about her. In my occasional vegetable gardens, weeds rarely got the death penalty.

'Hi, guys, I'm Barbara,' she greeted Hudson and me, opening the door for us while holding the collar of a tall, lunging black animal that was hands-down the ugliest dog I'd ever seen. Black hair stuck out of bald patches. There were dime-sized red sores on his back that appeared to be healing. 'Cricket, get back. Sorry, my teenage daughter has a thing for strays, and this one isn't trained yet. Also, he's not contagious, just ugly for life, according to the vet.'

I tried patting his bony, scaly head, bare of hair except for a tuft behind his ear, and he licked me appreciatively. Whatever happened to him, Cricket appeared to have sustained little psychological damage.

I'd called and introduced myself to Barbara only two hours ago, and she sounded busy but cheerful enough on the phone about helping. 'I gave all that up a long time ago for a more lucrative PR career,' she informed me. 'I'd met my first husband, and he didn't like the idea of taking death threats in the middle of the night.'

Still playing tug-of-war with Cricket, she gestured to a cozy room on our right, bulging with books, antiques, and stacks of *The Atlantic*, the *Utne Reader*, and *Scientific American*. Again, a good sign. Someone who reads about intelligent life.

'Have a seat. Let me crate Cricket.' She and Cricket disappeared into the back of the house, and I zeroed in on the cardboard box open in the middle of the floor. How could I not? It called out to me in large black Sharpie letters: *CHICAGO INQUIRER*.

'Don't even think about it,' Hudson said, pulling me with him onto a leather love seat. 'Just wait for her.'

The box spilled over onto the floor with what I presumed were the oddball accessories of a newspaper reporter's desktop – a dusty, tarnished trophy, a windup toy of a human peanut with Jimmy Carter's face on it, a stained coffee cup that advertised the paper, miscellaneous clippings, a bulging Rolodex, and – most fascinating to me – stacks of old notebooks.

'Hard to believe I didn't dump this stuff,' Barbara said. Unhindered by the dog, she stood an elegant five feet, eight inches in Manolo Blahnik heels and a well-cut black suit, vibrating with the kind of energy I'd seen in her reporting. I suspected that Barbara was a fierce competitor in the land of public relations.

She ran a hand through artfully chopped hair, too inky black to be anything but dyed, and picked up a lint roller from a library table, removing Cricket's hairs from her jacket.

'I suppose I kept it all because I never got closure.'

257

'When did you quit?' I asked.

'A lifetime ago. Right after the Marchetti girl's kidnapping. It was my last, and biggest, story. A career-maker, my editor told me. I didn't have the stomach for it or I wouldn't have let my husband talk me into quitting. Then, again, I was only twenty-five. What do you know at twenty-five?'

I nodded encouragingly. 'I read the column you wrote telling everybody off.'

'Oh, yes. The naïve rantings of a young reporter. It was like spitting into the ocean. By that time, my boxes were packed. The publisher was ticked that my editor even let that column see the light of day.'

'You got actual death threats?' Hudson asked.

'Just two. The same guy. It was long before caller ID. He called to tell me to drop the story or he'd kill me in an unpleasant way. Real scary, because he called my apartment after midnight when I was alone in bed. Liked to wake me up.'

She kneeled and pulled out four more notebooks I hadn't noticed, hidden out of sight on the floor behind the box.

'For you. I thumbed through these. There isn't much I didn't print.'

'It's OK for me to take them?' Even years later, I was surprised Barbara could hand her notes off so easily. Lyle would rather cut off an ear.

'I never really believed Rosalina's whole story. She was a drugged-out mess at the time, although she knew how to use her looks to pull the sympathy chain. I always doubted her, but the police thought she was telling the truth because of the witness to the kidnapping.'

I abruptly stopped flipping through the scratchings in her notebooks. 'I didn't know there were any witnesses.'

Barbara glanced at her watch. Platinum, I noticed. Not a reporter's accessory. It made me rethink her a little. Her earrings were expensive hammered silver squares that matched a cuff on her wrist.

'It was a detail kept out of the press,' she told us. 'I didn't find out until several days after the kidnapping, when a cop slipped up talking to me. The witness was a stripper friend of Rosalina's who claimed her pimp would kill her if he knew she spent an afternoon off-duty to be with Rosalina and her kid. She had one of those indulgent Italian princess names. Gabriella, maybe? I'm sure I wrote it in there. Her story matched Rosalina's word for word, maybe a little too closely. The police cut her a break and left her out of it, and so did I.'

Barbara started stuffing everything back in the box, including the cheap trophy engraved with the inscription 'Chicago's Rookie Reporter of the Year,' which she angled so I would be sure to see it.

'Sorry to rush you, but I've got to go sell a campaign for an erectile dysfunction drug.' She winked. 'That changes lives, too.'

This sophisticated, toned woman wasn't at all the slightly plump, gray-haired Barbara with a vague memory of distant events that I'd imagined on the way over here. Apparently, I wasn't what she imagined, either.

'I like you, Tommie,' she said. 'You're not what I expected. I've spent plenty of time on the couch. You're not the usual brand of psychologist. You get what you need by really listening. Not casting silent judgment. It's a better approach. Believe me, I know.'

She was gooping it on pretty thick. Maybe I hadn't pressured her enough. And she seemed oddly relieved. How far to go was always the psychologist's dilemma. It occurred to me that she hadn't asked any questions at all.

Barbara opened up a black patent-leather shoulder bag that cost more than most people's monthly mortgage and reached into a back pocket of a wallet, behind a lineup of shiny credit cards. She pulled out a tattered 3 x 5 photograph with a white creased line down the middle from being folded in half for a very long time, and handed it over.

It was a picture of a sweet-faced little girl perched behind a cupcake with a single lit candle. On the back, in faded blue ink, I could make out the name 'Adriana Marchetti.' I'm pretty sure my face remained blank, something I'd become better at in the last week.

Barbara Monroe continued to contradict herself. A powerhouse PR woman and a matter-of-fact caregiver to down-and-out strays. A $1,600 purse, and a photograph memento of someone else's probably dead little girl.

Barbara hesitated for a second and then reached inside her purse again, this time for a large manila envelope.

'I've decided to give you this, too. My husband – my *third* husband,' she corrected with a wry smile, 'thinks I'm a little nuts to do this. But about two years ago, I did a press packet for a start-up company that specializes in age progression. You know, for missing kids and stuff. I asked him to age Adriana forward as one of the press kit samples. She was so young when this picture was taken that it's a bit of a crapshoot. But if she's alive today, she might look something like this.'

Before I could lift the flap on the envelope, Cricket howled from his gut – the slow, pitiful howl of a dog that knows he'll soon be without human company – and Barbara hustled us out the front door. 'Every time we leave, he's still sure we're never coming back. My daughter will be home from school to walk him in a minute. Or rather, Cricket will walk *her*.'

Barbara flicked her remote at the blue Audi sitting in the driveway, eyes now hidden behind dark, sexy sunglasses that gave her an instant pass into her forties.

She vanished behind the tinted glass, with words that I'd wonder about later.

'Don't disappoint me,' she said.

CHAPTER 22

I kept the manila envelope sealed until Hudson and I were crammed onto the Chicago El in two plastic blue seats that were sticky with a substance I thought best not to identify. We sat directly across from a public service ad recommending the use of pink condoms for Breast Cancer Awareness. I guess that isn't much odder than NFL players wearing fuchsia shoes on a field where they are trying to kill each other.

Hudson had chosen our mode of transportation for the morning. He'd been quiet, almost sullen, ever since I ran the slide show for him back at the hotel. He didn't like being a sitting duck in a cab he wasn't driving, but a crowded train that allowed us to dodge and duck and leap from car to car was apparently acceptable. Just one of his many control issues.

Then again, I felt lucky that he agreed to this side trip to see Barbara Monroe at all and that at this moment his thigh was pressed against mine like a hot waffle press. It was a bonus that either one of his fists could concuss someone with a glancing blow.

While Hudson casually scoped the occupants of our car, I did the same. In one corner, a man and woman in jeans and matching turquoise Cancer Fun Run T-shirts were quietly arguing. In the other, a businessman in an ugly tie read a weathered John Grisham paperback. Everybody else appeared equally harmless, but then, I'd lost my instinct for this sort of thing.

I turned my attention to the envelope.

Actually ripping it open turned out to be a letdown, not the dramatic eureka moment in the movies. I realized that a tiny part of me wondered whether the face inside would look like Sadie, a sure sign my senses had left me, since I held her the day she was born. Rosalina's missing daughter would be older anyway. My age.

'Barbara Monroe was ripped off,' Hudson said, leaning over to look. 'The nose is crooked. Sort of Michael Jackson-y.'

'She didn't pay for this,' I said, but Hudson had already started a conversation with the middle-aged Hispanic man nursing a Starbucks next to him. They slipped into a highly animated stream of Spanish about last night's Cubs game.

I stared at the computer-generated color composite in my hand. An unhappy woman in her late twenties with short black hair and funky red highlights stared back. She had Rosalina's eyes and a small, pursed mouth that looked like it wanted to spit out, 'Who the fuck are you?' The nose tilted up and left, as if the artist couldn't quite decide what to do with it. There was no resemblance to the gleeful copper angel in Rosalina's fountain.

The image radiated an unreal quality, like someone improperly embalmed.

Waxy, shiny skin. Parts that didn't fit together. The hair, stiff, like it had been sprayed to death. How in the hell did the artist commit to red highlights?

I flipped over the picture and found a note that Barbara had scribbled to me, saying that she'd provided the artist with a picture of Rosalina and a blurry police mug shot of the guy she says raped her. What a crapshoot. She signed off with, 'Hope this helps!' and a giant *B* scrawled underneath like two perky cartoon boobs.

Age progression had advanced significantly beyond the scope of the amateurish portrait in my hand. How did Barbara Monroe think this could possibly help me?

The sweaty, extra-large man on my other side stunk like a combination of Old Spice, onions, and garlic. His thigh crept onto my side of the blue plastic seat by about two inches. I smiled politely and pulled out the first of Barbara's notebooks.

They were a newspaper lawyer's worst nightmare. Barbara used a bastardized shorthand that was, at best, cryptic: sweeping, curlicued handwriting with bursts of short phrases or words and the occasional full quote, often marked with three or four exclamation points. Like her stories, the notebooks read a little fast and loose, mostly posing questions and notes to herself.

Lttle grl's white shoe.

Rosalina drunk???

Blck sedan.

I knew psychologists who worked like this – scribbled diligently, using their notebooks more as a prop than anything else. But they also backed themselves up with a tape recorder. Then again, maybe I was being too hard on her. I'd met and envied a few people with photographic memories, including an autistic nine-year-old able to describe the peacock tattoo of the man who mugged his grandmother in such exquisite detail that the jury returned a verdict in ten minutes.

A name stood out amid the rubble of words: Rosalina's witness.

Not Gabriella, but Gisella. Gisella Russo, which looped at a slant across a whole page, along with the single descriptive phrase *pretty fat for a stripper.*

And the name of the first cop on the scene – Milt Dobrzeniecky with a large *SP? Check it!!!* by his name. At least she was careful about some things. I tried to make out the near-illegible phrase beside his name, holding the page up to the window as a row of track houses zipped by, playing havoc with the shadow and light in the train.

I nudged Hudson, now dozing with his head slumped as if he'd had sex all night with me instead of sleeping for nine straight hours.

'What do you think that says?' I demanded, pointing to the words. He picked up the pad and gave it a cursory glance before tossing it back in my lap, confirming what I thought.

'It says "nose hairs,"' he said. 'What's for lunch?'

I stepped inside my hotel room, suddenly overwhelmed with the certainty that Mama was taking her last breath, right now, a thousand miles away from me. I tapped out the number to the hospital with shaking fingers.

The nurse on duty was calm.

No change. Wade was sitting with her.

No change, I thought bitterly.

I threw the phone with such force that it bounced off the bed and onto the floor. Childish, I knew, but I was consumed with anger. Hot, bitter anger, stoked a little more every day by the knowledge that the woman staring blankly at the cracks in a hospital ceiling had waited too long to ever tell me the truth.

Were there moments when the words hung on her lips? When we swung high in the hammocks staring at the stars or at spectacular cloud shapes? When she helped me with a genealogy tree in sixth grade? When I took off for college? I'd never know.

I heard the faint clicking sound of a keycard in the lock and the door burst open, slamming into the wall. It happened so fast, I only had time to slip halfway behind the heavy curtain at the window.

Hudson.

Back from his trip to the vending machine, Coke in hand. I didn't remember giving him a key.

'Where the hell is the guard?' he asked angrily.

'Do you ever, *ever* make a quiet entrance?' I emerged from the curtain, my heart still knocking around. 'I have no idea why there isn't a guard anymore.'

'We'll see about that.'

He went to work on his phone.

'Agent Waring? Hudson Byrd.'

Even four feet away, I could hear the high chatter of a female voice rolling in an uninterruptible stream.

'Right,' Hudson said finally. 'Yes. I do want to be there. About twenty minutes. Where's the detail on Tommie's room? Sorry to hear that. Uh-huh. I agree. She can stay in the room while I'm gone.'

This lit a little fuse in me.

'Thanks. Be there soon.' He tucked the phone back in a case hanging off his belt. I caught the glimpse of a gun tucked into the band of his jeans underneath his loose-fitting fishing shirt. A Hawaiian shirt or a fishing shirt on a Texas man was a big clue that he was concealing a piece. Fashion be damned.

'Louie's lawyer showed up. They're inviting me to sit in on the second round of questioning. Your guard was called off to a school shooting.' He held up his hand when he saw my expression. 'Nobody hurt bad. As for Louie, the safest place for you is right here. He was caught in the act. All they need for now is the statement you gave them. I've got the feeling they want to use your kidnapping to get Louie to roll on something bigger. Like his family's drug op.'

He tugged open the nightstand drawer and pulled out a Gideon Bible, blue with gold lettering. In perfect shape, like it had never been touched. Placed in hotel rooms since 1908. Gideon, I remembered, did whatever God wanted him to do. No matter what.

'Swear you'll stay in the room. That you'll throw the deadbolt when I leave.'

The tough-guy soldier stood in front of me holding a Bible.

Pleading.

'Swear on this Bible and the soul of the Virgin Mary.'

I'd forgotten he was a devout Catholic. He'd forgotten I couldn't always be trusted even when there was a Bible involved.

I nodded imperceptibly.

He glanced at his watch. 'I'll be back at five. That will be enough time to navigate the security lines at the airport.'

As soon as he left, I sucked in the feeling of a hotel room nipped and tucked into shape and reminded myself to leave a big tip for the tired maid I'd seen in the hallway.

Then I imagined the tiny skeletal bone of a finger under the rigid eye of an airport X-ray machine.

In the bathroom, I stuffed the little red box into my cosmetic bag, hoping it would blend in with the mess of lipstick tubes and mascara.

I was itching to get out of the room. Instead, I popped open my laptop and stuck in an old flash drive I'd found in the bottom of my computer bag, copying the slide show and carefully zipping it into a side compartment of my purse.

With even less enthusiasm, I tackled the canvas book bag that held the disarray of clips I had copied at the library the day before. I painstakingly separated the stories about Adriana Marchetti's kidnapping and the stories about the Fred Bennett murder case, then arranged them in chronological order and highlighted the names of people whose brains I might want to rattle out of retirement. More phone numbers to chase down. This was like cleaning the oven – drudgery coupled with the nagging feeling that it wouldn't matter a bit if I didn't do it at all.

I sat down at my laptop again and randomly typed 'Gisella Russo' into a Google search. I found a thirty-year-old obituary notice within five minutes. Gisella was survived by her mother and two younger sisters. In lieu of flowers, the family had requested donations be made to a local Catholic church's antidrug campaign. Rosalina's friend had lived only one more year after Adriana's kidnapping.

Still restless, I Googled 'Ellis Island.' I clicked on the nonprofit website, created a password and username, and started a search for a passenger named Ingrid Margaret Ankrim, the great-grandmother of my mother's legend. No matches. What a surprise.

On a whim, I typed in Ingrid Margaret Roth, the surname Jack dropped in the hotel room. To my surprise, I got a hit. I clicked on the manifest. There she was. Ingrid Roth, sixteen, left the German port of Bremen in 1892.

Something that was true.

I was overcome with a profound longing to talk to Sadie and Maddie, to connect with the people I loved. I still hadn't heard from them, which worried me.

I glanced at my watch again. Two and a half hours to go. It seemed wrong to break my promise to Hudson. But I was packed. Agitated.

I needed to *do* something.

It didn't take long to find the phone number the old-fashioned way, through telephone information.

Or to convince him to meet me.

He made a stark and poignant figure at the top of the hill, bent like a tree seedling fighting the wind. I spotted him immediately as the cabbie rounded the corner, eliminating the need for the cemetery map I picked up at the gate. The old man was my guidepost.

I slid up in the backseat and pointed. 'Stop as close as you can to that gentleman.'

The cabbie pulled over next to a stone mausoleum

with a rusty lock and a crumbling shepherd guarding the door to a family's forgotten bones.

The old man was several plots away. He didn't turn around, now kneeling and pulling away weeds creeping like spiders over a grave.

The sky seemed bigger here. The cemetery, dotted with trees and thousands of headstones, stretched out in all directions. Clouds swirled like black smoke in the eastern sky, and the cabbie told me to hurry, that the radio was predicting a nasty surprise storm.

I stepped awkwardly over the gravestones, thinking what a perfect target I'd make for a sniper, briefly but seriously considering throwing open my arms and screaming, *Shoot me now!*

Get it the hell over with.

Instead, I slowed down, a perfectly respectful mourner carrying a semi-tasteful plastic wreath of white orchids that I'd picked up at one of the flower shops ubiquitous around Chicago cemeteries.

The wreath seemed silly now, fake in every possible way.

The saleswoman instantly made me as a novice, presenting me with a laminated card of '10 Flower Rules You Must Follow for Chicago Cemeteries' and leading me to a greenhouse of artificial plants and buckets of tiny plastic Virgin Marys and Josephs and angels perched on top of sticks. I looked obediently through the buckets, thinking the plastic Christian icons were probably mass-produced in China by Buddha worshippers.

I skipped the Virgin Marys, who gazed at me reprovingly, and picked a gold plastic angel, wondering how many thousands of these were not decomposing in the ground at local cemeteries.

Now I wish I'd stuck to my original thought of a single rose, cliché as it would be, Chicago cemetery rules about live flowers be damned. My foot sank on top of a soft, grassy space where a head rested ten feet under. I shivered and silently apologized to Peter Theodore Ostrowski, who'd been camped out there since 1912.

By the time my shadow fell over her grave, the old man had yanked most of the grass and clover away from the tiny square marker lying flat in the ground.

Susan Bridget Adams
Our angel, still climbing
Jan. 3, 1977–Jan. 19, 1980

'She loved to climb trees,' Susie's father said. He was still kneeling, facing away as if he couldn't bear to look at me. 'If you didn't watch, she'd go all the way to the top of the old oak in our backyard. I was supposed to watch. But I went inside, just for a second.'

Just for a second.

I'd once counseled a grieving young girl whose one-year-old sister drowned at a backyard pool party while the adults stood around talking and drinking wine.

Six months ago, a Cheyenne first-grader chased his soccer ball into the path of a UPS truck when his mother stepped inside to get her ringing cell phone off the front hall table. He insisted we lift him out of his wheelchair onto a horse his first day at the ranch.

Just for a second, his mother told me, and now he'll wear a prosthetic leg forever.

'She stayed in a coma for three months,' Mr Adams said. 'I think that made it worse. To have hope.'

He made the sign of the cross and then struggled to pull himself up with his cane. My arms instinctively reached out to help. Abruptly, I remembered he was only in his sixties. Not that old. Grief had chiseled away at him.

I don't know who moved first.

We stood there, two strangers clasped in a tight embrace on a lonely hill, until a light rain began to fall.

CHAPTER 23

I promised the cabbie an extra fifty dollars to stop honking and for the use of a green-striped golf umbrella in his trunk that some passenger had left behind.

The rain pelted down insistently, but rather than tell our stories while an impatient cabdriver eavesdropped, Albert Adams and I walked toward a wrought-iron bench a few feet from his daughter's grave.

It hadn't been hard to convince him to show up, even though I was a stranger's voice on the phone with an implausible story. I had given him a small truth and a small lie, saying that I'd recently found out that my Social Security number matched Susie's in some kind of government screwup. I said I wondered if I'd been adopted and hoped he could help me find some answers.

He didn't seem surprised. He said he'd been meaning to get up to the cemetery. He'd be happy to meet if he could be home by five for dinner with one of his daughters.

'I haven't been here in years,' he confessed, wiping off the bench for me with a handkerchief.

'It's different. But just as painful. I think this will be my last trip.'

I sat down beside him, the wet wind tossing the pieces of hair coming loose around my face, briefly grateful that I'd taken the time to twist my hair into a long braid and wrap it around my head. Hudson had always said that this prairie-girl look of mine reminded him of his Catholic middle-school days. In other words, kind of hot.

Susie's father introduced himself with a firm grip of bony hand and paper-thin skin. 'Please call me Al,' he said.

He insisted on putting his old brown sweater around my bare shoulders, holding the umbrella over our heads.

'I've been waiting for this phone call for years,' he said.

'You knew about me?'

'I knew someone in witness protection had been given Susie's number. But I always wanted confirmation, with my own eyes, that Susie's life had gone on in someone else.'

'Well, here I am,' I said awkwardly. I didn't pretend surprise when he mentioned witness protection and he didn't seem to notice.

'Yes, here you are.' Al's eyes were shining. 'I like to think I can see people's souls through their eyes. You've got a good one.'

The rain let up and he rested the umbrella on the ground. He opened up his wallet, bulging with bright-eyed school pictures of his thirteen grandchildren, so I could admire them. His faux Hush Puppies, probably from Walmart and not in the greatest shape to begin with, were soaked. He'd have to hurry, he said. He didn't want to miss the 4:13 bus at Addison and Narragansett.

He appeared to be shrinking before my eyes. The rain was spitting again, and I didn't want him to catch pneumonia. I insisted on taking a turn with the umbrella, worried that I'd waited too late for my questions.

Then the girl with the good soul pushed for just a little more.

'Before you go, can you tell me if you know . . . why I had to disappear?'

Al closed his eyes, transporting himself back to the freezing January day that he buried his daughter.

A man showed up a couple of hours after Susie's funeral, he said. Slipping in among the neighbors loading up the kitchen table with chicken casseroles and red velvet cakes.

'He was a big man. Powerful-looking. He didn't appear comfortable in his suit. I guess he wore it out of respect for Susie. I went over to introduce myself, to thank him for coming. I thought he was one of my wife's co-workers.'

'But he wasn't.'

'He asked if there was somewhere we could speak privately. It was a small house. We've built on since. Anyway, we put on our coats and stood on the back porch and he offered me a smoke. He told me he was working in witness protection. He said he was very sorry about Susie and the timing of all of this but that the government needed to take her Social Security number. It was going to be used for another child. His team didn't want to go through formal government channels for a clean number. He didn't say it, but I knew it had to be Mafia. He seemed real worried that government clerks could be bribed.'

The thunder was like bass rumbling through a loudspeaker, making it hard to hear. The rain shot needles at us sideways. I tilted the umbrella for more protection and leaned in.

'. . . he told me he was trying to save a little baby who wasn't even born yet. That only a handful of people knew about you. It felt desperate to me, and also believable. You couldn't pick up the paper back then without reading about a politician who'd been bribed or an unidentified body in the water. I'll never forget Daniel Seifert, that fiberglass dealer in Bensenville ready to testify against the mob. They shot him right in front of his wife and kid. They didn't get Joey the Clown for it until five years ago. Remember that trial?'

I nodded, but he didn't seem to notice.

His face turned a shade paler. The small voice in my head urged me to stop, for decency's sake, to let him go on to a cozy dinner with his daughter.

'I asked him, "Why did you come to me?" He

277

said that I was the right person at the right time. He said I was an honorable man. He knew I was a Vietnam vet.'

He cleared his throat. 'I wanted to believe him. As angry as I was at his intrusion . . . our Susie was barely in the ground . . . I needed to do something to redeem myself. I had just killed my daughter.'

'You can't blame yourself . . .' I began, a meaningless platitude, one I hardly ever used with patients.

But Mr Adams was lost in his past, not even hearing.

'I didn't want to hand over my daughter's life but he was a hammer going at me. I had the feeling it was going to happen no matter what and if I didn't cooperate I'd put everyone in more danger, including my wife.'

'So you agreed?'

'I would be lying if I didn't say he clinched it when he held out an envelope with ten thousand dollars in twenty-dollar bills. He knew we were struggling. I'd gotten laid off from my job. My wife was six months pregnant. She started bleeding three days after Susie died. So much stress. The doctor told her to quit work or she could lose this baby, too.'

His daughter. Maybe the one who was making him supper. The one who would hang his wet clothes to dry when he got there, who would chide him for sitting in the cemetery in the rain with a strange woman. But, then, he would probably not tell her that part.

'He said we'd only get the money if we gave our complete cooperation. We needed to turn over a few things. He told me to talk to my wife. That night, *she's* the one who convinced *me*. It was the lowest point in our marriage. We were fighting over whether we could afford four extra words on Susie's gravestone. She told me, "We have to move on for this baby," and put my hand on her belly. Mary Elizabeth kicked. I'll never forget that moment.'

'So the man came again? With the money?'

'Two days later. I called the number on his card. He showed up in an hour and we exchanged envelopes. I gave him everything he wanted. Susie's birth certificate, Social Security card, anything official with her name on it. For the next fifteen years, a certified letter came to the house on the day she died with more cash. At least five thousand, sometimes more. No note. No explanation. More money wasn't part of the deal. But we knew it was from him.'

'Do you remember the postmark?'

'Different places. Towns I hadn't heard of. Once I called the number he gave me to thank him. It was disconnected. I was afraid to pursue it any more. We were being paid to keep a secret. I needed to protect my family, too.'

'Do your children know? Or anyone else?'

He shook his head. It stunned me that a man

could keep so much inside for so long. He was a secret keeper, like my mother. Maybe they weren't as rare as I thought.

'Susie came to me last night in a dream,' I blurted out. 'I thought she was someone else but . . . it was her. She was happy.' I shifted uncomfortably on the bench, aware how crazy that sounded outside the safe perimeter of my family of believers.

Al Adams touched my cheek, just as jagged lightning lit his face and the headstones behind him. It occurred to me that I was holding a death pole over our heads.

'We better leave,' I said hurriedly. 'My cab can take you home. Or we can still make the bus stop. Whatever you want. My treat.'

'I need to say goodbye,' he said, and I understood.

We walked to Susie's grave and Mr Adams stuck the metal prongs of the wreath I brought into the mushy ground in front of her headstone. I pushed the gold-angel-on-a-stick into the middle and stood back. Not so bad really. The wreath looked prettier, almost real, with raindrops glittering on its plastic leaves. The angel appeared happy to be on the job.

Before we dropped Al at the bus stop, he opened up the wallet stuffed with grandchildren and gave me a faded picture of Susie, a toddler with brown curls and chubby knees. My sad little collection of dead girls was growing.

'You can have this, too.' He handed me a dog-eared business card. 'I've carried it with me since the day I met him. I don't need it anymore.'

As the cab pulled away, I read the name on the card.

William T. McCloud. Federal marshal. Baseball fanatic. Rancher. Oilman. Father to a boy named Tuck and two girls named Tommie and Sadie.

William Travis McCloud, the man who raised me, had only one true name. It honored the infamous commander of the Battle of the Alamo.

Before Texas became a punch line, native Texans felt that kind of pride in their roots and most still do. Daddy took us to San Antonio one spring break and showed Sadie and me the approximate spot at the north wall of the Alamo where his namesake fell, shot in the head.

Commander William Travis, he told us, had drawn a line in the sand with his sword before the battle. Travis gave each of his men the choice to cross that line and fight against terrible odds or to retreat with honor. We didn't have to ask which way Daddy would have gone. Retreat was not his nature.

Because of Daddy, I've always divided the world into two kinds of people: people who will jump off a boat into choppy water to save you, and people who won't.

My father set that standard one summer afternoon at the lake when I was ten. We'd been waterskiing and tubing all day, when the wind started playing havoc with the water. Mama and I yanked Sadie and her inner tube from the water so Daddy could motor us back to the dock.

A boat of laughing teenagers blew by, spraying us and hitting the white caps with such force that I was sure their boat would flip. And then, only a hundred feet away, it did.

Before I could even process what I'd seen, Daddy hit the water with a clean, strong dive that seemed a physical impossibility for a 220-pound man. Mama had grabbed the wheel and yelled at us to get the cushions that doubled as life preservers. Three of them blew out of my hands as soon as I pulled them off, skipping across the waves uselessly. We could see two heads bobbing in the water, disappearing under the waves, bobbing up and disappearing again. Another kid was trying to hang on to the flipped boat. As we drew closer, Mama killed the motor, now afraid of running over someone in the water.

'The rope,' Daddy yelled at us. I threw the thick rope always tied to the back ring for just this purpose but it plopped into the water a pitiful three feet from the boat. Daddy reached it with monster strokes, then swam it out thirty yards to the two teenagers, now drifting dangerously away.

'Pull,' he yelled. The three of us pulled, while Daddy surged toward the boy holding on to the boat. As we helped the other boy and girl on board, Daddy was already swimming toward us, his arm around the third kid's neck in a lifeguard grip.

'Lisa. My sister—' The girl barely choked out the words as Daddy reached the boat. He was spent, exhausted from fighting the angry water.

The girl could see this and was frantic. 'There are *four* of us! You have to get Lisa!'

'Will . . .' I could hear the plea in Mama's voice. She wanted him to stay.

But Daddy was already gone, disappearing under the waves. It was the longest three minutes of my life before his head broke the water, pulling Lisa with him. She was a smart girl. She found an air pocket under the flipped boat and prayed the Lord's Prayer over and over. Most of the time Daddy spent out of our sight was in that air pocket, working up her courage to swim to the surface with him. Lisa's mother sent Daddy a Thanksgiving card every year until she died of cancer. Lisa is now a neonatal nurse saving other children's lives.

I followed a raindrop as it made a wiggly path down the cab window. I had wanted so much to believe that it was Daddy's heroic blood flowing through my veins. Even as questions about his part in this rose up again and again, I had pushed them away. I'd let myself be consumed by Mama's betrayal, because it was much easier to believe. But there was too much to ignore.

The argument Sadie overheard between Mama and Daddy. Jack Smith's suspicion that I was born in witness protection. Charla's bizarre phone calls from prison. Rosalina's wild tale. The enigmatic

Anthony Marchetti. Al Adams and the card I held in my hand. I ran my thumb over the embossed seal.

William Travis McCloud.

Your father says he is protecting you.

Right words. Wrong father.

Daddy would risk his life for a perfect stranger. I'd seen him do it. I now knew that once, that stranger was me.

The finger made it through the X-ray machine without a hitch, but I lost an $8 pair of cuticle scissors.

'You're in a dark mood,' Hudson remarked, as he crammed my laptop bag into the overhead compartment. 'You haven't said two words since the hotel. Except "Dammit" when you had to say goodbye to your toenail clippers.'

I didn't tell Hudson I'd left the hotel to meet Albert Adams. I wanted to, but I knew he'd be furious. He described his own afternoon as a complete waste of time. He waited two hours for Louie's lawyer to show up and tell Louie not to answer most of the questions in the interview.

'I'm just tired,' I said, standing on my tiptoes to pull down the blanket at the very back of the overhead bin.

Hudson gestured me toward the window seat, and I buckled myself in, closing my eyes. An extra-enthusiastic flight attendant began her show, reminding me of an old *Saturday Night Live* skit with Tina Fey. My thoughts drifted.

Memory is a funny thing.

Perspective is so much more.

Now I knew why Mama dressed us like boys and cut our hair short.

Why she named a girl Tommie.

Why she colored away her distinctive gray streak.

Why she built a hidden storm shelter in a bedroom closet.

Why she loved and married my father.

Why that man, whom I trusted more than anyone in the world, held on to her secrets until the day he died.

Hudson flipped the pages of a *Sports Illustrated*, and I turned my attention to a glorious orange and gold sunset putting on a private show for everyone on the left side of the plane. My knee felt a gentle squeeze, and I looked down to see Hudson's big hand, offering comfort, taking a chance. I thought about confessing everything I knew while we floated above the earth. Instead, I put my hand on top of his and left it there.

Every 'why' on that list hurt. I had to stop counting the deceptions, or I'd go crazy. I had to stop parsing every memory, knowing I could imagine things that weren't there.

In college, I studied a civil case brought by a twenty-year-old woman who claimed to have 'recovered' a memory about her childhood piano teacher. She said that the image of him standing behind her with his hands cupped over her breasts while she played 'Für Elise' came to her in the shower ten years later. The case turned on the defense testimony of a middle-aged college professor who told the jury about a study of sixteen young adults who had witnessed the murder of a parent as a child.

The memory of the murder burned like a brand, imprinted forever in their brain matter.

Not one of them, no matter how young at the time it happened, ever forgot it. Many of them could still recount the horror in precise detail. Yet another reason, the defense lawyer argued, to believe that repressed memory is a crock. The moments we remember without exception, he insisted, are unfortunately the horrible ones.

As I saw it, my problem was that what I needed to remember was probably very small, a single grain in a sea of waving wheat. If I could take over this plane and fly back to my childhood, I'd find that tiny grain and know what to do with it. My head bumped along on an insufficient airplane pillow beside a man who I believed cared for me deeply, who wanted to keep me safe. That didn't stop the dread curling up in my stomach. The airplane banked steeply, tipping me on edge so that for a few seconds I had the eerie sensation that I could fall right out my window and into one of the tiny sparkling blue swimming pools below.

That might be a blessing.

Every mile we flew closer to the Texas border, my chest grew tighter and tighter like the screw of a vise.

CHAPTER 24

Hudson dropped me off at the Worthington, clearly torn about leaving me. He ordered me to stay put in the room and open the door only for room service.

He'd left a client in the lurch to chase me in Chicago. He didn't say whom. But when he finished up the job tomorrow afternoon, he would be all mine.

All mine.

While we were flying up in the heavens, a familiar space developed between the two of us that held all the things we wouldn't say to each other. Like that I couldn't bear the thought that Hudson had been to war and back, but that he could die, here, because of me.

So that made calling Victor the second I closed the hotel room door a lot easier.

I didn't want to risk anyone's life but mine.

I didn't want to be manipulated anymore.

Not by Hudson, not by Mama, not by madddog12296.

I wanted some clean underwear and my gun.

I wanted to go home.

★　　★　　★

287

Victor let me off at our mailbox at the bottom of the road around midnight, the security lights of the house blinking through the branches of the trees.

Not Victor's preference, but mine. I needed the walk up the road to clear my mind. I wanted to feel open black sky above my head, to see it twinkling like Christmas in summer, to remember when a hot Texas night felt like a security blanket instead of a threat.

About halfway there, I was sweating buckets, wishing I had let Victor drop my suitcase and backpack on the porch like he suggested. I noticed a vehicle half-parked under the branches of a tree near the house. Not Daddy's pickup, which had been wheezing a little under the hood. I'd parked it in the garage before I left, deciding to take a shuttle to the airport. Could Sadie be back already from Marfa? No lights shone through the windows of the house. Maybe she was in bed. Why the hell didn't she stay at the hotel like I'd asked?

A few minutes later, I stopped short. Not Sadie's SUV. A small green Jeep parked recklessly, the front end on the grass. A security light shone directly into the front window, the necklace dangling from the mirror glinting gold.

The Jeep that was parked beside my pickup in a garage a few days ago.

The one stuffed with boxes and papers.

The hoarder.

No effort to hide the Jeep's presence. And no one inside it.

I dropped my suitcase and backpack onto the grass and crept forward as close to the shadow of the tree line as I could.

Connecticut plates.

I ran the last yards across the open drive, kneeling down on the passenger side, tugging at the door. Locked.

I crouched perfectly still, held my breath, and listened. No sound, except the buzzing of cicadas near the lights as some of them met an early death. I crawled on my hands and knees through the gravel to the driver's side, acutely aware that I was now an open target to anyone on the porch or in the house.

I lifted the door handle. Bingo.

I opened the door a quarter of the way and hurriedly shut it behind me to cut off the light. Then I threw myself flat over the passenger seat, the stick shift punching me in the gut, and stared at a pile of McDonald's wrappers on the floor, waiting for a gunshot.

When it didn't come, I groped for the glove compartment. Nothing much useful. No paperwork like an insurance card or registration that would tell me who owned the Jeep. No weapon. Just a dog-eared Jeep manual. And a mini Maglite. I punched the button. It worked. I raised my head cautiously. Something slithered across my cheek and I screeched.

The damn necklace. Heart thudding, I glanced outside. If anyone heard me, he was biding his time. I pinched the medallion between my fingers and held it under the beam of the flash-light.

St Michael.

Patron saint of police officers.

Patron saint of fending off evil.

Maybe I should put it on.

I ran the light over the papers piled in the backseat. Some folders were thin, others stuffed. Randomly, I pulled at one folder and the entire pile slid toward me.

Shit. I let it fall, papers slipping loose and skittering onto the floor of the backseat. I grabbed several sheets on the way down and shone the light on them. A document from the Stateville Correctional Center. A handwritten account of a 1983 incident in the shower between Anthony Marchetti and an inmate named George Meadows. Meadows ended up in the infirmary for three weeks with a punctured voice box, but every naked man in the shower that day insisted that he started it, not Marchetti.

I scanned the next sheet. An application from Anthony Marchetti for permission to use the internet in the Stateville prison library once a week. April 8, 2004. Signed and approved. *And probably monitored 24/7 by the FBI.*

I grabbed at a few more papers. WITSEC documents. Almost every word blacked out. Mama's? How had all of this wound up at my doorstep?

Swoosh.

I jumped and turned back in time to watch three more stacks topple over, papers sliding out like a waterfall. Their demolition exposed a slick, ultra-thin black laptop computer and an old shoebox on the seat. I dropped the folder and leaned over the back, butt in the air, to reach the shoebox. Not light, not heavy. Facing forward again, I let it sit in my lap, thinking of the wonderful and terrible things it could hold.

The answers to all of my questions.

The souvenirs of a serial killer.

Maybe the rest of Adriana's fingers.

I ripped off the lid. Old audiotapes. Some with the tape tangled and coming loose. Labeled with people's names I didn't recognize. Interviews? The final minutes of dying murder victims?

I tossed the box down by the hamburger wrappers, panic snuffing out the air in the Jeep. I rolled down a window and sucked in a deep breath of hot, humid air.

I stared at the front door.

Was it pure crazy to venture into the house alone?

Distractedly, I opened the folder I'd dropped onto the seat beside me. On top, a bad photo, snapped from a distance, blurred by motion and age.

Something about it felt voyeuristic.

Maybe because I recognized the girl.

It was me, at sixteen, on the back of a bull.

★   ★   ★

291

He was sitting in Daddy's chair with a huge grin on his face, like nothing could be more normal.

Jack.

There was a little pop of electricity when I saw him there, a thousand questions like lightning strikes.

He was not a reporter chasing a random story.

The Jeep was his.

Everything was shifting.

It took half a second for me to realize that Jack was sloppy drunk. The sprawl of his body, the eight crumpled beer cans on the floor. Cheetos crumbs littered an orange trail down the front of his sweaty white Tommy Hilfiger shirt.

'Long time, no see,' he slurred, although it sounded more like, 'Lun ti, no seep.' He let out a long, textured burp.

'Comm eeer,' he coaxed, reaching out his arms.

Not what I expected. Not at all what I expected.

'I'll be right back,' I said politely, as if, yes, indeed, finding him in Daddy's chair in the dead of night was perfectly OK.

It took less than a minute for me to grab my .45 out of the safe in Daddy's office, check the chamber, and fast-walk it back to the living room, tripping over three more empties and fossilized evidence of pepperoni pizza.

Jack hadn't moved an inch.

'Whatcha got that for?' His eyes jittered over the .45. He seemed genuinely confused.

'Is that your Jeep? Are you alone?'

'Oh, my Jeep! Didn't want to pay another week on rental.'

'Are you alone?' I repeated.

'Jus' you and me, baby.' His right hand moved like a snake along the seat cushion.

'Uh-uh. Get up. Keep your hands in front of you.' I pointed my gun at the center of his chest.

He pushed himself to his feet, grinning. 'Whatever you say, Miss Tommie.'

'Jesus, Jack.' I waved the .45 in the general area of his crotch, averting my eyes.

'Oops.' He laughed sloppily, zipping up, nearly toppling over. 'Don't think my aim was so good in the pisser.'

'Move,' I said impatiently, gesturing with my gun toward the kitchen.

When we reached the kitchen table, I shoved him into a chair.

Now I had a dilemma. Too drunk and he wouldn't stay focused. Too sober and I wasn't sure. So far, no aggressive behavior. But with a drunk, that could change in a beat.

'Put your hands flat on the table and keep them there,' I said. 'You move, and I will blow your head apart like that Jack in the Box antenna ball.'

With one hand on the gun and one eye on Jack, I opened the pantry door and pulled out a monster-sized Costco can of Maxwell House. The expiration date was two years ago. Mama had written it on the lid with black marker. So she wouldn't forget. I ripped off a paper towel for a filter and, without measuring, dumped a liberal amount from the can into the coffeemaker, the blacker the better.

While it brewed, Jack's head drooped on the table. He started to snore.

I filled his mug to the top with sludgy liquid and slammed it down in front of him.

Jack's head popped up. His eyes were glassy.

'Drink,' I said, my voice friendly. 'Tell me, what are all those papers in the back of your Jeep?'

'Stuff.' He obediently tipped the mug up, making a face and doing a spit-take across the table. 'This is yucky.'

I tried not to let the frustration enter my voice. This was like interviewing an unhappy Maddie. 'You mean stuff related to Anthony Marchetti?'

'Useless,' he slurred. 'All that work. Every damn thing you ever wanted to know 'bout that son bitch except why he's a big fat liar. I know. I was there. I *saw*.' He stood, wobbled, raised his fist, and then thumped the kitchen table so hard I thought it might crack the ancient wood.

He missed the chair entirely when he decided to sit back down, falling flat on his butt onto the tiles and popping the last button on his fly. Calvin Klein boxer briefs. No surprise. Like every good drunk, he apparently didn't feel any pain.

I knelt beside him cautiously.

'Jack. Look at me. Focus. What do you know? What did you see?'

'A Hobbit man. *Mean.* A giant. Big heart.'

Jack drew wildly concentric circles in the air with his finger.

'Like that.'

Then he crumpled, and laid his cheek flat on a cold tile, the one with the little bluebird etched on it that I'd found as a prize at the bottom of a dusty box in Tijuana. Mama had let me pick a spot for it when she had workers redo the floor with old Saltillo tile from Mexico. Sadie had pressed her orange dragonfly into the corner under the window so it could feel the sun.

'Pillow,' he ordered. 'Nice down here.'

I pulled the necklace, the one I'd unhooked from the Jeep's rearview mirror, from my pocket. I used the chain to tickle his cheek.

'Who are you, Jack Smith?'

His eyes flickered open. 'Mommy's. Thank you.' He grabbed the necklace with one hand and curled it up in his fist. Then Jack lived up to every other encounter I'd ever had with him. He passed out.

I rolled him over and pulled a wallet out of his back pocket, the one I tried to dig from a plastic bag hanging on a hospital gurney what seemed like years ago. Preppy, of course. A Tommy Hilfiger flag in the corner. Where was his phone?

The wallet held a liquor store receipt dated yesterday, $162 in cash, and six credit cards in the name of Jack R. Smith. Nothing else. His other back pocket held the keys to the Jeep.

No driver's license or ID of any kind.
No explanation.

Nothing, nothing, *nothing* made any sense.

Jack Smith was a goddamn drunken mess, passed out on my kitchen floor. Before that, he'd been babbling like he stepped out of a J.R.R. Tolkien novel.

I sat in Daddy's chair in the living room with my gun in my lap and punched in my cell phone's voicemail password. Nine unplayed messages since I stepped on the plane in Chicago. I hurried through them – four from Charla from prison that were all versions of 'Shit, she's not there,' two from Lyle that asked me to call as soon as possible, one from my boss at Halo Ranch, one from Wade asking where the hell Sadie and I had lit off to. Desperately punching away, I finally found what I wanted.

Hearing Sadie's voice was like drinking in air after a punk kid held your head under water.

'Hey, Tommie. This is awful, isn't it? I'm on my way back from Marfa now. I left Maddie with Nanette. I had to get her out of there. Hudson has promised me one of his war buddies as a companion for the next few days. Anyway, my first stop will be the hospital. Love you. See you soon.'

I stared at my hands, willing them to stop shaking. I took in the mess Jack had made: newspaper scattered all over the floor, crumbs smeared into the Oriental rug, a slice of half-eaten pizza under the sofa, what appeared to be a little throw-up on the arm of the chair. Jack was like the potbellied pig that my East Texas cousin let roam her house. My hand followed a hard lump near my butt and found a cold steel handle.

Jack's gun was wedged between the cushion and the frame. Had he been reaching for it before I made him stand up?

I emptied the chamber, stuck the bullets in my pocket, and placed it on the mantel. Fully wired, I glanced at my watch. Ten till one.

Jack said the answer wasn't in his Jeep. I tended to believe him. The thought of hauling those files in here and pawing through them was over-whelming. It could take days, and I'd still be nowhere.

I walked back into the kitchen and nudged Jack with the toe of my boot. Still out.

I pulled up the leg of his jeans and carefully removed his backup weapon, emptied the chamber, and stuck it in the refrigerator.

The door to the laundry room was shut.

I never left it shut.

I kicked it open and crouched down. Nothing sprang out. Jack didn't budge.

Gun drawn, I flipped the switch in the laundry room.

Nobody.

I breathed.

I was facing the map tacked to the wall and the jagged black route I'd drawn across it.

Two of the newspaper articles began to nag at me: the one about a city councilman's race in Norman, Oklahoma, and, of course, the tragic story of Jennifer Coogan's murder in Idabel. They were the only two clippings from the same state and were No. 1 and No. 2 on the map going chronologically by date.

The thought slammed into me like things often do when you've thought too hard about them, as if it had always been there, just waiting for a lull.

The University of Oklahoma was in Norman. Jennifer Coogan was a student at the University of Oklahoma, waitressing for the summer back home in Idabel. That had to mean something, didn't it? Was the crooked line the path of a serial killer? Why, why, why would my mother know anything about that? And how could it have anything to do with Anthony Marchetti? Or Rosalina? Or the man snoring on my kitchen floor? Or me?

I headed to the computer. Obsessively, I raked through the archives of newspapers located in the cities on my map. I searched the FBI official missing persons list, along with a number of other sites. No murders, and no girls went missing in the month before or after the dates on the clips. The city councilman in Norman was squeaky clean and long retired. His name popped up as an elder at the First Presbyterian Church.

The time on the computer screen read 3:08 a.m.

I got up and kicked Jack again, noticing for the

first time that he no longer had a sling. Was that a fakeout, too?

'Ow,' he grumbled, turning over, never opening his eyes.

Back in the laundry room, I flipped off the computer and leaned in to lift the blind on the window, staring into the inkiness of the backyard. Empty, open space.

Jack R. Smith appeared to be on an obsessive quest. Like me.

I didn't think he was my primary enemy, but how many times did the plucky heroine get that part wrong?

A half an hour later, I was creeping down the hill, Daddy's hunting backpack slung over my shoulder, stuffed with my laptop, two pairs of my new lace underwear, a T-shirt, a pair of jeans, the Beretta, and a toothbrush.

'I need a rental car,' I told Victor when he cheerfully pulled up in his taxi to our rusty mailbox on the main road ten minutes later. 'Find me one at this hour and you'll get my undying gratitude and a hundred-dollar tip.'

'Where the hell are you?'

The fury in Lyle's voice through my cell phone was the jolt I needed to stay awake. I was driving through a rare Starbucks-free zone, my eyes drooping dangerously with jet lag and the monotony of navigating country roads for two and a half hours with very little sleep.

'I'm in Melissa. No, wait, that was a while ago. I'm just outside of Paris. *Oui, oui.*' I offered up a weak laugh.

'What the hell are you doing up near the Oklahoma border?'

You couldn't throw Lyle, not even for a second. It wouldn't surprise me if he had every city and town on the U.S. map memorized, along with their latitude and longitude.

Paris, Texas, was a fly speck on the map, a place to grow up and leave. Its importance in the universe shot up mildly when the enterprising Boiler Makers Local #902 constructed a sixty-five-foot Eiffel Tower replica in the center of town. As I whizzed past, I noticed the addition of a large red cowboy hat perched jauntily on top of it.

'I'm going to Idabel,' I said in a small voice. 'Alone.'

The deep silence that followed hurt my ears more than the yelling.

'Lyle? Say something. This is my life, you know. I'm going to lose my mind if this goes on much longer.'

He made his usual grunting sound. Good, bad, or indifferent, I couldn't tell, but I was pretty sure he was tussling with himself. He let his reporters do stupid, dangerous things all the time in pursuit of truth and you rarely found their skeletons hanging from trees.

He finally spoke. 'You're talking to Jennifer Coogan's parents?'

'I spoke with them a little while ago. They're expecting me. So is the sheriff. He's pulling the file. Very cooperative.' I hesitated. 'I told them I was a journalist.'

'That's just dandy,' he shot back sarcastically. 'I expect a call as soon as it's over. In fact, I want a call every twenty-four hours, just to know you're all right. I'm extremely pissed off that you are doing this on your own.'

'Sorry,' I said meekly.

After we hung up, my guilt got the better of me. I dialed Hudson, knowing he wouldn't answer because he let everything go to voicemail when he was on a job. I told him that Jack was laid out drunk on my floor with a Jeep full of documents parked out front. I said I was taking a little trip, but not to worry, that I would see him soon. It was like dropping a little bomb into his cell phone. I was glad I wouldn't be there when it went off.

Two hours and a Big Gulp Dr Pepper later, I pulled up to a renovated green storage unit with a flashing red 'vacancy' sign. A white banner stretching across the low-slung building advertised itself as the 'Sunset Motel, Idabel's Bargain Bed, Under New Management.'

The Sunset Motel sat across the street from the Charles Wesley Motor Lodge, a palace in comparison, but the Lodge was booked solid with a bunch of Eagle Scouts. Only in Oklahoma would a religious icon get his own motor lodge. Wesley wrote six thousand hymns, including Granny's favorite, 'Christ the Lord Is Risen Today,' which she belted out a cappella.

The bare-bones, photo-free website said the Sunset Motel had plenty of its rooms available – I could now see why – and a customer review raved about 'good heat, AC, and hot water' although, unfortunately, 'there isn't a good place to pull your boat and four-wheelers up to your door.'

The strip of rooms faced the main road with barely enough concrete parking in front to keep the end of the cars out of traffic. No office in sight.

As I crammed my car sideways into the lot, searching for a sign of life, I decided it was probably as good a place as any to hide from the mob. Bullets wouldn't fly through steel, for one thing. I'd kept one eye on the rearview mirror all the way here, looking for more Louies. I was sure there were more ants in the pile he crawled out of.

I honked twice, and after a few minutes, a scraggly man in a white T-shirt and jeans came out of one of the units. He stuck his head in the car window, providing a suffocating whiff of bad breath and body odor.

'Sixty dollars a night, cash,' he said. I opened my purse and handed over $120. From his happy expression, this didn't happen very often.

'Two nights,' I said. 'I have a reserva—'

'Don't need to know who you are.' He thrust a metal key at me through the window. It dangled off a crudely whittled pine bear, a homey touch, maybe what he did in his spare time.

'Key says thirty-two,' he said, 'but you're in number five. No service after eight.'

Uh-huh.

I watched him walk back to his unit, which probably served as both office and home, before making a tight U-turn into space No. 5.

I opened the door to a room more pleasant than its manager – a wood-paneled space right out of the 1960s, including a red phone with an old-fashioned round dial. I liked the clicking noise when I stuck my finger in a hole and gave it a whirl. I thought briefly about calling Hudson again. The room smelled musty but not too bad. And it was deliciously cool.

The king-sized bed sank easily from the weight of a thousand bodies before me and boasted a scratchy polyester bedspread with a pinecone motif, a few mysterious stains, and pillows that were hard as rocks. I fell asleep instantly.

CHAPTER 25

Jennifer Coogan's childhood home was a small gray box on the outskirts of town. It looked sad, like it gave up after her murder. Slack curtains hung in the windows on either side, making me think of weeping eyes. A wreath with faded yellow daisies that should have been tossed years ago hung on a front door with black paint peeling off in little curls.

Granny said black doors kept demons in. Or encouraged them to come. I couldn't remember which.

Before I got out of the car, I wondered for the hundredth time why Mama would save a story about a college girl's murder that took place more than two hundred miles away.

I knocked on the door, my stomach protesting a breakfast of a melted Snickers bar and a warm can of Coke from the Sunset's vending machine. A woman with bright red hair opened up instantly, as if her hand had been on the knob. Unsmiling, wary.

'Are you the reporter?' A slight Oklahoma twang.

'I'm Tommie,' I said. With effort, she stretched her mouth into something resembling a smile.

'I'm Jen's mother. Come on in. I got my family here waiting.'

The living room was painted a harsh yellow, an unsuccessful attempt to make the room appear cheerful. While most people reserved the shrine for the bedroom, the Coogans had crowded the tiny living room with everything Jennifer – soccer and pageant trophies, track ribbons, framed finger-paint drawings, even a dusty volcano science project with a blue ribbon hanging off it.

The pictures of her that covered the walls and the tables and the mantel were an assault. There was no other way to describe it. I couldn't turn my eyes without seeing Jennifer as a baby, as a pageant contestant, as a graduate.

Jennifer wasn't just pretty, I realized. She was at least five steps up from pretty. Big green eyes, softly curling auburn hair that fell past her shoulders, and a permanent, genuine smile. I wondered what tiny flaw made her the Miss National Teenager runner-up instead of the queen.

'Please. Sit down.' Jennifer's mother gestured toward a high-back rose-and-vine-printed chair with dark wood trim that matched the small couch. It held a weary-eyed gray-haired man and a plain young woman who looked ready to run from the room.

'I'm Leslie. This is my husband, Richard, and our daughter, Amanda. Amanda took off from her job at Wood's Auto to be here. She was eight when Jen died.' I did the math. That would put Amanda in her early thirties. And desperately unlucky to have to grow up in this claustrophobic house with a ghost she could never live up to.

I let an awkward silence lay among us and studied the three of them, now in a prim row on the couch. Above their heads, a large silver crucifix hung between two Olen Mills portraits of a smiling Jennifer in the head-tossed-over-the-shoulder pose, probably taken shortly before her death. She was one of the few people I'd ever seen who took to that pose naturally.

Leslie Coogan's red hair, surely gray underneath, was bottled. My hairdresser said anyone could be a redhead, you just had to find the right color red, but he hadn't met Leslie Coogan. Another morbid salute to Jennifer? Amanda's left hand sparkled with a tiny diamond. She was getting out, thank God. Richard Coogan's grimace reminded me of a patient whose morphine had worn off.

Still, I felt something that resembled hope emanating off that couch. It was as if all three of them were waiting for me to tell them that, twenty-five years later, it was all just a big misunderstanding and that Jennifer wasn't the bloated thing dragged out of the river, after all.

'Do you think you'll be able to find the killer after all these years?' Mrs Coogan asked, eagerly leaning forward, saving me from an introduction.

'I can't even begin to promise you that,' I said. Richard Coogan contemplated me as if I were another giant disappointment in a life crammed with them. 'Nothing could make it worse. Our lives have been over for years.'

I'm not sure anybody but me noticed the slight twitch of Amanda's lips when he said that.

Richard spit out the saga of Jennifer's murder like a well-rehearsed speech, mostly things that matched my internet research. But I didn't interrupt. I needed to feel his pain for myself, a part of my process. Sadie had warned me for years that it was dangerous for me to carry around so many people's hurt.

'Jen always closed up alone every third Saturday night,' Mrs Coogan told me. 'I told Richard he should go up and check on her when she wasn't home by midnight. But Richard said nothing bad ever happens in Idabel. And we went to sleep.' Tears welled in her eyes.

'Tell me about her boyfriend at OU. The one who disappeared. Did you meet him?'

Mrs Coogan pulled a tissue out of her sweater pocket and dabbed her eyes.

'No, but she really liked him. They talked on the phone a lot. His name was Barry. They'd been dating for about five months. Jennifer said he didn't like his picture taken so we never knew what he looked like. The police found that real suspicious.'

'What about the letter?' Amanda prodded her, in a barely audible voice.

'Oh, yes.' Mrs Coogan got up and opened a

drawer in an end table stuffed with letters and cards. 'He did write her letters over the summer. I couldn't find them anywhere when the police asked for them, not in her room or her car, but this one arrived a few days after she died. The police fingerprinted it but couldn't find anything. Maybe he used gloves. Here it is.'

I tried not to appear too eager as she handed over a small white envelope with Jennifer's name and address in clean, bold printing. Not cramped and distressed, like a maniacal killer of young women. No return address.

I scanned the one-page letter written on a spare sheet of notebook paper. It was a short, funny note about his landlady's obsession with her poodle, Queen Anne Boleyn. He liked his new bartending job. He missed Jennifer.

No misspellings or grammatical errors. Based on this single piece of evidence, I liked Barry.

I handed the letter back and Mrs Coogan placed it carefully in the drawer.

'He signed it with six X's and ten O's,' she said.

I stood up. 'Thank you so much for your time. I'll let you know right away if I find anything that sheds light on your daughter's case.'

'That's it?' Red splotches spread like a weather map over her face. 'You've got nothing for us?'

Amanda was up in a flash, moving toward the door, pulling me with her.

I hesitated as we reached the door and decided it was worth the risk.

308

'Just one thing. Do any of you know an Ingrid McCloud? Or did Jennifer?'

All three of them stared at me blankly.

'An Ingrid Mitchell? A Genoveve Roth?'

They shook their heads.

'Um, well, thank you, anyway, for your time.'

'Don't mention it,' Mrs Coogan said sarcastically. 'Really, don't.'

Amanda pulled me with her onto the stoop, and the door shut a little harder than it needed to behind us. I wondered briefly whether her parents were getting out a gun or a bottle of vodka to put themselves out of their misery. The statistics on couples staying together after the loss of a child were staggeringly depressing.

'I call it the House of Pain.' Amanda slid on a pair of cheap drugstore sunglasses as we walked down the concrete walk. I noticed she stepped carefully over each crack.

'I got that line from my high school trigonometry teacher. He used to greet us at the classroom door with "Welcome to the House of Pain." Only it was funny when he said it. My therapist thinks it's kind of funny when I say it. At least, he thinks it's a positive sign.'

I wondered about the credentials of a therapist who set up shop in Idabel, but, then again, it looked like there was plenty of ripe material here.

We had parked back-to-back on the street in front of the house. A pink rabbit's foot dangled from the rearview mirror of Amanda's canary-yellow beater

Toyota. I wanted to tell Amanda that I'd lost a brother, but I didn't. I didn't know which was worse: for her to live in that horrid museum to Jennifer or for me to exist in a home wiped clean of any sign that Tuck ever existed.

Amanda opened the Toyota's door and tossed in her purse. All fingers present and accounted for. Amanda was about the right age to fit Adriana Marchetti's profile if she'd lived. This new habit of counting strange women's fingers had obsessed me for an hour in the Chicago airport. That placed me on the scale of crazy an inch or so below Rosalina.

'I'll tell you what I told the cops,' she said. 'They didn't listen because I was just a kid. Jennifer loved that guy Barry. I always thought that whoever killed Jennifer killed him, too. They just did a better job of making sure he wasn't found.'

I waited forty minutes in the 'interview' room of the McCurtain County Sheriff's Office, a small, stuffy space crammed with an old school lunch-room table, a microwave that predated my birth, a coffeepot, and a humming refrigerator with a sign that read, 'To Prevent BIOHAZARD, All Leftover Sack Lunches and TUPPERWARE Will Be DUMPED Daily at 5 p.m. ON THE DOT. NO EXCEPTIONS.' I decided the author upper-cased the appropriate words.

Aging posters, the only attempt to spruce up blinding white walls, warned against the perils of alcohol, pot, and getting in cars with strangers. Too late for me.

When Sheriff Joe Bob Woolsey entered, he radiated nuclear Oklahoma heat. His body raised the room's temperature five degrees.

'Sorry I'm runnin' behind.' He sounded slightly out of breath. 'I been out workin' cattle on my ranch. This sheriff deal don't pay enough for me to give up my day job.'

This is something I love about native southerners – a hello includes more personal information than a Yankee would parse out in an hour. Actually, the hello often doesn't include the word *hello*.

Sheriff Joe Bob, who had run unopposed for twelve years running, was a large red-faced man on his way to a coronary. Tributaries of burst blood vessels on his cheeks and nose were a better advertisement for not drinking than his own posters.

He stood well over six feet and was dressed in jeans, a pair of scuffed brown Justin boots, a sweaty blue plaid work shirt, and a crooked badge that I suspected he'd stuck on in his pickup on the way over. The holster and gun that rested comfortably around his hips like a second skin – those he probably wore to bed.

Big, calloused hands that reminded me of my father held a thin file, which he slid across the table to me before he took a swig of some black, oily-looking coffee. He slurped from the Styrofoam cup like a needy alcoholic.

'I'd offer ya some, but it might kill ya,' he said, grinning. 'That there is the case file for Jennifer Coogan. Biggest thing that ever happened here, but you wouldn't know it by lookin' at that. I got bigger files on the town drunks. The way I hear it, the FBI guys took it over almost from the git-go, pissin' everybody off.'

'Is the sheriff who worked the case still alive?' I asked.

'Nope. Died a few years back. Most everybody who had an inside track to that case is in the ground. We live hard and die young 'round here. If cancer don't git you, your wife's naggin' will.' He winked as if I'd never heard that one before. 'Nope, pretty much what you got is those few pieces of paper.'

He wiped his forehead with a dirty handkerchief. 'It's hotter than my Meemaw's griddle out there.'

I flipped over the ten or so single pages of the file, thinking that I'd driven a lot of miles for a few folksy metaphors. The meager police report didn't even mention the cans of hominy and nacho cheese sauce. Jack said they'd been strapped to her body to weigh her down in the river. The coroner's report was incomplete. Interviews were sketchy. Useless.

I reluctantly turned over the second to last page, feeling a lousy dead end.

A blurry, mimeographed picture stared up at me. I had to look twice, then one more time to be sure. I glanced up at the sheriff, wondering if this was a joke and he was in on it, but common sense said that was impossible.

It seemed more logical that Idabel, Oklahoma, was just a shortcut to Oz.

I blinked, and the men were still there on the page, unaware they'd been caught by the camera.

A hobbit and a giant.

A giant with a big heart tattoo.

CHAPTER 26

I heard a commotion outside the door, but it seemed miles away from the fantasyland where I'd retreated with a giant and a dwarf.

Hudson snapped me right back.

He stood at the door to the interview room, radiating his own kind of nuclear energy, instantly raising *my* temperature ten degrees. The man kept showing up no matter what. Not letting go. 'What do you think you're doing, Tommie?' Controlled rage. The tip-top of Hudson's temper scale.

Sheriff Woolsey surprised me by rising with the quick grace of an old movie cowboy, his hand resting on the .45 in his holster. 'Ma'am, do you want me to draw?' he asked politely.

'No. No! I know him. He's a friend. It's OK.' The sheriff didn't move, his eyes traveling to the bulge at Hudson's waist.

'We're in a relationship,' Hudson said, tossing over his security firm's card.

'Who says?' I spit at him, while inside I hoped that he meant it.

'Oh.' Sheriff Joe Bob relaxed, as if that explained

314

everything, sitting back down and propping his boots up on the table. 'Go right to it.'

'We're leaving.' Hudson gestured for me to get up.

Uh, have you met me before?

'How did you find me?' I asked, not moving, trying to keep my voice level. Then, grudgingly, 'I was planning to check in with you again shortly.'

'Well, let's see,' he said. 'You rented a car under your real name with your MasterCard. The car had a GPS device in the trunk. I have enough special abilities to charm minimum-wage rental car agents.' His voice grew more sarcastic, which I didn't think was possible. 'Oh, yeah, and Lyle called and told me where you were. My ten-year-old nephew could have found you, Tommie.'

Hudson was always good with reality checks. I'd been playing a dangerous game on this trip, fooling myself. Thinking I'd left my hunters behind.

Before I could respond, Sheriff Woolsey flipped his chair around and sat it down hard inches from me, probably one of his tried-and-true witness intimidation techniques. One move closer and I'd get poked by the toothpick getting a workout in his mouth. His breath smelled like Skoal and bitter coffee.

'She can't leave yet. If I'm not mistaken, she recognized these boys.' He tapped the paper in front of me.

It wasn't like I'd forgotten. Dear God.

'Do you know these men?'

With the sheet in my hand, I moved over to the light by the window, buying a little time for Hudson to calm down. In the old days, I timed him at sixteen minutes but this was a fairly egregious offense on my part. I examined the men in the picture closely, thrilled I'd found a connection but even more confused. How was Jennifer Coogan's death tied to Jack Smith and Anthony Marchetti?

Less than twenty-four hours ago, Jack had rambled drunkenly to me about a seemingly mythical hobbit, a giant, and the lying ways of the Chicago mobster who just might be my father. Now here, in the murder file of Jennifer Coogan, in a small Oklahoma town, the Hobbit and the Giant had sprung to life.

The Hobbit stood about three feet tall. 'Little person' would be the politically correct term. Because I'm rarely politically correct, he looked to me like a malevolent Sneezy, with a bulbous red nose and pockmarked cheeks. Genetics had not been kind. The Giant stood four feet taller and two feet wider, with tree trunks for arms and an enormous shaved vegetable of a head.

I imagined a gentle tap from him would send me into outer space. He wore size giant jeans that he must have special-ordered and a cutoff white Harley T-shirt that bared pumped-up arms. A cupid's heart tattoo the size of a baseball curved around his left bicep. I couldn't read the name that arced around the top of it.

'I don't know these men,' I said firmly, now that I could catch my breath. That was true. 'Who are they?'

'Strangers in town who got caught on a video exiting a local bar two nights before Jennifer's body was found. Their looks made folks remember them. The bar owner had just put in a newfangled camera outside his dump to keep the drug pushers away. He watched every frame for the first month until he got bored of it. He brought this in right away.'

'Did the FBI know about these two? I didn't read anything about these guys as suspects.'

'Nope. Don't think so. Like I said, they treated us like a bunch of local yokels with our heads up our asses. So the sheriff kept a few clues to hisself.'

Great, I thought. *Prove the FBI right by hiding information that could lead to solving Jennifer's murder.* It occurred to me that Sheriff Joe Bob knew this meager case file surprisingly well.

'How old were you when this happened?' I asked.

'Sixteen goin' on thirty. Scared the pee out of all of us. Shut down our Saturday night make-out and beer parties for a month or so.' For a second, I felt the panic of trying to get the beer and cigarette smell out of Sadie's favorite jeans before Granny got hold of them for Monday's wash. I was familiar with the thrill of illicit parties that spilled into hay fields from the backs of pickup trucks, the cheap beer, the amateur groping.

'Her younger sister was a wild thing when she

317

was growing up.' The sheriff paused. 'Not pretty like Jenny, but she put out. I hear she's finally settling down. Some psychologist fellow in Broken Bow.' My hope for Amanda took a hit. 'Y'all want to see where they pulled Jennifer out of the water?'

Now he sounded like a forty-year-old going on sixteen.

There seemed to be no reason, other than morbid fascination, to say yes. Hudson gave a mute nod. His face was unreadable.

Minutes later, the three of us sat in intimate discomfort bumping along in the front cab of the sheriff's fully loaded shiny black Eddie Bauer Ford truck, the portable flashing red cherry on the roof giving us the eighty-mile-an-hour right-of-way down the highway. I was squashed in the middle and none of us smelled very good.

The speedometer tipped up toward ninety.

'All the sudden, I'm guessin' you're not a reporter,' the sheriff said.

'No.' The right tires caught the rough, unpaved berm and he swung the wheel back, but his focus stayed on me, the speedometer holding steady. 'But I do have a legitimate reason for being here.'

'That's what they all say. You leaving town soon?'

'Yes. Soon. Very, very soon.'

'Then I reckon I don't need to know about your legitimate reasons.' He gunned the motor. This seemed to be the general approach to law enforcement in Idabel. Machismo and benign neglect.

Minutes later, the sheriff brought the pickup to a halt on the side of the road right before an old bridge that hovered over a slow-drifting, rusty river. We sidestepped broken beer bottles as we worked our way down a marshy path of trampled grass toward the water. I remembered that two boys out fishing had discovered Jennifer's corpse.

'Can't keep the kids out, unless I physically post somebody here. Her ghost brings 'em. Freshman football initiations, séances, first-time lovers, double-dares – you name it.'

Surely, I thought, swatting at mosquitoes, *anyone idiotic enough to lose their virginity at a murder site must wind up with some pretty big hang-ups.*

It took about five minutes to walk the path, five minutes for my anxiety to start thrumming again. My white T-shirt, soaked with sweat, clung to my breasts. The mud-caked leopard-print cork wedge sandals on my feet appeared to be yet another piece of my new Nordstrom wardrobe headed for a hotel trashcan. Thorns found their way up the hem of my jeans and bit my ankles.

I stepped into the clearing with a sense of dread and involuntarily grabbed Hudson's hand. To my surprise, he didn't pull away.

Someone had stuck a small white cross in the ground near the water's edge. A used, cream-colored candle lay toppled on its side, wet with river muck and dripping with hard tears of wax. Candy wrappers, diet drink cans, and a couple of broken tequila bottles littered the area. I saw three used condoms and a pair of muddy purple thong panties.

Almost as soon as we got there, I asked to leave.

Hudson and I silently shared wrinkled hot dogs and soggy crinkle fries in a green plastic booth at Burger Barn, a small converted dry-cleaner shop smack in the middle of the Idabel loop. We probably should have been dissuaded by the fact that the word 'Burger' on the sign had been changed to 'Booger' by some spray-paint-happy teenagers. At least we were smart enough to pass on the special of the day, jalapeño tater tots.

I did venture a hesitant question.

'Did you . . . see Jack?'

'The Jeep was gone by the time my friend got there.' He said it curtly.

That's all he was giving me. He knew a lot more, I was sure. He was Hudson, the legend.

In as few words as possible, we determined that the most sensible thing was to spend the night at my motel before heading home. We stopped at Walmart on the way back so I could buy a pair of pajamas. The choices in my size were covered with ducks, cupcakes, or Britney Spears's face. I picked cupcakes.

When we stepped through our motel room doorway, I announced I was taking a shower. Anything to avoid him.

Every molecule in the room was charged with the potent combination of anger, cheap pine-scented air freshener, and sexual tension. Hudson ignored me. He flipped on the TV, trying to find something other than gray fuzz. While I dug through my backpack for clean underwear, he adjusted the aluminum foil on the rabbit ears for a recognizable image of Diane Sawyer. Or maybe it was Brian Williams.

I yanked out a T-shirt. That's when my gun hit the floor.

But he didn't seem perturbed at all. He picked it up off the floor and handed it back to me, butt first.

'I used to love watching you shoot Miller Lite cans off the fence at twenty-five yards,' he said.

'Thirty-five yards,' I corrected. 'And I can do it on a horse at full trot.'

'I don't think I can do this again, Tommie.' His voice was tired, not angry. He sat on the edge of the bed, eyes wet. 'I thought we could make it work this time, but I was wrong. As soon as we get back, I'm assigning a friend of mine to see you through this. He owes me a favor. And he's almost as good as I am.'

I stood there, stunned, feeling an awful weight in my stomach, not at all sure I believed him.

'What do you mean, "again"? I asked. 'You said you couldn't do this *again*.'

'This push-pull thing. I think I've made my intentions pretty damn clear all along but you still go your own way at the end of the day. This time, you might get yourself killed. Go on, take your shower.' He lay back, faceup on the bedspread, eyes closed.

'I want to know why *you* think we broke up.'

He opened his eyes and regarded me thoughtfully. 'Partly because you were too young. Partly because I'm an ass. But mostly because I was never going to live up to your Daddy.'

I looked around for something to throw at him but the choices were limited. The pillows weren't hard enough and the bedside lamps were screwed to the tables. I stalked off and slammed the bathroom door.

I waited to cry until I stripped and leaned into the tepid stream of water, so Hudson couldn't hear. I didn't indulge myself for long.

The shower was the size of a coffin standing on end. It took all my concentration to wash myself while dodging alien life-forms that grew in black patches on the walls. The mildewed shower curtain brushed up against my skin like a dog's cold wet nose. With evil timing, the shower spurted boiling hot water down my spine, followed shortly by an icy blast. I let out a tiny shriek. At least it sounded tiny to me.

Not three seconds later, a shadowy figure hovered outside the curtain. I screamed.

The bathroom erupted in a stream of angry words. Hudson, busting in on me again. Thankfully, the scummy plastic shower curtain obscured his view. Until he slung it open.

I scrambled to cover myself with the Sunset's

rag of a washcloth and pointed wordlessly to the showerhead. He couldn't help himself. He laughed, a sound I loved.

He whipped the curtain back across and I heard him mutter either, 'Oklahoma's version of *Psycho*,' or 'Omigod, she's a psycho,' before making his exit. I figured on the latter.

The shower had settled on a temperature right below freezing, and I reached for a towel. The air-conditioning draft from the gap left by the open door woke up every goose bump on my body. I shivered into the pajamas and then took a good half-hour to blow out my hair into the long, soft mane that Hudson used to bury his face in.

Push. Pull.

I stared at my face in the milky mirror. A small, good nose, defined cheekbones, pearl-white pore-less skin that needed the regular attention of a self-tanner, green eyes, arched eyebrows. And fear. I saw fear.

By the time I exited the bathroom, it was after nine. All the lights were out, except for a small lamp shedding a half-moon glow on my side of the bed. I say *my* side because Hudson's long lean form took over the other side. No chivalrous pallet on the floor for him, I guess. He lay under the tiny pinecone forest, his back to me speaking volumes.

The door chain was in place and a brittle-looking unfinished pine chair, the only one in the room, was jammed under the doorknob. The setup didn't give me confidence that it would hold a determined person from getting in, but maybe just long enough for us to draw or hit the floor. I slipped the gun out of my backpack and placed it as quietly as possible near the lamp, although I imagined the evil outside transforming into wisps of smoke and snaking under the crack of the door. In that scenario, a bullet would not help.

I glanced at Hudson's still form on the bed. I knew he was awake, the jerk. I slipped in beside him, a foot of sexual tension between us. I turned over and faced the wall, making out the face of a monster in the knotty pine. Maybe he *was* asleep. Oh, God, was that a brown recluse crawling on the back of my neck? I thought I'd seen a carcass in the bathroom. I slapped at it, the worst thing to do with a legendary poisonous spider that eats a hole in your skin.

'Hmm, I guess that's not one of your top ten erogenous zones,' Hudson said. 'I was misinformed in eighth grade by my sister's *Cosmo*.' His finger continued to trail up my neck, disturbing every nerve ending in my body.

'Turn around,' he urged, pulling me over. 'Let's not go to sleep angry.'

The window air conditioner was rattling like a truck. My body, still cool, melted against his warm one. He wasn't wearing a shirt, and my hands moved on his back, feeling the hard curve of muscle. I couldn't tell what, if anything, he was wearing below the waist.

This simple hug in Idabel's Bargain Bed with scratchy 100-thread-count sheets was the safest place I'd been in days. Maybe years.

When he finally bent to kiss me, I lost track of everything. It was like falling into an endless stream. We came up for air and he tipped my chin and planted a light kiss on my forehead.

'Good night,' he said gently, and turned over, his back now a wall, leaving me wide awake, body pulsing, thinking I was screwing this up again.

Push. Pull.

I woke to my cell phone vibrating like a giant cockroach on the bedside table.

It was Lyle, and 'unhappy' didn't begin to describe him. I had broken my promise to call.

'Hold on,' I whispered, pressing my finger over the tiny speaker, trying not to disturb Hudson, still rolled over, sleeping like a tank. I wrapped the top sheet around me and sat with my knees up in the corner of the room. A real spider made its move down the wall inches from me. At the moment, it seemed less scary than Lyle.

As soon he stopped berating me, I apologized, rattling on about Hudson's arrival, the gloomy decorating habits of Jennifer Coogan's parents, Amanda's conviction that Jennifer's boyfriend had been murdered by the same killer, the makeshift memorial site where Jennifer washed ashore, the Hobbit and the Giant as possible suspects, the surreal connection to Jack, his drunk presence at my house. It all seemed ludicrous in the pale light of dawn, now trying to get in through the dirty picture window that looked out on the parking lot.

'I need to tell you something about Jack Smith,' Lyle said when I finished. 'My friend at *Texas Monthly*'s back. He'd never heard of a Jack Smith, so he checked it out. An IT intern was bribed to set up a voicemail and email for Smith. A kid from Princeton. You think he'd know better.' Princeton. Jack's supposed alma mater.

'Tommie, you need to stay away from that guy. Seriously think about taking Sadie and Maddie and going somewhere. The next step needs to involve the police.'

'I'll talk to Hudson about it,' I said noncommittally.

'Good. One more thing. Did you happen to read about Barbara Monroe?'

It took a sleepy second to jog my memory. Barbara Monroe, previously known as Barbara Thurman, star reporter. It seemed like years since I'd talked to her about Adriana's kidnapping.

'Someone broke into her house. The *Chicago Tribune* ran the story this morning.'

'What happened?'

'They are using it as the centerpiece on the *Tribune* home page. It would have been a Metro brief but a rescue dog bit a chunk out of the intruder and saved the day. Readers love that kind of thing.' This last part came out a little annoyed.

'Let me call you back, Lyle. No, really, I promise.'

I clicked off before he could start up with the yelling again.

My laptop was still in my backpack. I pulled it out, flipped it open, and sat cross-legged on the bed while the living, breathing lump beside me didn't budge. The wireless internet connection worked right away, a freak gift courtesy of the Charles Wesley Motor Lodge across the road, which boasted such amenities.

RESCUE DOG RESCUES RIGHT BACK, the headline read, over a picture of a familiar grinning black dog with a white megaphone cuff around his neck and a new patch taped over one eye. The story, posted two hours and twenty-three minutes ago, had 400,342 hits.

The *Tribune* photographer made the heroic effort to take Cricket's best side, without any scabs showing. The night before last, a man in a navy ski mask entered the Monroe house, apparently expecting it to be empty. But one of Barbara's daughters was home alone, heard a noise, and wandered out of her bedroom, where she had been studying. The intruder grabbed her and Cricket went wild, banging against his crate door in the kitchen until it fell off the hinges. Cricket bit a chunk out of the guy, which was being tested for DNA.

I scrolled down more, skimming quickly. One of Cricket's eyes was damaged. He might lose some sight. The police believed it to be a random break-in.

The story finished with Cricket's sad history of disease and abuse at the hands of a previous owner, his rescue by the SPCA, and the numbers and addresses of three of Chicago's primary animal shelters.

Good for Cricket. Hundreds of people would scurry to the shelters this weekend to save lives on doggy death row. Unfortunately, a third of them would return the dogs two weeks later after deciding that their cute fuzzy faces weren't worth all the poop and pee, that actual work was involved to love something that was damaged.

I punched my cell phone.

'Lyle?'

'I was sleeping.'

'I told you I was calling back.'

He grunted sarcastically.

'Do you think I'm the reason Barbara's house got hit? That they're looking for something?'

'Maybe. I went over those Bennett crime scene pictures again. We've still been unable to trace the sender. Can you call up the slide show wherever the hell you are?'

I clicked on the icon reluctantly. I didn't really want to ever see these bloody images again.

'You got it up, Tommie? Are you there?'

'Yes. To both.'

'A source of mine faxed the crime scene and coroner reports on all six of the victims. Here's something surprising: The FBI woman and Fred Bennett weren't shot. The woman was hit in the head and strangled. The father was beaten with, and I quote, "a narrow lead object, probably a pipe."'

'Why wasn't this reported?'

'According to my friend, cause of death was inked out in the reports handed out to the press. He had to really dig for the original reports.'

'Who is your friend?'

Lyle acted as if he hadn't heard me. 'This couldn't have been a one-man job. Really look at the pictures. Fred Bennett didn't go down easily or quietly. The wife, the kids, would have jumped out a window while that was going down. There were at least two attackers. I think one man took out the FBI agent in the laundry room while she was pulling out a load of clothes. Then he moved on to the father, in the kitchen. The rest of the family was attacked simultaneously at the back of the house *by someone else.*'

'The kids and the mother were killed by a Sig semi-automatic.' It was a detail I remembered from one of the *Chicago Tribune* clips. 'It was left at the scene.'

'As far as I can tell, that's true,' Lyle said. 'But there were *three* different methods of killing. There's a psychotic quality to this. Like a Coen Brothers movie. A thrill kill.'

I wasn't even really sure why any of this mattered. So what if Anthony Marchetti had an accomplice?

'This wasn't Marchetti's style,' Lyle insisted, determined to make his point. 'There's nothing in his history about killing women and kids. This job was inefficient. Messy. Beneath him.'

'Damning with faint praise,' I said softly. 'But thanks.' I understood now. Lyle believed that Anthony Marchetti was my father. He was trying to make it as OK as it could be.

After we hung up, I stared at the photograph of the blood-spattered kitchen. Fred Bennett had been preparing a bedtime snack for his kids. An attempt to make their uprooted lives in a safe house feel a little normal? Did he pretend that they were on a big adventure? Or did he tell them the truth?

Plastic bowls with cartoon figures were lined up on the kitchen counter. Three glasses stood untouched, in a neat row, poured to the brim with juice. The popcorn, though, was everywhere. On the floor, on the counters, some of it dyed red like for a Christmas tree chain. The white cabinets slashed with blood.

A Jackson Pollock canvas.

A Coen Brothers movie.

I said their names softly.

Alyssa. Robert. Joe.

My breath grew more shallow, a rope of dread spinning tight around my chest.

Focus. Don't give in.

I drew my knees up, settling my eyes on one of the printed cupcakes running down my pajama legs.

Pink frosting, lots of sprinkles.

Imagine something happy.

The taste of tart strawberry icing, a table piled with presents, a balloon floating away.

Suffocating to death on this hard, filthy floor.

All the oxygen in the room was suddenly gone, as if someone had shut off a valve.

And then, nothing.

Twenty minutes later, I found myself shivering on the bathroom floor.

CHAPTER 27

The next morning, for a crisp hundred-dollar bill, Hudson talked the man behind the motel desk at the Charles Wesley Lodge into returning my rental car to a branch in Durant so we could ride home together in his company-owned, late-model black Ford F-350 with a high-end blinking GPS device wired to God knows how many satellites roving above our heads.

It was custom-built into the dash with an oversized screen and so many buttons and lights that I wondered if it also had the capabilities to shoot lasers and grill a hot dog. The tinted windows, Hudson told me, were bulletproof and the outside was armor-plated. The truck was a loaner, headed for Afghanistan in a month. As soon as we sped by the Idabel city limits sign, I closed my eyes and tucked myself into a corner of the passenger seat with a pillow I'd spied in a plastic bag under the truck bed cover, neatly stacked beside a built-in firearms safe and a first-aid kit.

But Hudson had other ideas. Like a conversation.

'You recognized those two men in the photo at the sheriff's office.' It wasn't a question.

'Not exactly. Jack mentioned them. At least I think he did.'

'Jack.'

'Yes, Jack. Before he passed out on my kitchen floor, he mumbled something about a hobbit and a giant. And Anthony Marchetti being a liar. The men in that picture fit the bill.'

'I can't believe you went back to the house.'

I ignored his anger. 'The Jeep was parked out front. Packed with documents. Lots about Marchetti. I found a picture of me in one of the folders from when I was still competing. Jack was too drunk to explain. You're swerving.'

'You went in alone.'

'I think you're missing the point.'

'According to you, I usually do.'

He stuck the cord of an iPod into an auxiliary plug, adjusted earbuds, and turned his attention to the road. It struck me that we were not a very good team. I wadded myself back into the corner and shut my eyes again.

Almost immediately, my cell phone sang out from the depths of my backpack. I pulled it out on the fourth ring. Private caller.

'Hello?' I asked hopefully. I'd left the phone on because I didn't want to miss a call from Sadie. Hudson had wanted me to shut it off, worried that it could be tracked.

'I thought you were strung up somewhere! Like,

dead.' I held the phone tightly against my ear so Hudson couldn't listen in on Charla's wailing. I shouldn't have worried; his iPod was turned up so loud that I could hear Johnny Cash walking the line.

'No,' I told Charla. 'Not strung up.' Not yet.

'It's an emergency. *An emergency.* Your dad wants you to come to see him tomorrow during visiting hours. My lawyer called to say an anonymous donor is going to put ten thousand in my defense fund if I cooperate. If you don't come, it will be *big* trouble for me.'

When did I become responsible for the fate of this squeaky death row inmate who had me on speed-dial?

I tried to speak calmly. 'That's not going to happen.'

'What? The trouble? I'm damn sure it is if you don't show up.'

'*I'm not coming.*' My tone was not to be reckoned with. I didn't care what Anthony Marchetti had to say, I would never believe a word of it. I glanced at Hudson. His head was bopping, eyes on the road.

'I'm supposed to tell you that you were lucky in Chicago,' Charla whined. 'That you won't be so lucky again.'

'Is that a threat?'

'No. Supposably, it's a fact.' The word *supposably* always set my teeth on edge. It was a Texas colloquialism used by a quarter of the state. It's probably in the dictionary now a few skips ahead of Sarah Palin's *refudiate*.

'Are you listening to me? He says to tell you they're following you all the time, even if you can't see them. He says to trust *no one*.'

'I got that loud and clear the last time you called.'

I couldn't help but glance over my shoulder at the rear window. Summer wheat grass rippled on either side of a retreating ribbon of black highway, empty except for a rusted green pickup on the verge of passing us. I really ought to be driving. That pickup should not be taking us down.

I returned to Charla. 'Are they threatening you?'

'Are you not hearing me? Lordy. Although the guard who's my contact is not bad. He drops good stuff on me. Like a box of Whitman's Samplers and that Dove lotion that turns you tan real gradual so nobody knows it's fake. People just say you look healthy.'

Exasperated, I tried to get her back on point. 'You know that if you take money, you are theirs forever. Did you ever wonder why Marchetti chose you? Because the guards think you are susceptible. I am probably not the last assignment they have in mind for you.'

'Mmmmhhmmmm,' Charla said, noncommittally. 'I don't know what septi-whatever means. Here comes my keeper. I don't want to scare you or nothing. At this point, you're like my dear third cousin and I'm thinking you'd be a good character witness for me at my appeal. But I'm supposed to tell you one last thing.' I heard the muffled sound of voices before she came back on the line.

'You're currently ten or so miles outside of Melissa, Texas. Going about fifty-five. Why so slow?' Then, wistfully, 'I wonder who Melissa was. I bet she was pretty. A natural blonde. She was probably so beautiful that her Daddy named a town after her. I wished my Daddy had named a town after me. Instead, he was just a shitty, lying drunk.'

A slight commotion, and then a click.

'Who was that?' Hudson asked, a full ten minutes after I hung up.

I debated where to start. Maybe with the truth.

'Charla Polaski.'

Hudson turned his head sharply.

'The woman on death row who shot off her husband's genitals in a middle-school shower?' Was everyone in my life a virtual Wikipedia of crime information?

'The one and only. Currently in the same prison as Anthony Marchetti. She's been turned into a messenger. Calling me. I figure Marchetti is bribing the guards to make it happen.' I hesitated. 'There's a tracer on this car or those guys behind us aren't on our side because she just told me our exact location.'

'Or they tracked us by the signal in your damn phone, which you left on even though I asked you *nicely* not to.'

'Well, there's that possibility, too.'

'How many times has she called?'

'Three in the last seven days if you don't count the ten times I didn't answer.' I was making this sound perfectly logical, the sudden liaison of a Texas murderess and a Chicago mobster legend with me, the magnet in the middle. 'Charla says Marchetti wants me to come see him tomorrow during visiting hours.'

I stole a look at Hudson's face. Redder. About five or so on the volcano scale.

'I'll go,' he said stiffly. 'You won't.'

'I think she needs protection.' I didn't mention that he'd announced last night that he was done with me. 'Maybe to be moved to another facility. Also—'

'I can't even express how angry I am with you.'

'She told me to trust no one.'

'Hell, you didn't need her to tell you that. You've been operating that way for years.'

'Hudson . . .'

'Just shut up and turn off that phone,' he said, his eyes on our tail in the rear-view mirror. 'I need to think.'

When I was small, I pictured God sticking His finger down through the clouds into the dust of the earth and drawing all the roads in lines and loops, circles and zigzags, so that we could go wherever we wanted but always end up back in the same place.

I never expected Tuck to die violently on one of those roads while I slept on my favorite pony sheets. Tuck left and I never got to say goodbye and the little girl in me won't forgive God for not bringing him home.

I never knew Roxy Martin in life, but it was her car wreck on a moonless Wyoming night twenty-two years after Tuck's death that gave birth to the panic attacks buried inside me.

I was only a hundred yards away shortly after Roxy's spirit abandoned her body in the ravine. I felt a connection, as if she'd swept by and tried to help me catch my breath before she flew off for good. Sometimes I imagine she still visits me, her ghost as gauzy as the dress she died in. Tuck visits, too, but his energy is dense and thick, like the air before a thunderstorm.

For a week after Roxy's death, I became her primary voyeur. I walked in a dream through my job at Halo Ranch and devoured every newspaper article about the investigation into the crash, every word of her obituary. She was the best setter on her high school volleyball team, a part-time worker at Burger King, her single mother's best friend. Ordinary and not, like most of us.

I attended her funeral even though she was a complete stranger, even though the thought of a funeral overwhelms me with dread, like when the bar clamps down before the roller coaster takes off.

I knew, of course, that Roxy broke something

loose in me, that my brief obsession with her was rooted in pent-up grief for my brother, who died the same way, a teenager on a night of celebration.

My larger fixation with death is more complicated. The therapist in my head says it is because I was left alone with Tuck's closed casket when I was six and looked inside.

I don't know why I am thinking about this now, in the middle of Texas nowhere, whizzing by fields fried gold by the heat, as Hudson gives me the silent treatment.

Granny would call it a premonition.

I had my finger poised to power off my phone when it began to vibrate.

Private caller. *Please, not Charla.*

One press of a button, and my world hurtled out of control again.

Sadie's voice. Two words, the last ones I expected.

'Mama's dead.'

The next twenty-four hours were a blur of tears, anger, denial, and the tedious business of death.

I learned that Hudson was, in fact, extremely good at speeding. It turns out that his team in Afghanistan drove a 'controlled' hundred miles an hour everywhere they went to avoid getting ambushed. With warning lights flashing and the speedometer pushing ninety, he scooted every vehicle to the side of the road like an obedient row of ants. He stopped only when we reached the hospital, where Sadie and I sat numbly in the office of a suited nerd who'd been through this routine way too many times to still successfully fake sympathy. I almost appreciated that.

Would we like Mama to stay in a comfort room in the hospital morgue for the night (translation, on a steel table covered with a sheet) or had we already picked a funeral home?

He shoved a permission form across the desk. The hospital sometimes conducted autopsies in cases like this when the cause of death was uncertain. Would we please sign off? The hospital would pay, of course, although it could take up to a month for the results from UT Southwestern. I tried to turn off the mental picture of medical students cutting away on our mother, trading sick jokes to make it seem like a less awful way to learn.

'It's not *CSI*, where cases are solved in forty-five minutes,' the administrator said, a line he probably used five times a week.

My head throbbed under the fluorescent lights. I let my attention wander to his name tag. 'Martin Van Buren, senior afterlife counselor,' a title surely tried out first on some stupid focus group.

I'd bet Mr Van Buren was one of the last kids picked for games in elementary school and things hadn't improved much for him since. His dark suit hung on a thin frame that held no hint of muscle. Fuzzy red hair sprouted out of his balding head. He wore smudged wire-frame glasses. No wedding ring. A brutal analysis, but I needed a target for my anger.

'How did this happen?' I demanded, making him jump. 'Who had access to her room? To her IV?'

My fury bounced off. I would have to do better than that to ruffle Mr Van Buren, whose plaque on the wall boasted fifteen years of counseling to unreasonable, grief-stricken customers like me.

In a practiced gesture, he took one hand and flipped out his polyester tie, a colorful bouquet of hot air balloons.

'Ma'am, you will need to speak to the authorities about that. The hospital is not admitting to any fault or culpability. Her doctor believes she suffered a stroke, a risk of one of her medications. The autopsy is just a matter of routine.'

A visibly upset Sadie put her hand on my knee. 'Tommie – let's talk in the hall for a second.

'Don't do this, please,' she pleaded, outside the door. Thirty feet away, Hudson and two of his bodyguard friends stood like gladiators in a protective semicircle around a teary Maddie. Our cousin Nanette had brought her back from Marfa an hour ago.

'Mama's dead, Tommie. Let's bury her peacefully. Send her off with good karma.'

'Good karma?' I looked at her in disbelief. 'This isn't about karma. This is about what's *real*. About whether our mother was murdered.' I spit out this last part as quietly as I could, but Maddie captured the tone and planted her face in her protector's chest, a man with the ridiculous name of Bat whom we hadn't even known yesterday.

I couldn't stop myself, hurtful words rolling out of my mouth way too easily. 'Why do you just accept things as fate?' And then, with a disgust that surprised me: 'Grow up, Sadie.'

From the corner of my eye, I watched Hudson urge Maddie and the rest of the group down the hall, away from my explosion, a good decision because Sadie immediately fired back with dead-on arrows. She'd always been a good shot.

'You're kidding, right? Look at yourself, Tommie. You rescue those kids. But you won't lift a finger to rescue yourself. Your personal life is a sea of denial. Maybe you're not dependent on alcohol now, but if you keep going this way, in ten years you will be. And where's a lasting relationship? For that matter, where's mine?'

I started to interject, but Sadie was just warming up.

'Did you really just figure out now that our childhood was a little odd? That Mama was depressed? That Daddy wanted a better marriage than he got? That we lived in a state of paranoia? How many grandfathers do you know who place their elementary school granddaughters in the trunks of their cars, close the lids, and tell them to kick out the taillights while lying there in the dark, then wave their hands out of the holes like a white flag? Remember how Daddy used to make us get in on the passenger side of our car

342

in a parking lot if a van had parked next to the driver's side? You know, a safety precaution so the bad guys couldn't toss us in.'

Her voice had begun to shake. 'I still do that with Maddie today even though he always said it was a game. *A game!*'

The tiny white cross on her forehead, usually invisible, flared red, a warning sign to anyone who knew my sister well. The scar resulted from Sadie refusing to wear a seatbelt on the way home from a dance lesson. Almost as soon as Mama hit the gas, a car pulled out in front of us and Sadie hit the dashboard.

When Sadie arrived home with a pink balloon and a neat cross of black stitches on her forehead, Granny said that it was a sign that God had personally stamped Sadie with the Gift. Mama had disappeared for the rest of the night.

Mr Van Buren poked his head out the door. 'Ladies? It's closing in on five p.m. Decisions should be made.'

I swallowed hard. My anger was about something else entirely. The person I wanted to talk to most in the world, who could shed light into all the dark places, was gone, forever. No more living with the hope of a new drug or the fantasy that Mama would just snap out of it.

No more music.

'We're ready,' I told Van Buren.

Sadie, surprised, raised her eyes. Her face was splotchy and pale.

'You're right,' I said quietly, squeezing her hand. 'You're right about everything. We need to say goodbye to Mama. I'll leave it alone. Turn it over to the police.' I didn't know yet if this was a lie.

Sadie and I had survived bitter fights like this as teenagers because every hormonal word we spoke melted away by morning. But I couldn't count on that now. I couldn't be sure of anything, except that I couldn't lose Sadie, too.

CHAPTER 28

I sat alone on the front porch swing at the ranch, lulled by the gentle clanking sounds of dishes being washed by hand. Three former high school basketball teammates I'd barely seen in the last ten years carried on an easy conversation about their kids that floated out the cranked-out kitchen window, over the stretch of burned-out lawn and into a fiery summer sunset.

They'd shown up every morning for the last three days with something in their hands. One of them had even paid the grave-digger, driving the money I gave her to the old frame house over the tracks where Ronald 'Gippy' Gillespie had lived with his mother since dropping out of Ponder High School's special ed classes. Gippy's mother, a horse-faced woman who preferred flowered sundresses, took care of the financial end. She stopped playing online poker only long enough to collect it, and you usually had to knock five minutes before she'd open the door. A crude system, but in Ponder it worked.

Ingrid McCloud was a name in the small towns around Ponder, so there was a good turnout. She taught piano. She slipped people cash when they were hard up. She and Daddy owned a hell of a lot of land.

Lyle wore the first collared shirt and tie I'd ever seen on him. Wade wandered the background in boots and a vintage jacket with western lapels, attending to pallbearers and a thousand other details. Sweet old ladies patted our hands and told us the funeral went 'real fine.' That Lonnie Harbin had done a terrific job with Mama's hair, which had always been so beautiful.

They gossiped, of course, but well out of our earshot. How could they not? At this point every person in town had heard wild tales about Mama's last strange days, and the First Baptist Church of Ponder literally rolled out a red carpet for the gawkers, possible souls to save.

W. A. Masters, Mama's counsel for thirty years, took a day off from lawyering to deliver a eulogy to a house packed to the rafters of the balcony. The only other time I'd seen the church that full was on Christmas Eve, with the lights out, everybody holding a candle sparked by a single flame.

W.A.'s eulogy made me weep and laugh, but later I couldn't remember a single word of it. He finished by reciting an Emily Dickinson poem Mama loved, threaded with exquisite pain, although W.A.'s twang made it bearable.

Last night, Hudson showed up at the visitation dressed in a beautiful black suit, a modern knight.

He told me that the nursing staff swore up and down that no one had entered Mama's room but hospital personnel.

'My guys are on the case,' he had told me, lowering his voice. 'Contacting FBI sources. Tracing Smith. Trying to figure out . . . with your mother's death . . . if this is over.'

I had nodded and continued shaking hands, carrying on my hosting obligations well away from the casket, trying to avoid the sliver of Mama's face, like the top of a white mask. Trying to reconcile an electric buzz for Hudson with my grief and numbness and duty.

I stared out now from my perch on the swing to the orange horizon casting its glow over our land. I could hear one of my friends in the kitchen asking someone for one of the casserole recipes.

The sun was slipping down, closing out this awful day.

My mind was spinning back.

To another shiny coffin.

When I ventured into the house, only a few stragglers remained, most of them strangers to each other, hanging out in the sprawling living room in that twilight moment before anyone thinks to turn on the lights.

Despite his rotten father, cousin Bobby of the tall tales had grown up into a decent, hardworking truck driver with two kids and a sweet-faced wife who'd brought a large pot of homemade chicken and noodles that she sat in her lap for the hour and a half drive it took to get here.

'Bobby, honey, we should head out to the Best Western soon and put the kids to bed,' she said while her hands scooped up used paper plates and cups scattered around the room.

At the visitation, it took several seconds for me to recognize Bobby White when he arrived with his small parade. We'd lost touch years ago when he'd moved to a town ninety miles east.

'Your ma was always real nice to me,' he said, ambling over with his cowboy hat in hand, after a moment with his head bowed at the casket. 'She used to write me a note on the first of every month, like clockwork, with a ten-dollar bill inside. I saved for the glove that I used for years, even at the state 2A championship. It always brought me luck. She was about the only person to make a point to compliment me on a regular basis.'

He grinned. 'I know I was ornery.'

He shifted his feet, probably composing what he wanted to say next. His physical awkwardness in that moment took me back to one of the purest athletic sights I'd ever seen, of Bobby flying through our fields. Granny told Sadie and me he was running off his demons.

'She was the best person I ever knew,' he said, patting my shoulder awkwardly. 'Once, she gave me a lecture on Daddy and adversity. Said I could either let it break me or turn me strong. She said there was no other person on earth more proud of me than my Daddy but that he couldn't show it.'

I had a sudden picture of that boy berated and humiliated on the pitcher's mound by the man who was supposed to support him most. I fought back emotion, unprepared for Bobby White tearing into my armor today the way no one else had.

'Does your son play sports?' I asked, wiping my eyes. 'Maybe I could drive out to a game sometime.'

'Naw.' He shook his head. 'I don't make him. He likes to paint. He's real good at it.'

I thought about those words now as I saw Bobby stretched back on our old couch, his youngest son, Nate, spread-eagle on top of him, asleep, mouth open, as if there were no safer place on earth.

Bobby had flinched every time his father walked in a room.

'Here.' Sadie jarred me back to the present. 'Drink this.' She touched my bare arm with a sweaty, chilled can of Coke. 'You look like you're about to pass out.'

Sadie gestured behind me, toward the door.

'There's a man here to see you. Says he used to work on the ranch for Daddy and Mama. I don't remember him.' She waved and smiled to a group making their exit before turning back to me. 'After that, when people clear out, W.A. wants to give us the gist of Mama's will. He says there's a surprise. Like we need another surprise.'

She rolled her eyes and chugged wine from a plastic cup. She had tapped it directly from the spout of a box of Franzia Cabernet on the kitchen counter, dropped off anonymously on our doorstep last night along with three cases of Bud Light, a common gesture of sympathy here in Ponder.

'Where's Maddie?' I asked.

'Back at our place, trying to beat Bat at a game of chess.' Bat, Hudson's friend who'd been at the hospital. Someone with a gun.

'Do you think that Mama's dying is the end of this mess?' Sadie asked me.

'Maybe.' I stared at the man moving confidently toward us. Dark suit. Official.

'That's him. The guy who said he worked for Daddy. Kind of hard to picture him getting his hands dirty. Have a good chat.' Sadie slid back into the crowd.

It took a couple of beats to recognize him. He was older, heavier, a solid block of muscle with an overlay of fat from sitting behind a desk.

Federal marshal Angel Martinez, former agent of WITSEC.

The 'migrant worker' who protected Mama that long-ago summer. Who flirted with her a little too much when Daddy wasn't around. My crush.

Another liar.

He put his hand out genially. 'Tommie, I'm not sure you'll remember—'

'I remember,' I interrupted. 'The jack of clubs. Deceit.'

'What?'

'You showed up in Granny's cards.' I knew that

I wasn't making sense to him, but I didn't care. 'You lied to me. All of you lied to me. I need to know why. Right now.'

My voice traveled up, enough that Sadie turned her head sharply across the room.

'I'm not here in an official capacity,' Martinez said. 'I came to express my condolences.'

'Tell me why,' I insisted, shaking off his grip on my elbow.

'Tommie, there's no reason to dredge it up. Let it go with your mother. I didn't know everything myself. I was just brought in to do a job.'

'You liked my mother so much all those years ago that you showed up at her funeral.' My voice was ugly with sarcasm.

'Yes. Also out of respect for your grandfather, who trained me.'

I opened my mouth, then closed it, hearing Granny's warning.

The jack of clubs.

'You know more than you're saying.' I kept my voice steady. 'I don't think my family is safe. Can your marshals offer us protection?'

'I'm sorry. I'm no longer involved.'

'So that's a no.'

'There's no reason—'

'For you to be here,' I finished. 'Show yourself out, Agent Martinez.'

I sat, spent, in one of the rawhide easy chairs facing the fieldstone fireplace. The living room that once hosted our birthday parties and Christmas mornings felt as if its soul had drained away.

Sadie lit the kerosene lamp on top of the mantel while W.A. got papers together in the other room. Then she poured out three glasses of Merlot from a good bottle someone working in the kitchen tonight had thoughtfully tucked away for us.

My eyes were drawn to the flame.

I saw Tuck's face.

It was my fault.

I had faked a sore throat to get out of school that day.

Because of my lie, Mama and Granny took me with them to the funeral home before visitation to write down the names on the cards pinned to the floral arrangements. I sat in a corner, cross-legged, forgotten. The casket was closed and would stay that way.

When they slipped out without me, I stood up, running my hand over the shellacked, gleaming maple box. In that instant, I realized Tuck wasn't dead. That it was all a big mistake.

And I'd prove it.

I pushed up on the top half of the coffin lid as hard as I could. It didn't budge. Determined, I dug my heels into the carpet and tried again. On the fourth try, I raised the coffin lid for six inches before losing my grip. It slammed shut with a deafening bang that brought Granny and Mama running. Granny said it was a miracle of God that

I'd pulled my small fingers out of the way before they were crushed.

What I found inside that casket would layer the fabric of my dreams.

Rivers of white gauze wrapped around and around Tuck's head like a mummy, smothering him, covering his burns. A baseball in his left hand. His baseball jersey, red and gold. I knew that a black 9 on his back was pressed into the white satin.

Mama and Granny carried me out of the funeral home screaming that he couldn't breathe.

Tuck couldn't breathe.

'Tommie.'

Thank God for Sadie's voice, always bringing me back.

My gaze moved from the lamp to my sister. She gestured to W.A., who was spreading documents on the oak coffee table. I had to return Tuck to his black coffin.

I vaguely wondered if it was true that W.A. shot the rattle-snakes whose skin graced his briefcase, if we'd eaten some of the insides of those nasty reptiles years ago at his legendary rattlesnake fries. It had tasted like tough chicken.

'First, each of you gets a letter from your mother,' he said, sounding officious, unlike himself. 'They were sealed when I got them. I suggest you read them in private, when you can take some time.'

He handed each of us a vanilla-colored envelope. Our first and middle names were scrawled across the front. *Tommie Anne. Sadie Louisa.* An unbroken wax seal on the back. I thought of the pink envelope from Rosalina, the piece of paper that had ignited everything.

'Second, I'd like to do a brief overview of the will. I'll be direct. You girls get the ranch and every inch of the land, about five thousand acres, most of which includes the oil and gas rights. In addition, there's about forty million dollars in the investment portfolio.'

He waited a second for this to sink in, but neither Sadie nor I cared much about money, maybe because we always knew it was there. Daddy had been open about our inheritance and how he expected us to handle it. Spend a little, give a lot.

W.A., a man who had defended murderers, drummed his fingers nervously on the arm of his chair.

Here it comes, I thought.

'The money in your parents' investment portfolio will be divided into thirds,' W.A. said. 'One third to Sadie, one third to Tommie. The other third goes into a trust to be divided between two undisclosed heirs.'

'I don't understand.' Confusion flickered over Sadie's face. I said nothing.

'I sure as hell don't, either.' W.A. unwrapped a cigar from his pocket, more relaxed now that he'd delivered the news. 'Your Mama and Daddy created an elaborate financial labyrinth with a financial adviser in New York. Didn't include me.'

He snapped open a silver lighter. 'I'm not saying it's a code that can't be cracked. I just don't think they wanted you to.' Three perfect smoke circles rose in the air between us, a magic act that used to delight us as kids. 'She slipped once, though. Later on, when she wasn't quite right. Indicated the heirs are children. Under eighteen.'

'That's interesting,' I said. *Just go,* I screamed silently.

'I asked her once, if she was so intent on being secret about it, why she just didn't give the money away privately before her death so you girls wouldn't have to know,' W.A. continued. 'She thought that would be deceptive. She said you girls wouldn't care about the money.'

I laughed at this, an artificial sound in the room that once echoed with Mama's music.

You were right about one thing, Mama. It's not about money.

Hours ago, as they lowered her body into the red sandy earth, I'd been in the process of forgiving her.

That was my mistake.

CHAPTER 29

While W.A. roared his old white Cadillac to life outside, Sadie blew out the kerosene lamp and we headed into the kitchen with the dirty wineglasses. It was better in here. The low light over the sink was on, casting friendly light. The room had been whipped into perfect order, with damp dishtowels hanging neatly on Mama's wooden towel rack, and foil-wrapped cookies and half-eaten cakes lining the long table.

'Whoa,' Sadie said, peering inside the refrigerator, crammed with Tupperware, Cool Whip fruit salads, and King Ranch casseroles. 'Take me home and let's deal with this tomorrow. Or never.'

Ten minutes later, I dropped Sadie in front of the trailer, armed with a slab of Marjory Adams's double fudge cake and a generous serving of Waynette Sanders's homemade macaroni and cheese, very specific requests from a text sent by Maddie.

Hudson appeared under her porch light as I started to pull out, tie loose and hanging around his neck, dress shirt wrinkled and untucked, a relaxed smile on his face. So this is where he'd disappeared to. To keep an eye on Maddie.

I waited with the engine running while he walked over.

'Scoot,' he said, opening my door and throwing his jacket across the bench seat. 'I'm driving. I left my truck at the barn.'

I thought about protesting, my conditioned response to Hudson. I thought about asking why his truck was at the barn. Instead, I scooted.

'Are you going to forgive me?' I asked, my eyes straight ahead, following the headlights as they illuminated the deep tire treads in the dirt road.

'Probably,' he said.

I hadn't really cried all day. Not like this. Embarrassing, hiccupy gasps. Hudson yanked the truck over to the side of the road and held on to me while I let out grief and fear and an unfortunate amount of snot.

'She's gone, and I don't even know who I am,' I said, sobbing.

Hudson pulled back, tilting up my chin.

'I know who you are. You're this scar.' He touched my wrist. 'And this one.' He stroked the hair at my temple. 'You're kind. Beautiful. Brave. You save children.'

The hug rolled into something carnal and primitive, nothing but sensation, hands and mouths roving, neither of us able to get enough fast enough.

'Wait,' he said thickly. He pulled off the brake

357

and hit the gas but I couldn't stop touching him and he couldn't stop kissing me and it was a bumpy, chaotic ride until he turned off on one of the flattened grass four-wheeler paths to the pond.

If predators of any kind waited for us in the dark, so be it.

Dying right now in Hudson's arms, without the answers, in the fields where I grew up, would be OK.

This is what always happened when I surrendered my body to Hudson. Every brain cell was suddenly drunk. I stood blithely on the edge of a cliff, hoping it wouldn't hurt too much when I fell but 100 percent sure that it would.

We only made it about a third of the way to the pond before Hudson turned the truck crookedly into the field, jamming on the brake. He pushed me flat against the back of the seat, and I knew from experience that he had the bad end of this deal.

'Ow,' he said, backing into the steering wheel. 'I'm a little out of practice. In a pickup.'

'You had to add that last part.' For a second I wondered about all the women he made love to after I let him go, if it was like this, fierce and fast, all-consuming, so intimate it hurt.

My black nylon funeral dress was somewhere up around my waist, his hands busy, warm, stripping off my underwear, losing them on the floor. I'd done my part on the drive over, unzipping his pants, pulling at his new shirt until buttons clicked off the dashboard. This was only going to end one way.

Hudson paused to kick open his door, letting in the dense, hot perfume of our land and the ghosts of my past summers. I adjusted my body underneath him. 'Is that better?'

'Much better.' Hudson leaned in and pushed back my hair, damp with sweat and tears.

'I've heard about you McCloud girls. Isn't now when I'm supposed to ask if you want me to stop?'

'Shut up,' I answered, and for a little while everything bad disappeared.

'Who's still here?' Hudson asked, stopping short of the drive.

I lifted my head from his shoulder, groggy, sated, ready to collapse in my bed.

Through the windows of the darkened living room, shadow and light played a spooky game. A steady pulse, a single, timed beat between each movement like a blinking traffic light.

Light, dark.

Light, dark.

'No one,' I said. 'Everybody should be gone.'

'Stay here,' he said brusquely, and I nodded, my heart knocking.

Hudson, already halfway up the walk, had entered another zone and I wasn't invited.

I pulled the keys out of the ignition and threw open the pickup door, careful not to slam it behind me.

'Wait!' I whispered loudly, running up the walk in my bare feet.

'This one,' I said, one key poking out from the jumble on a tarnished key ring that declared me 'World's Best Aunt.'

Hudson motioned me to back up and in one smooth gesture slipped in the key, pushed open the door. He took three cautious steps inside the entryway.

'What the hell?' he muttered. I slipped beside him.

Hudson's gun pointed at a motionless form slumped in my father's chair. Two framed landscapes were lying on the floor. We had stepped into the path of an eerie slide show projected on the wall behind us. Oversized, out-of-focus images stained our clothes and our faces with flickering light.

I'd seen these pictures of Fred Bennett and his murdered family enough for twenty lifetimes.

A gray blur hovered on my black dress and up my arm. Part of the image on the wall.

The dead little girl's face or a doll or the pattern in a couch. I slapped at it like a terrible insect I had to get off. My eyes frantically scanned for a projector and settled on a laptop computer propped up on a stack of books.

I moved farther into the room, away from the wall. The man in the chair dangled an empty bottle from one hand. I didn't think a dead person could dangle. He lifted his other arm and pointed to the photograph on the wall. A bloody kitchen countertop.

'Get back, Tommie,' Hudson said. 'Now.'

'It's Jack,' I said softly, moving toward the chair.

No visible weapon. I knelt beside him. Something was horribly wrong.

'Jack, this is my friend Hudson. He isn't going to hurt you. Let's turn this off and we can talk.' No response. I shook Jack by the shoulder, and Hudson took three steps closer, his weapon aimed at Jack's head.

Jack had deteriorated. He smelled rancid. Stubble grew out of his chin. His hair, usually so perfect, was oily, wild.

'How many glasses do you count up there?' Jack asked. He didn't appear to care whether Hudson shot him or not.

I glanced up against my will.

'Three,' I said.

'Good girl,' Jack mumbled. 'Smart girl.'

The bottle in his hand was one of those over-priced fancy designer waters. Not whiskey.

Not drunk.

Jack pressed the remote, sweeping us into the tornado after a child's bath. Wet towels on the floor, the cap off the toothpaste, a pile of dirty clothes in the corner.

He fast-forwarded. Images, melting into each other. 'Here it is,' he said.

It was like someone had dumped a can of red paint in the open dishwasher. Fred Bennett's blood. His body, slumped on the floor.

Jack wasn't interested in the blood or the body.

He zeroed in, blowing up the focus on the refrigerator and a two-door cabinet above it.

One of the cabinet doors hung open.

Jack stumbled over to the wall, Hudson's gun tracking him. Jack's shadow loomed across the image, the dates from a calendar on the refrigerator reflected on his forehead like a tattoo.

'See that little white thing right there inside the cabinet? That's my foot.'

I didn't process it right away. All of the Bennett children *had died*. Hadn't they?

I moved toward Jack and he staggered toward me, grabbing my hair, his whiskey breath heating my face.

'Shhhhhhh,' he said, his eyes empty, one finger in front of his lips, the other hand gripping my hair and pulling me close. The stubble on his chin scratched my cheek.

'Play dead. Do you hear me?'

He twisted my hair harder when I didn't reply.

'My brother told me to do that. He told me to play dead when the Hobbit came to our window. He saved me.' He scrunched up his face.

'It's OK, Hudson,' I said. 'Put the gun down. I've got this.'

'Please don't be mad,' Jack pleaded. 'He shot us. My bubby wouldn't wake up. I had to find Daddy. As soon as Daddy saw me, he stuck me in the cabinet. "Shhhh," he said. "Keep the door closed." But I couldn't. I was afraid of the dark. I saw the Giant come out of the living room with a big stick. I thought Daddy would win. Good guys *win*.'

Three children. Two died. One lived. A cabinet door cracked open three inches, not one, not two, meant a lifetime of Jack playing and replaying the murder of his father like a bloody video game in his head.

A part of me was enraged by this man in front of me. But this wasn't a man. This was a bewildered child.

'The Hobbit is at the window.' Jack stared frantically at the shut blinds across the room, his mouth an open circle, an expression of pure terror on his face. Maddie's face as a toddler, before a shot needle punctured her skin.

The silent scream, I called it.

The silence before a terrible wail.

When it came, I wondered whether Jack or the house would implode first.

Wait, I urged myself. *Let it go. He needs to let it go.*

In less than a minute, he was crying quietly.

I took a breath. 'Jack, you're in my living room. You're safe. The bad things happened a long time ago. The Hobbit can't hurt you anymore.'

His eyes flicked back to the window, suspicious. 'He's out there somewhere. You're lying.'

'He's not coming in here. Hudson won't let him. You will be OK. You did the right thing. Hiding.'

'Fuck that!' He pushed me roughly, throwing the remote hard against the stone of the fireplace, cracking it into pieces.

'PTSD,' Hudson mumbled to me. 'I've seen it enough.'

'I have an idea,' I said. 'Not textbook exactly. I have to go upstairs. Please talk to him.'

I ran to my bedroom, flipping on lights as I went. I spilled everything out of my backpack until I found what I wanted. Downstairs, I could hear Hudson speaking quietly.

Then I was back on my knees in front of Jack, forcing the piece of paper from Idabel, Oklahoma, into his hands.

'Are these the men, Jack? This picture has been sitting in Jennifer Coogan's police file in Idabel. Jack, do you remember Jennifer?'

Do you remember where you really are? Come on, Jack, snap back.

Something in his eyes flickered.

'These two men were strangers in the area at the time of her death. No one ever tracked them down.'

'I drew that heart tattoo,' he said softly, pointing to the giant's shoulder. 'I went through boxes of crayons. They took all my crayons away.'

I felt a rush of anger that he'd been forced to leave those pictures inside his head.

That adults – *caretakers* – felt the need for such destructive control.

I placed my hand on his knee.

'Jack, your family's murders, Jennifer's murder . . . were six years apart. A thousand miles away from each other. But they're connected. Can you help me, Jack?'

CHAPTER 30

Single blow psychic trauma.

A profound violent act that, when witnessed by someone so young, can lead to structural abnormalities in a developing brain.

Drugs and therapy, even if started the day after little Jack watched his father die, might not have rewired his head. Healed him. And now? Now it would be like stitching up a wound with a thread of hair.

I walked Jack to the bathroom and pulled out a clean towel and washcloth. I dug in the drawer for a new toothbrush and a comb. His blue Polo was soaked with sweat stains and smelled like old cheese. I found one of Daddy's shirts in the back of his closet and hung it on a hook on the bathroom door.

Then I closed the door for him, and waited.

Jack emerged with bloodshot eyes, slicked-back hair. Embarrassed.

'I'm sorry about that in there.' He gestured toward the living room. 'That's never happened before.'

I didn't believe him.

'OK,' I said. 'Hudson's making coffee.'

He shrugged. The wall was up.

Hudson planted three steaming mugs in front of us at the kitchen table. I ran my finger in circles around a white imprint on the wood where Granny used to set her glass of iced tea every afternoon at three.

'You are madddog. You emailed me that slide show. You spread rumors about my mother to some very bad people.' *You put everyone I loved in danger.*

'I thought you deserved a little clarity. I wanted to piss off your father and find out the truth about who killed my family. Anthony Marchetti wasn't there that night. But he confessed.' Blunt, unrepentant. No longer a child.

'Clarity? I have no clarity! Why didn't you just tell somebody what you saw?'

Hudson nudged my foot under the table. But I knew what I was doing.

'Who believes a distraught four-year-old?' he shot back. 'I read the psychiatrist's report on me. She wrote that I was putting everything in the context of a fairy tale to make it more bearable. I invented the Hobbit. It represented me, blaming myself for my brother's death. The tattoo was my broken heart. A bunch of psychobabble shit. I'm sure you're familiar.'

He looked beat-up, exhausted. Skin bone-white. Dark smudges under his eyes. I wondered how far to push this outside the safety net of a clinic.

'My life has sucked since they pulled me from that cabinet and carried me out in a body bag,' he said. 'They buried my family a week later. Five coffins. Mine was for show. Filled with a bag of sand, topped with a little headstone. They changed my name and stuck me in foster care instead of witness protection. None of my extended family wanted to take me. Too dangerous.'

'You said you were a reporter,' I said, steering him away. 'That you went to Princeton.'

'I did go to Princeton. Scored 1590 on the SAT. Tragic childhood produces overachiever. How can you say I'm not a reporter? This is my story, Tommie. *You* are my story.'

He leaned in with a bitter grin.

'So many years and so many dead ends. Until I had a piece of luck a few months ago. Someone in the Stateville prison system told me that Marchetti had a special interest in some girl on the outside. Someone had sent photos of you. *For years.*'

The first thought that rushed at me: Would Mama do that? Send pictures of me while I was growing up, to a killer?

'I'm out of here,' Jack said suddenly.

'Don't go yet,' I pleaded. 'Talk to my . . . to Marchetti . . . I can get you help.'

'Are you not listening? After my last visit to your father, he sent those redneck freelancers to the garage to tell me to back off. I don't need your help. I finally have their faces. Proof of the Hobbit and the Giant. It's the first time in years I've been absolutely certain they weren't a figment of my imagination. That I wasn't crazy. That might be enough.'

Before I could react to this, the kitchen phone, the landline, began to ring on the wall by the refrigerator.

Once.

Twice.

Three times. The three of us sat there, no one making a move, the tension in the room holding us in place like dolls arranged for a tea party. The answering machine picked up with my father's rough voice, like he'd been here listening all along. And then, another voice. Irritated.

'Tommie? Pick up. Are you there? Is this the right number? This is James. You know, the guy you FedExed a finger to?'

That broke the spell. I jumped from the chair, knocking it to the floor, and ran to grab the receiver.

'It's me. I'm here.' I slid down the wall to a sitting position, holding one hand over my ear to hear better, to shut out Jack and Hudson, although the only sound in the room was the hum of the refrigerator.

'Want to know about your baby finger, the finger I put ahead of six other cases that I'm actually getting paid for?' James, a fellow UT grad who thought he should be curing cancer instead of figuring out the DNA tree of rich people's dogs, was pretty much annoyed at the world all the time.

'Tell me,' I said. 'Please.'

'It contains a high concentration of calcium sulfate hemihydrate. Or let me put it in layman's terms. Your finger is plaster of Paris.'

I hung up the phone, my face hot and perspiring.

'A friend,' I said awkwardly.

Jack stretched and stood. Hudson gathered up the coffee cups and put them in the sink. We both followed Jack to the front door, Hudson casually holding his gun.

This couldn't be over.

'Where's your car?' I asked Jack suddenly.

'I parked it at the pond.' I wondered if he had considered driving it into the water, sinking away with everything inside it.

Jack turned at the door, a pitying look on his face.

'You and me,' he said, 'we're the same now.'

'What do you mean?'

'You'll never feel safe again.'

And then he was gone, striding toward the fields, melting into the trees.

It is a cancerous myth, that children are resilient.

For the next twenty-one hours, I slept.

I woke to the air conditioner thumping on, whispering a breeze across the half of my body uncovered by the sheets.

I glanced at the clock radio by the bed: 6:08 a.m.

Hudson was a long lump lying several feet away in Sadie's twin bed, breathing in and out in a steady rhythm.

The first thought punched its way through.

I wondered whether Jack would chase down his monsters. Get rid of them for both of us. The picture of the Hobbit and the Giant had disappeared with him.

The second thought: I should read Mama's letter.

I slid out of bed, shivering in my T-shirt and underwear, and wrapped the Peter Rabbit comforter tighter around me before heading down the stairs.

The kitchen was spotless. The three coffee cups from the other night were washed and draining on a dishtowel. An old mayonnaise jar filled with fresh yellow daisies and purple dianthus from Mama's garden sat in the center of the table – cheery flowers victorious against the wicked heat, not a cloying refrigerated arrangement left over from the funeral.

Sadie's work. A little purple Post-it in her artistic scrawl stuck to the side of the jar said: *I ♥ you. Call me if you ever get up.*

I pushed aside congealing casseroles to find a lone Dr Pepper, then ventured to the laundry room and opened the middle drawer in Mama's desk. The letter was faceup, exactly the way I'd left it before taking Sadie home.

I stuck the envelope under my nose, hoping for

a whiff of her perfume, or the garlic she planted every year or the wax she used like a religion on her grand piano. It smelled . . . anonymous. I ran my finger under the seal, pulled out a single page:

Dear Tommie,

Already, I can feel my mind slipping away. You were here today, sitting across from me drinking a glass of tea. It would have been the time to tell you everything, but I couldn't do it. I'm ashamed to say I am not that brave even now. But you are the bravest girl I know. Whatever you discover about me, about your father, about your-self, I hope that the only answer you need is that we loved you.

Be happy.

Love, Mama

It figured. She wasn't going to tie things up in a pretty little bow.

I stuck the letter back in the drawer and walked over to my cell phone, both plugged in and charging. Sweet of Hudson to do that.

Five messages on my phone.

I was a little leery of reconnecting to the world, but what the hell. Maybe Rosalina Marchetti had another fake body part for me.

W.A. wanted to know when Sadie and I could meet to talk over more details of the will.

Donna had a dermatologist appointment at 2 p.m.

tomorrow. I'd been getting Donna's messages for two years even though I wasn't Donna.

Wade, pushing his agenda, asked if I'd like to take some horses out to the wind farm this week for a ride.

Halo Ranch wanted to know whether I'd picked a moving company to haul my stuff home. I'd resigned by phone the day before Mama's funeral for three good reasons: Sadie. Maddie. The weight of our inheritance.

Charla Polaski sounded the most desperate I'd heard her, with voices and clanking noises in the background almost drowning her squeak.

'I hate to leave this on a voicemail,' she said, *'but, word is, your Daddy is planning to kill himself.'*

CHAPTER 31

My pickup spun down Highway 377, a hot wind blowing through the open windows like God had turned on his giant blow-dryer.

It had been four days since I ignored the last phone call from Charla, ten days since Mama had died, one month since I opened the letter that said I was someone else.

Hudson was sleeping with me every night at the ranch. The pony sheets often ended up tangled and sweaty on the floor. One of Hudson's war buddies remained a constant at Sadie's trailer, but something more than a professional relationship was developing there, too.

I didn't like driving alone. *Being* alone.

Nothing about my life was resolved since Jack walked out the door.

I took a fast glance at the map on the seat beside me and turned left onto the next county road, stirring up a flock of grackles, a species of black birds invented by the devil. Not a thing to recommend them, Granny would say. They devoured crops, dropped bombs of poop, and were too damn noisy. Nature's reality TV stars.

The birds flew higher, black dots guiding my eye to a neat row of wind turbines stuck into the earth like white toothpicks. At this distance, the turbines were tiny, almost invisible against the clouds, but I knew that was just a trick of the eye, that they towered forty stories into the sky and weighed hundreds of tons.

Texas leads the way on wind farms, but we've been wrong about a lot of things. I don't yet know what is best for my pieces of the earth, I'm only certain that Wade is about to tell me.

I urged the pickup forward and finally up a dusty hill, three enormous white blades rising up abruptly in front of me, a rotating sculpture against the blue sky. In seconds, the full turbine emerged only yards ahead, and I braked at the top of the rise, absorbing the scene. Seventy-four more turbines spread out into the fields beyond, spinning hypnotically, peacefully, a modern-day Stonehenge. They made a low hum, like a small jet flying overhead.

A herd of cows chewed grass obliviously in the field across the road. A long black horse-trailer was parked on the right side of the road in front of me. Wade. Our meeting spot on the land where Daddy, an oil and gas tycoon, agreed to try to harness the wind.

I pulled in behind the trailer and steeled myself for Wade's hour-and-a-half lecture about grasping the future. As I stepped out of the truck, Maddie burst from behind the cab, rushing me with the force of an eighty-pound linebacker.

'Surprise! We got Mel!'

Wade appeared from inside the back of the trailer, leading a gray horse.

Mel. Or, formally on paper, Unchained Melody. A gift from Daddy on my thirtieth birthday. Mel arrived at Halo Ranch two years ago with a big red bow, like a Lexus.

I was stunned. Thrilled. If this was a bribe, I was happy to take it.

'We road-tripped to get her,' Maddie said. 'Me and Wade.'

I threw one arm around Maddie and buried my face in Mel's mane before lifting my head to speak. Wade gave me a curt nod.

'Thank you,' I told him. 'I didn't want to hire someone for that long ride. They cram them into those trailers. Mel goes crazy if she can't ride backward.'

'She let me know that pretty fast,' he said. 'Happy to do it.'

'I fed her carrots and apples on the way,' Maddie said. 'And I patted her a *lot*.'

'Lucky horse,' I said. 'It sounds like a pretty cushy limo ride.'

Her face lit up with a grin. 'Wade said I could ride with y'all today. I brought my helmet.'

The fact that she said this so earnestly broke my heart a little. At her age, I rode bareback, bareheaded, hair flying behind me like crepe-paper streamers, the kind of freedom everybody should feel at least once as a child.

Most sensible parents don't let their kids do that anymore and certainly not Sadie. Maddie's helmet was custom-made, reinforced, to cushion her brain and its small tumor in case of a fall. It was the invention of a medical equipment manufacturer and a professional hockey goalie with a brain-injured son. Still, it was heavy and hot. A precaution, doctors said. If she wanted to ride, she had to wear it.

She strapped it on, in all its pink and purple glittery glory, and for fifteen minutes, we worked to get the other two horses out of the trailer and saddled up.

'We need to ride on ahead several miles to a turbine that isn't behind a cattle gate,' Wade said, as he tightened the last strap on Maddie's saddle. 'I want you to get a look inside at the computer that runs them.'

Fair enough. He delivered my horse. I could look at a computer.

We trotted a mile down the road, barbed-wire fences and wild cactus stretching into the horizon, until we reached a long, low picket gate. Wade rolled off his horse, jiggled a key in the padlock, and swung the gate open for Maddie and me to ride on through.

I pointed to a large rock ahead and she got the message. Race. We pushed the horses to a gallop,

Maddie staying inches ahead, before we halted short at the finish line and turned around to wait for Wade as he finished securing the gate.

Did I see the black Jeep on the road first or hear the shot? Suddenly, Maddie's horse was out of control, up on its haunches. Maddie was a still form in the dirt, her horse spinning, hooves dangerously near every precious part of her. I half fell, half jumped off Mel to pull Maddie away from the frightened horse and cradle her in my arms.

Blood on Maddie's face, on her shoulder, her helmet in shattered pieces.

Eyes shut like a baby doll's.

Smack in the middle of open land with nowhere to hide.

In three seconds, Wade had dropped to the ground and pulled a gun out of the waist of his jeans. God bless him, always carrying. The Jeep now blocked the gate. Tinted windows. Wade shot five times at the vehicle, shattering two of them. The driver gunned the engine and roared down the road, kicking up angry dust. Maddie's horse shot off across the field.

Wade ran over to us, hunched, with a plan. A former federal marshal. My Daddy's keeper to the end.

'Get on my horse,' he ordered. 'She's faster. I'll hand Maddie up to you. Head to the truck. I'll distract them.'

Surreal. His words, his twang, the giant machines

whirling behind him on barren soil. A bad Western shot on Mars.

'I don't know if we should move her—' I protested, futilely scanning the bare terrain.

'She's sure to die if we don't. Hurry.'

'That shot was meant for me. They're after me, not you or Maddie. You take Maddie. I'll ride Mel off somewhere. Let them follow me. I'll beat them.'

Wade didn't appear shocked that we were being shot at like a family of ducks. How much did he know? No time to ask.

'Please,' I begged. *'Take Maddie.'*

As we argued, the Jeep rounded the curve of the road where it had disappeared, flooring it, heading back.

Wade was nothing if not a practical man. He whistled and his horse obeyed, instantly at his side. In my next life, I would have him teach me that. He stuck his foot in the stirrup and threw his bad leg over. I lifted Maddie and he leaned down and pulled her up in front of him, steadying her limp body with one hand, the reins in the other.

'I'll call for help as soon as I can get a cell signal.' He tapped his horse lightly on the rear and clicked his tongue. Wade's instructions to his obedient horse to get the hell out of there.

Mel and I were flying in the other direction by the time I heard the next shot.

I was suddenly airborne. It's always a surprise

when you got tossed, but the instincts kicked in, and I willed my body to stay loose. If I knew nothing else, I knew how to fall. I hit the ground hard and rolled. Mel whinnied, reared back, and charged across the field, scared out of her mind, trying to find the door out of this alien landscape. I prayed she wasn't hit.

I stumbled up and started running. Another shot struck the air. I ran toward a row of turbines, stopped at the first one, and raced up the five metal steps, jiggling the door before realizing it was padlocked. I glanced behind me. Two small black figures climbed the gate, staring a hole in me. One of them lifted his arm and fired again. He was too far away, wasting ammunition. *Keep it up, asshole.*

I ran zigzag. The way Hudson recommended to his suburban mommies, I realized, and almost laughed.

The next turbine in the row was locked and the next one and the next. I wanted to scream out in frustration but I didn't have enough breath. Another shot. Much closer. There was only one more turbine close by, and it appeared half-finished, the enormous blades still lying on the ground. But the door was a black hole.

Open.

I almost fell inside and slammed it, searching frantically for an inside lock or something to block the door. Nothing.

I stood, wheezing, inside a white tube large

enough to hold several people. The shell of an impressive computer planted in the center, unfinished. It was too late to get out, to run again. They were close now. My eyes followed a ladder up, two hundred feet or more, a round tunnel to the sky.

A bullet pinged off the side of the turbine. I started to climb. The next shot bit into the outside steel near my ear, but I did not stop. I hit the middle landing and stepped off the ladder, legs trembling. I had a decision to make. Cower here or keep climbing. It was stifling hot inside the tube, my body dripping, palms slick with sweat.

I pushed the hair out of my face and glanced down a hundred feet.

Bad idea. Dizzying. Terrifying.

I looked up. Equally terrifying. A closed metal hatch, a hundred feet up, taunted me at the top.

It would either open when I got up there or it wouldn't. I imagined pushing uselessly against it, clinging to the ladder while they shot at me until I tumbled down, down, down.

Up, I urged myself. *Up.*

I could see the hooks on the turbine wall to attach a safety harness that I didn't have. It made me giggle, the silly horribleness of it all.

Rung after rung, hand over hand. Keep moving. A foot from the top, the door below me kicked open, and I willed myself not to look down.

I slammed at the metal hatch, a desperate submariner emerging from a sinking ship. It flung open so easily I nearly sobbed.

A bullet ricocheted off the inside of the turbine.

'Shit!' someone yelled. 'What the hell are you doing?'

Foolish boy to shoot in a fish barrel.

I clambered up into the open air, the hatch clanging shut behind me.

For a second, I stared, blinded, dizzy, hair whipping into my eyes.

Rapunzel standing on the roof of her high-tech castle.

A 360-degree-view of pinwheels in motion.

I fell to my knees and crawled to the side of the platform.

Sweaty. Wild-eyed. Furious.

I pulled Daddy's Beretta from the holster latched to my ankle, cocked it, gripped it with shaking hands, pointed it at the hatch, and waited.

Lucky me, I was carrying, too.

There are monsters rising out of the ocean in the gray waters off the Dutch coast, giant wind turbines drilled deep into the seabed. The wind's force against the enormous blades is said to be like the rush of semi-trucks charging them at full speed.

Someday, wind turbines will fly in the air like kites, capturing the highest, fastest currents.

People dream about these things, and they happen.

I dream about surviving this.

It took four minutes for him to climb up, to savagely throw open the hatch. It took one second for me to pull the trigger and forever for him to fall, screaming down the rabbit hole.

From the top of the world, I watched his friend run across the field, a skittering bug. Zigzag.

I wondered who taught him that.

Then I heard a crack, like a twig snapped.

He fell and didn't get up.

They were both waiting at the bottom.

The dead guy I sent down the barrel.

And someone else.

He held his hands up in the air, relaxed, a willing prisoner, even though my gun was holstered, too far down to reach. He was tall and ripped with taut muscle, not young, not old, dressed in silver and white Asics running shoes, desert camouflage pants, and a skintight tan T-shirt. His face was so nondescript I could stare at it for five minutes and not be able to describe it.

'Your father sent me,' he said, and I wondered which father.

'Did you shoot him?' I nodded to the dark lump in the field. 'Is it over?'

'Can you walk?' he asked.

'I think my arm is broken.'

His face blurred and I swayed.

I felt surprisingly cold.

And then I was on the ground, mesmerized, the blades spinning overhead and lulling me away.

CHAPTER 32

I heard a voice from far away, up at the top of the well, and I tried pushing through the blackness to reach it, but I was so tired and someone had placed a large rock on my chest.

Get this rock off of me. I tried to scream it but there was no sound. Maybe it wasn't a rock. Maybe my soul was stuck, a grackle in my chest, pressing, unable to get out.

No white light. Did I not make it to heaven? Could I try again?

My eyes flickered at shadows. I worked my lids harder, opening and shutting, until all the lines and colors filled in. The rock floated off.

Not heaven. I was lying on a gold and red plaid couch that smelled of wet dog. An unshaven man on crutches hovered, peering down, perplexed about what to do with me. He held a rifle. Oddly, I could picture exactly where I was. An old farmhouse with a tin roof and a yard littered with abandoned farm equipment. A rusty basketball hoop attached to the garage, a wheelchair sitting under it. At least, that's how it used to be. I reached back for his name.

Arless. A Vietnam veteran with two Purple Hearts. Twenty years ago, Daddy and Arless shook on a long-term rental agreement that he would live free on our Stephenville property until he died.

'He just dropped you off,' Arless told me. 'Kicked in the door with you in his arms. I nearly shot him.'

'Maddie . . .' I said, suddenly remembering, wishing I hadn't, tears stinging.

'Don't say nothin'. You don't look too good. They're comin' for you.'

I woke up in the hospital, and Daddy was there. The smell of cigarette smoke embedded in the fibers of his work shirt, the rank and delicious fragrance of the barn. His hand like an oven mitt covering mine, one of the few parts of my body that didn't cry out.

When I opened my eyes to greet him, I saw Wade, and grief choked me, my mind suddenly locked on Daddy in the casket, shrunken and delicate, a wax doll in a neatly pressed blue suit. In life, Daddy was never neatly pressed.

'I was just filling in,' Wade said, pulling away, embarrassed. 'Sadie's down the way with Maddie. Maddie's doing real good. She's going home in the morning. Your boyfri – Hudson is getting some coffee.' He hesitated, brushing his hand over his head, smoothing back the few hairs left on it. 'The police are all over this.'

He put a finger to his lips. 'Uh-uh, don't talk.

The doc doesn't want you to.' I figured it was more likely that Wade was the one who wanted to stunt any conversation but I was struggling to move my lips. They felt enormous and tingly, as if they were triple-loaded with collagen. Wade glanced at the closed door, edgy.

The thought floated up like a dead fish. Was he going to smother me? His hand dug into the tight front pocket of his Levi's. Maybe a knife.

He removed a familiar object and held it in front of my eyes. I could see the letters. *BOWW*. Bank of the Wild West. How did he get the key to the safe deposit box?

'Your Mama gave me this, Tommie. Said to burn everything in the box it goes to when she died. I was going to give it to you yesterday out at the wind farm.' I was still staring at the key and registering the numbers. New numbers.

Another key. *A second key. Another box?*

I struggled to push away the haze settled around my brain like mosquito netting.

It was Mama that Wade was protecting. Not Daddy.

Something delicious was streaming through my IV.

'If it's OK with you, I'm going to reach into your purse right here and put this on your key chain. For when you're up to it.' While he threaded it on my key chain, he focused his eyes down on his task, away from me. 'I think you know where to use it. This is the first time I've ever gone against your Mama's wishes. I don't like the feeling.'

Wade tossed the keys back in my purse, stood up stiffly, and reached for his cowboy hat upright on the chair next to him.

'I know you never liked me,' he said, 'but I always liked you, and I'll tell you why. You never once looked down on my son even when you were a brat.'

He smiled.

A few things hit me right then.

The time Wade found me and a friend hitch-hiking from a nearby town in our high school track uniforms, how he pulled over and yanked us into his truck and yelled until I thought the windows in the cab would explode. How he never told on me to Daddy.

How he taught me to shatter skeet in the sky and to stick a hook into a wriggling minnow and to bank a tough shot on a pool table. How I thought he was mean because he never offered anything but criticism, but when I stepped outside the perimeter of the ranch I could beat a boy at anything Wade had taught me.

When Rusty, his son, erupted in a seizure in the barn two days after I turned ten, I knew to cushion his head with a horse blanket, not to restrain him, just reassure him, that he'd take his cues from me like any other animal, all because Wade hammered it in my head. I used the lesson of that experience to treat the little people who'd streamed into my life since, broken and flailing, terrified about what to expect.

'We don't get to pick things the way we want them,' Wade said now. 'I didn't want Rusty to be autistic. But he's the best thing in my life. I guess you know that.'

I didn't know that at all. I'd never heard Wade talk like this before, to bare a single emotion. A minute ago, I thought he was going to smother me.

'We don't get to pick things,' he said again.

He reached the door, and turned back.

'I don't know if the answers in that box will hurt you more or set you free, Tommie. But I figure it's your decision to make.'

I tried to get comfortable in the passenger seat of Hudson's truck, but the sling on my arm got in the way. Any movement to adjust positions either shot fire up my chest, taped like a corset to hold together three bruised ribs, or through my shoulder, which, it turned out, just needed one faint-inducing pop back into place by a qualified medical professional. My head ached steadily.

'You were lucky,' the emergency room doctor told me, after a short torture session. 'It's just a mild concussion.'

In the backward way that life operates, Maddie's tumor had helped save her life. If she hadn't been wearing the helmet, if the shooter's aim had been better, the bullet would have pierced her brain. Instead, it ricocheted and dug into our land, a trinket to be discovered by post-apocalypse hunters and gatherers thousands of years from now. Maddie was scratched up, but the brain scan deemed her no worse for wear.

Both of us stayed the night in the hospital for observation. Sadie and Maddie were now headed back to the ranch, while I remained stubbornly fettered to a course of possible self-destruction. The key clutched between my fingers felt weighted, full of portent.

'Could you maybe slow down a little?' I asked Hudson. 'And try not to hit big holes like that one?'

'Sorry. But this is stupid. You should be going home to bed, not to the bank.' His mouth was set in a grim line. He leaned over me to flip down the mirrored visor. 'Have you taken a good look at yourself lately?'

I barely recognized the wild being reflected back. I looked worse today than yesterday, like a rotting piece of fruit. Half of my face was tie-dyed a mottled purple and blue, and a tire track of a scab was forming. My hair stuck out in oily straggles. I leaned the mirror forward and took in the sling, which stretched across my body. I snapped the mirror up.

'Perfectly normal from the waist down,' I said, although Hudson hadn't seen the stream of bruises down my right side or watched my excruciating effort to slide into these jeans. Just speaking sent an avalanche of hurt down my body, each word like a little punch.

I reached for the bottle of pain pills in my purse and swallowed one dry, closing my eyes, replaying the last two days.

Only an hour or so had passed from the time the first shot was fired at Maddie until the police and emergency crew barreled into Arless's home. They had wasted a little time at the site of the Jeep after discovering a man on the driver's side with his head taken off by a nasty hollow point. Then they got Arless's 911 call.

A bullet from the same gun was found in the man in the field. He'd been shot in the back. I readily confessed to the splattered mess at the bottom of the turbine. All three men were identified as worker bees for the Cantini crime family, two cousins and a brother of the man who had dragged me from the library in Chicago.

When the police asked, I described the anonymous gentleman who had carried me off in his arms like John Wayne as 'beige.' Arless just kept his mouth shut.

Hudson interrupted my thoughts, grumpy, pulling the truck to a halt in front of the discreet glass door of the Bank of the Wild West. I wasn't sure how to deal with this Hudson, overprotective, loaded with guilt for not being there.

'You know, Wade is a closemouthed bastard,' he

said. 'I don't trust him. He couldn't have waited until you were better to hand over the key?' Hudson didn't seem to be expecting a response from me. 'Are you sure you don't want me to stay?'

'No, go on to the meeting. You've put it off twice because of me. Pick me up in about two hours.' I winced as I reached for the door handle.

'I'm having lunch with the guy at Reata. Two blocks away. I can cut it short if I need to. He just wants a tail on his daughter's ex-boyfriend.'

And maybe a warning from a guy who could snap his neck. Once upon a time, like a month ago, this would have bothered me. I would have held Hudson's willingness to cross the line against him, as a reason not to get close.

Not anymore. Snap away.

I put my hand on his shoulder. 'Stop this. None of this is your fault. I won't move an inch outside the bank until you come back.' I reached for the door handle again.

'Wait,' Hudson said, leaning over me to open the glove compartment.

'You're double-parked,' I protested. 'I don't need a gun. It will set off the bank alarm.'

'It's not a gun.' Whatever it was, it was very small. He turned over his hand and opened his palm like a magician, revealing a lovely band of gold filigree lit by tiny rubies.

'Your grandmother's ring,' I said, my heart flipping.

'You wore it once. Fourteen years ago. For forty-one days. This time I'm hoping you won't give it back.'

He slipped the delicate band onto the ring finger of my left hand.

'It's a promise,' he said.

Hudson waited until I disappeared behind the opaque door before pulling away from the curb. Ms Billington appeared at my side instantly, invisible antennae wiggling, her face contorting into a series of comical expressions as she took in my appearance. I'm pretty sure the last one said, 'Serves you right.'

'Your lawyer has it all set up,' she said briskly, recovering, guiding me back to her spotless desk. I avoided my reflection in the glass. Once was enough for today.

'ID, please. You are not listed as an agent to get into the box in case of emergency. Your lawyer cut through a few layers of protocol with my boss.' Clearly, Sue Billington did not approve of such favors tossed over a cell phone line.

'Can you tell me something, please?' I kept my voice neutral, pushing my driver's license across the desk. 'Did my Daddy know about this second box?'

'Signature here at the X, please,' she said briskly, separating one of the papers from the pile in front of her. 'And initial here. And here. Pretty ring, by the way. Unusual.'

'Please help me.'

Sue Billington popped up her head and connected with my eyes, now pooling with tears. As she whipped out a Kleenex from under the desk, her face melted into an expression probably reserved for her beloved cat, and she leaned in conspiratorially.

'No. I do not believe your father ever knew about this box. This is pure speculation based on twenty-five years of loyal bank service and observation of human behavior. The paperwork indicates that your mother opened this box alone. There is no joint renter or appointed agent for emergency access. If I've learned anything in this business, it's that people, especially people who sit all shiny in church every Sunday morning, are quite deceitful to their spouses. It's one of the reasons that I've never married.'

It's also because no one in his right mind has asked you, you nosy little fruitcake.

We repeated the Bank of the Wild West security rigmarole: keycard, palm scan, spy cameras, a greeting from Rex and his unholstered gun, and I was back in a room I had hoped to never step foot in again. Today, without Sadie, the room seemed even more claustrophobic. I imagined tiny dead bodies stored behind each metal door.

We inserted our keys and Ms Billington slid Mama's box out of its place from a lower corner nowhere near the other one. She placed it almost

393

tenderly on the table, reminded me to push the red button when I was finished so she could retrieve me, and left.

I dropped into one of the giant chairs and let it swallow me up like a leather womb.

The box contained two envelopes. One big, one small. It wasn't too late to let Wade burn them. My heart, for a change, felt perfectly still; my hands, ice cold.

My fingers reached for the larger manila envelope. No markings of any kind. I ran my nail under the flap and pulled out the few sheets inside.

The police report of Tuck's accident.

I jumped, dropping it from my fingers like it was flaming, my chair swerving backward on its rollers, sending me off balance. The report floated to the floor along with a series of stark black-and-white photographs.

There were photographs.

How cruel was Wade to send me here?

I don't know if the answers will hurt you or set you free, Tommie.

I reached over and picked up the pictures first, one by one, and examined the smoking black skeleton of Tuck's car.

A panic attack was banging in my chest, screaming. *Let me out, let me out.*

The police report was stuck under one of the chair's rollers. I extracted it, careful not to rip it. The words blurred, until my eyes halted abruptly like the Ouija mouse, settling over two words.

Explosive device.

Not an accident.

Tuck had been blown away.

CHAPTER 33

My brother, murdered.
Everybody covered it up.
My family.
The marshals.
Even the cops, no small feat in our town.

I was queasy and light-headed, reaching for the last thing in the box. A white business-sized envelope, addressed to my mother in bold black print. No return address. An Illinois postmark.

The next few sheets were simple notebook paper, folded and smudged and crammed with bold, stylized print.

I could still feel grit from the crack in the wall or the old pipe where he hid it in his cell.

Dear Gennie, it began.

I let that sink in.

Jack Smith was right.

She was Genoveve first.

When I finished the letter, I believed three things.

Anthony Marchetti was a complicated man.

My mother once loved him.

An eleven-year-old boy, my brother, was at the heart of everything.

He was the witness.

More than thirty years ago while doing his home-work in the wine cellar of the Chicago bar where my mother waitressed and played piano, Tuck overheard Azzo Cantini order the hit on Fred Bennett, the undercover agent about to blow the lid off of Cantini's heroin operation.

Unfortunately, Tuck was seen. Like Fred Bennett, he had to die.

Anthony Marchetti confessed to the Bennett murders to save my brother. To save my mother. To save me, growing inside her. He did this even though Marchetti was from a rival family. Even though he didn't do it.

Marchetti knew that a mobster, *a monster,* would never let Tuck live.

After all, he was one.

He agreed to confess to a crime he didn't do, to a plea deal – but only if the Feds would arrange witness protection for Tuck and Mama.

The Feds were happy to do it. Eager to close a nightmare case even if the lid didn't fit just right.

At least that is how the letter read.

Anthony Marchetti, a hero.

I stared out the passenger window of Hudson's truck, lulled by two hours of monotonous highway driving. A twenty-five-foot electric security fence began to run along the right side of the car, a sign that we were close.

Hudson's face was grimmer than I'd ever seen it, his eyes steady on the road. My body suddenly ached for him, rushing blood to the nasty gash in my cheek so it throbbed and hurt even more. Love in all its painful glory.

Not for the first time, I wondered about pursuing this tiny crack in time. Ten minutes. It was all that Hudson and his connections could get me on less than twenty-four hours' notice.

A welcome sign appeared announcing the Trudy Lavonne Carter Center for Felons. Most rich people in Texas wanted their names fixed to museums and hospital wings but the late Trudy Lavonne Carter had spent her millions on this fully air-conditioned, high-tech maximum security home for murderers and rapists. Trudy believed God demanded humane treatment of all living things. Its thousands of detractors sarcastically dubbed the prison TLC. The name stuck.

Except for the ten sharpshooters in the four corner towers and on the roof, TLC reminded me of a mini-mall on a Sims game. Hudson handed over our IDs at a massive steel gate while two heavily armed men checked the trunk and the backseat.

In less than five minutes, we stood inside the front entrance, cheerful and flooded with light. A smiling woman behind a glass window gestured for me to sign in, like I was arriving for a mammogram. Upholstered chairs and couches lined the walls. Helpful signage directed us to bathrooms and waiting areas. An erase board declared Roasted Red Pepper and Chicken Fettuccine as today's special in the visitors' cafeteria.

Hudson's cell phone rang.

'Sir, you need to turn that off.' The guard frowned. 'You can't go in with her. I'll take you to the waiting area.'

'I guess we part here,' Hudson said. 'You ready?'

I nodded.

'Ten minutes with Marchetti,' the guard said to me. 'No more. Marcy will take you from here.'

A female guard wearing lemon-sized biceps and J. Lo perfume led me down a maze of halls to a cubicle with a curtained-off dressing area and a plaque with an admonishment from Turkish poet Nazim Hikmet: 'And don't forget, a prisoner's wife must always think good thoughts.'

I wondered how many wives, in a humiliating state of undress, had longed to smash his words against the wall and if any of them knew who in the hell Nazim Hikmet was.

Marcy tried to be considerate of my injuries during the pat down, but I winced through it nonetheless. She allowed me to keep one personal item: an old Walmart receipt with five questions scribbled on the back, winnowed down from a long list in my head.

Two minutes for each answer. For closure.

Impossible.

She guided me to a small, white, windowless room, stark and stripped of any charm. Two steel chairs faced each other, bolted to the concrete floor. I began to shiver as soon as my thighs hit the chilled metal seat. It was like sitting on a glacier.

A guard in a tan uniform stood upright in the corner, ignoring me, as if I didn't exist.

I stared straight ahead at the chair in front of me, at the rings in the concrete that would chain him in place, the most scared I have ever been.

Waiting.

Full of what? Hope? Anger? Fear?

All of the above?

I focused my eyes on the door, trying to stir up the girl inside, the bull rider who was so much gutsier than the woman in this room. Would he look me in the eyes? Speak first? Beg forgiveness? Threaten me? Say he loved me?

The mob was supposed to be dead. Fiction. Cliché fodder for television and movies. And yet here I sat, tapping my boot nervously, about to confront a man who knew guys on the outside named Nerves and Baby Shanks, Vinnie Carwash and Jack the Whack.

I grew up with names like Sug and Dub, Butelle and Waydeen, Coody and Willie Pearl. Even without the three fingers he lost in a farm equipment accident, I'd bet Butelle could take down Nerves and Baby Shanks at the same time.

The door clicked. I yanked my attention back. He was coming.

As he shuffled through the door, blinding in a highlighter orange jumpsuit, shackled, cuffed, and led by two men in full riot gear, I reacted like I would to any powerful, leashed animal. I stayed perfectly still, struck again by his potent dark looks.

Neither of us spoke, wasting precious seconds, while one of the men unshackled his feet, reattaching the cuff on his right foot to the hook in the floor. Throughout this process, Marchetti's eyes traveled over my face, furious, reminding me what a horror show it was.

'I am innocent,' he said.

Out of more than a million words to pick from in the English language, he chose those three to say first, to the daughter he might never see again, who had presented herself to him like a hurt rabbit.

It was and forever would be about him. Ten minutes would be plenty.

To hell with my list. I really only had one question. One thing to say.

'Why are you here? In Texas?' I drew in a shaky breath. 'I want you to go back.'

He gazed at me steadily, not reacting.

'I wanted to breathe the same air as your mother. I wanted to know she was close.'

'Jack?'

'He was interfering. Raising the dead. It wasn't that hard to get here. I still have a few connections.'

My eyes dropped to the floor, locking onto the

black patch of hair I could see between the cheap prison-issued blue deck shoe and the hem of his jumpsuit.

'You are safe now,' Marchetti said. 'I've made sure.'

I met his pupils, receding into vertical slits, reminding me of a copperhead that once wrapped itself around my boot. Daddy had taught me, only inches from a rattlesnake curled on a rock, that elliptical pupils in a snake meant venomous. Back away.

'Who murdered Tuck?' My voice trembled, amplified by the close space, the thick walls.

It took just a second for me to travel the few feet between us, to grab his chin and turn his face up so he was forced to look at me, unflinching. My fingers were hot against his skin, a current pulsing between us. The guard leapt up, maybe surprised that a 107-pound woman with a braid down her back was going to be today's problem.

I didn't flinch as the correctional officer grabbed my arm. 'Ma'am, no contact. Sit down.' He was giving me a chance to behave.

'You owe me,' I said fiercely to Marchetti, not letting go. Wasn't that what Rosalina had said to me not that long ago?

It occurred to me that he probably hadn't been touched like this in more than thirty years. That he might like it.

Everything around us was happening in slow

motion. The guard yanking me back, barking into his walkie-talkie, the human black bugs running in.

'I don't know,' Marchetti said quietly.

One of the bugs pulled me by my sling and the pain dropped me to my knees.

My father didn't move. His face twisted into something inhuman.

And I knew.

Unchained, he would have killed the man who hurt me.

We were halfway home before Hudson spoke.

'You remember that phone call I got at the prison?'

I roused myself from half slumber.

'Your library kidnapper got a toothbrush shiv to the throat last night in jail.'

I sat up straight, ignoring the pain. 'Is he dead?'

'Very dead. Coincidentally, his father, Azzo Cantini, died in his sleep last night.'

You're safe, my father had told me.

'Marchetti told me he is innocent of the Bennett murders,' I said dully, face pressed against the window, brown scenery whirring by.

'Marchetti was knee deep in their blood.' Hudson said it sharply. 'Those murders benefited every single mobster dealing drugs in Chicago. Who knows how much the Feds had on him?'

He hesitated.

'I've been able to trace Jack Smith, aka little Joe

Bennett. He did survive a crappy childhood in the foster care system. He did go to Princeton on a full-ride scholarship. Until six months ago, he was a computer software engineer at one of the large insurance companies in Hartford. That's when he took an extended leave of absence, claiming a family tragedy. His boss was talkative on the phone. Smith is very gifted with computers, apparently. Nobody knows where he is right now.'

I nodded, absorbing this. A brilliant guy. A computer expert. Jack Smith was probably his own best source.

Hudson rested a hand on my knee, concerned, and asked the question of the day.

'Are you all right?'

'Almost,' I said.

I still had a little dead girl to find.

CHAPTER 34

Maddie and I stood, hand in hand, in front of Rosalina Marchetti's gate. Up the hill, I could glimpse one of the mansion's shiny copper turrets, barely visible above the forest of trees and thick green vegetation. A September chill blew through our paper-thin Texas skin, and we huddled a little closer.

I wondered how we looked in the fish-eye lens of the security camera. Harmless, I hoped.

I pressed the buzzer again. We weren't expected. So when the electronic gate swung open, I was surprised, but only a little.

Rosalina had unfinished business with me, too.

I'd been sling-free for a week. The bruises painted on the right side of my face were now a poisonous yellow and green.

My niece had returned to her joyful little self and this weekend in the city was our personal celebration of survival. We cursed out the Cubs like natives, made faces in the Bean, and checked out the American Girl store although Maddie insisted she was too old and just wanted to take a brief look inside. We left with a red bag. Of course, I had ulterior motives for picking Chicago.

Maddie and I climbed the driveway that wound like a wide ribbon to the top of the hill, arriving a little breathless at the mansion.

'This place is awesome.' Maddie's face was enthralled. 'A fairy tale. I feel like we're coming to visit the queen.' She pointed up. 'There she is!'

On a small, curlicued balcony, Rosalina struck a pose like a 1930s movie star, her silky red robe glimmering in the sun. She pretended not to see us, her profile turned, staring off at something only she could see. I prepared for her to swoon and wondered how we'd catch her. Something white flashed briefly in the upstairs window beside her. A nurse?

A black-uniformed maid met us outside, leading the way up a curving staircase to the balcony in the back where Rosalina and I first met. Like magic, our hostess was already in place, sitting near the ledge at a table set with two martinis and a crystal dish of mixed nuts.

'Hello again, my dear,' she said, not getting up.

As we reached the table, her gaze drilled into Maddie, clearly an unexpected nuisance. 'Run on down to the garden and play in the maze. Little girl, when you get lost, just yell. There are cameras. Someone will lead you out.'

'Don't go far,' I added, not sensing any real danger. I now believed the cameras were there more to keep Rosalina in than to keep anyone out.

Maddie bounced off with the maid, who was already offering up chocolate chip cookies and milk, and I confronted this woman whose vanished child had made a permanent home in my dreams.

'Where is Adriana?' I asked.

She sighed, and pointed to her heart. 'She's here, and . . .' pointing melodramatically down to the fountain, '. . . she's there.'

It took me a second to get it.

Adriana wasn't missing.

She was buried below us.

The fountain was her tomb.

Maddie was roaming the gardens. Alone. What the hell else was buried there?

I tried to keep my voice steady. 'She wasn't kidnapped. How did she die?'

'It was an accident. I was high on something. Some of Cantini's special juice. I was about to put her in her crib and I dropped her. She hit her head. Wouldn't stop crying. Then she went to sleep. The next morning, she wouldn't wake up.'

Her lack of emotion chilled me.

'Anthony knew, of course. He was in constant contact from jail. His lawyers are always busy maneuvering his money and I'm always signing things. I think that's why he married me. Not to protect your mother – to hide all his dirty business.'

That had occurred to me, too.

'One of his men came up with the finger thing. Did the chopping. Mailed the package.'

I winced at the word *chopping,* but Rosalina appeared unbothered.

'And then there was that pesky little reporter. Barbara Thurman. She couldn't stop bugging me about the kidnapping. I let something slip once, and she wouldn't let go. She never liked me.'

Rosalina twirled the olive to marinate it and gracefully popped it in her mouth, the perfect socialite, the studied actress. She and Jack, co-stars.

'So what made her stop pursuing the story?'

'Money, what else? Lots and lots of money.'

'So you were responsible for the break-in at her house?'

'One of my boys followed you. I wanted to know if Thurman broke her word. She was paid too much for that. I planned to tell you in my own good time. Or not.'

'You shouldn't have worried.' I thought of Barbara's misdirection, the drawing of a woman with funky red highlights who had never existed.

Poor Adriana. I felt the finality of her small death, the immense sadness that came with it, and a weight lifting off of me, rising like a balloon.

You didn't die in place of me.

'Why the hell did you give me that fake finger?' I asked Rosalina. 'Why did you beg me to come up here?'

'Honey, I didn't really think you'd take it. What kind of person would? It was for effect. I made it in my ceramics studio one day when I was missing

Adriana. The real one is buried with her. When the police gave it back to me, they said it had been chopped off after death. Of course, I already knew that.'

I shivered at the image of Rosalina casting the finger of her baby, maybe singing a lullaby as she worked at it.

'You know, your mother had everything.' Her voice grew ugly with bitterness. 'A daughter who lived. Men who adored her. A nice reporter doing a piece on Anthony told me all about it. He suggested that you and I should meet. The letter was his idea.'

Jack. Of course. Jack's fingers were everywhere. Pulling me down with him.

Rosalina's face took on a dreamy quality. 'I thought maybe you'd believe me. That you could become the daughter I never had. That reporter told me your mother had lost her mind. So the timing was perfect. You were the same age as my Adriana. You'd have been like sisters if all of this had never happened.'

She reached across the table to cover my hand with hers, a creepy albino spider.

'It was absolution,' she said. 'A full circle.'

I felt a deep, urgent need to find Maddie.

'Don't you judge me,' Rosalina said petulantly, sensing my abrupt mood change. 'Everybody's always judging me.'

I stood up to go, knocking my half-finished martini across the table, bitter liquid spilling onto

Rosalina's red silk, the stain spreading, reminding me of blood.

So much blood.

'I've spent years atoning with my charity work. I'm a good person!' Rosalina's voice was rising now, out of control.

Peering down on the shiny copper Adriana, I frantically called Maddie's name.

Seconds later, she appeared out of a path on the opposite side of the courtyard from which she'd disappeared, looking pleased with herself.

'She's the first one to find her way out,' Rosalina said, surprised.

I hoped those words were prophetic.

CHAPTER 35

I couldn't let go of Jennifer Coogan.
The last piece.
I knew that her story was linked to mine.
I like to think that she led me here, to this spot,
on this snowy January night in Rochester, New
York. I stared across the street through the icy film
on my rental car window at a boy shooting hoops
in the driveway of a blue Victorian house painted
with cheerful yellow trim. I closed my eyes and
listened to the ringing echo as the ball hit the
concrete, a steady pound, pound, pound. Then I
drove away.

Thirteen hours later, I waited at a table in a
coffee shop on a quaint little street called Park,
twisting Hudson's ring on my finger, nervously
smoothing the newspaper articles Mama had so
carefully safeguarded. I sipped a fully leaded
mocha cappuccino. The caffeine was a tough call.
I'd been trying to clean up my act.
Less tequila, more whole grains. Less oil, more
wind.
Anthony Marchetti had lost his parole hearing

in Illinois and asked to be moved back to his cell at Stateville. He hadn't killed himself. I didn't think he was the type. I decided against requesting a DNA test.

Charla Polaski still calls me once in a while, asks my advice and never takes it.

It took sixty-three hours and twenty-nine minutes for the Hobbit and the Giant to pop out of face recognition software at Hudson's security firm. Ernest Lowalsky and Reuben Fierstein, two minor contract guys who died in a shootout three years earlier when they wouldn't surrender to the police. Wherever Jack was, I hoped he knew.

As for Hudson and me, we are nudging our way toward permanent, working steadily on my dream to build a horse therapy ranch on our property in the Hill Country. He helps me assess every horse I buy as if they were for his own children. Maybe they will be.

Mama's autopsy revealed she died of natural causes. A stroke. Slowly, I have begun to grieve her and Daddy the way I was supposed to, saving the best parts of them.

Still, I wish they had trusted me. Told me. Instead, they let Tuck lie like a cement block in my gut. I think of all the master secret keepers who come to me, old souls in little bodies, kids who never had a tight hug, a single peaceful night of sleep, or a place in the hay to disappear and have a good cry. For these children, the hard part isn't getting them to keep a secret, it is getting them to tell.

In my free time, I made a trip back to Idabel and dug up the names of every person alive who might know something about Jennifer Coogan's life and death. I hit upon Holly Bender, an acquaintance who'd gone to the University of Oklahoma at the same time and now managed the local Walmart.

Holly told me what she could about Jennifer's mysterious boyfriend, including the name of an OU professor who'd taken a special interest in him. It was easy to find the professor's phone number and picture on the university website. He genially offered up little but a description – good-looking, dirty-blond hair, blue eyes, thin frame – the first thing that tickled the back of my mind.

W.A. knew a lot more than he let on about the anonymous heirs in my mother's will, but I guess he couldn't stop protecting her after all these years. His dear secretary, Marcia, took pity on me and surreptitiously combed his files for the name of the New York lawyer who set up their trust. Instead, she found the actual names of the teenage heirs: Troy and Amy Merchant, who coincidentally lived in the same city as one of Mama's newspaper articles.

It was Maddie who dug up their profiles on Facebook. I keep no secrets from her, for better or worse. She tried to unsuccessfully 'friend' them when I wasn't looking. No response. They had parents with strict rules.

Sometimes at night, I dreamed about Jennifer Coogan and the man she thought she loved.

So when he walked into the coffee shop, announced by the jangling Indian bells on the door, I knew him at once, because I'd obsessively examined his picture on the Eastman School of Music website.

A tenured professor of classical music studies. A composer. The father of two young heirs to a considerable fortune.

He looked the part – an erudite, tall, good-looking, middle-aged man with wire-frame glasses, wearing a brown tweedy coat and jeans. He ordered a plain cup of black coffee as he did every morning at 7:25 a.m. on his way to work.

His eager young teaching assistant had been very helpful on the phone with details about her boss's routine. She thought I was an old friend who wanted to surprise him. At the Eastman School of Music, they aren't expecting killers.

He dropped a few coins in the tip jar, picked up his coffee, and turned. I was hard to miss. I'd left my hair down on purpose.

I was a ghost. One of his ghosts.

He moved first.

Once again, I found myself in the arms of a strange man in a strange place. Except he wasn't a stranger.

He was Tuck.

'You look just like her,' my brother said into my ear, my wet face pressed against the scruffy fabric of his coat. He smelled clean and safe, like he'd showered with Ivory soap and then eaten an orange for breakfast. These are the silly things we remember. He used to smell like boy sweat and too much Drakkar cologne.

'I'm so sorry,' he said.

The people in the café stopped gawking and went back to their coffee, figuring us for over-wrought lovers. Tuck and I sat down in awkward silence. His hands fingered the yellowed news-paper articles, picking them up one at a time, hesitating the longest over the one about Jennifer's murder.

'Is this how you found me?' he wanted to know.

'Not exactly. Some legal documents helped. But once I found you, I finally got a hint of what they meant.'

'I mailed them to Mama. Every time they relocated me, I sent her a newspaper article so she'd know where I was. Nothing else. Just a clipping.'

He reached a hand across the table, hesitant.

'Let's just sit here for a while.' I dropped my hands to my lap. 'You don't have to explain. I've figured out most of it.'

It didn't matter that a homeless man was prob-ably buried in Tuck's grave. Or that Tuck was once an OU student named Barry.

What did anything matter when my dead brother sat across from me, pulsing with life, wanting to fill the space between us?

'I was a left-handed pitcher,' he said. 'A bookie

for Cantini tracked every high school team with a left-handed pitcher my age. The Feds found out they were stalking two players in other states. William thought it was just a matter of time.'

William. Daddy.

Tuck picked up the clip with Jennifer's photo, her smile forever frozen in newsprint, and in a sad little house in Oklahoma.

'I'll never forgive myself,' he said. 'I loved her. That summer, they tracked me down at OU through a leak in the field office. Found Jennifer first. Tortured her to get my address. I'm pretty sure she died without saying.'

His voice faltered. 'The marshals kept moving me. Eventually here.'

Tuck leaned back and pushed his glasses up with the long, graceful fingers of a pianist. 'I met Nora as a student at Eastman and she saved my life. We've been married twelve years. She teaches flute. We have two kids.'

'I know.' I wondered whether I should confess to last night's spying, to months of spying. I wasn't sure he knew about the inheritance. The financial documents Marcia found said his kids wouldn't be notified until they turned twenty-five.

I studied his face. Up close, he looked older than forty-four. Wrinkles feathered out from the corners of his eyes. Two deep lines creased his forehead. Only his hands were smooth and young. The pale yellow shirt under his tweed coat was slightly wrinkled, unstarched. The jeans were worn to a pale blue, the hem a little ragged against white Nikes. Things he didn't care about.

I wondered what kind of man he was.

I imagined that he was two kinds.

The kind who sat patiently on a piano bench for hours with a struggling student.

And the kind who shut himself away in a rehearsal room to forge thunderous compositions of terror and loss, angry notes slamming the walls, trapped in a tiny space, trying to get out. Like him.

'Tommie, did you hear what I said? I saw Mama before she died. She called me. She was frantic. Asked me to clean out a safe deposit box. Gave me the name of a bank. I said no. Too risky to come home. Two days later, I dialed the number back. I told the nurse I was a distant relative just checking in. She said that Mrs McCloud was being treated for dementia. That her husband had recently passed away. I flew down to Texas the next morning.'

He tapped his finger nervously on the edge of his cup, still full, growing tepid. His eyes were expanding and contracting mirrors, a kaleidoscope of emotions I couldn't identify. Shame, maybe? Grief for Daddy? Had he known and chosen not to come to the funeral? Before I could ask, maybe so I wouldn't, he continued.

'It was a mistake. A woman at the bank barely let me past the door. And Mama . . . she didn't know me, of course. I sat there anyway and held her hand and talked about the kids. I left after about half an hour. She was screaming my name by the time I hit the front door. I didn't go back.'

I hadn't guessed that. Tuck had been the visitor in Mama's nursing home, not some goon of Cantini's.

'I'm sorry,' Tuck repeated. 'About not being there for you. I know the lies bothered . . . Daddy. Even when you were young, before everything went to hell, he wanted to tell you.'

'Anthony Marchetti is my father,' I said flatly.

'William McCloud was your real father. He was *my* father. Genetics has nothing to do with it.'

He had no right to say this.

And every right.

It stirred up things I was still desperate to bury.

I ducked my head and brought my backpack up to my lap from under the table, unzipping a small compartment.

'Do you remember this?'

I laid a worn playing card, a joker, in front of him on the table and watched the recognition dawn on his face as he turned it over to reveal two pink swans entwined on the back.

'Something wild.' He looked up at me with a wry grin I remembered. 'Something unexpected. Granny was never wrong.'

I laid down one more card. I'd pulled it out of the deck at random in the hotel room last night after compulsively shuffling the deck for hours.

Granny's fast and loose method of answering a single burning question.

It was the reason I was sitting at this table and not in an airplane on the way home, leaving the past alone, turning my back on the unanswered questions.

One card, one answer.

The three of clubs.

For Tuck and me, a second chance.

EPILOGUE

I am sitting on the floor of Tuck's old room, a pile of treasure in front of me. A blue jay's feather, a dried stem of lavender, a grocery store slip, a smooth pebble from the driveway, a fork, a photograph. I don't know what these objects meant to my mother, but she hid them here under the mattress in the childhood room of the son she had to let go.

It is a breezy, cloudy October day, almost a year since my brother and I sat together in that New York coffee shop. We are preparing the house for his first visit home to the ranch with my niece, nephew, and sister-in-law. I didn't expect to find Mama's collection while I cleaned, but I remember Daddy saying that, at the end, this had become her habit. To hide inconsequential things.

'What's that stuff?' Maddie asks, appearing beside me. Her face and hands are thick with dust, her tennis shoes caked with cow manure, all part of her ritual that she calls 'cleaning the barn.'

'Some things your grandmother kept in here.'

'Cool,' she says. 'Can I have the feather?'

'Sure.'

She grazes it across her cheek, then picks up the photograph on top of the pile.

'Is this you?'

I am startled that she can see it instantly when I could not.

'No, that's your grandmother. I think she must be holding your uncle Tuck's hand. He looks about three.'

'Are you still mad at her for lying?'

'Not exactly mad, no.'

She studies my face solemnly. 'You know, Mama lies to me.'

'Don't say that, Maddie. You mother would never lie to you.'

'She tells me that the tumor in my head is nothing to worry about.'

I feel an ache all over. We didn't use the word *tumor* with Maddie. Ever.

'What do *you* think?' I ask, cautious.

'I think Mama doesn't know what will happen. Nobody knows.'

'You can talk to me about it anytime.' I reach over, smoothing her hair. 'But it would be better if you talk to her.'

'Mama feels better like this. Thinking I don't know. Protecting me.' She bounces up, handing me the photograph, not ready yet for more. 'Do you think my cousins will want to play croquet? I found an old set in the barn. I can put it up.'

'I think they would love that,' I say, and Maddie

skips out the door, unaware that she has opened the door to my prison.

I stare at the picture of Mama, not begging her to speak like in my childhood game with Etta Place, but hoping she can hear.

'I know who you are,' I say aloud, softly, repeating Hudson's words. 'You are kind. Beautiful. Brave. You save children.'

Not one of us who loved Mama ever saw the whole, but the piece I have of her is jagged and beautiful. I can see the sun shining through it.

The curtains at the open window dance and the photograph flutters out of my hand, skittering across the floor. The air fills the room with the intoxicating, earthy smell of our land. I close my eyes, drinking it in.

I could swear I heard music in the wind.